AN AMISH
CHRISTMAS GIFT

Other Novels by the Authors

Amy Clipston

The Amish Homestead Series
A Place at Our Table
Room on the Porch Swing
A Seat by the Hearth (Available November 2018)

The Amish Heirloom Series
The Forgotten Recipe
The Courtship Basket
The Cherished Quilt
The Beloved Hope Chest

The Hearts of the Lancaster Grand Hotel Series
A Hopeful Heart
A Mother's Secret
A Dream of Home
A Simple Prayer

The Kauffman Amish Bakery Series
A Gift of Grace
A Promise of Hope
A Place of Peace
A Life of Joy
A Season of Love

A Plain and Simple Christmas
Naomi's Gift

Young Adult
Roadside Assistance
Reckless Heart

AN AMISH CHRISTMAS GIFT

Three Stories

Amy Clipston

Ruth Reid

Kelly Irvin

Published in Nashville, Tennessee, by Zondervan. Zondervan is a registered trademark of HarperCollins Christian Publishing, Inc.

Zondervan titles may be purchased in bulk for educational, business, fund-raising, or sales promotional use. For information, please e-mail SpecialMarkets@ThomasNelson.com.

Scripture quotations marked NIV are taken from the Holy Bible, New International Version®, NIV®. Copyright © 1973, 1978, 1984, 2011 by Biblica, Inc.™ Used by permission of Zondervan. All rights reserved worldwide. www.zondervan.com. The "NIV" and "New International Version" are trademarks registered in the United States Patent and Trademark Office by Biblica, Inc.™

Publisher's Note: This novel is a work of fiction. Names, characters, places, and incidents are either products of the author's imagination or used fictitiously. All characters are fictional, and any similarity to people living or dead is purely coincidental.

Library of Congress Cataloging-in-Publication Data

An Amish Christmas gift: three Amish novellas / Amy Clipston, Ruth Reid, Kelly Irvin.
pages cm
ISBN 978-0-7180-3965-3 (paperback)
ISBN 978-0-3103-5348-5 (mass market)
1. Amish—Fiction. 2. Christian fiction, American. 3. Christmas stories. I. Clipston, Amy. Naomi's gift. II. Reid, Ruth. Unexpected. III. Irvin, Kelly. A Christmas visitor.
PS648.A45A34 2015
813'.01083823—dc23
2015015189

Printed in the United States of America

18 19 20 QG 6 5 4 3 2 1

CONTENTS

NAOMI'S GIFT

AMY CLIPSTON

For Lauran

GLOSSARY FOR PENNSYLVANIA DUTCH WORDS USED IN LANCASTER COUNTY, PENNSYLVANIA

ach—oh
aenti—aunt
appeditlich—delicious
Ausbund—Amish hymnal with only printed words
bedauerlich—sad
boppli—baby
bruder—brother
daed—father
danki—thank you
dat—dad/daddy
dochder—daughter
Englisher—a non-Amish person
fraa—wife
Frehlicher Grischtdaag—Merry Christmas
freind—friend; *freinden*—friends
froh—happy
gegisch—silly
gern gschehne—you're welcome

Grischtdaag—Christmas

grossdaddi—grandfather

grossmammi—grandmother

gut—good

gut nacht—goodnight

Ich liebe dich—I love you

kapp—prayer covering or cap

kind—child

kinner—children

kumm—come

liewe—love, a term of endearment

Lob Lied—song of praise

maedel—young woman

mamm—mom

mei—my

mutter—mother

naerfich—nervous

narrisch—crazy

onkel—uncle

schee—pretty

schtupp—family room

schweschder—sister

Was iss letz?—What's wrong?

Wie geht's?—How do you do? or Good day!

wunderbaar—wonderful

ya—yes

NOTE TO THE READER

While this novel is set against the real backdrop of Lancaster County, Pennsylvania, the characters are fictional. There is no intended resemblance between the characters in this book and any real members of the Amish and Mennonite communities. As with any work of fiction, I've taken license in some areas of research as a means to create the necessary circumstances for my characters. My research was thorough; however, it would be impossible to be completely accurate in details and description, since each and every community differs. Therefore, any inaccuracies in the Amish and Mennonite lifestyles portrayed in this book are completely due to fictional license.

CHAPTER 1

Caleb sucked in a deep breath as the taxi van bounced down Route 340 toward Bird-in-Hand, Pennsylvania. After nearly a decade, he'd returned to the town of his birth. He clasped his hands together. Why was he nervous? This was supposed to be a happy reunion with his family, and yet, his palms were sweaty with anticipation despite the biting December wind.

"*Dat*," Susie said, grabbing the sleeve of his coat and yanking with one hand while pointing toward the indoor farmers market with the other hand. "*Dat*. Can we stop there? Can we? Please? Please?"

"Why would we stop there?" he asked. "We have a farmers market back home that's much the same."

She blew out an exasperated sigh and glowered with annoyance. "To get a gift for *Aenti* Sadie, of course. Teacher Linda says that you should always bring a nice dessert to dinner. Please, *Dat*? I'll pick something out fast like we do at the market at home." She batted her eyelashes and gave her prettiest and cutest smile. "Pretty please, *Dat*?" She looked like a mirror of her beautiful mother, and his heart turned over in his chest. At the tender age of eight, Caleb Schmucker's daughter already knew how to wrap him around her little finger.

He gave a sigh of defeat, and Susie clapped her hands while grinning with triumph.

"Driver?" Caleb asked. "Could we please make a quick stop at the farmers market?"

The middle-aged man nodded and merged into the parking lot.

"We have to make this quick," Caleb said as the van steered into a parking space. "Your *aenti* and *onkel* are expecting us. They know that our train arrived less than an hour ago and will worry if we don't get to their house soon."

"I'll be quick. I promise." Susie nodded, and the ties to her black winter bonnet bobbed up and down on her black wrap.

"We should find a nice pie to bring for *Aenti* Sadie."

"That sounds *gut*." Caleb touched her nose and smiled. Oh how he adored his little girl. There was no greater love in his life.

Except for Barbara.

Pushing the thought from his mind, he took Susie's little hand in his and they climbed from the van. He glanced across the parking lot toward the highway, and his eyes fell on the Kauffman & Yoder Amish Furniture Store, owned by an old family friend, Eli Kauffman. Caleb's elder sister, Sadie, had married Robert, the oldest of the Kauffman sons, while the youngest Kauffman son, Timothy, had been Caleb's best school friend. He wondered how his old friend was doing these days. He would have to stop by and visit him before he and Susie returned to Ohio.

"*Dat*!" Susie yanked Caleb toward the entrance to the farmers market. "Let's go."

Caleb stifled a laugh. The little girl had her mother's impatience too. "I'm coming, *mei liewe*."

They stepped through the double doors, and the holiday smells of freshly baked cookies and breads, spices, and pine assaulted Caleb's senses. The market bustled with customers, English and Amish, rushing to the many booths. Scanning the area, Caleb spotted booths for baked goods, jellies and jams, crafts and gifts, and paintings. A sea of shoppers pushed past Caleb, and he dropped his hold of Susie's hand as he approached the baked-goods counter.

"What kind of pie did you want to get, Susie?" Caleb asked. "Do you think a pumpkin pie or apple?" When his daughter didn't answer, he turned around and found a group of English customers pushing toward the counter.

"Susie?" he called. "Susie?" He glanced through the crowd, finding only unfamiliar faces. "Susan? Susan?" Caleb's heart raced as he pushed through the knot of holiday shoppers, searching for his only child. "Susan!"

. . .

Naomi King straightened a king-size Lone Star patterned quilt and glanced at her best friend Lilly Lapp, who was glancing through the order book. "I can't believe Christmas is next week. Where has the year gone?"

Lilly shook her head. "I don't know. That's a very good question." An English customer approached and began asking Lilly questions about custom ordering a queen-size quilt as a gift.

Turning her back to the counter, Naomi hummed to herself while mentally listing all she had to do before Christmas. She still needed to shop for her parents and her eight siblings. And then there was the baking for the cookie exchange. And she had to—

"Excuse me," a little voice asked, interrupting her mental tirade.

Naomi spun to find a little girl leaning over the counter and pointing toward the king-size Lone Star quilt Naomi was draping over a wooden dowel. "May I help you?"

The girl adjusted the black bonnet on her head. "Did you make that?"

Naomi nodded. "*Ya*, I did."

"It's *schee*." The girl studied the quilt, her eyebrows knitting together in concentration. "My *mamm* made a quilt like this once, only she used blues and creams instead of maroons."

Naomi smiled. "I bet that was *schee*."

"Can I touch it?"

"Of course." Naomi held the quilt out, and the girl ran her hand over it.

The girl studied the quilt, her eyes trained on the intricate star pattern. "My *mamm* promised she would teach me how to quilt someday."

"I bet she will. I think I was about your age when my *mamm* started teaching me."

The girl looked up, and Naomi was struck by her deep-green eyes. They reminded Naomi of the deep green the pasture turned every spring.

"My *mamm* is gone," the girl said, her expression serious.

"Gone?" Naomi set the dowel in the rack and leaned over the counter. "What do you mean?"

"She's in heaven with Jesus." The girl ran her fingers over the counter.

Naomi gasped, cupping a hand to her mouth. "I'm so sorry. You must miss her."

"I do. I was only—" she began.

"Susan!" A man rushed over, his expression full of fear. He placed his hands on the girl's shoulders and angled her to face him. He crouched down and met her at eye level. "I turned my head for a moment and you took off. Do you know how much you scared me? I thought I'd lost you. What were you thinking?"

"I'm sorry, *Dat*." The girl shook her head, tears filling her striking eyes. "I saw the quilt stand, and I wanted to come see the quilts."

The man sighed and closed his eyes for a split second. Standing, he took her hand in his. "Don't do that ever again." His voice pleaded with her. "Promise me?"

"*Ya*." A tear trickled down her rosy cheek, and she sniffed. His expression became tender, and Naomi's heart swelled.

"Don't cry, Susie," he said, brushing her tears away with his fingertip. "It's okay, *mei liewe*. You're all right, and that's all that matters." He glanced toward the clock on the wall. "We need to get going. Your *aenti* is expecting us." He turned to Naomi. "I'm sorry for creating such a scene. My *dochder* took off and scared me so."

Naomi opened her mouth to speak, but her voice was stuck in her throat for a moment. Her eyes were lost in his, which were the same deep shade of emerald as the girl's.

"It was no bother," Naomi finally said. "We were having a nice discussion about quilts. I'm sorry she scared you."

"*Danki.*" He glanced at his daughter. "We must be going." He turned back to Naomi. "*Frehlicher Grischtdaag.*" He smiled, and his handsome face was kind. Yet, there was something sad in his gorgeous eyes. Naomi surmised it was the loss of his wife. Her heart ached for him.

Before she could respond to his Christmas greetings, the man and the girl were gone. He held the girl's hand as they turned the corner. The girl waved at Naomi, and Naomi waved back, her heart touched by the sweet gesture.

The customer who had been chatting with Lilly walked away from the stand.

"What happened?" Lilly asked, leaning over to Naomi.

"What?" Naomi asked, searching the crowd for the man and girl.

"What was all the commotion with the man and the girl?" Lilly closed the order book.

"The girl wandered off from her father, and he was worried about her." Naomi leaned against the counter. "She told me that her mother made quilts."

"Oh, that's sweet."

"*Ya*, it is." Naomi lifted a twin-size quilt from the bag below the counter and began to fold it. "But she also said her mother had died."

Lilly frowned and shook her head. "How *bedauerlich*."

"*Ya*, I know." Naomi glanced toward the door, wishing she could see the girl just one more time. "There was such sadness in her eyes. I saw it in her father's eyes too."

"I can imagine that the sadness was from losing her." Lilly straightened the pens by the register. "I know how hard it was to lose my *mamm*, and I'm much older than she is."

Naomi touched Lilly's arm. "I know. There was just something . . ." She let her voice trail off and pushed the thought away. She'd been burned more than once by misreading her own thoughts and feelings. It was silly to even consider she'd felt something for the man and the girl, but the feeling was strong, deep in her gut. She'd wanted to hug the girl and ask her how long her mother had been gone, to take away some of the pain in her eyes.

But that wasn't Naomi's business. She didn't even know the girl or her father. She'd never seen them before. She wondered which district they belonged to. Were they from Lancaster County or were they visiting for the holidays? Now she would never know. The moment was gone and so were the girl and her father.

"What is it?" Lilly asked, a grin splitting her pretty face. She jammed a hand on the hip of her purple frock. "You're scheming something, Naomi King."

"Don't be *gegisch*." Naomi draped the quilt over a dowel. "I was just thinking about that poor little girl without a mother. My heart goes out to her."

"Is that it? Or were you thinking about her father who misses his wife?"

Naomi frowned. "Please, Lilly. I don't know his name or even what district he's a member of. There's no such thing as love at first sight. Love is a feeling that grows over time. It can't just appear out of thin air."

Lilly's expression was pensive. "You're different than you were when you were seeing Timothy Kauffman."

Naomi shrugged. "No, I'm not different. I just matured. My *mamm* told me I was boy crazy and made a fool of myself the way I ran after Luke Troyer and then Timothy."

Lilly touched Naomi's shoulder. "That's not true. You were never a fool."

"*Ya*, I was." Naomi cleared her throat to prevent a lump from swelling as the humiliation rained down on her. She could still feel the sting of her mother's harsh words after she and Timothy broke up. "My *mamm* told me that I need to concentrate on my family and stop worrying about finding a husband. So, my focus now is my siblings. If I'm meant to find love, God will bring it into my life. But honestly, I think God wants me to help my *mamm* raise my eight siblings."

Lilly shook her head. "You don't honestly believe that, Naomi. God wants us to get married and have *kinner*."

Naomi busied herself with hanging the quilt onto the rack in order to avoid Lilly's probing stare. "*Ya*, I do believe it. I tried love twice and failed. That was the sign that I wasn't meant to find true love, if there even is a true love for me."

"Naomi." Lilly took Naomi's hand and gave her a gentle smile. "Listen to me. I didn't think there was a true love for me, but I was wrong."

Naomi raised an eyebrow in surprise. "You found love?" Lilly's cheeks flushed a bright pink.

"Why haven't you told me?" Naomi asked. "I thought I was your best friend."

"You are." Lilly sighed and sat on a stool. "We were going to keep it a secret until we get published next year."

Naomi gasped. "You're getting married?"

Lilly smiled, and Naomi shrieked and hugged her. "Is it Zach Fisher?" Naomi asked.

Lilly nodded. "I wanted to tell you, but we're trying to keep it a secret."

Naomi smiled. "That's *wunderbaar*. You deserve to be *froh*."

Lilly touched Naomi's arm. "You do too. God will lead you to the path He wants, and I believe He wants you to find true love. You've been hurt in the past, but that doesn't mean you're meant to be alone." She gave a gentle smile. "Just remember this verse from Corinthians: 'And our hope for you is firm, because we know that just as you share in our sufferings, so also you share in our comfort.'"

Naomi nodded in agreement, but she struggled to believe she was meant to be with someone.

"Excuse me," an English customer said, approaching

the counter. "I would like to pick up a couple of quilts for my kids for Christmas. Do you have any queen-size quilts available that are Christmassy?"

"Yes, ma'am, we do," Lilly said, moving to the rack. "Let me show you what I have here."

As Lilly pulled out two quilts, Naomi glanced toward the market exit and wondered where the handsome widower and his daughter were headed when they left.

CHAPTER 2

The van bumped and rattled down the long rock driveway to his sister's large white farmhouse. The dairy farm had been passed down through the Schmucker family for four generations, and Caleb's parents had lived in the apartment at the back of the house until they passed away.

The white clapboard home still looked the same as he remembered from his childhood. The vast three stories sprawled across the front of the property, while one large white barn and three smaller barns sat behind it, housing their livestock and farming supplies. The white split-rail fence outlined the large pasture, and Sadie's gardens—her pride and joy that she replanted every spring—ran the length of the enormous house.

Happy childhood memories swirled through Caleb's mind. He'd spent many hours on the porch with his parents and extended family during the warm months. The back pasture was where he and his cousins would play baseball.

During his teenage years, the pasture became the site for impromptu volleyball courts during youth socials. And it was at one of those socials where he'd met Barbara, who'd been visiting her cousin for the summer. Caleb had taken one look at Barbara's beautiful smile, and he knew he'd met his future bride.

"*Dat*?" Susie's little voice brought him back to the present. "We're here, *ya*?"

Caleb leaned over and touched her chin. "*Ya*, we are." He glanced toward the porch and found his seven nieces and nephews filing out from the front door. "You go ahead and greet your cousins. I'll grab our bags and pay the driver."

"I can't wait to meet them!" Gripping the pumpkin pie in her hands, Susie trotted up the front steps to the circle of cousins.

After grabbing their two bags, Caleb paid the driver and then made his way up the front steps, where he was engulfed in hugs from his nieces and nephews.

"Caleb!" Sadie's voice rang through the crowd. "It's so *gut* to see you!" She pulled him into a tight hug. "How was your trip?"

"*Gut*," he said.

"We were beginning to worry about you," Sadie said.

"We made a stop on the way," Caleb said, glancing at his daughter, who bit her bottom lip. "Susie wanted to bring you a pie."

"This is for you, *Aenti* Sadie." Susie handed her the pie. "We stopped at the farmers market for it."

"Oh, it smells *appeditlich*." After hugging Susie, Sadie motioned for them to come into the house. "*Kumm*! Let's eat!"

. . .

Caleb sat between his nephews, Samuel and Raymond, at his sister's long kitchen table. Across from him, Susie was engrossed in an animated conversation with her cousins about school.

Robert cleared his throat and Caleb bowed his head in silent prayer. The aroma of baked chicken and freshly baked bread filled his senses and he smiled. Being surrounded by family warmed his soul, and he thanked God for the opportunity to spend Christmas with them.

When Robert's fork scraped the plate, Caleb glanced up at the gaggle of arms resembling an octopus reaching for the dishes and bowls of food in the center of the table. Voices rang out around him as the children discussed the upcoming Christmas plans.

"Caleb," Sadie said, raising her voice above the discussions swirling around them. "It's so *gut* to have you here with us. How does it feel to be home again?"

"*Gut.*" Caleb glanced at his daughter, who was laughing while her cousin Janie shared a story. "Real *gut.*" He loved seeing Susie so happy. He wished they had close relatives back home, but Barbara's cousins lived in a neighboring district and rarely visited.

"How are things in Middlefield?" Robert asked.

"Going well." Caleb grabbed the serving fork for the chicken.

"Is the carriage shop keeping you busy?" Robert asked while cutting up his chicken.

"*Ya,*" Caleb said. "The buggy orders have been steady." He filled his plate with chicken and then grabbed a roll. "The Lord is blessing us with plenty of business. How is the dairy business?"

Robert shrugged. "The same. Every time we get ahead, something happens to set us back, like the rising cost of diesel to run the milkers. There's always something holding us back."

Sadie beamed at her husband. "However, the Lord always provides."

Caleb asked Samuel about the youth gatherings, and soon their plates were clean and the serving dishes were empty. While Sadie and the girls cleaned up the kitchen, Caleb joined Robert and the boys in the family room. The conversations spanned the hours as Caleb caught up with the latest community news. Susie rushed by, laughing and talking with her cousins as they stomped up the stairs to the bedrooms. Sadie brought in large hunks of pumpkin pie covered in whipped cream, and Caleb ate until his stomach was sore. "We better get these *kinner* to bed," Sadie said when the clock struck eight. "Service is early in the morning tomorrow."

"*Ya.*" Caleb stood and stretched. "I'll tuck Susie in over in the apartment, *ya?*"

Sadie shook her head. "The girls want Susie to stay with them, but you're welcome to stay in the apartment if you'd like."

"That sounds *gut.*" Caleb carried Susie's bag up the steep stairs to the hallway lined with doors. He felt as if he'd been transported back in time since he'd climbed these stairs thousands of times during his childhood.

He found Susie giggling on a double bed with Janie and Linda. When she spotted Caleb in the doorway, they sat up. "Girls!" Sadie bellowed, joining him in the doorway. "There's no need for all of this noise. You know that your *dat* likes some quiet in the evenings. You don't want him yelling, do you?"

Sadie's daughters silently shook their heads in response. "*Gut*," Sadie continued. "Have you gotten your baths?" They shook their heads no.

"It's time." Sadie stepped into the room and yanked nightgowns from the bureau.

The girls moaned their disappointment.

"Church comes early in the morning." Sadie pointed toward the hallway. "Go get your baths and then come to bed." She glanced at Caleb and smiled. "Let me go check on the boys. I'll be back."

Caleb turned to Susie. "Let's find your gown. You can take a bath too." He placed her bag on the bed and rummaged through it.

He tried to suppress his smile. "*Ya*, but you were also cooped up on a smelly train overnight, and we have services tomorrow. Do you want the other *kinner* in the district to call you the stinky girl from Ohio?"

"No!" She laughed.

"Here." He pulled her bed clothes from the bag. "Now remember to keep your voice down. Your *onkel* doesn't like a lot of noise. We don't want to wear out our welcome on the first night. Go wash up."

Susie removed her prayer covering and unwound her long, light-brown hair from its tight bun. She started for the door and then faced him, her pretty face pensive. "*Dat*, I'm sorry for scaring you at the market."

Caleb lowered himself on the bed and sighed. "I

forgive you, *mei liewe*. I may be a bit overprotective, but it's my job to make sure you're safe." *Like I failed to do with your mother . . .*

He pushed the thought away. He needed to suppress that regret and concentrate on enjoying Christmas with his sister's family.

"I know." She bit her lower lip and then smiled. "Did you see that pretty lady at the quilt stand?"

"What pretty lady?" Sadie rounded the corner with her eyes wide with excitement.

Caleb swallowed a groan. While he loved his sister dearly, he'd learned a long time ago that she was a hopeless gossip, who enjoyed sharing the latest community news at her weekly quilting bees. Rumors of his courting Barbara spread like wildfire after Sadie caught Caleb and Barbara chatting on the porch late one night during the summer they met.

"At the farmers market, where we got the pie," Susie said, hugging her nightgown to her chest. "She was at a quilt stand, and she said that her *mamm* taught her how to make quilts when she was about my age."

"Quilt stand?" Sadie tilted her head in question. "That must have been Naomi King or maybe Lilly Lapp. They both work there. Naomi's *mamm* owns the stand. She's had it for years, and it does a good bit of business. I quilt for her sometimes."

"Really?" Susie's eyes were wide with excitement. "Would you teach me how to quilt, *Aenti* Sadie?"

"*Ya*." Sadie touched Susie's nose. "Now you run along and get your bath. We must rise early in the morning."

"Okay." Susie trotted down the long hallway.

"She needs a *mamm*," Sadie said, shooting Caleb a stern look. "It's been two years."

Caleb frowned. He'd expected a lecture with Sadie's unsolicited advice, but he'd hoped she'd wait a day or two before starting in on him. "She has plenty of female role models in our community. She loves her teacher, and we have many friends at church."

"That's not the same as a *mamm*." Sadie's expression softened, and she stepped toward him. "She needs someone to be there when she has questions that only a woman can discuss."

Caleb pinched the bridge of his nose in hopes of stopping the tension headache brewing behind his eyes. "I know you mean well, but you can't tell me how to run my—"

"Naomi King wouldn't be a good match for you." Sadie talked over him while shaking her head. "She's a bit too eager for a husband. You know the type—always mingling with the men after service and trying to get them to go for rides with her."

"Sadie," Caleb said, attempting to interrupt her, but she continued her monologue as if she'd never heard him.

"Naomi ran after Luke Troyer, who married Sarah Rose, Robert's youngest sister, a couple of months ago." Sadie frowned. "Then she enticed Timothy Kauffman, but they broke up." She smiled. "I have just the *maedel* for you. There haven't been any rumors about her, and she's very sweet."

"Sadie," he repeated, standing.

Her grin widened with excitement. "Her name is

Irene, and her *daed* owns a carriage shop. She'd be a *wunderbaar mamm* for Susie. You could move back here and go to work for her *daed* and—"

"Sadie!" His booming voice caused her to jump. "I'm sorry for startling you, but you're not listening to me. I'm not looking for a *mamm* for Susie just yet. Barbara was the love of my life, and I'm not ready to try to replace her."

"You won't ever replace her, Caleb." Sadie touched his arm. "You'll find a new *liewe*, who will help ease the pain and give Susie the guidance that only a *mamm* can give her. I know it's hard, but it's time to move on."

What do you know about loss? He swallowed the thought and glanced toward the door. "I think I'm going to go get ready for bed. Will you call me when the girls are ready to be tucked in?" He started for the door.

"*Ya*," Sadie said. "Caleb."

He faced her, hoping she wouldn't lecture him again. "*Ya*?"

"Please think about what I said." She stepped toward the door with a hopeful expression. "You and Susie are more than welcome to stay with us. You can move into the apartment, and Susie would love to go to school with her cousins. She needs her family, Caleb. Barbara was an only child, and her parents are gone. Who do you really have in Ohio?"

Caleb folded his arms in defiance. "We have family. Barbara had cousins, and our church district is *wunderbaar*. We're not alone."

"Think about it." She clasped her hands together. "I want you to meet Irene and consider my offer."

He nodded, knowing she wasn't going to let this issue die until he agreed. "Fine. I'll consider it."

"*Gut!*" She hugged him. "I'll call you when it's time to kiss Susie goodnight."

As Caleb descended the stairs, he hoped Sadie wouldn't spend his entire visit trying to play matchmaker. He wasn't ready for another relationship, and he believed Susie was receiving all the female guidance she needed. While Sadie had the best intentions, her meddling was misguided. He was a grown man and capable of making the best decisions for his child; Sadie needed to concentrate on her own family.

Caleb plucked his bag from the family-room floor, then stepped through the doorway and into the apartment at the back of the house.

He moved through the small sitting room to the bedroom. As he placed the bag on the bed, he thought of the young woman at the farmers market. While he didn't know her name, he'd noticed her beautiful face and captivating brown eyes. She seemed to have made an impression on Susie. He wondered if he would run into her again during his visit.

Deep in his heart, he hoped he would.

CHAPTER 3

Naomi sat with the other young unmarried women while she sang along with the familiar German hymns in the *Ausbund*. Keeping with tradition, the three-hour service was held in the home of one of the church district families on every other Sunday. With the living room and bedroom moveable walls removed, the downstairs of Eli and Elizabeth Kauffman's home was spacious. Backless benches were lined up for the district members, and later they would be converted to tables for lunch.

The congregation was seated by age and gender, and the service area was plain. There was no altar, no cross, no flowers, nor instruments. They sang the hymns slowly, and a male song leader chosen at the beginning of the service would begin the first syllable of each line.

While the ministers met in another room for thirty minutes to choose who would preach that day, the congregation continued to sing. They returned during the last verse of the second hymn, which was always *"Lob Lied,"* and when the ministers hung their hats on the pegs on the wall, it symbolized that the service was about to begin.

The minister began the first sermon, and Naomi clasped her hands. Her eyes scanned the congregation, and she tried to concentrate on the minister's words. However, her thoughts kept fluttering to the scene at the farmers market yesterday. She could still visualize the little girl's sweet face when she shared that her mother had died. The fear mixed with relief on the father's face was still fresh in Naomi's mind—along with his expressive eyes.

She was still thinking of him when her stare moved to the married men sitting across the room. She spotted Robert Kauffman, and her gaze stopped when her eyes focused on the man next to him. She blinked, but the figure didn't transform. The man from the market was sitting next to Robert Kauffman.

How can this be?

The man's eyes met hers, and he looked as surprised as she felt. A smile turned up the corners of his mouth, and Naomi felt her cheeks burn with embarrassment.

Why was this stranger causing her to blush? She didn't even know him! She quickly looked away in order to break the trance.

The first sermon ended, and Naomi knelt in silent prayer along with the rest of the congregation. During her prayers, she pushed thoughts of the stranger from her mind and thanked God for the blessings in her life. She also asked for health and happiness for her family during the upcoming holidays.

After the prayers, the deacon read from the Scriptures and then the hour-long main sermon began. Naomi tried in vain to keep her eyes off the stranger during the sermon, but her glance kept moving back to him. He occasionally met her gaze with a pleasant smile, and each time, her heart fluttered and cheeks flushed. She stared at her lap and willed herself to concentrate on the sermon, which was always spoken in High German, keeping with Amish tradition.

She swallowed a sigh of relief when the kneeling prayer was over. The congregation then stood for the benediction, and the closing hymn was sung.

When the service was over, Naomi moved toward the kitchen with the rest of the women to help serve the noon meal. The men converted the benches into tables and then sat and chatted while awaiting their food. As she headed for the kitchen, Naomi averted her eyes from the group of men talking in the corner since she'd spotted the mysterious widower speaking to Timothy Kauffman.

"The service was beautiful, *ya*?" Kathryn Beiler asked Naomi as she moved a tray of pies and cakes over to the counter covered in the desserts.

"*Ya*, it was," Naomi agreed, filling a pitcher of water.

"Are you ready for Christmas?" Kathryn asked.

Naomi laughed. "No. I still need some things to finish my gifts. How about you?"

Kathryn shook her head. "No, I'm not ready either. Perhaps we should go shopping to—"

"Hi!" a little voice screeched. "Hi!"

Naomi glanced over just as Susie came trotting toward her with Robert and Sadie Kauffman's two youngest daughters trailing close behind. "Susie?"

"I remember you from the farmers market!" The little girl beamed. "So this is your church district?"

"*Ya*, it is." Naomi gestured toward Janie and Linda. "I see you know Janie and Linda Kauffman."

Susie took their hands in hers. "They're my cousins. I just met them for the first time yesterday, and we're already best friends."

Naomi plastered a smile on her lips as she inwardly gasped—Susie and her father were related to the Kauffmans! She hoped that meeting Susie wouldn't become awkward. While the Kauffmans had been gracious after her breakups with Luke and Timothy, she still felt uncomfortable. She could only imagine the rumors that were still flying about her and how forward she was with the boys.

"You know Susie?" Kathryn asked, sidling up to Naomi.

"We met at the farmers market yesterday," Naomi said.

Susie beamed. "She makes *schee* quilts like my *mamm* did."

"*Ya*," Kathryn said, smiling. "She does." She turned to Naomi. "Susie and her *dat* are visiting from Ohio for the holidays. Her *dat* is Sadie's *bruder*."

"Oh," Naomi said with a nod while suppressing an inward groan. "That's so nice."

"What's your name?" Susie asked.

"I'm Naomi," she said, shaking the girl's hand. "It's nice to meet you."

"You too," Susie said.

A chorus of voices sounded as a group of women entered the kitchen laughing, including Beth Anne Bontrager, one of Timothy's sisters, and Miriam Lapp, Timothy's fiancée.

Beth Anne's eyes widened as she approached. "Susie!" She hugged the little girl. "I saw your *dat*, and I was looking for you. How are you?"

"*Gut*." Susie gave her a shy smile.

Beth Anne smiled. "You don't know me, do you?"

Susie bit her bottom lip and shook her head. "I'm sorry, but I haven't met you yet."

"She's *Aenti* Beth Anne," Janie said.

"I'm your *Onkel* Robert's sister," Beth Anne said. "And this is Miriam. She's *Onkel* Timothy's fiancée."

Naomi slowly backed up toward the counter. She wanted to sneak away and hide somewhere far away from this uncomfortable moment. Pushing thoughts of Susie and her father out of her mind, she crossed the kitchen and found her mother. She planned to help serve lunch and forget her idea of getting to know Susie.

. . .

"Caleb!" A voice bellowed. "Caleb Schmucker!"

Caleb turned just as Timothy Kauffman smacked his back. "Timothy!"

"How are you?" Timothy gave his hand a stiff shake. "It's been what—ten years?"

"It feels that long. I'm *gut*." Caleb examined his face and found it clean-shaven. "You're not married yet?"

Timothy smirked. "I'm working on it."

"What are you waiting for?" Caleb asked. "You're thirty now. We're getting old."

Timothy laughed. "*Ya*, we are, but I'm getting there. I think next wedding season I'll be taking my vow with my *liewe*. How's Susie? I believe I saw her running off with Robert's girls."

"She is doing well," Caleb said. He patted Timothy's shoulder. "It's so *gut* to see you. I've missed my family here."

Timothy shrugged. "So move back. You can build buggies here just like you do in Middlefield."

Caleb scanned the room, spotting a host of familiar faces. "It's tempting."

Timothy guided Caleb to a table where they sat with Timothy's brothers and a few other men Caleb recognized. "I think a new start would be *wunderbaar* for you and Susie."

"How are you, Caleb?" Daniel Kauffman asked, leaning over and shaking Caleb's hand.

"It's so *gut* to see you," Eli Kauffman interjected. "I was so sorry to hear about Barbara."

"*Danki*," Caleb said with a nod.

"How are things in Ohio?" Eli asked.

He updated the men on his life, and out of the corner of his eye, he spotted the woman from the farmers market. She approached the table with a tray of potato salad, and he tried to make eye contact.

"*Danki*, Naomi," Daniel said as she filled his plate with potato salad.

Naomi. Her name is Naomi.

Caleb let the name roll through his mind while he

tried to remember what Sadie had told him about her. According to Sadie, the woman was too eager for a husband and she had run after Luke Troyer and Timothy. However, she looked very sweet and humble with her pretty face and deep-brown eyes. He couldn't imagine her running after any man.

While the conversation at his table continued among the men, Caleb tried again to make eye contact with her. However, she quickly served each of them and then moved on to the adjacent table. He wondered if she'd even seen him. He'd noticed her during the service, and she'd met his gaze. Why was she avoiding it now?

Naomi headed back to the kitchen, and Caleb felt the unfaltering urge to follow her. He set his fork on the table and stood.

"Caleb?" Timothy asked, looking confused.

Caleb nodded toward the kitchen. "I'm going to go check on Susie. I'll be right back." He headed toward the kitchen but was waylaid by David Beiler, who stepped in front of him, blocking the doorway.

"How are you, Caleb?" David shook his hand. "It's so good to see you."

"It's nice to see you too. I spoke to Kathryn earlier." Caleb glanced past him, spotting Naomi chatting with an older woman while filling another pan with potato salad.

"Caleb!" Sadie said, appearing with a tray of rolls. "I've been looking for you. I have someone I want you to meet."

Caleb glanced back toward the kitchen doorway just as Naomi stepped through it. She met his stare and then quickly turned away. Before he could step toward her, Sadie grabbed his arm and yanked him to the other side of the room, causing him to stumble along behind her.

"Sadie, I was going to—" he began.

"Caleb," she said, bringing him to a jolting stop in front of an attractive young blonde, who smiled. "This is Irene Wagler. Irene's *daed* owns Wagler's Buggies in Intercourse."

"*Wie geht's*?" Irene held out her hand.

Caleb gave her hand a quick shake. "It's nice to meet you." Irene glanced toward the kitchen. "I better get back in and finish serving the drinks."

"Don't be silly," Sadie said, waving off the comment. "You two get acquainted, and I'll bring out the drinks." She winked at Irene, and Caleb wondered if she'd meant to be discreet. However, he was certain his older sister had never been subtle a day in her life.

"Sadie tells me you're visiting for the holidays," Irene said as she leaned against the wall behind her.

"*Ya*." Caleb fingered his beard and glanced across the room where Naomi was scooping potato salad onto a man's plate.

"You should come by and see my *daed's* shop. It's very nice."

"Maybe I will," he said.

Susie raced over, narrowly missing running into a man who was headed in the opposite direction. "*Dat! Dat!*"

"Calm down," he told her, leaning over to take her hand in his. "You almost crashed into that man."

"*Dat!*" Her eyes were wide with excitement. "*Aenti* Sadie told me that I'm going to a cookie exchange tomorrow! Isn't that *wunderbaar*?" She squeezed his hands. "I love it here."

He laughed. "That sounds *wunderbaar gut*. I'm so glad you're having fun." He nodded toward Irene. "This is my new friend, Irene. Can you say hello to her?"

"Hi. I'm Susan Schmucker, but my friends call me Susie."

"Hi, Susie. I'm Irene, and I'll be at the cookie exchange tomorrow too." Although Irene smiled down at his daughter, Caleb couldn't help but notice that the smile didn't reach her eyes.

"I'm going to go back in the kitchen and help with the dishes," Susie said. "Bye!"

Caleb grinned after her. Oh how that little girl warmed his heart.

"So, tell me about Middlefield," Irene said.

He shrugged. "What do you want to know?"

Irene smiled, and this one was real. "Everything."

CHAPTER 4

"How are you really?" Timothy asked. "You said things are *gut* at work, but how are you really coping?"

Caleb shivered while sitting on the porch at Eli Kauffman's house later that evening. Most everyone had left, except for a few families, the bulk of them related to the Kauffmans. He was disappointed that he hadn't managed to speak with Naomi before she exited with her family. However, he'd shared a brief gaze with her from across the crowded room. She'd given him a shy smile, and he noticed she had an adorable dimple on her right cheek. He hated how cliché the smile across the crowded room felt, and he hoped he'd meet her personally soon.

"Caleb?" Timothy asked. "Did you hear me? I asked how you truly are. You can be honest with me."

Caleb buried his frigid hands in the pockets of his coat. "I'm living, day to day. Susie keeps me going."

Timothy frowned. "How's Susie coping?"

Caleb shrugged. "She seems okay to me. She loves school, and her teacher is *wunderbaar*." He shook his head. "Sadie told me last night that Susie needs a *mamm*, but it's not that simple. I can't just order one from a catalog."

Timothy gave a bark of laughter. "Mail-order *mamm*, eh?"

"Right." Caleb chuckled.

"There's no one special waiting for you back in Ohio?"

"No." Caleb shook his head. "One of Barbara's cousins tried to set me up with a couple of her friends, but we really didn't have anything in common. Her cousin finally gave up on me."

Timothy turned to him, looking intrigued. "Don't you want to find a *mamm* for Susie? I don't mean to sound like your *schweschder*, but why would you want to raise Susie all by yourself?"

"It's not that I choose to be alone, but it sort of feels like I'm supposed to be alone." Caleb paused, gathering his thoughts. He'd never opened up about this subject before and it made him uncomfortable. However, he trusted Timothy and he wanted to get the emotions out in the open. "I feel like I don't deserve to be *froh* after what happened to Barbara. I feel like it's my fault."

Timothy frowned. "It's not your fault, Caleb. It was an accident."

"I know," Caleb said with a sigh. "But it's not fair that I'm still here, and she's not. I feel like I should be punished or suffer somehow." He thought about the nights spent alone in bed, thinking of her and all they'd lost. "I feel like I'm stuck in this lonely cloud sometimes just floating around all by myself."

"Maybe you and Susie need a new beginning." Timothy brightened. "You can come back here and start over. That would cheer you up a bit and help you move on."

"It's not that easy. I also feel guilty about moving on with my life. How is it fair that I can move on, but Barbara can't?"

Timothy was silent for a moment. "What's keeping you in Ohio? What do you have there?"

"Susie has a few of Barbara's cousins that we see occasionally," Caleb said. "That seems to be the right reason to stay. But to be perfectly honest, I'm not sure why we are stuck in the same old routine. I guess it's easy because I don't have to think about it. I just continue through the daily grind. The reminders of Barbara all over the house are painful, but I try to let go of my emotions and just remain distant. It's the only way I know to cope with it all for Susie's sake."

"So you're the shell of the man you once were?" Timothy shook his head. "That's sad."

Caleb paused, touching his beard while considering Timothy's words. He knew his friend was right, but he didn't want to talk about it anymore. He needed to change the subject. "I'd rather hear about your life, Timothy. When do I get to meet your future *fraa*?"

Timothy jammed a thumb toward the door. "Miriam is here. She was talking with my sisters earlier."

"How'd you meet her?"

Timothy shook his head. "It's a long story. We met at a singing."

"A singing?" Caleb sat up straight on the bench. "Your district has singings for folks our age? I definitely need to move back home."

"Ha, ha," Timothy muttered, his voice seeping sarcasm. "That's not what I meant. We met when we were younger, and then we parted ways. Miriam moved to Indiana for a few years and then came back last year. We worked things out, and now we're finally on the right path. I guess God needed us to grow up a bit before we were ready to get married."

"That may be so." *Is that why God took Barbara from me? Is there a lesson I need to learn before I find happiness again?* Caleb stared out at the small snowflakes beginning to fall from the sky while the thoughts floated through his mind. "We may have a white Christmas," he finally said.

"*Ya*," Timothy said. "It's supposed to snow a few times before Christmas Eve."

Caleb wanted to ask Timothy about Naomi. However, he didn't want to make it sound like he was interested in her. He didn't even know her, but he found her so intriguing. There was something about her, something subtle that he couldn't put into words. She was nothing like the women back in Ohio that Barbara's cousin had tried to push him to get to know.

"You should come by the furniture store," Timothy said, rubbing his hands together. "We rebuilt it after the fire, and it looks a bit different. It's a little bigger. We've been really busy this year. My *daed* hired a few more carpenters."

"I'm glad business is *gut*. I'd heard about the fire," Caleb said. "I'm sorry about Peter."

"*Ya*, that was a tragedy." Timothy frowned. "Much

like what happened . . ." His words trailed off, but Caleb knew he was speaking of Barbara.

Caleb didn't want to talk about the accident now and run the risk of getting emotional. "On the way in yesterday, Susie and I stopped at the farmers market, and she spoke to a woman at a quilt stand." He gestured toward the door. "The woman was here today. Her name is Naomi, and Susie has really taken to her. Do you know her?"

Timothy smiled. "*Ya*, you could say I know her."

Curious, Caleb raised an eyebrow. For some reason, he'd hoped the rumors Sadie had shared weren't true.

"I feel bad because I sort of broke her heart." Timothy shook his head. "You won't be proud of me, *bruder*."

"I'm certain it's nothing that you should be ashamed of, Timothy," Caleb said, hoping he wasn't going to regret asking about her.

"I guess you could say I led her on." Timothy stared off toward the falling snow. "We courted for a while, and I guess I sort of used her to get my mind off Miriam when Miriam came back into town. I feel terrible about it. I was going to keep my word and stay with Naomi, but she set me free, saying she knew I loved Miriam and not her. Naomi seems so sad now. I feel bad about it, but I couldn't live a lie either. If I had married Naomi, we would've wound up resenting each other."

Caleb nodded, letting the words sink in. As usual, Sadie had it wrong. From what Timothy had described, Naomi wasn't a desperate woman; she'd simply had her heart broken.

"But Naomi is a real nice *maedel*. We're still friends."
Timothy hugged his coat to his chest. "It's cold, *ya*?"

"It is December," Caleb said. "What did you expect—a
heat wave?"

Timothy chuckled. "I'm glad to see you're still a wise
guy."

The door opened and banged shut, and Robert
stepped out. "It's cold out here. How can you sit out here
and talk?"

"We can hear our thoughts out here, unlike in
there," Timothy said with a smile.

Robert chuckled. "*Ya*, the women and *kinner* are
loud."

He looked toward the road. "I guess we better get
going. The animals will be hungry." He stepped back
toward the door. "I'll gather everyone up."

Timothy stood. "We'll get the buggies hitched."

Caleb followed him to the barn. "It was *gut* visiting
with you."

"You should come by the shop and see me this
week," Timothy said as he opened the barn door.

"*Ya*, I will." Caleb led Robert's horse from the stall.

"You really should think about moving back here,"
Timothy repeated, leading his horse out of the barn. "I
know you could get a job building buggies here, or you
could even start your own business. I'm certain you
could get a loan and find some land." Timothy snapped
his fingers. "In fact, there's some land with a big shop
for sale by the furniture store. If you'd like, I could contact the owner and tell him—"

"Whoa!" Caleb held his hand up to silence his

friend. "Slow down, Timothy. I just arrived yesterday, and I didn't come with the intention of moving back."

Timothy grinned. "I know you didn't come with that intention, but you could leave with it."

"Timothy!" a woman's voice called. "Are we leaving? It's getting late."

"Caleb," Timothy said with a sweeping gesture as the brunette approached. "This is Miriam Lapp. Miriam, this is Caleb Schmucker, my best friend from boyhood. He's visiting from Ohio for Christmas."

Caleb shook her hand. "It's nice to meet you."

"You too," she said with a smile. "I met your daughter, Susie. She's a cutie."

"*Danki*." Caleb hitched Robert's horse to the buggy while Timothy hitched his. "I guess I'll see you again," he said, climbing into the buggy seat.

"*Ya*," Timothy said. "I expect to see you."

"You will." Caleb drove the buggy up to the porch, and Robert, Sadie, and the children piled in. As he steered onto the main road and headed toward their house, the children chattered about the upcoming school Christmas program.

He smiled as they talked, their voices filled with excitement, and he watched the snowflakes pelt the windshield. His thoughts turned to Naomi and Timothy's story of how he broke her heart. He longed to talk to Naomi, to get to know her. But why? Why should he think of this woman when he was only going to be in town a short while?

Unless he took Timothy's advice and stayed . . .

He pushed the thoughts away as the horse

clip-clopped down the road. He would only concentrate on spending time with his family. That was all that mattered. His family would get him through the second anniversary of Barbara's death. He needed them now.

CHAPTER 5

"Why do I have to go?" Naomi asked as she placed more cookies into the five-gallon bucket at her feet. "You can take my sisters and then bring them back when it's over."

Lilly tapped her finger on the counter with impatience. "Naomi, we discussed this. You're expected to be at this cookie exchange."

"No, I'm not." Naomi continued to drop cookies into the bucket. "I don't belong there. Sarah Rose and Miriam will both be there for sure. It's going to be at the Kauffmans' bakery, so it's a Kauffman event."

"So?" Lilly threw up her hands. "You're a friend of the Kauffman family."

"But you were invited, not me," Naomi said, dropping the last of the sugar cookies into the bucket, filling it to the brim. "You're Miriam's sister. I'm just an ex-fiancée. You can't get much more awkward than that."

Lilly swiped an extra cookie from the counter. "You're the only one who thinks it's awkward. My sister happens to like you, and all the Kauffman sisters talk to you every time they see you. The only awkwardness is what you perceive in your head." She bit the cookie and moaned. "These cookies are delicious. You really outdid yourself."

"*Danki*," Naomi muttered.

"You really need to get over this idea that the Kauffmans don't like you. It's simply not true," Lilly said, lowering herself into a kitchen chair. "My sister is going to be a Kauffman, so that makes me a Kauffman by default. You're my best friend, so you're going to have to hang out with me and the Kauffmans."

"You could never understand how I feel," Naomi's voice quavered as she swept the crumbs from the counter into the palm of her hand. "Every time I see them, I think of how I made a fool of myself. It's hard to relive it over and over again."

"You didn't make a fool of yourself," Lilly said. "You were just immature."

Naomi nodded. "I know. I pursued Luke in a very unladylike way by running after him and bringing him lunch all the time. I never should've chased after him."

Lilly gave a sad smile. "You didn't realize you were doing that. You thought you were in love with Luke, but it was really a crush. On the other hand, you didn't pursue Timothy. He courted you." She pointed to Naomi for emphasis. "He proposed to you and then changed his mind, breaking your heart in the process."

"That's true," Naomi began, "but I think I went about it all the wrong way with both of them. I was so eager, and I was trying to make my future happen instead of waiting for God's plan." She sniffed.

"*Ach*." Lilly stood and touched Naomi's shoulder. "I didn't mean to upset you."

"It's okay." Naomi wiped away her threatening tears and shook her head.

"The Kauffmans are members of your church district," Lilly said softly. "You can't avoid them unless you stop going to church."

Naomi leaned against the counter and swiped a cookie from the bucket. "Sometimes I dream of marrying someone from another district, so I don't have to see them every other Sunday. Is that *gegisch*?"

Lilly snorted. "*Ya*, it's *gegisch*. How can you marry someone from another district if you don't visit other districts? Do you think an eligible bachelor will fall from heaven and transport you into another church district?"

Naomi glowered.

"I'm sorry." Lilly smiled. "Naomi, I'm just trying to tell you that you have every right to go to this cookie exchange. The Kauffmans like you, and they want you there. How will it look if I show up with your sisters and you're absent?"

"Tell them I'm ill." Naomi bit into the cookie. "These cookies aren't half bad."

"It would be a lie if I told them you're ill, and lying is a sin. I'm not going to knowingly sin this close to Christmas." Lilly crossed the kitchen to the doorway heading into the family room. "Lizzie Anne! Levina! Sylvia!" She bellowed each of Naomi's sisters' names.

The girls raced into the kitchen, chattering all at once. "Lilly!" Lizzie Anne, who was fifteen, hugged her. "*Wie geht's*?"

"Is it time to go yet?" Sylvia, who was eight, whined. "I want cookies!"

"We're going to be late!" Levina, who was ten, pulled on her wrap and bonnet and headed out the door, announcing she was ready to go.

Lilly shot Naomi a smile. "Are you ready?"

"No," Naomi muttered. She snatched her wrap from the peg by the door and moved to the doorway, where she spotted her mother sitting in her favorite chair quilting. "We're leaving," she told her mother.

"Have fun," her mother said with a smile.

"*Ya.*" Naomi crossed the kitchen and grabbed the bucket of cookies. She instructed Lizzie Anne and Sylvia to carry the two covered dishes to the buggy. "Elam should have the buggy waiting for us. *Daed* told him to hook it up earlier."

"Your *mamm's* not coming?" Lilly asked as she tied her bonnet under her chin.

"No," Naomi said, heading for the door. "She has some last-minute quilts to finish. They're Christmas orders that an English customer is going to pick up later in the week. We're going to have a quilting bee at Sadie's on Wednesday to finish them up." She sighed as her sisters rushed out the door. "Let's get this over and done with."

"Naomi," Lilly began with a condescending smile. "It's Christmas. Get in the Christmas spirit."

Naomi rolled her eyes. "I can't wait until this Christmas season is over, and we can get back to our normal lives."

Lilly's smile faded. "You don't mean that."

Frowning, Naomi placed the bucket on the counter. "No, I don't mean it, really. The *kinner* are excited."

Her eyes filled with tears, and she suddenly felt like a heel. "I'm very blessed. I have a *wunderbaar* family and *freinden* like you. But sometimes I feel selfish and wish I had someone special to share the holidays with." Clearing her throat, she lifted the bucket. "But that's a selfish and *gegisch* thing to say. Let's go."

"No, it's okay." Lilly touched Naomi's arm. "You'll find your special someone."

"Naomi!" Sylvia's voice shrieked. "It's cold out here!"

Shaking her head, Naomi headed for the door. She hoped the cookie exchange would be quick and painless.

. . .

With her sisters laughing and chattering in the back, Naomi guided the horse as the buggy bounced along the road leading to the Kauffman Amish Bakery. The terrain was hilly, and the roads were winding and rural. Soon she spotted the Kauffman farm with a cluster of large houses set back off the road and surrounded by four barns, along with a large pasture dotted with snow.

The property was owned by Elizabeth and Eli Kauffman, Timothy's parents, and included their house, Timothy's house, and Sarah and Luke Troyer's house. The bakery was the fourth house, the one closest to the road. Timothy and his five siblings had grown up in the biggest house, where his parents still lived.

Naomi steered into the parking lot and brought it to a stop by a row of buggies. A tall sign with Kauffman Amish Bakery in old-fashioned letters hung above the door of the large, white clapboard farmhouse with the sweeping wraparound porch. Out behind the building was a fenced-in play area, and beyond that was an enclosed field. The three other large farmhouses and four barns were set back beyond the pasture. The dirt road leading to the other homes was roped off with a sign declaring: Private Property—No Trespassing. A large, paved parking lot sat adjacent to the bakery.

"Cookies!" Sylvia yelled, trotting toward the steps.

"Yay!" Levina chimed in.

"Wait!" Lizzie Anne called. "You can carry something." She pulled the covered dishes from the back of the buggy. "Here. Take these."

The girls took the serving platters and hurried toward the bakery.

"Slow down!" Lizzie Anne called. Shaking her head, she hefted the bucket up from the buggy floor.

"*Danki*," Naomi said while she and Lilly unhitched the horse. "You take the empty buckets, and I'll bring the cookies."

Lizzie Anne started toward the door, carrying the empty buckets that they would fill with cookies. "I'm going to see if Lindsay is here."

While Lilly led the horse to the pasture to join the other horses, Naomi grabbed the bucket of cookies and started toward the stairs. A sign on the door read: Bakery Closed at 4 p.m. for Private Party.

Lilly fell in step beside her. "Smile, Naomi," she said as they approached the door. "It's Christmas."

Plastering a smile on her face, Naomi yanked the door open and stepped into the bakery. The room was rearranged with a long line of tables placed in the center of the room with piles of cookies lined up from one end to the other. The counter was filled with a variety of covered dishes, which Naomi assumed were desserts other than cookies. Women and girls of all ages were gathered around the table chatting. Naomi inhaled the delicious scents of cookies, cakes, breads, and casseroles.

"Naomi!" Susie yelled as she ran over and reached for the bucket. "Can I help you?"

Naomi couldn't stop the smile forming on her lips. "Hello, Susie." She handed the little girl the bucket. "Are you certain you can lift this? It's sort of heavy."

"I got it." Susie huffed and puffed, but she couldn't lift it. Grinning, Naomi grabbed the handle. "Let me help you."

"That's a good idea. We'll work together." Susie put her little hand on the handle next to Naomi's, and they lifted together. Walking slowly, they moved to the table.

"On three, we'll lift the bucket onto the table," Naomi said. "One, two, three!"

They hefted the bucket onto an empty spot on the table and began to carefully remove the cookies.

"Teamwork," Susie said with a smile.

Elizabeth Kauffman stepped to the center of the room and clapped her hands. "Hello everyone!" she said. "I'm so glad you all could come to our cookie exchange. I'm sure you all remember the rules. We'll file around the table and fill our buckets until all of the cookies are gone." She motioned toward the counter behind her. "And then we'll enjoy our delicious desserts. *Frehlicher Grischtdaag!*"

Chattering and laughing, the women and girls lined up around the table.

Susie looked up at Naomi. "Can I help you get cookies?"

Naomi's heart warmed. "I would love it," she said.

Susie beamed and held up the bucket. "I'll get us the best cookies."

Touching Susie's shoulder, Naomi smiled. "That sounds *wunderbaar gut.*"

As they moved around the table grabbing cookies, Naomi wondered why Susie had latched onto her when there were a host of other women and Susie's cousins in the room. And would Susie's father approve if he saw Susie with her? Her thoughts turned to Susie's father, and she wondered what he was doing while they filled buckets with cookies.

. . .

"This is nice," Caleb said. He glanced around the showroom of the Kauffman & Yoder Amish Furniture Store and marveled at the dining-room sets, bedroom suites, entertainment centers, hutches, end tables, desks, and coffee tables. All were examples of the finely crafted pieces that Timothy and the other carpenters created.

Timothy's father, Eli, had built the original store with his best friend, Elmer Yoder, before Timothy was born.

"*Danki.*" Timothy looped an arm around Caleb's shoulder. "Let's go in the shop and you can see everyone."

Timothy led Caleb behind the counter and through the doorway to the center of the work area. Caleb scanned the sea of carpenters and waved at Timothy's brother, Daniel. The large, open warehouse was divided into nearly a dozen work areas separated by workbenches cluttered with an array of tools.

The sweet scent of wood and stain filled his nostrils. The men working around him were building beautifully designed pieces that would be favorites among Lancaster County tourists and residents alike. Hammers banged and saw blades whirled beneath the hum of diesel-powered air compressors.

Eli approached and shook Caleb's hand. "*Wie geht's?*"

"I'm doing well," Caleb said. "This is a *wunderbaar* shop you have. It's bigger, and the furniture is still *schee.*"

"*Danki.*" Eli folded his arms and glanced around. "We're pleased with it. Business has been very *gut* this year. The Lord is *gut* to us."

Daniel approached with another man at his side. "Caleb! This is Luke Troyer, my sister Sarah's husband. Luke, this is a dear old friend, Caleb Schmucker. He abandoned us and moved to Ohio several years ago."

Caleb chuckled as he shook Luke's hand. "It's nice to meet you, and I didn't abandon anyone."

Luke laughed. "Nice to meet you too."

"Caleb builds buggies," Timothy said. "He's known in Middlefield as one of the best."

Caleb waved off the comment. "You're exaggerating."

"We could use your talent around here," Timothy said.

"You should have your own shop." Daniel patted Caleb's shoulder. "You need to move back here."

"That's funny." Caleb nodded. "I keep hearing that."

"I'm serious," Daniel continued. "Did you see that shop just down the road?" He pointed in the direction of the showroom. "It's not far from here. An *Englisher* owns it." He glanced at Eli. "What's his name?"

"Parker," Eli said, rubbing his beard. "Riley Parker."

Daniel snapped his fingers. "Right! He's been trying to sell it for quite a while. I bet you could get a great deal on it."

"That's a great idea," Luke chimed in. "We could help you fix the place up."

"*Ya*, we could," Timothy said with a grin.

"Hold on a minute!" Caleb held his hands up. "Slow down. I have a life in Ohio."

Timothy raised his eyebrows in question, and Caleb glanced away.

"Let's introduce you to the rest of the carpenters," Eli said. "Elmer would enjoy seeing you. It's been a long time."

• • •

After meeting all of the carpenters, Caleb sat in the break room with Timothy and Daniel. "Your *dat* has done well for himself."

Timothy passed a bottle of water across the table to Caleb. "*Ya*, he has. It's hard work, but it's paid off."

"Is Susie at the cookie party today?" Daniel asked while opening a bottle of water.

Caleb took a sip and nodded. "She was excited about it this morning. She loves being with her cousins."

Timothy raised his eyebrows.

Caleb shook his head. "Timothy, please don't start nagging me about moving here."

Timothy feigned insult. "I didn't say a word."

"Don't you think it would be good for Susie to be around her cousins and her family?" Daniel asked.

Caleb nodded. "I know it would be. I'm just not certain it will be good for me." He tore at the label on the bottle. "I'm not certain I'm ready to leave the memories."

"*Ach*," Timothy said. "Look at the time. The cookie exchange will be over soon." He stood. "I told Miriam I'd pick her up." He glanced at his brother. "Are you going to get Rebecca and the girls?"

Daniel nodded. "I am."

"Do you want me to get them?" Timothy offered.

"Will you have room for everyone?" Daniel asked. "Rebecca has Lindsay and Daniel Jr."

Timothy shrugged. "I think we'll have plenty of room."

"That would be fine," Daniel said. "I can finish this project I started. *Danki.*"

Caleb stood and shook Daniel's hand. "It was *gut* seeing you again."

"*Ya*," Daniel said. "Think about what I said about the property nearby. You'd have plenty of business here. I think a new start would be *gut* for your soul."

"I'll consider it," Caleb said.

He followed Timothy through the shop, where he said good-bye to the carpenters. Daniel's words were still fresh in his mind as he climbed into Timothy's buggy. Would moving be good for his soul? Would it be good for Susie, or would uprooting her from all she'd ever known cause her more emotional pain after losing her mother only two years ago? He thought back to the conversation he'd had with Timothy after the church service. While Caleb felt guilty about moving on, he was beginning to wonder if it was time to take the plunge and do it. Perhaps he should consider breaking free of the holding pattern he'd been stuck in since he'd lost Barbara. The questions rolled through his mind as they headed toward the bakery.

. . .

Susie sat across from Naomi at a small table and bit into another cookie. "I love chocolate chip cookies. They're my favorite. What's your favorite, Naomi?"

Naomi glanced beside her at Lilly, who grinned in response. "I think peanut butter is my favorite," Naomi said.

"Oh," Susie said. "I love peanut butter too. I guess I have two favorites." She turned to Janie beside her. "You like peanut butter, right?"

Janie nodded. "*Ya*, I love peanut butter. My *mamm* makes the best peanut butter cookies."

Susie glanced back at Naomi. "I like to bake. Do you like to bake?"

Naomi nodded. "I do."

"Do you bake a lot?" Susie asked between bites of cookie.

"*Ya*, I do. I have a big family, and I do a good bit of cooking." Naomi sipped her cup of water.

"How many brothers and sisters do you have?" Susie asked.

"I have five brothers and three sisters," Naomi said.

Susie's eyes widened. "Oh my. That is a big family. You're so lucky. I'm an only child." She frowned. "My *mamm* was going to have another *boppli* when she died."

Naomi dropped her cookie, and Lilly gasped.

Susie nodded. "*Ya*, my *dat* was so sad when my *mamm* died. I was sad too. I cried for my *mamm* and also for the *boppli*."

Naomi was stunned into silence for a moment. "I'm so sorry," Lilly said softly.

"I am too." Naomi reached over and touched Susie's hand.

"*Danki*. I'm still sad sometimes, but mostly I try to be *froh*. I like to think of the fun my *mamm* and I had. We used to bake cookies and she would read me stories at bedtime." Susie picked up another cookie. "My *dat* said that Jesus needed my *mamm* and the *boppli*, and I'll see them again someday."

"That's right," Naomi said, forcing a smile. "You'll see them, and you can hug them again in heaven."

"Right." Susie's smile widened. "And I can tell them how much I love them." She sipped her water. "I loved watching my *mamm* when she quilted. I used to sit on a stool next to her and she'd teach me how to make the stitches. I loved all of the colors she used. My favorite quilts were the ones that had blues and maroons in them."

Naomi nodded. "I love those colors too. They look very *schee* together."

"I saw those at the farmers market," Susie said. "That's why I ran over to meet you. It reminded me of my *mamm*."

Overwhelmed by emotion, Naomi smiled. *The quilts and memories of her mamm are what drew her to me. It makes sense now.* "That's very nice, Susie. I'm so glad that you like my quilts."

"Will you teach me how to make a quilt?" Susie's eyes were filled with hope. "I really want to learn how."

"*Ya*," Naomi said. "If we have time during your visit, I would—"

"Susie!" Sadie yelled from across the room. "Susie, will you come here, please?"

Susie stood. "My *aenti* is calling me. I'll be back." She and Janie ran off to where Sadie stood with Irene Wagler, Miriam, and Sarah Rose.

Naomi turned to Lilly, whose eyes were wide with shock.

"That poor *kind*," Lilly whispered. "She's been through so much." She wiped her tearing eyes. "And her *mamm* was pregnant. I wonder what happened. How did she die?"

"I don't know," Naomi said. "I was wondering too."

She looked across the room. Sadie gave her a nasty look that seemed to say she should stay away, which sent a cold chill up Naomi's spine. Sadie then said something to Irene who glanced down at Susie and gave her a forced smile. She wondered what Sadie was saying, and for a split second she felt a pang of jealousy. She wanted to spend more time with Susie, but she pushed the thought away. Why should she feel any connection to a child who would soon return to her home in another state?

"What's on your mind, Naomi?" Lilly asked.

"Nothing." Naomi turned her attention back to the plate of cookies in front of her, but her appetite had evaporated after hearing the story of Susie's mother.

"You like her, don't you?" Lilly asked.

"What do you mean?"

"Susie," Lilly said. "You care about her."

"Of course I do," Naomi said simply. "She's a sweet little girl who lost her *mamm*. It's difficult not to care about her. I feel sorry for her."

"But you feel something deep for her," Lilly pressed on. "I can see it in your eyes. And she's attached to you as well."

Naomi avoided Lilly's stare by examining the crumbs on her plate. "Maybe Susie will want to write letters to me. Hopefully she will come to visit again soon."

"Naomi." Lilly touched her arm. "It's okay to say that you care about the *kind* and want to get to know her better. Perhaps you should talk to her *dat*."

"What are you trying to get at?" Naomi asked with suspicion.

"You and the girl get along." Lilly shrugged. "Maybe the *dat* needs some company too after losing his *fraa*."

Naomi sighed. "We've discussed this. I'm not looking for love, and it's wrong to prey on a widower."

"Prey on him?" Lilly laughed. "How is it preying on him if you go and talk to him and tell him that you enjoy spending time with his *dochder*?"

Naomi glowered at her. "I know what you're

thinking. You want me to try to court him, and I won't do it. I refuse to be called the *maedel* who runs after every eligible bachelor. My *mamm* called me that, and it didn't feel nice at all. Besides that, he's connected to the Kauffmans. I think it's time I give up on the Kauffman men. If I ever do court again, it will be a man who is in no way related to the Kauffmans. Maybe he won't even know the Kauffmans." She turned back to Susie, who was smiling up at Irene. "Please just drop it."

"Fine," Lilly said with a sigh. "But I have a feeling about this, Naomi. I can't shake the idea that you and Susie's *dat*—"

"Lilly," Naomi seethed. "Stop."

"Fine, fine." Lilly waved off the thought.

Naomi shook her head and wondered if Lilly could somehow be right about the connection Naomi felt toward Susie.

. . .

Caleb climbed the steps to the bakery. "It feels like I was just here yesterday," he said, glancing around the wraparound porch. "It looks the same as it did when we were kids."

"*Ya*, my *mamm* loves it and keeps it running with several of her daughters. We fix it up and repaint every spring." Timothy yanked the door open and they stepped into the bakery, which was bustling with women and girls who were laughing while straightening, sweeping, and cleaning.

"I guess we missed the party," Timothy said.

Caleb chuckled. "*Ya*, it sure looks like—"

"*Dat!*" Susie ran over, interrupting his words. "*Dat!*"

He bent down, and she wrapped her arms around him and kissed his cheek. Holding onto her, he closed his eyes and smiled. Oh, how he cherished his sweet little girl. "Did you have fun?" he asked.

"*Ya!*" She beamed. "I ate so many cookies! And I sat and talked to Naomi, my new *freind*." She pointed across the room to where Naomi stood with another young woman. "She's the one who makes the quilts at the farmers market." Taking his hand, Susie yanked him. "Come meet her."

"Okay," Caleb said. "Slow down."

Holding her hand, he followed her across the room. Naomi's gaze met his, and he was almost certain he glimpsed a flash of panic in her eyes before she glanced away. He wondered what that brief expression meant. Did his presence bother her?

"You'll like my new *freind*," Susie said, pulling Caleb toward Naomi.

"Caleb!" Sadie's voice called as she approached.

Caleb stepped toward Naomi, who looked up at him. As he opened his mouth to speak to Naomi, Sadie stepped in front of him and grabbed his arm.

"I'm so glad you're here," Sadie said, turning him toward her. "Irene is here too. I know she would love to talk to you." She pushed him toward Irene, who stood with Sarah Rose Troyer and Rebecca Kauffman.

Susie grabbed his hand and tried to pull him backward. "*Dat*," she began with a huff, "I wanted you to meet *mei freind*."

"Susie," Caleb said, looking into her disappointed eyes. "I'll be just a moment."

"Irene was just telling me that her *dat* does have an opening for a new buggy mechanic," Sadie continued. "Right, Irene?"

Irene's smile was almost coy. "*Ya*, that's true, Caleb. I would be *froh* to introduce you."

"She's leaving!" Susie said. She stamped her foot and marched back toward Naomi.

Caleb opened his mouth to correct Susie's disrespectful display, but he didn't get a chance to speak. Instead, Irene continued chatting on about her father's shop, and Caleb wanted to interject. He waited for her to take a breath, but her words were strung together like a buggy wheel: no beginning, no end. He nodded, feigning interest, but his mind was set on a polite escape. He turned in the direction of Susie, and he spotted his daughter waving to Naomi as she headed out the front door with a woman about her age and three younger girls. He gave a sigh of defeat as he looked at Irene, who was still talking.

. . .

"I wanted you to meet *mei freind*," Susie said to Caleb while snuggling down in the bed next to her cousin later that evening.

"I know, but you were very disrespectful when you yelled and stamped your foot like a *boppli*." Caleb brushed a lock of brown hair back from Susie's forehead. "I'm certain I will talk to her before we leave."

"I'm sorry I acted like a *boppli*, but I was just disappointed. Naomi is really nice." Susie nodded with emphasis. "She said she's going to teach me to quilt."

Caleb smiled. "Is that so?"

"*Ya*." Susie glanced at Janie, who also nodded. "She's very pretty."

Ya, *she is*. He pushed that thought away.

"Tomorrow is the school program," Susie said. "I hope Naomi is there. Maybe you can meet her then."

He nodded. "Maybe so."

"Naomi will be there. Her sisters, Levina and Sylvia, go to the school. The Christmas program will be fun," Janie chimed in. "Susie is going to help us with the singing."

"That's *gut*." Caleb smiled at his niece. "It's time to get some sleep." Leaning over, he kissed Susie's cheek. "I'm glad you had fun today." He said goodnight to his nieces and then headed for the door.

As he descended the stairs, he contemplated Naomi. Susie was correct: Naomi was pretty. And he hoped his next encounter with the mysterious woman wouldn't be hijacked by his elder sister. In fact, he decided at that moment that he would make it a point to speak to the young woman who had his daughter so captivated.

CHAPTER 6

The following afternoon, Naomi shivered and pulled her cloak closer to her body while she trudged through the blowing snow from her family's buggy toward the one-room schoolhouse. Levina stumbled beside her, and Naomi grabbed her arm, steadying her younger sister on her feet as they moved through the swirling snow.

Irma, Naomi's mother, fell in step beside her. "I didn't think this snow was predicted for today. I thought the paper said the snow would start tomorrow."

Shaking her head, Naomi tightened her grip on her bag filled with treats and candies for the children who would perform the Christmas program. Each year, the teacher wrote the program, and the students practiced to get it just right. "No, I didn't think the snow was supposed to start before this evening."

Her brothers ran ahead, laughing and slipping through the snow.

"Slow down, boys!" Titus, her father, bellowed. He shook his head. "They have such energy."

"*Ya*," Irma said, taking his hand. "They do. They get it from you." She gave Titus a sweet smile.

Naomi swallowed a sigh at the sweet sign of affection. She'd always admired the relationship her parents shared. She hoped that someday she'd find that kind of love and affection in a husband. She pushed the thought away since she believed in her heart that love wasn't in God's plan for her. Thinking about it too much would put her in a blue mood, and she needed to stay upbeat so she could enjoy the program.

A line of families moved slowly up the road through the snow toward the schoolhouse. Naomi couldn't help but think that the scene looked like a painting. The sky above them was gray, and the snow resembled a beautiful white fog engulfing the families who moved through it like apparitions dressed in dark cloaks and coats, some carrying gas lanterns, which glowed in the dark winter afternoon. The white, one-room schoolhouse was covered in the blowing snow, and buggies peppered with large white flakes surrounded the little building.

They reached the schoolhouse at the end of the path, and Naomi shivered while stepping into the large room. A coal-burning stove provided warmth from the blustering, cold afternoon. Rows of desks, benches, and folding chairs filled the center of the room, which was packed with children and their families. Paper snowflakes hung like mobiles fluttering from the ceiling, and drawings, including nativity scenes, angels, wreaths, and candles decked the walls. Similar drawings filled the blackboard at the front of the room. A makeshift curtain consisting of a few sheets hanging over twine hung at the front of the classroom in front of a raised platform that served as a stage next to the teacher's desk.

Naomi, Lizzie Anne, and her mother sat on an available bench. Her father and Elam, her eldest brother at the age of nineteen, joined the men at the back of the room. Since Lizzie Anne had completed eighth grade last year, she'd graduated and was no longer a student at the school. Naomi greeted friends and chatted about the cold weather, while scanning the crowd consisting of members of her church district and families she'd known since her family moved to this district when she was sixteen, eight years ago.

Sylvia, Levina, and a group of their schoolmates hurried through the room, passing out handwritten pieces of paper with the schedule of program events, including Christmas-themed poems, songs, and skits. Naomi smiled, remembering her own happy memories of Christmas programs she'd participated in during eight years of school. She'd relished participating in the program with the other children. It was one of the highlights of every school year.

A mutter fell over the crowd and then the voices were silent.

"Good afternoon," Lena, the teacher, said. "*Danki* for coming to our program. The scholars have worked very hard, and we hope you enjoy it." She then glanced around the room. "Okay, *kinner*. Let's begin!"

The students lined up at the front of the classroom, the older children in back and the younger up front. Naomi spotted Susie standing with her cousins. When her gaze met Naomi's, she waved and grinned, and Naomi's heart warmed.

While the children sang a round of Christmas

carols, Naomi couldn't help but join in, as did many of the adults surrounding her. After the carols, the teacher rang a bell, and the children began acting out their skits and reciting their poems.

When Naomi's youngest brothers and group of friends presented impressions of their favorite animals, Naomi laughed and glanced at her smiling mother. She cut her eyes toward the men in the back of the room and found Caleb watching her, his eyes intense. With her cheeks blazing, Naomi turned back to the front of the room. She wished the sight of the widower didn't turn her insides to mush, but his eyes had mysterious power over her.

After several more skits, the program came to an end with another round of Christmas carols. The children invited the audience to join in, and Naomi tried to concentrate on the songs. However, her thoughts were focused on Caleb's intense green eyes and how they caused her body to warm.

As "Joy to the World" came to a close, the audience clapped and the children beamed. Lena moved to the front of the room, her young face shining with a smile. "*Danki* for coming to our program," she said. "Please don't forget that Sadie Kauffman has invited us to come to her home for a little party. *Frehlicher Grischtdaag!*"

While conversations broke out around her, Naomi's stomach flip-flopped. She hoped she could convince her mother to skip the party in order to avoid more idle and awkward conversation with the Kauffmans.

Her mother leaned over. "I didn't know that we were going to Sadie's or I would've brought a covered dish."

Naomi shrugged. "Oh well. We can give out the candy and then head home. I'm sure the children are tired and—"

"Naomi." Her mother squeezed her hand. "It's Christmas. I'm certain Sadie will understand that we forgot a covered dish. It's about fellowship. The *kinner* will love being with their *freinden* awhile longer."

Naomi shook her head, determined to avoid fellowship at Sadie's home. "*Ach*, I don't—"

"Naomi!" Susie rushed over and grabbed Naomi's sleeve. "I'm so *froh* you're here! I was hoping you'd see the program. Wasn't it great? What's your favorite Christmas carol? Mine is 'O Little Town of Bethlehem.' When I was little, I used to sing it all the time. How about you? Do you like to sing?"

Susie's father approached with a gentle smile. "Susie, you have to give her a chance to answer a question before you spout off six more."

The little girl giggled. "*Ya*, I guess you're right. Let's start with the most important question: What's your favorite Christmas carol?"

Although she was aware of Caleb's stare, Naomi kept her eyes on Susie. "My favorite is 'O Little Town of Bethlehem' too."

"That's *wunderbaar gut*! It was my *mamm's* too!" Susie grabbed Caleb's hand and yanked him closer. "This is my *dat*. His name is Caleb." She glanced up at her father. "*Dat*, this is *mei freind* Naomi I've been telling you about. She likes to quilt, bake, and sing, just like *Mamm* did!"

"It's nice to finally meet you, Naomi." His smile was

warm as he held out his hand. "I've heard an awful lot about you." With her heart in her throat, Naomi hesitated for a split second before taking his hand. The warm feel of his skin caused her breath to pause as her eyes locked with his.

"Are you coming over to my *Aenti* Sadie's house?" Susie asked, breaking the trance.

"Oh," Naomi said, pulling her hand back. "I don't know. I think I—"

"Please?" Susie's eyes were hopeful. Naomi glanced up at Caleb.

"I think it's going to be a nice time," he said.

Nodding, Naomi finally gave in and smiled. "I'll be there after I help my *mamm* round up my siblings."

. . .

Gripping two mugs of Robert's homemade hot cider, Caleb weaved through the crowd in Sadie's family room for a second time and then back into the knot of people in the kitchen. He scanned the faces in search of Naomi's pretty smile. She'd seemed hesitant to join him and Susie at Sadie's house; however, she'd gathered up her siblings and steered them out the schoolhouse door and into the falling snow.

While her parents took their buggy to the house, Naomi and her siblings had walked the short distance from the schoolhouse to Sadie's home. He'd lost track of her amongst the group during the trek down the road toward Sadie's house, but he'd seen her younger sisters running around the house with Susie and a group of children. He hoped Naomi had chosen to stay with them. He was determined to speak to her for longer than that brief introduction they'd shared at the schoolhouse. He'd been captivated by her beautiful brown eyes and dimple while he'd watched her smiling and laughing during the children's program. Her warm handshake stirred something deep in his soul, a feeling he hadn't experienced since he'd lost Barbara.

When he spotted Naomi standing by the back door, his steps quickened. She was still wearing her cloak, and he hoped she wasn't planning to hurry out the back door before they spoke again.

Moving toward her, he cleared his throat. "Naomi," he said, slipping between two laughing little boys.

"Oh, Caleb," she said. "Hi." Her cheeks flamed a bright pink. It seemed she was always blushing. He couldn't help but wonder if she always blushed in a man's presence. Whatever the reason, he found it adorable, and he was certain Naomi wasn't the temptress his sister had described.

"I hope you aren't planning on leaving." He held out one of the mugs. "I brought you some of Robert's famous hot cider. It's the best I've ever had."

"*Danki.*" She sipped from the cup and smiled. "*Ya*, it is *gut*. It's even better than my *dat's*, but I would never tell him that."

Caleb laughed. He opened his mouth to speak but was interrupted by a group of young girls who ran by screeching through the kitchen on their way to the stairs leading to the second floor. Leaning in close to

Naomi, he inhaled her flowery scent that must've been from her soap or shampoo. "Do you mind the cold?" he asked.

She shook her head. "Cold is fine."

"Want to go sit on the porch so we can hear each other speak?" He nodded toward the back door. "Then we don't have to compete with the *kinner.* I'm surprised Robert hasn't yelled for the *kinner* to keep it down, but I guess he knows he can't control the crowd."

"It is loud in here. Sitting outside sounds *gut,*" she said.

He held the door open for her and followed her out onto the sweeping, wraparound porch. She lowered herself onto a bench and shivered.

"Bad idea?" he asked.

She shook her head. "It's nice out here. The house was getting stuffy." She gestured toward the snow flakes dancing across the white pasture. "From the looks of those clouds, this snow may not stop any time soon."

"I think you're right." He sank onto the bench beside her and swallowed a shiver. He should've grabbed his coat from the peg by the door, but he was more focused on having an uninterrupted conversation with her than how he would weather the crisp December air. "We'll definitely have a white Christmas this year."

"Do you prefer white Christmases?" she asked before sipping from the mug.

"*Ya.*" He shrugged. He hadn't thought much about Christmas since he'd lost Barbara. "How about you?"

She mirrored his shrug. "*Ya.* I figure if it's going to

be so cold, it might as well snow and make the scenery *schee* as a celebration of God's glory and our Savior's birth."

"I have to agree with that." He drank the hot cider and watched the snowflakes for a moment while trying to find a way to keep the conversation going. "What are your family Christmas traditions?"

"*Ach*, you know, nothing out of the ordinary." She set the mug down on the bench beside her. "We have the Christmas table with a place set for each of my siblings. I'm the oldest, and I love helping my mother set it up the night before. We put out little toys and candies for each of the *kinner*. I love seeing their faces Christmas morning. We have a big breakfast and then my *dat* sits in his favorite chair and tells the Christmas story from the book of Luke. It's *wunderbaar*. I look forward to it every year. How about you?"

Caleb studied the flakes that fluttered down onto the snow lining the wooden porch railing while he considered his answer. In all honesty, he and Susie hadn't really practiced any traditions since they'd lost Barbara. Last year, he gave her little gifts Christmas morning, and they'd placed a poinsettia on the mantel. But they didn't sing Christmas carols or share the Christmas story like they'd done when Barbara was alive. Beyond the Christmas program at school and a dinner shared with a neighbor, it seemed like just another day without Barbara.

"Susie and I don't really have any traditions anymore," he finally said. "We seem to just take things day by day with God's help."

Naomi's expression was sad. "I'm sorry for your loss." Her sweet voice was a mere whisper.

"I appreciate how nice you've been to my Susie," he said, placing his mug on the seat beside him. "You've taken a lot of time to talk with her, and not many adults seem to care enough to do that. *Danki.*"

Her smile and dimple were back. "Oh, it's nothing." She waved off the comment. "She's an easy girl to love."

"She's quite taken with you," he said, studying her eyes. "You seem to have a gift with *kinner.*"

Her cheeks were pink again, and he was certain it was more than just the cool breeze that colored them. "I've had a lot of experience with my siblings. My *mamm* once said I should've been a schoolteacher, but I thought quilting was the talent God wanted me to share." She paused as if gathering her thoughts. "Susie is a very special little girl. I've enjoyed spending time with her."

He nodded. "I believe she feels the same way about you. She's talked about you constantly since we met at the farmers market." He shook his head, embarrassed. "I'm sorry we made a scene that day."

"You didn't make a scene. It's scary when you think you've lost a *kind.* I took my siblings to the park one day last spring. My littlest brother, Joseph, was only four and wandered off while I was tying Leroy's shoe." She frowned. "I was scared to death with worry. There's a little stream that runs through the park, and I was certain he'd drowned." She laughed. "It turned out he was hiding behind a nearby tree, pretending to be a squirrel." Her expression was serious again. "But I understand how you felt at the farmers market. When you've lost sight of a child, your mind runs away with the most horrible possibilities of what could've happened to them."

The understanding in her pretty eyes touched him. "I feel like I've become even more protective of her since I lost Barbara," he said. "I guess it's because she's all I have left."

Naomi hugged her cloak closer to her body. "You must miss her so."

He nodded. "Every day."

"May I ask . . . ?" Her voice trailed off.

"What?" He rubbed his arms as the frosty air seeped into his skin. He wished he could run in and snatch his coat without losing a moment of conversation with Naomi.

"Nothing." She cleared her throat and glanced back toward the pasture. "The snow is beautiful, *ya*? I could watch it all night." She looked at his arms. "You should go get your coat. You don't want to spend your Christmas visit in bed or at the hospital with pneumonia, do you?"

"Naomi, you don't have to change the subject," he said with a smile. "You can ask me anything."

Standing, she pursed her lips. "You're going to catch a cold." She slipped in the door and returned a few moments later with a coat. "I grabbed one from of the peg by the door. It's my father's, but I don't think he'd mind if you borrowed it during our visit."

"*Danki.*" He pulled it on. Although the coat was a little large in the shoulders, it was warm. "What were you going to ask me?"

She bit her lower lip as if choosing her words. "I was wondering what happened to Barbara." She held a hand up, palm out. "But if it's too painful to share, I understand. I don't mean to pry into your life."

"It was Christmas Eve two years ago," he began, staring across the pasture. "We were so *froh* and excited back then. She was pregnant with our second *kind* and due at the end of January. Although she was feeling tired, she insisted that we celebrate with her cousins who lived on the other side of town. She'd baked a torte . . . Susie had helped her while they talked and laughed."

The memories flooded his mind like a rushing waterfall, with every detail bubbling forth, from the smell of her baked raspberry dream torte to the sight of her honey-blond hair sticking out from under her prayer *kapp*.

"I'd wanted to stay home because Barbara said that she had some back pain, but she'd insisted we go," he continued, lifting the mug of cider. "She'd even invited our neighbors to join us, and looking back, I'm certain she did that to give herself an excuse to go no matter what." He chuckled to himself. "Barbara was good at that—finding ways to get what she wanted. Not that she was deceitful. She had a heart of gold. She knew our neighbors were celebrating Christmas alone that year, and she wanted to give them *froh* memories."

"She was very caring," Naomi said softly.

"*Ya*, she was." He glanced over at her, and her lip twitched as her eyes filled with tears. He hoped she didn't cry. He didn't want to cause her any sadness while they visited together. He also didn't want to cry and show too much emotion in front of her and seem as if he were weak.

"We'd spent all afternoon with her cousins and had a *gut* time," he said. "We ate too much, and the *kinner* played well together while sharing their Christmas candy and toys. We stayed much later than we should've, but Susie was having so much fun with her cousins."

He sipped the cider and looked back over the pasture as the memories of that tragic night gripped him.

"On the way home, I was riding in a buggy behind her and witnessed the whole thing." His voice quavered. He cleared his throat before continuing. "Barbara had wanted to ride back to our house with our neighbor and her family. For some reason, Susie insisted on riding with me. She said she was afraid I would get lost if I rode home alone." He snorted at the irony.

"She's such a thoughtful *kind*," Naomi whispered, wiping a tear.

"A pickup truck ran a red light and . . ." His voice trailed off as the graphic images of the crash flooded his mind. He shook the memories away. "My neighbor and her family suffered bruises and scrapes. But my Barbara and our unborn baby took the brunt of the impact." His voice fell to a whisper. "They were killed instantly."

"I'm so sorry." Tears glistened in Naomi's brown eyes. "I can't imagine how difficult it was for you and Susie."

He wiped his eyes, hoping to prevent any threatening

tears from splashing down his cheeks. "The month that followed her death was a blur. Of course, God was with me the whole time, and I believe He still is." He paused and pulled at his beard while gathering his thoughts. "To be honest, the most difficult part has been the day-to-day routine, the things we do without thinking twice. You know, getting Susie ready for school, making her lunch, combing her hair, going to bed alone at night. That's when I miss Barbara the most."

Naomi wiped her eyes again. "That would make sense. You miss her the most when you're alone with Susie or just plain alone."

He nodded, impressed by her understanding of his loss. "That's it exactly. It's funny how your life can change in a split second. One minute I was riding down a road thinking about how much fun I'd had at the little party and listening to my little girl chatter endlessly about Christmas. Then the next moment I was trying to hold my emotions together while I held my little girl at the scene of the accident."

"Life does have a tendency to change on us in a split second," Naomi said, holding her mug in her hands.

He raised his eyebrow. "You sound like you speak from experience."

She shrugged while studying the contents of the mug. "I've made plans that haven't turned out the way I'd thought. Of course, it's nothing like you've experienced. My heartaches have been on a much smaller scale."

"Your heartaches?" he asked, his curiosity piqued. "Do you want to share?"

Naomi shook her head. "I'd rather not. It's just silliness." She sipped more of her drink. "This is the best cider I've ever tasted. Makes me thirsty for Robert's summer root beer. It's especially tasty with some vanilla ice cream."

"*Ya*, it is good. We'll have to do that next time we come visit," he said. "Susie and I will be sure to have the floats ready."

She gave him a surprised expression. "Okay."

He studied her eyes, wishing he could read her thoughts. "I've talked your ear off," he said. "Tell me about your life here in Bird-in-Hand."

She shrugged and cleared her throat. "It's nothing out of the ordinary. You already know that I work at the quilt stand in the farmers market and I help care for my siblings."

"What do you like to do for fun?" he asked, crossing his ankle onto his knee.

She laughed. "For fun?"

"That's right." He nodded. "You have fun, right?"

"Hmm." She gnawed her bottom lip and hugged her cloak closer to her body. "I enjoy reading with my youngest siblings. Leroy and Joseph are learning quickly how to sound out words." Her fingers moved to the ties of her black bonnet, and she absently moved them on her chin. "I love to quilt, and we sometimes have quilting bees." She turned to him, her eyes full of excitement. "In fact, we're having one here tomorrow, and I hope Susie will attend. She's asked me to teach her to quilt, and I'd love to give her some instructions."

He grinned. "She'd love that."

"*Gut*." She smiled. "I guess that's about it."

"So everything you enjoy is for someone else?"

She laughed. "I guess so. But isn't that what God has instructed us to do—to give of ourselves?"

"*Ya*, He has." Caleb wondered why she wasn't married yet. He surmised she was in her midtwenties. Why hadn't some eligible bachelor swooped her up?

She gestured toward the front door. "You grew up here, *ya*?"

"I did."

"What took you to Ohio?"

"Love." He folded his arms across his chest. "I met Barbara while she was visiting her cousin here one summer. We courted through letters and the phone for a while, and I made a couple of trips up to visit her. She didn't want to leave her *mamm*, who was alive when we first met, so I moved there."

"Are many of Barbara's relatives still there?"

He shook his head. "No, just a handful of cousins in neighboring church districts."

"What do you do for a living?" she asked.

"I'm a buggy maker."

"Do you ever miss living here?"

He nodded. "Sometimes I do. Sometimes I wish I'd convinced Barbara to come live here, but when I think about that too much, I make myself *narrisch*, wondering if she'd still be alive. Then again, it's not our place to question God's will, is it?"

Naomi shook her head. "No, it's not." She then tilted her head in question, her eyes thoughtful. "Do you believe that God only gives us one chance at true love?

Or do you think He provides us the opportunity to love more than once during a lifetime?"

"That is a very *gut* question." He idly rubbed his beard while considering his answer. "I would say that God gives us second chances. I think Timothy's youngest sister is a great example of that." He was almost certain he saw her flinch at the mention of his best friend's name.

"*Ya*," she said softly. "That is a *gut* point."

Her eyes were full of something that seemed to resemble regret or possibly grief. He wanted to ask her what had happened to her to make her so sad, but the back door opened with a whoosh, revealing Sadie. Did his sister have a sixth sense when it came to ruining perfect moments?

"Caleb!" Sadie exclaimed, her face full of shock. "What are you doing out here in the cold?" She turned to Naomi and her eyes narrowed slightly, looking annoyed. "Oh, Naomi. *Wie geht's?*"

"I'm fine, *danki*." Naomi rose and stepped toward the door. "How are you?"

"Fine, fine. You must come in out of this cold before you both get sick." Sadie motioned for Naomi to enter the house. As Naomi stepped through the doorway, she shot Caleb a quizzical expression as if to ask what he'd been doing on the porch with Naomi. "That's not your coat, is it?" she asked.

Caleb stood and shook his head. "No, this coat belongs to Naomi's *dat*. She grabbed it for me when I started shivering." Once Naomi was through the door, Sadie stepped back onto the porch and closed the door. "What are you doing out here, Caleb?"

"Just talking with my new *freind*." He moved past her. "We were discussing the snow and Christmas." He shrugged. "That was all."

She took his arm and pulled him toward the door. "I have plenty of families I want you to meet, so you must come back inside."

"Yes, *schweschder*." He forced a smile and she steered him through the door. As he walked by Naomi and her mother, Caleb rolled his eyes and then smiled. Naomi laughed, and he gave her a little wave.

Sadie guided Caleb toward Irene Wagler who stood with her father and another couple. Caleb nodded a greeting and then glanced back at Naomi, who blushed and looked away.

"Caleb," Sadie said with a sweeping gesture, "this is Hezekiah Wagler, Irene's father."

Caleb shook the middle-aged gentleman's hand. "It's nice to meet you."

"You too," Hezekiah said. "I hear you are a buggy maker. I've owned my own shop for thirty years."

While the man began to describe his shop, Caleb glanced toward Naomi standing with her mother, and his mind wandered back to their conversation on the porch. He wished he could've sat with Naomi for much longer, perhaps hours, while they continued their conversation. She was so beautiful and so easy to talk to, and he felt a connection to her, as if she could be a kindred spirit.

While he missed Barbara so much his heart ached some days, he felt something new when he looked at Naomi. She ignited a glimmer of hope that he might somehow find love again. Although he could never replace Barbara, he suddenly wondered if he could find happiness and build a life with a woman as special as Naomi. He had the suspicion he could love again, and Naomi King could possibly hold that key.

A smile turned up the corner of Caleb's lips. The possibility of finding a life mate again filled him with a joy he hadn't felt in years. He looked forward to exploring that future, but he knew he had to move slowly and make sure it was right. He didn't want to do anything to hurt Susie or Naomi.

Caleb turned back to the Waglers, and Sadie shot him a curious look.

Ignoring his sister, Caleb continued to smile and nod while Hezekiah discussed his booming business. He tried his best to look interested and engaged in the discussion, even though his thoughts were on the other side of the room with Naomi.

Caleb would keep his excitement about his evolving feelings for Naomi King to himself and let God lead him. He believed that with God, all things were possible, even the potential of a widower finding love again.

CHAPTER 7

"The word quilting refers to the hand stitching of three layers: a pieced top, a layer of batting, and a bottom fabric layered together, then stitched together in a pattern to hold the layers together," Naomi began while holding up a quilt and showing it to Susie the following morning while they stood together in Sadie's kitchen.

Deep in thought, Susie scrunched her nose and swiped her hand over the cream, blue, and maroon quilt created in a log cabin pattern.

"See here?" Naomi ran her hand over the pattern. "The top layers were pieced together on the treadle sewing machine I have at my house in my room. The quilting is always done by hand. Then a binding is sewn onto the bottom layer by the machine and hand stitched to the top layer." She smiled at Susie's little tongue, sticking out of her mouth as if she were contemplating the meaning of life. "I'm sure you already know that we use what the *Englishers* consider an old-fashioned sewing machine powered by a pedal and no electricity." She felt her admiration for the little girl growing by the minute.

Naomi had arrived at Sadie's that morning along with her sisters, mother, and Lilly. As soon as Naomi stepped in the door, Susie ran over and began chatting without taking a breath—asking question after question about Naomi's quilt, which she held in her hands. Naomi brought it in order to explain how a quilt was created.

While Naomi was excited to spend time with Susie, she couldn't help but be disappointed that Caleb had already left for a day of visiting his friends and acquaintances in town. She'd spent all evening thinking about their conversation on the porch.

Throughout the night, she'd tossed and turned, analyzing his words and remembering the sadness in his eyes while he'd discussed his beloved wife. She knew that she was developing feelings for the man, and she wished she could suppress them. However, her stomach fluttered at the thought of seeing him and speaking to him again.

Susie ran her hand over the stitching. "You sewed the top layer and then you hand stitched it all together?"

"That's right." Naomi nodded toward the family room where the women sat around a frame that held Sadie's latest creation. "See how all the women are stitching that quilt your *aenti* made? My *mamm* and I stitched this one. Since it's only a twin size, we didn't need a whole group to help us."

Susie studied the creation in her hands. "Who did you make this one for?"

Naomi shrugged. "This one was really just for fun. I was experimenting with the colors. Do you like it?"

Susie's eyes were bright. "I love it."

Naomi smiled. Perhaps the quilt could be a surprise Christmas gift for her little friend. She gestured toward the family room. "Did you want to go help the women with that quilt your *aenti* is finishing for the English customer?"

"No. Let's talk instead." Susie sat on a kitchen chair. "Did you have any of my *onkel's* cider last night?"

Naomi sat across from her. "I did. It was *appeditlich*."

The little girl nodded. "*Ya*, it was *wunderbaar*. I told my *dat* he needs to learn how to make cider like that."

Naomi laughed while standing. "That would be nice, wouldn't it?"

Susie tilted her head in question. "Do you believe in Christmas miracles, Naomi?"

Naomi's smile faded as she crossed the kitchen, grabbed two cups of water, and brought them over to the table. "Sure, Susie. Why do you ask?"

"*Danki*," Susie said, taking the cup. "Janie and Linda said that one of their cows was born on Christmas Eve last year, and their *dat* said it was a miracle because it was so cold." She sipped her water.

"I imagine it was a miracle." Naomi sipped the water, wondering where this conversation was headed.

Susie glanced toward the women in the family room next to the kitchen and then moved closer to Naomi. "May I tell you a secret?" she whispered.

"Of course," Naomi said softly, leaning closer to her.

"There's a Christmas miracle I've been praying for." Susie wiggled her chair closer to Naomi. "My dream is for my *dat* to be *froh* again on Christmas. I want to see him smile. I mean really smile. He smiles now, but I don't think he's truly *froh* since *Mamm* is gone. I want him to be really and truly *froh*."

Naomi smiled as tears filled her eyes. "That's very sweet, Susie."

"Do you think it's possible?" Susie asked, still whispering. "Do you think God will grant me that one miracle?"

Naomi pushed a lock of hair that had escaped Susie's prayer covering away from her face. "With God, all things are possible," she whispered.

"What are you two scheming?" Sadie asked, stepping into the kitchen and shooting Naomi a suspicious expression.

"We're just talking, *Aenti* Sadie," Susie said. "Naomi was telling me all about quilts."

Sadie grabbed a stack of dishes from the cabinet. "I thought you wanted to learn how to make them. If you want to learn how, then you need to come join us in the *schtupp* and not sit out here gabbing with Naomi."

Naomi bit her bottom lip to hold back the stinging retort she wanted to throw back at Sadie. Why did Sadie have to nag Susie when they were having a nice time together?

"Let's serve lunch, Susie," Sadie said.

Naomi and Susie helped Sadie spread out the food for lunch, including chicken salad, homemade bread, pickles, and meadow tea. The women gathered around the table. After a silent prayer, they discussed their upcoming Christmas plans while eating.

Naomi was filling the sink with soapy water for the

dirty dishes when the back door opened and shut with a bang. She spotted Caleb following Robert into the family room, and her stomach flip-flopped. She was glad that Irene Wagler hadn't come to the quilting bee. Although she knew it was a sin, she couldn't ignore the jealousy she'd felt when Caleb had spoken to Irene and Irene's father last night. She'd felt a special connection with Caleb during their conversation on the porch. She knew that she had no future with the widower since he and his daughter would soon return to Ohio. However, she couldn't stop the growing attraction that bubbled up in her every time she saw him.

"*Dat!*" Susie rushed over and hugged Caleb, nearly knocking him over. "We've had such fun!" She began rattling off details of her new knowledge of quilt-making.

Grinning, Caleb shucked his coat and hung it on the peg by the door. Turning, he met Naomi's stare, and her pulse skittered. She looked back toward the sink and began scrubbing the dirty utensils as a diversion from his captivating eyes.

Conversations swirled around her while she continued washing the dirty serving platters and bowls. A tug on her apron caused her to jump with a start. She glanced down at Susie smiling up at her.

"Naomi?" Susie asked, her big green eyes hopeful. "My *dat* and I were wondering if you would go shopping with us."

"Shopping?" Naomi wiped her hands on a dish towel as she faced Susie and Caleb.

Sadie stepped behind Caleb and studied her

brother. "Shopping?" she echoed. "Where are you going shopping?"

He shrugged. "Susie wants to go Christmas shopping, and it sounds like fun to fight the crowds. I don't care where we go. I'll leave the location up to Susie and Naomi."

"Will you come with us?" Susie grabbed Naomi's arm and tugged. "There are some things I want to get for my cousins."

Sadie gave Naomi a hard look, and Naomi paused. She knew how Sadie relished sharing gossip at her quilting bees, and that was the reason why Naomi had enjoyed staying in the kitchen with Susie instead of listening to Sadie's latest news.

Naomi met Susie's hopeful eyes and silently debated what to do. She didn't want to hurt the little girl's feelings, but she also knew the possible consequences. Going shopping alone with Caleb and his daughter could start rumors that would upset Naomi's mother.

"Well, I don't know." Naomi turned back to the sink. "There are an awful lot of dishes to be cleaned up, and then I need to help finish the quilt. Sadie has a customer who is going to pick it up tomorrow since it's a Christmas gift for her daughter."

"I'll help finish the dishes," Caleb said, grabbing a dish towel.

Stunned, Naomi stared at him. "You will?"

He chuckled. "Believe it or not, I cook and do dishes back home."

"I just don't know." Naomi felt Sadie's scrutinizing stare. "I think I need to stay and help with the quilt."

Susie frowned. "Are you certain?"

Once Sadie had walked away, Caleb sidled up to Naomi and began to dry a serving platter. "Would you feel more comfortable if one of your sisters or perhaps one of my nieces came along with us?" he asked her under his breath.

Naomi studied him, wondering how this man could read her mind. "How did you know?"

He gave a small smile. "I know how *mei schweschder* works."

Naomi leaned closer to him. She couldn't help but inhale his manly scent, like earth mixed with a spicy deodorant. "What do you mean?" she asked.

He placed the dry platter on the counter. "She had spread the news about my proposal to Barbara before I had even decided to propose. She should've been an editor for the local paper instead of a quilt maker." He snatched a handful of clean utensils from the sink. "I'll finish the dishes, and Susie can help me put them away. Why don't you see if one of your sisters or my nieces wants to join us? That will quell any rumors about our shopping expedition."

"Are you certain?" Naomi placed the dish towel on the counter.

"I'm drying the dishes, aren't I?" he asked with a grin.

She couldn't help but smile. His handsome face was nearly intoxicating. "*Danki.*"

"No need to thank me," he said, opening the utensil drawer. "You're going to help me more than you know. Shopping is not one of my strengths."

CHAPTER 8

Caleb walked through the flea market with Naomi by his side while Susie, her cousin Janie, and Naomi's sisters, Levina and Sylvia, skipped ahead toward a candy concession stand.

The ride over to the indoor flea market in Robert's borrowed buggy had been noisy, with the four girls chatting all at once in the backseat. Caleb had stolen several glances at Naomi and found her fingering the ties on her black bonnet and the hem of her cloak. He wondered what she was thinking and if she was enjoying her time with him as much as he enjoyed his time with her.

"How come we haven't met before now?" he asked, falling into step with her while holding the bags containing a few small gifts he'd picked up for Sadie and Robert.

She gave him a confused expression. "Excuse me?"

"You didn't go to school with the Kauffmans, right?" he asked.

She shook her head. "No. I grew up in a district that's a few miles away. My *dat* decided to move to a larger farm when I was sixteen." She paused, gathering her thoughts. "You're close to the Kauffmans, *ya*?"

He nodded. "Timothy's been my best *freind* for as long as I can remember."

"Oh." She frowned.

"You don't like the Kauffmans much, do you?" He felt like a liar for asking the question. He knew part of the answer since Timothy had shared that he'd broken Naomi's heart. However, he wanted to hear her version of her past with Timothy and Luke. He knew in his gut that Sadie was wrong about Naomi. She seemed like a quiet, honest young woman, not a woman who was too eager to find a husband.

"It's not that." Her cheeks were pink again. "I just. *Ach*. I sort of—"

"Naomi!" Levina's loud voice interrupted Naomi. "Can I have some money? I want to get some licorice."

"Oh." Naomi pulled out her small black handbag.

"I got it." Caleb touched her warm hand and then pulled out his wallet.

"Oh no." Naomi shook her head. "That's not necessary. I don't expect you to buy candy for my sisters."

"It's my pleasure." He handed Levina a ten. "Please buy for all of the girls."

"*Danki*, Caleb." Levina smiled and trotted off to the candy counter.

"*Danki*," Naomi said.

"*Gern gschehne*." He motioned toward a bench near the candy stand. "Let's sit for a moment. What were you saying about the Kauffmans?"

She smoothed her skirt. "It's rather embarrassing."

"I'm certain it can't be that bad."

She frowned and placed her plain, black handbag on her lap. "I'd rather not talk about it."

"That's fine," he said, glancing toward the girls, who were busy ordering candy at the stand. "What do you want for Christmas?"

"Me?" Naomi laughed. "*Ach*, I don't need anything."

He studied her deep-brown eyes. "There must be something you'd like. There's always something we don't need that we'd like to have, even if it's considered unnecessary or frivolous."

"Well." She tapped her chin and glanced toward a bookstand. "There's a pretty Bible that I looked at a few weeks ago. I'm still waiting for it to go on sale. The binding on my Bible is falling apart, but I don't necessarily need a new one. However, every night when I open it for my devotional time, I feel the fraying binding and think about how nice it would be to have a new one."

"Interesting." He smiled. "You'll have to show it to me before we leave."

Naomi shrugged. "Alright. So what about you? What do you want for Christmas?"

At first he waved off the question because he couldn't think of anything he wanted. But then the answer hit him like a speeding, oncoming freight train. The truth was that he did want something, and it was as if a light-bulb went off in his head and in his heart. The feeling was overwhelming and it was brand new, something he hadn't felt in a long, long time. What he wanted for Christmas was something he'd probably never experience again. He wanted a companion. Someone to share his life with. Someone to tell his hopes and dreams to and to help him through the tough times. Someone to help him raise Susie in a faithful, Christian home.

He wanted a life partner.

He wanted a wife and a mother for Susie.

But finding that wasn't as easy as Sadie had made it sound. Besides, worrying about his own needs was selfish and self-serving, since he knew his focus had to be on being the best parent he could for Susie. Aside from God, she was the center of his life now. Concentrating on finding a new wife would only take his focus away from Susie, which would be wrong.

Therefore, he couldn't tell Naomi the truth about what he wanted for Christmas because it was too embarrassing.

"I don't need anything." Grinning, he raised an eyebrow. "Sound familiar?"

She mirrored his grin, and she was adorable. "There must be something you want, no matter how unnecessary and frivolous it may sound, Caleb. Isn't that what you told me?"

He glanced across the large flea market toward a booth with antique tools they'd passed earlier. "There was a tool I spotted over there that would be a great one to add to my collection, but it's nothing I necessarily need."

She touched his hand. "I'll make a deal with you. I'll show you my dream Bible if you show me that tool you want but don't need."

He shook her hand. "It's a deal."

Her smile was bright, revealing her dimple. "*Wunderbaar.*"

"*Dat*," Susie asked, approaching them. "Can we get some fudge?"

Caleb glanced at Naomi, and she shrugged while pulling out her wallet. "Let me pay this time. You paid for the licorice."

He leaned close to her and inhaled her flowery scent, wondering briefly if it was her shampoo. "Put your money away," he whispered. He then turned to Susie. "That's a *gut* idea. Let's all get some fudge."

Stepping over to a fudge stand, he ordered a slab for the girls and then some for himself and Naomi.

"You're much too generous," Naomi said before breaking off a piece from the small block. "I could've paid for my sisters and me."

He shook his head. "Don't be *gegisch*. It was just fudge."

"*Danki*," she said.

He wished he could get her to open up to him, but he didn't want to push her. He and Susie would head back to Ohio soon, so any thoughts of a relationship would be preposterous. Yet, he was captivated by her.

She smiled and then nodded toward the girls, who were disappearing in the crowd. "We'd better catch up to them."

He nodded. "You're right."

They weaved through a knot of shoppers and caught up with the girls at a toy stand.

"Did you have a nice day in town today?" she asked.

"*Ya*," he said. "I ran some errands with Robert and visited some old *freinden*."

"I bet your friends were *froh* to see you," she said, wiping her mouth with a napkin.

"I think so." He shrugged while biting into the chocolate. "We stopped by the Kauffman Furniture store so Robert could talk to his *dat* and brothers." He shook his head as he recalled the conversations. "Timothy and his brothers are mounting a campaign to get me to move back here. They were trying to get me to go visit a shop that's for sale near the furniture store."

"Oh?" Her eyes rounded with interest. "Did you go visit it?"

He shook his head. "Not yet. But I might."

The girls sat on a bench outside the toy stand and giggled while eating their fudge, and Caleb wondered if he should go visit the shop owner. Would moving Susie closer to his family be a way to help her heal after losing her mother?

He motioned toward a bench near the girls. "Should we sit and finish our chocolate?"

"That's a *gut* idea." Naomi sat down. "I didn't mean to be rude before."

"Rude?" He sank down next to her. "What do you mean?"

"When you asked me what I thought of the Kauffmans."

She studied her remaining square of fudge, and he wondered if she was avoiding his eyes. "It's just that I've made some mistakes that I regret, and they aren't easy to talk about."

Guilt rained down on him for pushing her to discuss it. He didn't want to make her uncomfortable. "You don't have to tell me. It's none of my business."

"No," she said, frowning as she looked up at him. "You've been honest with me, so I need to be honest with you. Timothy and I courted for a short while, but we broke up when we realized that we weren't right for each other. I also courted Luke Troyer for a short time. *Mei mamm* said I was too eager with them, and I know she's right." Her cheeks blazed a bright pink, and he wished he could ease her embarrassment. "But I was young then. I'm almost twenty-five and I know better now. I won't rush into another relationship. In fact, I think God would prefer I help *mei mamm* raise my siblings rather than court."

He raised an eyebrow in surprise. "Don't you think you're being a bit too hard on yourself? We've all had our hearts broken at one time or another, but God still wants us to get married and have a family. You said yourself that God can give us a second chance at love."

She shook her head. "That's not what I said. I asked you if you believe God gives us a second chance, but I never said I believe it."

"But you agreed that God gave Sarah Rose a second chance with Luke."

"*Ya*, I did," she said softly. "But I'm not so sure He'd be willing to give me a third chance."

"What makes you think God puts a cap on how many chances we can have to find love?"

Naomi looked away from his stare. "I don't know. It's just a feeling I have."

"You're young," Caleb said. "Don't give up on love so quickly. Barbara had an *onkel* who didn't marry until he was almost fifty. He never gave up on love."

She gasped. "Really? He was almost fifty?"

"I'm not saying you'll have to wait that long," he added, wiping his beard with a napkin. "I would imagine you'll be snatched up quickly with that *schee* smile of yours."

Looking embarrassed, she bit into the fudge. He wondered what on earth Timothy did to shatter her heart into pieces. Timothy had hinted that he wasn't proud of how their relationship had ended. He must not have let her down too easily.

They ate in silence for a few moments. The girls finished their fudge, and Susie came over and got money from Caleb in order to purchase a few small toys. While the girls shopped, Caleb and Naomi finished their chocolate.

"How about we go into that antique place?" she asked, wiping her mouth. "I want to see that tool you need."

He took her used napkin from her and tossed it into the trash along with his. "You forgot what I said. I don't need it. I would like to have it."

She grinned as she stood. "I meant to say, show me the tool that you would like to have."

"That's right." They walked over to the toy shop together, and he approached the girls. "We'll be right next door looking at the antiques. When you're finished shopping, come over and join us."

The girls agreed, and he and Naomi entered the

antique shop, where he led her over to the tools. Her eyes widened as she glanced over the assortment of gadgets.

"Wow," she said. "Are these the tools you use for your buggy projects?"

He grinned. "No, I actually use modern tools, but I like to collect antiques. I can use them, and sometimes I do. But mostly, I collect them for fun."

She picked up an antique saw and studied it as if it were a precious piece of glass. "How did you start your collection?"

He picked up a hand drill. "My *grossdaddi* started the collection. Actually, he used the tools in his carriage shop. I like to add to it every now and then. It's not really a frivolous expense because I can actually use them." He turned the drill over in his hand, examining the craftsmanship.

"Is that the one you want?" she asked as she stepped over to him.

Caleb nodded. "*Ya.* Like I said, I don't need it, but it would be nice to have." He placed it back on the counter. "I guess we should go find the girls and see if my *dochder* is finished spending my money yet."

"Are women ever finished spending a man's money?" Naomi's smile was coy.

He grinned. "If I answer that question truthfully, will I get smacked?"

She tapped her chin, feigning deep thought. "I don't know. I suppose it depends on the answer."

He laughed and suppressed the urge to put his arm around her shoulders and pull her into his arms for a hug. He enjoyed her easy sense of humor. Spending time with her was akin to relaxing, a feeling he hadn't enjoyed in months—no, more like years.

"*Dat!*" Susie rushed over, her three shopping bags rustling against her cloak. "I think I'm finished. I got some candy and toys. Want to see?" She held open one of the bags and found a plethora of lollipops, chocolate coins, ring pops, candy canes, marbles, small rubber balls, and little toy cars.

"Very nice, Susie." He touched her cheek. "I think you're going to make your *freinden* and cousins very happy on Christmas."

"Are we heading home now?" Susie asked. "I think I have to help my *mamm* start supper."

"*Ya*," Caleb said, placing his hand on Susie's shoulder. "I believe your *dat* may send out a search party if we don't head home soon." He glanced at Naomi. "You need to show me that Bible you were talking about earlier before we head out."

"*Ach*, it's not something I need." Naomi waved it off as they weaved through the crowd.

Levina sidled up to Naomi and took her hand. "That pretty Bible you always visit when you come in here?"

Naomi swung her sister's hand and smiled down at her. "It's not something I need. I can still enjoy God's Word with the Bible I have."

Caleb smiled at the tenderness between the sisters and he took Susie's hand. "We'll stop at the bookstore on the way out."

They entered the little bookstand, and he followed her over to a display of Bibles.

Sylvia pointed to a plain but elegant black Bible. "This is the one she wants."

Naomi's cheeks were pink again. "But I really don't need it." Caleb glanced at the price tag. "Would you want your name engraved on the front?"

Naomi shook her head. "Oh, it's just too much. I couldn't expect you to—"

"*Ya*, she does," Levina chimed in. "*Mamm* and *Dat* have one that was engraved for them on their wedding day, and Naomi has always thought that was a nice gift. She said she wants one with her name on it too."

"Levina," Naomi gently scolded. "You need to mind your own business."

Janie glanced toward the clock on the wall. "We better go," she said, starting toward the door. "I don't want my *dat* angry with me. You know how he gets."

Caleb nodded, knowing how short his brother-in-law's temper could be. He distinctly remembered the early years of Sadie's marriage to Robert, when he'd yell at her for things as simple as supper not being ready at his requested time.

Once the girls were loaded into the back of the buggy, Caleb climbed into the buggy seat next to Naomi. "Do you want me to drop you and your sisters off at home?"

She nodded. "That would be *wunderbaar*."

While the girls chatted about snow and Christmas, Caleb and Naomi rode in silence. He wondered if she'd had as much fun as he'd had today. He wished the afternoon didn't have to end. The idea of moving back to Bird-in-Hand swirled through his mind. Should he go look at that shop? Should he make an offer on the place if it was a good deal? Did he want to uproot Susie? Was he entitled to the happiness he could possibly have here in Lancaster County?

Out the corner of his eye, he spotted his daughter laughing with her cousin and Naomi's sisters. If he moved her here, he wouldn't so much as uproot her as give her a sense of family. Surely, she would miss her friends back in Ohio, but she would also make new friends, including Naomi's sisters and Naomi herself.

"Turn here," Naomi said, breaking through his thoughts. "Then go about half a mile and turn right."

"Oh," Caleb said with a smile. "You're not far at all from Sadie's house."

Naomi shook her head. "Just a little ways, really."

"Close enough to walk," he said, steering around a corner.

"*Ya*," she said, lifting her purse from the floorboard. "I think Susie got all that she wanted today."

"I think so," he said.

She pointed toward a large white farmhouse. "That's it."

"*Danki* for coming," he said as he steered toward her driveway.

"*Danki* for the invitation," she said, turning toward him. "I had a nice time."

"I did too." And he hoped that they could get together again sometime soon.

"Let's go, girls," Naomi said, facing her sisters. "We have to get started on supper." She opened the door, hopped down from the buggy, and helped her sisters down. After saying goodbye to the girls in the back, Naomi turned to Caleb. "Have a nice evening."

"You too," he said. "I hope to see you again soon."

She smiled. "*Ya*, I do too." She said goodbye to the girls and then hurried toward the house with her sisters in tow.

As Caleb steered toward Sadie's house, he decided he needed to check into that shop that Timothy had recommended, and an unfamiliar excitement filled him.

CHAPTER 9

"Go wash up," Naomi told her siblings as she set the table later that evening. "Supper is almost ready."

The children filed out of the kitchen, and Naomi lined the plates up on the long table.

Her mother placed a large bowl of mashed potatoes at the center of the table. "Did you have fun today?"

"*Ya*," Naomi said, snatching a handful of utensils from the drawer. "Susie wanted to shop for Christmas gifts for her cousins and friends. She, Janie, Sylvia, and Levina had a *gut* time shopping, and Caleb and I just walked around and talked."

"What did you and Caleb discuss?" Irma began to fill a platter with homemade rolls.

"Oh, nothing much." Naomi lined the utensils up by the place settings. "We talked about Christmas and things like that. He's very easy to talk to. We had a nice time together." She didn't want to admit they'd talked about her doomed relationships.

Irma gave Naomi a hard look, and Naomi wished she hadn't even mentioned Caleb's name.

Rather than argue about Naomi's track record with dating, Naomi decided to change the subject. "How did the quilt turn out? Did you get it finished before the customer arrived?"

Irma placed the platter next to the rolls and glowered. "I hope you're not getting any ideas about this widower, Naomi. You know he's going back to Ohio after the holidays and you're just going to get your heart broken if you get too attached."

Naomi breathed out a deep sigh. "*Mamm*, I know that. He's just a *freind*."

Her mother continued to frown. "Don't make a fool of yourself again. You never should've gone out with him today. You know how that will look to the rest of the community."

"He invited me," Naomi said, pointing to her chest. "It wasn't my idea. In fact, I think it was Susie's idea. She really likes me, and I enjoy spending time with her too. You know she lost her *mamm* only two years ago. For some reason, she's latched on to me, and how can I turn her away?"

Irma wagged a finger at Naomi. "You can't be her *mamm*. That's not your place."

"I never said I wanted to be her mother. I just want to be her *freind*. Is that so wrong?"

"*Ach*, no." Irma shook her head. "But I know you, Naomi. You get too attached, and that will only lead to trouble."

Naomi shook her head. "I can't do anything right in your eyes, can I, *Mamm*? The way you see it, I mess up completely when it comes to love, and I'm destined to be alone."

"I wasn't speaking of love," Irma said, pulling the

broccoli and rice casserole from the oven. "I was talking about perceptions. It just didn't look right for you to go out shopping with that widower and his *dochder*. It looked very inappropriate, and you know how people talk."

"I don't see how any of my behavior was inappropriate, *Mamm*." Naomi wished her voice wouldn't quaver with her frustration. She grabbed a handful of napkins and began adding them to the place settings in order to keep busy and stop her threatening tears. She was tired of her mother's constant criticism. "It was Susie's idea, and I didn't want to disappoint her. I even invited Levina, Sylvia, and Janie to join us in order to quell any rumors that Sadie Kauffman might feel the need to start about me."

Irma set the casserole dish on the table and pursed her lips. "I know you're not trying to give people the wrong impression, but I know how they think. If you even go for a walk alone with a man, some women assume things they shouldn't about you."

"Why should I care what people think of me?"

"It reflects on this family, Naomi." Irma set the potholders on the counter and then lowered her voice. "How do you think your *dat* will feel if he hears people call you 'too eager'?"

Naomi shook her head. "He would know that I'm not those things, and he would defend me."

Irma touched Naomi's shoulder. "I know you. I know your heart and how you get too attached too soon."

"I'm not attached," Naomi insisted, even though she knew it wasn't the whole truth. "He's *mei freind, Mamm*. What's wrong with being *freinden* with him?"

Irma gave her a sympathetic expression. "I've seen the way you look at him and the way you blush when he's around. Your feelings for him are written all over your *schee* face, Naomi."

Naomi cupped a hand to her mouth. "They are?"

"*Ya*." Irma touched Naomi's cheek. "I don't want to see you get hurt again. I remember clearly the pain you suffered when you had your heart broken by Luke Troyer and then Timothy Kauffman. I don't want to see you suffer that again, and I don't want you to get a reputation."

"Caleb and I are just *freinden, Mamm*," she repeated, her voice quavering.

Irma raised an eyebrow in disbelief. "Is that what you're trying to convince yourself?"

A lump swelled in Naomi's throat as tears filled her eyes. "It's the truth, *Mamm*."

"He's a widower, Naomi," she said. "He's not ready to give his heart away."

"I know," Naomi whispered. "I've already considered that, and I respect his feelings for his *fraa*."

Her siblings returned to the kitchen with a roar of footsteps, chatter, and giggles, and Naomi breathed a sigh of relief. She longed for her mother's focus to turn to someone other than her.

"Lizzie Anne," Naomi called over the noise. "Would you please grab the glasses from the cabinet?" She glanced at her younger sisters. "You can put the glasses out by the dishes."

Lizzie Anne instructed Amos to go out to the barn and call Elam and their father to come in for supper. She then gave Naomi a concerned expression, but

Naomi quickly looked away and turned toward the refrigerator.

Irma grabbed Naomi's arm and pulled her back. "Caleb will go home to Ohio soon," she whispered in Naomi's ear. "Don't let him take your heart with him. You've been hurt enough."

Naomi sighed with defeat. "Yes, *Mamm*," she said before grabbing the pitcher of ice water and the tub of butter. She took a deep, cleansing breath, pushing away the emotions rioting within her. She knew her mother was right about Caleb's plans to return to Ohio. However, Naomi also couldn't squelch the notion that the feelings she had for Caleb were different from anything she'd ever felt for Luke Troyer or Timothy Kauffman. What she felt for Caleb was deeper, something that touched her soul.

Lizzie Anne sidled up to Naomi. "Are you okay?" she whispered.

Naomi nodded. "*Ya*. I'm gut."

Lizzie Anne frowned. "You look upset."

"*Wie geht's?*" Titus's voice boomed as he entered the kitchen. "It smells *appeditlich*."

Naomi forced a smile and touched her sister's arm. "*Danki*," she whispered, "but I'm fine."

Lizzie Anne gave her a look of disbelief.

"It's all ready," Irma said. "*Kinner*, please take your seats." Naomi delivered the pitcher of water and the butter, placing them near her father's seat, and then sat in her usual place, which was between Lizzie Anne and Elam. As she bowed her head in silent prayer, she asked God to guide her in her confusing feelings for Caleb Schmucker.

• • •

"Did you have a *gut* day?" Caleb asked Susie as he sat on the edge of her bed and tucked her in.

"Of course I did, *gegisch*." Susie grinned, hugging her favorite doll to her white nightgown.

He smirked and rubbed her brunette head. Glancing toward the hallway, he wondered how much time he'd have alone with Susie before her cousins came clambering in from the bathroom down the hall. He leaned in close. "Susie, how would you feel about selling our house in Ohio and moving here?"

She gasped, her big green eyes rounding with excitement. "You mean, like live here forever, *Dat*?"

"*Ya*." He touched the tip of her little nose. "Forever."

She screeched, and he pressed a finger to her lips shushing her.

"Your *onkel* will get very upset if he hears you yell like that," he said.

"Are we going to live here?" she asked, sitting up and gesturing around the room. "Then I can stay in this room with Janie, Nancy, and Linda, and I could go to school with them." Her smile widened. "And maybe I could learn to quilt with *Aenti* Sadie and Naomi. And we could go shopping again with Naomi, and I could play with her sisters. Right, *Dat*?"

He brushed his fingers through her long brown hair. "*Ya*, maybe so." *And I could spend more time with Naomi as well.*

She leaned forward and wrapped her arms around his neck, hugging him. "*Ich liebe dich, Dat.*"

"I love you too, *boppli*," he whispered before he kissed the top of her head.

Closing his eyes, he sent up a prayer to God, asking Him for help with this decision. While he felt in his heart it was time to move back home, a small part of his mind was apprehensive. It seemed all the signs were there leading him back home: his family, his friends, the welcoming of the church-district members, and the possible opportunity of a job. But was he moving for the right reasons? Would this be a new start or would he be trying to outrun the loneliness that had overtaken his soul when Barbara died? Was he doing this for selfish reasons or did he have his daughter's best interests in mind?

"*Dat*?"

Opening his eyes, he found Susie studying him. "*Ya*?" Wrinkling her nose, she gave him a confused expression.

"Were you sleeping or praying?"

He touched her cheek. "I was praying."

"What were you praying about?"

"I was asking God if He thought we should move back here."

"Oh." She nodded, her expression serious. "And what do you think God's answer was?"

He smiled. "I'm not certain yet, but I'll tell you when He gives me a sign."

"Do you think He'll give me a sign too?"

"Maybe."

She leaned closer and lowered her voice. "You know what Naomi told me?"

"What?"

"She told me that she believes in Christmas miracles," Susie whispered. "Do you believe in them?"

Sighing, he gave her a gentle smile. "Sure I do, Susie." Muted giggles and loud thumping footsteps echoed down the hallway, announcing the arrival of Susie's cousins. Caleb stood as the girls entered the room and jumped into the beds.

Sadie appeared in the doorway. "It's time to settle down." Crossing the room, she kissed them all on their foreheads.

Caleb wished them each a good night and then followed Sadie down the stairs to the family room. "Would you like some cocoa?" she asked.

"*Ya. Danki*," Caleb said.

"Have a seat. I'll be right back." She disappeared into the kitchen.

Caleb sat in a chair in front of the fire, which crackled, popped, and hissed.

Across the room, Robert sat in his favorite chair, reading the paper. Fingering his beard, Caleb wondered what to say to his brother-in-law. Although he'd known Robert since he was a teenager, Caleb never felt much of a connection to him. Not like he did with Timothy and Daniel, anyway. Robert was the least friendly of the Kauffman men. Caleb used to wonder why Robert was so different from his brothers, but he'd finally decided Robert was just stoic. He was more focused on work and running a smooth household and farm than on fun and games.

"I was thinking about going to see that house and

workshop that are for sale," Caleb blurted out. "Daniel and Timothy mentioned it was near the furniture store."

Robert peeked at Caleb over the paper. "Really?"

Caleb nodded. "Timothy mentioned that the owner wanted a fair price, and I have some money I've been saving up to rebuild my barn."

Looking intrigued, Robert folded his paper and placed it on the table beside him. "You're considering moving back here, *ya*?"

"I think so." Caleb shifted in the chair. "I mentioned it to Susie, and she's very excited. I think it would be good for her to be with her cousins."

Robert was silent for a moment, fingering his beard and considering Caleb's words. "That makes a lot of sense. It would be *gut* for you and Susie to have a new start, and we would love for you to join our church district."

"*Danki*." Caleb glanced around the room as memories of his childhood cluttered his mind.

It seemed as if only yesterday he was sitting in this same wing chair and looking at the mantel. The same old, plain cherry clock sat in the center and ticked over the crackle of the fire. The Christmas decorations consisted of a large poinsettia and some greenery, just as when he was a child. For a moment, he expected his father to flop into the armchair across from him, open his Bible, and begin to read aloud while his mother knitted in the love seat next to him.

"Did you have a nice time at the flea market?" Sadie asked, returning from the kitchen holding a tray with three mugs of hot cocoa.

"*Ya,* I did." Caleb lifted a mug from the tray. "*Danki.*"

"*Gern gschehne.*" She handed a mug and napkin to Robert and then sat across from Caleb in their *daed's* favorite chair.

Caleb sipped the mug and felt the whipped cream in his beard. "*Appeditlich.*" He swiped the napkin across his whiskers.

Sadie cradled a mug in her hands. "Susie seemed like she had fun today."

Caleb nodded, sipping more cocoa. "I think she has a *wunderbaar gut* time with her cousin and friends."

"And Naomi." Sadie tapped the side of her mug, a frown turning the corners of her mouth downward.

"*Ya,*" he said, ignoring her tone and her expression. "Susie loves spending time with Naomi."

She wagged a finger at him. "You remember what I told you about her."

"Sadie," Robert snapped. "Gossiping is a sin."

Caleb drank from his mug in an effort to suppress the grin threatening to curl his lips. This was one instance in which he appreciated his gruff brother-in-law.

With an indignant frown, Sadie sipped her cocoa.

An awkward silence fell among them as they enjoyed their drinks. Caleb searched for something to say but found himself only thinking of Naomi and wondering if she'd enjoyed their day together.

After a few sips of cocoa, Robert cleared his throat and glanced at his wife. "Caleb was telling me he wants to go look at the shop that's for sale near my father's store."

"What?" Sadie gasped and grinned. "You're going to consider buying a shop here?"

"Maybe." Caleb held up a hand as if to calm her from across the room. "Don't get your hopes up yet. I'm thinking about moving back, and Timothy and Daniel told me about the shop. Apparently it has a house on the property as well."

Placing her mug on the table beside her, Sadie clapped her hands together. "*Ach*, that's *wunderbaar*. We would love to have you and Susie here."

"Don't get too excited," Caleb repeated. "I discussed it with Susie tonight, and she likes the idea. But I need to do some research and some careful consideration. I have a little bit of money I've been saving to refurbish my barn, but it's only enough for a small down payment. I can't do anything until I get a buyer for my farm. And with today's economy—"

She waved off the thought as she interrupted him. "Your farm would sell easily, Caleb. From what you've told me, you have prime land that an investor would love."

"I'd be glad to take you over to see the shop tomorrow," Robert said. "The owner is Riley Parker, an *Englisher* who grew up here. He's a *gut* man, and he'll give you a fair price." Caleb nodded and studied the plain white mug while mulling over the notion of buying a place and setting up business after being gone from Lancaster County for so long. It seemed like such a hasty decision to look at a shop. Would it be prudent to put in an offer? But he wasn't necessarily going to buy it. He was only going to research it and weigh options.

"You know, Caleb," Sadie began, "you don't need to invest in a business quite yet. You could simply take a job working at Wagler's Buggies."

Meeting her probing gaze, Caleb swallowed a sigh, hoping his sister wasn't trying to play matchmaker again. Would she ever listen and respect his decisions? "It's a thought, but I'm not sure I want to be an apprentice anymore. I think I'm ready to open my own shop." His words surprised himself. He hadn't realized he'd wanted to branch out on his own until he said it out loud.

Sadie's eyes widened. "Really?"

Caleb nodded. "I've been working for Jonas since I moved to Middlefield, and as much as I admire him, I think I'm ready to run my own business. As a bonus, he taught me how to make Lancaster-style buggies, in addition to our Ohio ones. So I'd be well prepared to take on business here."

Sadie glanced at Robert, who looked equally shocked. Robert stood. "I'll take you by there tomorrow. I think I'm going to head up to bed. It's getting late."

Sadie glanced at the clock and popped out of her chair. "Oh my. It's after nine. I best head to bed too." She stepped over to Caleb and glanced at his mug. "Are you finished?"

He shook his head. "No, I've been savoring it." He smiled up at her. "I think I'll sit here for a few minutes and enjoy the fire. I'll clean up after myself."

She patted his shoulder. "*Gut nacht, bruder.* I do hope you decide to stay."

"*Danki.*" He frowned. "Don't start any rumors about my moving here, Sadie. Right now I'm trying to figure out God's plan for Susie and me."

She gasped. "I'll do no such thing, Caleb. I'll keep it to myself."

He raised an eyebrow with suspicion.

She made a motion as if to zip her lips and then headed into the kitchen.

Sighing, Caleb leaned his head back on the chair and closed his eyes. Opening his heart to God, Caleb silently asked Him to reveal the right path for him and his precious daughter.

CHAPTER 10

C aleb steered the horse toward the For Sale sign sitting at the edge of the property. Since Robert had to tend to business at the farm, Caleb had borrowed the horse and buggy and ventured out to find the place on his own.

Guiding the horse into a rock driveway, Caleb spotted a large cinderblock building containing three bay doors and an office off to the right. He stopped the horse by the office door, and his boots crunched across the snow as he walked around to the front of the building. Caleb climbed the stairs, and the door opened with a loud squeak, revealing a stocky middle-aged English man with dark hair and eyes.

"Good morning," the man said. "May I help you?"

"Yes," Caleb said. "My name is Caleb Schmucker, and I wanted to speak with the owner regarding the price of this property."

"I'm the owner, and it's nice to meet you." The man shook Caleb's hand. "I'm Riley Parker. Please come in." He gestured for Caleb to enter the shop. "I'm glad you came by. Do you live around here?"

"No. I'm visiting from Ohio. My sister lives in

Bird-in-Hand." Caleb glanced around the office, which was a small room that led to the large work bays. "My daughter and I are here for the holidays, and I'm considering moving back."

"Oh." Riley rubbed the stubble on his chin. "You're from around here originally?"

Caleb nodded. "That's right. I moved to Ohio about ten years ago after I got married. My wife passed away two years ago, and I don't have any family there, except for a few of her cousins."

Riley frowned. "I'm sorry for your loss."

"*Danki.*" Caleb smiled. "I'm thinking that I want to come back here so that my daughter has some family around her while she grows up."

"Yes, family is important." Riley leaned on the counter behind him. "I know quite a few Amish families around here. Who is your sister?"

"Sadie Kauffman." He jammed his thumb toward the door as if in the direction of the road. "Her husband's family owns the furniture store a few blocks down."

"Oh!" Riley nodded. "I know Eli Kauffman quite well. Nice family."

"Yes." Caleb stepped over to the door and looked toward the bays, imagining his toolboxes and supplies lining the walls while he built buggies. He could see himself coming here every day and working to make a living. "This is a nice place you have here. Have you owned it long?"

"Oh yeah." Riley limped toward the bays and motioned for Caleb to follow. "This land has been in my family for years. My father built this shop about fifty years ago, and I added on twenty years ago. I ran a towing company and did some minor car repairs on the side." He patted his thigh.

"I've got a bum leg, so I can't work much anymore. My kids have all married and moved away, and my wife and I decided it was time to retire and move to Florida. But we need to unload this place before I can buy my condo."

Riley gestured toward the row of toolboxes and workbenches. "I'll have all of this cleared out soon. My youngest son is supposed to come and get the tools at some point. I don't want to take any of them to Florida." He smiled. "Well, just a little box with the basics for the honey-do lists my wife likes to make to keep me off the sofa."

Caleb walked the length of the shop, imagining how he would set it up if it were his. The building was bigger than the shop he worked in back in Ohio. "This is quite spacious."

Riley moved the curtain and pointed toward a brick home behind the shop. "The house is out back if you'd like to see that too."

"*Danki*." Caleb followed Riley out a side door and down the driveway.

"We have a barn out back too," Riley said, pointing toward a small fenced pasture. "It's not big, but it's functional if you have a few animals."

"How many acres are here?"

"Six," Riley said as they approached the brick ranch house. "The house has three bedrooms and two bathrooms. The rooms are fairly big. We raised four boys without any problems. Would you like to come in? My wife is at the market right now, but I would be happy to show you around."

"That would be great," Caleb said.

While Riley led him around the house, Caleb imagined making a home for him and Susie. The bedrooms were a good size, and the woodwork on the trim in the little house was also nice. The house was nothing fancy, but Caleb didn't need fancy.

Before he could move in, he would have to have the electricity removed from the house in order to keep with his Amish traditions. He would also need to convert to gas appliances, but that wouldn't be a problem.

Caleb glanced around the kitchen, trying to imagine his table and chairs in the center of the room. His heart warmed at the idea of being home in Lancaster County, celebrating holidays and milestones with his sister and her family, worshipping with her church district and his old friends. He would also make new friends, and he would possibly get to know a very special friend better: Naomi King.

His last thought caused him to smile to himself. He would definitely enjoy spending time with Naomi, as would Susie.

Caleb turned to Riley, standing in the doorway to the family room. "May I see the barn?"

"Sure." Riley led him out through the small one-car garage toward the pasture.

Stepping into the barn, an overwhelming calmness enveloped Caleb. He glanced around at the horse stalls, and he knew—this was the house. This was meant to be for him and Susie.

This was the sign from God he'd been waiting for.

Smiling, Caleb faced Riley in the doorway. "What's your final price, Mr. Parker?"

. . .

Later that afternoon, Caleb steered the buggy into Sadie's driveway. After putting up the horse and buggy, he grabbed his armload of bags from his shopping trip and headed up the back steps. Entering the kitchen, he found Susie sitting at the table eating cookies with her cousins.

"*Dat!*" she called when she spotted him. "Look at the cookies we made at Naomi's today." She held up a plate with assorted Christmas cookies. "Levina and Sylvia invited us over after school. We had fun."

"Oh my." Dropping his bags on the floor, Caleb swiped a chocolate chip cookie from the plate and took a bite. "*Appeditlich!*" He finished the cookie in two big bites and then hung his coat on the peg by the door before kicking off his boots.

Susie leaned over and examined the pile of bags. "What's in there?"

He picked up the bags and held them close to his body. "Nothing for you to be concerned about." He backed out of the kitchen. "Enjoy your cookies, girls."

Caleb crossed the family room and into his parents' former apartment where he'd been staying. He walked through the small sitting room to the bedroom and dropped the bags onto the bed. He then opened the closet to make room for the gifts. He was placing the bag from the bookstore onto the top shelf of the closet when a knock sounded on the door frame.

Sadie stepped into the room with a curious expression. "How was your visit to the Parker place?"

"*Gut.*" Caleb lowered himself onto the bed, and it creaked beneath his weight.

"Oh?" She raised her eyebrows with curiosity.

He crossed his arms over his wide chest. "I made an offer."

She gasped and clasped her hands together. "My *bruder* is moving back home!"

He nodded and smiled. "I think so."

"*Ach!* This is *wunderbaar gut!*" Sadie gestured widely with an equally wide grin. "Our *kinner* will go to school together. We'll worship together and also celebrate birthdays and holidays together! This is a dream come true. I'm so *froh!*"

"Don't get too excited just yet," he said, standing. "I have to try to sell my farm, and then it will take some time to get my business going here. I'm hoping I can make a smooth transition from Jonas's shop to my own."

"Wait." She held a hand up. "You shouldn't open your own business just yet. You should work for Hezekiah Wagler until you have enough money to open your own business. That way you could—"

"Sadie," he began, his voice firm. "Stop trying to set me up with Irene Wagler."

"What are you implying, Caleb?" Her surprised expression was forced. "I'm not trying to set you up. I'm just looking after your finances."

He glowered at his older sister. "I can look after my own finances just fine, *danki*. I'm a grown man. I also will decide if and when I'm ready to court women."

She frowned, looking hurt by his words. "Caleb, I only have your best interests in mind. I want you to make the right decisions for you and Susie."

"I can make my own decisions, *danki*." He spotted Susie crossing the sitting room and heading for the door, and he bit back the angry words that were bubbling forth from his throat.

"*Dat!*" Susie bounded into the room. "Where did you go today? I thought you'd be home sooner."

"I told you," he said, forcing a smile for his daughter's sake. "I ran a few errands."

"Errands?" Sadie asked.

He nodded at Sadie and then glanced at Susie. "I just had a few things I needed to pick up at the store while I was out."

Susie looked curious. "Oh. Did you have a *gut* day?"

"I did," Caleb said. "Did you have a *gut* day?"

Susie nodded. "I had lots of fun with my cousins."

"I'm going to go start supper." Sadie stepped toward the door. "Did you tell Susie the exciting news?"

Susie's eyes rounded. "What news?"

"It looks like we're going to move here," he said slowly. "I talked to a man about a house today."

"Yeah!" Susie wrapped her arms around Caleb's neck, and he hugged her.

Caleb glanced toward the doorway. Seeing that Sadie was gone, he breathed a sigh of relief. While he loved his sister, he grew weary of her constant interference.

He hoped that moving closer to her wouldn't be a mistake. However, in his heart, he knew this was the best plan for him and Susie. Besides, he could get to know Naomi better and see if his growing feelings for her would turn into something more permanent.

And that was when Caleb realized the truth: he was planning this move for himself as much as for Susie. God wanted him to break free of the loneliness that had hung over him like a black cloud since Barbara's death. Caleb believed he was entitled to find happiness again even though Barbara was gone.

CHAPTER 11

I can't believe Christmas Eve is tomorrow," Naomi said as she walked through the indoor flea market on Friday.

"I know." Lilly stopped and glanced at the candy concession stand. "I should get some candy for Hannah's *kinner*."

She smiled at the clerk and began rattling off a list of candy.

Lizzie Anne sidled up to Naomi and tapped her shoulder. "Are you okay?" she whispered. "You've been sort of quiet since Wednesday. Is everything all right?"

Naomi held back a sigh. Her younger sister was quite intuitive. Naomi had been quiet since her discussion with her mother Wednesday night, after her shopping excursion with Caleb and the girls. And Naomi's reticence was caused by the conflicting thoughts swirling through her head. Her mother had warned her not to allow Caleb to return to Ohio with her heart. While Naomi knew that the advice was sound, she feared that Caleb Schmucker already had possession of it.

Naomi tried to smile, but her lips formed a grimace. "I have some things on my mind."

"Is something wrong?" Lizzie Anne asked, her brown eyes full of worry.

"No," Naomi said, glancing toward the counter, where Lilly stood talking to the candy clerk. "Everything is fine. I just have a lot to get done. I still have to make a batch of butterscotch cookies for *Dat* and then get all of the gifts together for the little ones."

Lizzie Anne tilted her chin in question. "Are you certain that's it?"

"*Ya.*" Naomi pulled her list from the pocket of her apron. "I need to pick up a few gifts for *Mamm*. She wants me to get some little gifts in case we go visiting tomorrow."

"For the Kauffmans, *ya*?"

Naomi's eyes snapped to her sister's face. "The Kauffmans?"

"*Ya.* We were invited to Sadie's tomorrow night for the Kauffman Christmas Eve get-together," Lizzie Anne said with a smile. "I have to pick up something special for Lindsay," she said, referring to Rebecca Kauffman's niece who lived with her. "You know she's my best *freind.*"

Nodding, Naomi had wondered when she would see Caleb again. Although the thought of seeing him again sent her stomach into a knot, she also couldn't wait. She'd enjoyed the time spent baking and laughing with her sisters and Susie yesterday afternoon. She felt her attachment to the girl growing, but she also knew the attachment wasn't limited to just the girl. She had deep, growing feelings for Susie's father, and it both scared and excited her at the same time. And this feeling was nothing compared to what she'd believed she felt for Luke Troyer and Timothy Kauffman once. This attachment was more meaningful. The risk of heartbreak was high, but for some inexplicable reason, Naomi felt a willingness to take the risk.

"Naomi?" a voice asked.

Naomi turned and found Lilly studying her. "You okay?" her friend asked.

"Funny," Lizzie Anne began with a grin. "I just asked her the same question."

Naomi blew out a defeated sigh. "I feel like I'm on trial here."

Lilly took Naomi's arm and pulled her through the knot of shoppers. "Let's go get some fudge and talk."

"Fine." Naomi gave in with a grimace. Getting fudge would bring back memories of her shopping day with Caleb. How ironic.

After ordering the chocolate, they sat at a small table. Naomi felt her sister's and her friend's eyes studying her as she broke off a piece of milk chocolate fudge.

"What's going on?" Lilly asked between bites of her dark chocolate fudge. "You're very distracted and quiet."

"That's what I said," Lizzie Anne said while wiping a piece of milk chocolate off her sleeve and balancing her slab of remaining fudge in her other hand.

"I have a lot on my mind," Naomi said with a shrug.

"Such as?" Lilly prodded.

Naomi knew neither of them would back down until she spilled her heart to them. It was time to confess her feelings, and she wasn't certain she could put them into coherent words.

"On Wednesday, I went shopping with Caleb Schmucker, Susie, Janie Kauffman, and my younger sisters," Naomi said, keeping her eyes on her block of fudge. "In fact, we came here, so Susie could do some Christmas shopping for little gifts for her cousins and new friends."

"What?" Lilly's voice nearly squeaked with shock. "Why didn't you tell me this yesterday?"

"I didn't think to tell you." Naomi felt wretched for telling a fib, but she continued, despite Lilly's hurt expression. "That night, my *mamm* gave me a lecture on not giving my heart to Caleb because he's a widower and also because he's going to go back to Ohio. She said I'm just setting myself up to get hurt."

"Why would *Mamm* say that?" Lizzie Anne asked while wiping more stray crumbs off her sleeve. "Why does *Mamm* think you like Caleb?"

"I don't know." Naomi's cheeks heated. She wasn't very good at lying.

"Oh," Lizzie Anne said with a wide smile. "You do like Caleb."

"*Mamms* have a way of knowing these things," Lilly said, patting Lizzie Anne's arm. "Sometimes they know before we do. It's their job." She then turned her gaze to Naomi. "How did shopping go? Did you have a *gut* time?"

Naomi nodded. "We had a *wunderbaar* time. He's so easy to talk to, and he's so very sweet and thoughtful." She frowned and shook her head. "I'm doomed. I never should've gone out with him."

"Why do you say that?" Lizzie Anne asked. She bit into the fudge, and the crumbs were finally under control. "It sounds like you're *gut freinden*. Why can't you be *freinden* with him? Susie obviously likes you. I've seen how she talks to you and follows you around."

"It's more complicated than that," Naomi said with a gentle smile. She ate more fudge and wished she could turn off her feelings for Caleb. But did she really want to turn them off? When she was with him, she felt a true happiness that she'd never felt before.

"You're not going to listen to your *mamm* are you?" Lilly asked before popping a final piece of fudge into her mouth.

"I don't know." Naomi shrugged. "I don't know what to do. My *mamm* is right about him leaving. He's going to go back to Ohio, and where will that leave me? I'll be right back where I was when Timothy and I broke up— alone and nursing a broken heart."

"Maybe not," Lizzie Anne said. "Maybe he'll want to court you, and he and Susie can move here." She shrugged. "He may like you, too, and he may want to be back by his family since Susie's *mamm* is gone." She looked between Lilly and Naomi. "It's a possibility, right?"

Lilly nodded. "You could be right."

Naomi shook her head. "That would be a big move for him."

"Or you could move to Ohio," Lizzie Anne said. "I would hate to see you go, but we could visit."

Naomi shook her head. "I don't know if I could leave *Mamm*, *Dat*, and all of you."

"It would be difficult, but my cousin did it," Lilly said. "She misses her family, but she keeps in touch with letters and occasional phone calls."

"Lilly is right." Lizzie Anne wiped her mouth. "If it feels right for you to go with him to Ohio, then you should think about it. You need to follow your heart, Naomi. That's what you used to say."

"I was wrong," Naomi whispered, thinking back on her failed relationships.

"No, you were never wrong about following your heart," Lilly chimed in with a knowing smile. "You simply did it at the wrong time. Don't judge your future by your past. Things happen in God's time."

"Ya!" Lizzie Anne snapped her fingers. "It's like the verse *Dat* read last night during devotions. Remember? I think it went something like: 'I wait for the Lord, my soul waits, and in His word I put my hope.'"

Lilly grinned at Lizzie Anne. "You are one smart *maedel*."

Lizzie Anne smoothed the tie of her prayer covering. "Sometimes I have a *gut* thought or two."

Naomi smiled while finishing her fudge.

"It's like what you told me the other day," Lilly said. "You said that in the past you were too eager and you didn't wait for God's time for love. Maybe now it's God's time."

Naomi nodded slowly while considering the words. "Maybe it is." *I hope you're right, Lilly.*

Lilly wiped her hands and stood. "Let's shop, *ya*?"

Naomi tossed her dirty napkins in the trash can. "I have a store I want to go into."

Lizzie Anne chatted about the weather report and threat of more snow as they weaved through the crowd toward the antique store.

"What are we doing here?" Lizzie Anne asked as they stepped through the doorway.

"I'll be fast," Naomi said and then rushed toward the tool section, holding her breath and hoping that the antique drill was still there. She picked up the contraption and smiled.

After paying for it, she hurried over to Lizzie Anne and Lilly, who were in a deep discussion about a desk and whether or not it was an antique or just an overpriced piece of furniture.

"Did you get what you needed?" Lilly asked as they headed back out into the flea-market crowd.

"*Ya*," Naomi hugged the bag to her cloak. "I'm all set. I just need to go to the toy store and find some little things for the *kinner*."

"What's in the bag?" Lizzie Anne reached for the bag.

Naomi swatted her hand away. "Nothing."

Her sister's eyes widened with curiosity. "*Ach*, then it must be *gut*. Is it for Caleb?"

Naomi nodded.

"What is it?" Lilly asked, looking intrigued.

"It's something he told me he wanted but would never buy himself," Naomi said, loosening her grip on the bag.

"What is it?" Lizzie Anne asked again. "Just tell us. We'll keep it a secret, right, Lilly?"

Lilly nodded. "You have my word."

Naomi moved out of the crowd and stood outside the toy store. She pulled out the drill, and Lilly and Lizzie Anne stared at the tool as if it were from another world.

"What is it?" Lizzie Anne asked.

"It looks sort of like a drill my *grossdaddi* had in his barn," Lilly said.

"That's exactly what it is, Lilly," Naomi said. "Caleb collects antique tools, and he uses them too."

"Wow," Lizzie Anne said, touching the handle. "He'll love it."

Naomi smiled. "I hope so."

CHAPTER 12

Caleb was reading his Bible when a knock sounded on his bedroom door later that evening. He opened the door and found Susie glowering. "*Wie geht's?*"

"Irene is here." She spat out the words. "I don't think I like her."

He raised an eyebrow. "Susan. What's gotten into you?"

"She doesn't even say hello to me," Susie said, her frown deepening. "She looked at me and said, 'Where's your *dat*?' It's like I don't exist."

Caleb touched her prayer covering. "I'm certain she didn't mean it. Remember your manners."

"Why?" Susie asked as they headed through the sitting room. "She doesn't remember hers, so why should I remember mine?"

He suppressed a smile. "You must always be respectful of adults, even when it seems as if they don't have any manners. Maybe she will learn by your example."

"Yes, *Dat*." She stopped at the doorway leading to the large family room. "But I'm certain she doesn't like me," she whispered, her pretty face twisted with a deep scowl.

He touched her nose. "Anyone who doesn't like you is misled, *mei liewe.*"

She scrunched her nose, and he laughed. Taking her hand, he steered her to the kitchen where Irene sat talking with Sadie. Sadie's younger children were seated at the table coloring on construction paper.

"*Wie geht's?*" Caleb said.

"Oh, Caleb," Sadie said, popping up from her chair. "I'll let you two chat." She shooed her children into the family room and then looked at Susie. "You come, too, Susie. Let your *dat* and Irene chat."

Susie frowned up at Sadie. "I'm staying with my *dat.*" Sadie lifted a finger in preparation to scold her.

"She's fine," Caleb said, his voice booming a little louder than he'd intended.

"Oh," Sadie said, looking surprised. She disappeared into the family room.

"*Wie geht's?*" Caleb repeated, sinking into a chair across the table from Irene.

"I'm *gut.* How are you?" Irene smiled sweetly at Caleb and then glanced past him, her smile fading.

Caleb turned to find Susie leaning in the doorway, looking unhappy. "Join us, Susie." He motioned for her to come to the table, but she shook her head. He could feel her uneasiness from across the room, and his heart ached for his usually happy-go-lucky daughter.

He turned back to Irene, and her sugary sweet smile returned. "What brings you out this way?" he inquired, hoping to ease the tension.

"I was going to ask you what you were planning for supper," she said, leaning across the table just slightly as if to share a secret. "Do you like Hamburg Gulosh?"

"*Ach*," he said, fingering his beard. "I'd have to count that as one of my most favorite meals."

"*Gut!*" She grinned. "Why don't you grab your coat, and we'll head out to my parents' house. I made a special dessert too."

"Sounds *appeditlich*." He turned to Susie, who was still in the doorway, twisting one of the ties from her prayer covering in her little finger. "Grab your cloak, Susie. We're going to dinner at Irene's."

"Oh," Irene said quickly. She leaned toward him and lowered her voice. "I thought maybe Susie could stay here with Sadie so that you and my *dat* could talk about the shop."

"See, *Dat*," Susie exclaimed, stomping into the room. "She doesn't like me!"

"Susan." Caleb stood. He gestured for her to calm down while working to keep his voice composed. "We just talked about this. Remember your manners." He turned to Irene. "I'd rather not have dinner without my *dochder*."

Irene bristled. "Oh. I thought you might like to discuss the buggy business without the interruption of a *kind*."

"I don't see my *dochder* as an interruption." He walked over to Susie and placed a hand on her shoulder.

Irene looked stunned. "But don't you want to discuss working at my *daed's* shop?"

Caleb shook his head. "If she's not welcome, then I'll politely turn down your supper invitation." He glanced down at Susie, and she smiled. Her eyes were so full of love that his heart felt as if it would melt.

Popping up, Irene crossed to the door and snatched her cloak from the peg on the wall. "I suppose I'll see you later." Scowling, she pulled on her cloak. "Please tell Sadie I said *gut nacht*."

"I will," Caleb said, gently squeezing Susie's shoulder. Irene rushed through the door, which slammed behind her.

"*Dat*!" Susie beamed up at him. "You didn't want to go without me?"

He shook his head. "How could I go without you? You're *mei liewe*. We're in this together, remember?"

She wrapped her arms around his waist and hugged him. "*Ich liebe dich*."

"I love you too," he said. "But you must remember not to talk back to adults, Susie. You can get your point across without being rude."

She grinned up at him. "Like you did."

He chuckled and rubbed her shoulder. "*Ya*, I guess I did."

She headed for the door. "I'm going to go tell Janie!"

"Susie!" He hoped to stop her from telling the family about his conversation with Irene, but she was gone. He heard her shoes clunking up the stairs to the bedrooms.

Stepping over to the window, Caleb glanced out at the sky, seeing snowflakes floating down to the porch railing and dotting the rock driveway.

"Did I hear a door slam?" Sadie asked behind him.

"*Ya*," he said, facing her quizzical stare. "Irene left."

Sadie stepped through the doorway. "Didn't she invite you for supper?"

He nodded. "She did."

"And what happened?" Her eyes searched his face.

"I declined her invitation."

"Why would you do that?" She stepped toward him. "I don't understand. Irene is young and attractive, and her father has a successful carriage shop. You don't need to invest in a new business." She gestured with her hands. "You could simply work for him, and you and Irene could get to know each other better."

He frowned, running his hand through his hair. Would his sister ever stop her interfering? "I'm going for a walk." He gripped the doorknob and wrenched the backdoor open with a squeak.

"Caleb?" Sadie called after him.

Stepping out onto the porch, the cold, moist air seeped through his shirt and into his skin. He took a deep, cleansing breath and walked over to the railing. Closing his eyes, he let the cool snowflakes kiss his warm cheeks while breathing out the frustration boiling in his soul.

He knew that allowing his sister's interference to upset him wouldn't help the situation. He remembered clearly how she tried to run his life when he lived with his parents. She was interested in all of Caleb's comings and goings, suggesting how he should spend his social life and even giving her unsolicited opinions of his friends. While he loved his sister, she was a hopeless meddler.

Opening his eyes, he stared up at the sky, wondering

how he would handle her when he moved back. How could he keep the lines of communication open with his sister without losing his temper?

He glanced toward the driveway, and his thoughts turned to Irene. He'd hoped that Susie was wrong when she'd proclaimed Irene's dislike for her. However, Irene's facial expressions and her blatant disregard for Susie's feelings were apparent. He'd never understand how someone could disregard a child the way that Irene did. Even if Caleb had wanted to discuss business with Hezekiah Wagler, he would've done it in front of Susie. She was old enough to be quiet while the adults were having a serious conversation.

He turned back toward the pasture. If he cut across the pasture and continued about a half mile, he would wind up on Naomi's road. He wondered if she was home. And if so, would she want to visit with him? He hadn't seen her since Wednesday, and he missed her. He wondered if she missed him too.

Caleb snickered to himself. He sounded like a love-sick teenage boy.

"*Dat?*" Susie's voice sounded behind him.

He faced her and swallowed a shiver. "Susie?" he asked with a smile.

She jammed a hand on her little hip. "You know you're going to catch a cold, *ya?*"

He nodded. "*Ya.* I know."

She smiled. "Janie says you're a *wunderbaar gut dat* for what you said to Irene Wagler."

He grinned. "I'm *froh* she approves."

"I like Naomi more than I like Irene," she said.

"*Ya*, I know," he said. "I can't blame you."

"Are you going to come inside or do I need to get you your coat?" She frowned, and her face reminded him of Barbara's when she disapproved of something Caleb had done.

"I'll be in shortly," he said, rubbing his arms.

She gave him a confused expression, shrugged, and closed the door.

He looked back up at the sky and prayed for strength and help for dealing with both his sister and the uncertainties of the upcoming move from Ohio to Pennsylvania.

CHAPTER 13

I t's a regular blizzard out here," Naomi commented, climbing from Lilly's buggy. She helped her siblings out of the back and then grabbed her bag of gifts. "Lizzie Anne and Levina, grab those platters of cookies and carry them in please. Sylvia, please take the bag with the gifts for the *kinner*."

"I can't believe the snow." Lilly tented her hand over her eyes to block the raging flurries. "I don't know how we're going to find our way home."

Stepping on the sidewalk, Sylvia slipped and then righted herself. "Maybe we'll have to stay the night."

Naomi chuckled. "I don't think Sadie has enough room for all of us."

Naomi, her younger siblings, and Lilly made their way up the steps to the porch. A buggy bounced up the drive, leaving tracks revealing its path, and Naomi spotted her parents and Elam emerging from the buggy into the snow. Elam stowed her parents' horse and Lilly's horse, and her parents began their trek through the blowing snow to the stairs. Naomi waited for her parents while Lilly and Naomi's siblings disappeared into the house, carrying the food and gifts.

"Naomi, you should go inside," Titus said on his way up the stairs. Moving past her, he held the door open. "Go on. You'll catch a cold."

"*Danki, Dat*," Naomi said with a smile. She gestured for her mother to go in first. "After you, *Mamm*."

"*Danki*." Her mother smiled as she stepped into the foyer. "I assume the *kinner* brought in the food and gifts?"

"*Ya*." Naomi followed Irma into the family room and then helped her remove her cloak.

They hung their cloaks on the pegs on the wall, jamming them on top of the pile, and then stepped into the family room, clogged with people talking and laughing. Irma disappeared into the crowd, shaking hands and greeting friends while smiling.

Naomi scanned the group, her stomach fluttering as she searched for one certain face: Caleb's.

"Naomi!" A little voice yelled as a hand pulled on the skirt of her frock. "*Frehlicher Grischtdaag!*"

Naomi glanced down into Susie's smiling face. "Oh, Susie." She hugged the little girl. "*Frehlicher Grischtdaag* to you too! I have something for you." She perused the crowd, looking for one of her siblings and her bag of gifts.

"I have something for you!" Taking her hand, Susie yanked Naomi toward the far side of the family room. "I'll have to find my gifts."

They crossed the family room, and Naomi glanced through another doorway into a smaller sitting room, where she spotted Caleb standing with Timothy Kauffman and Hezekiah Wagler. The three men were talking and laughing while holding mugs, which she assumed were full of Robert's famous hot cider.

Susie dug through a large shopping bag and then pulled out a small doll. "This is for you."

Naomi held the doll up and examined it. The tiny cloth doll wore a blue dress, black apron, and black winter bonnet, and held a little sign that said "Friends." Tears filled Naomi's eyes as she looked at Susie. "It's *schee*."

Susie beamed. "I got it for you because you're *mei freind*."

"It's perfect." Leaning down, Naomi engulfed Susie into a hug and squeezed her tight.

When she stood, she felt someone's stare focused on her. Glancing over, she spotted Caleb watching her. He nodded and smiled, and she returned the gesture before turning back to Susie.

"Now, I hope you don't think this is *gegisch*, but I got you something too." Naomi put the doll into the pocket of her apron and then reached into her bag and pulled out the quilt she'd shown Susie during the quilting bee. "This is for you."

"For me?" Susie gasped as she hugged the quilt to her chest. "I love this so much! I will sleep with it on my bed every night. *Danki*, Naomi."

"*Gern gschehne.* That's not all." Naomi then pulled out a flat box. "This was my favorite game when I was your age." She held her breath, hoping Susie would like it.

"Scrabble!" Susie's green eyes rounded with excitement as she draped the quilt over her arm. "Oh, Naomi!

Danki!" She hugged Naomi again, and Naomi chuckled. "Will you play with me?"

"Of course," Naomi said. "I think it's too crowded to play here now, but I promise we'll get in at least one game before you and your *dat* head back to Ohio."

Susie examined the box. "Then you'll play more when we get back, right?"

"*Ya,*" Naomi said. "If you bring it each time you visit, we'll play it. I don't think my game at home has all of the pieces anymore." She gripped the handles of her shopping bag, wondering when to give Caleb his special gift.

"Not when we visit." Susie looked up. "I mean when we move here."

Naomi gasped. "What did you say?"

Susie grinned. "We're moving here. My *dat* said he found a house."

Stunned, Naomi was speechless. She looked toward Caleb and found him nodding while listening to Hezekiah. Her heart filled with warmth and hope of a possible future with Caleb and Susie. Maybe they could be a family? Was this what Lizzie Anne had been talking about with her verse about waiting for the Lord and putting hope in Him? Was it God's time for her like Lilly had said?

She glanced back at Susie. "Are you certain?"

Susie nodded. "*Ya.* I heard my *Aenti* Sadie say something about *Dat* working for Irene's *daed.*" She frowned. "I hope that isn't true. Irene doesn't like me. She doesn't smile at me. She invited my *dat* over for supper and said I wasn't invited. She's not very nice."

Naomi swallowed a groan as her hopes evaporated. Caleb's plans included Irene, not Naomi. "Oh," she said, her voice barely a whisper over the conversations floating around them.

"Irene is always smiling around my *dat*," Susie continued, looking disgusted. "She always wants to be with him alone. She acts nice around him, but she's not really nice at all."

Speechless, Naomi listened as her frown deepened.

"She acts like I don't exist," Susie said, gripping the box and the quilt in her arms. "She doesn't even want me in the room with her and my *dat*." She glowered. "My *dat* says I have to respect adults and use my manners, but I don't want to use my manners around her." Her expression softened. "But you're always so nice to me. You're *mei freind* and I could never be friends with Irene. I know it's not Christian to say that, but it's the truth."

Naomi nodded again. She couldn't form the words to express the emotions that were weighing down on her shoulders. She felt her spirit wilting, like a thirsty flower in desperate need of water.

"I want my *dat* to be with you, not Irene. I don't understand why he even talks to her. Irene would never bake with me or quilt with me. She would never even play a game with me." Susie placed the flat box and the quilt on the bench next to her and began to open the box. "Can we play now?"

"I don't think that would be a *gut* idea," Naomi said, hoping her anxiety didn't show on her face. "There are too many people here, and I'm afraid the pieces will get lost."

"Oh." Susie looked disappointed. "I can't wait to play. Maybe we can go up to my room." She nodded toward the sitting room behind them. "Or maybe my *dat's* room on the coffee table? We could spread the game out and play."

Naomi glanced toward the sitting room and spotted Irene standing next to Caleb while her father chatted. Caleb and Timothy both laughed at something Hezekiah said, and Naomi's heart sank. She'd been so wrong about Caleb. And now that he was going to move here, she'd have to see him and endure the sting of her heartache just as she had to endure seeing Luke Troyer and Timothy Kauffman. She felt herself falling into a pit of despair, as if her heart were being smashed into a million pieces right before her eyes.

Her stomach twisted, and she glanced at Susie. "I'm not feeling well. I think I need to go get something to drink."

Susie hoisted her game and quilt. "I'll come with you. Let me just run these upstairs." She trotted through the knot of people toward the stairs.

Naomi moved past familiar faces, nodding and shaking hands on her way to the kitchen. She reached the kitchen doorway and stopped when she spotted Sadie speaking to one of her quilting friends.

"Oh, *ya*," Sadie said. "Caleb and Susie love it here. In fact, he put a bid in on Riley Parker's place. You know, the one by the furniture store."

"Oh, right," her friend said. "The one with the little workshop."

"That's right," Sadie said. "But I told him not to open

a shop. He can work for Hezekiah Wagler." She smiled. "Caleb and Irene would make such a *wunderbaar* couple. As we all know, Susie needs the guidance that only a *mamm* can supply." Naomi's stomach clenched and bile rose in her throat. She had to make a quick getaway before she became physically ill. She spun on her heel and rushed through the crowd toward the front door.

"Naomi!" a voice called.

Naomi forged ahead, ignoring the voice.

"Wait!" A hand grabbed Naomi's arm and pulled her off balance, causing her to stumble.

Naomi turned to find Lilly studying her. "Where are you going?" Lilly asked.

"I don't feel well," Naomi said. And it wasn't a lie. She felt as if she were going to be sick, and she couldn't allow herself to be sick in public, especially in Sadie Kauffman's home.

Susie rushed over to them. "Naomi! Let's go get a drink." She took Naomi's hand.

"I'm sorry, Susie." Naomi touched the girl's cheek. "I'm not feeling well, so I'm going to head home. *Danki* for the gift."

Susie frowned. "But I thought we were going to spend time together."

"Not tonight." Naomi glanced down at the bag containing Caleb's gift. She held it out. "Would you please make sure your *dat* gets this? Tell him that it's from me, *ya*?"

Looking disappointed, Susie took the bag. "Okay."

"Goodnight." Naomi leaned down and kissed Susie's cheek. She then hugged Lilly. "I'll talk to you soon."

Lilly shook her head. "You shouldn't go out into that blizzard alone. Let me find Elam for you."

Naomi touched Lilly's shoulder. "I'll be fine. When I was seventeen, I left the house alone to get some medicine for Amos because he was really sick. On the way back from the store, my buggy broke down in the snow not too far from here. I had to leave the horse and buggy and walk home in a blizzard. I found my way, and everything was okay." She pulled on her cloak. "I know I can do this."

Before Lilly could respond, Naomi slipped out the door. She almost slipped twice on her way down the porch steps. The snow swirled around her, blinding her vision and soaking her cloak as she slowly moved down the driveway.

I can do this. I have to do it. I can't fall to pieces in front of Caleb, the Kauffmans, and the rest of the community.

Stopping at the pasture fence, she considered which route to take home. Although she couldn't see much beyond the fence, she knew that if she crossed the pasture, she could then cut through two farms and find her way to her road. It looked similar to the route she'd taken when her buggy had broken down years ago.

Heaving a deep breath, she began to trudge through the snow, shivering and gritting her teeth. The farther she moved, the less she could see in front of her.

What was I thinking? This is a bad idea.

Naomi glanced back in the direction of what she thought was Sadie's home, but she couldn't see the outline of the house, not even the pitch of the roof.

She turned completely around in a circle and couldn't see anything except for snow. Her teeth chattered, and her eyes filled with frustrated tears.

I'm lost.

She looked straight up toward the white sky, and large, moist flakes blinded her.

Naomi gazed in the direction that she thought was the road and then trudged ahead two steps. She then moved forward, and her foot landed in a hole, causing her ankle to twist in an awkward direction. Screaming out loud, she wobbled, fell, and rolled down a hill. The sting of pain shot like lightning from her ankle up her leg.

She tried to lift her leg, but she couldn't move it. Taking a deep breath, she attempted to sit up, but the sting in her ankle forced her to stop.

Sobbing, Naomi rolled to her side and prayed that someone would come and find her while the bitter, cold air closed in around her, prickling her skin like thousands of tiny icicles.

CHAPTER 14

Caleb smiled and nodded, wondering if Hezekiah Wagler would ever take a breath. Irene stood across from her father and chimed in frequently, adding details to the man's endless stories about his business, mechanical techniques, old friends, and family memories. Caleb was surprised Irene was even speaking to him, but she acted as if nothing had happened the previous day.

Glancing toward the door, Caleb noticed that the crowd in the main family room was dissipating. Timothy had left the conversation to join his fiancée and her family quite awhile ago. Caleb had hoped Timothy would return and rescue him from the Waglers, but Timothy was a smart man and had stayed away. Caleb wondered how long it had been since his best friend had abandoned him. Had it been more than an hour? Had Caleb missed the entire Christmas party?

Susie, Janie, Nancy, and Linda scampered into the sitting room and gathered around the coffee table where Susie opened a Scrabble board-game box. Taking out the contents of the box, the girls giggled while setting up their letters. Caleb swallowed a sigh of relief. This was his chance to break away and try to find Naomi. He couldn't wait to give her the special Christmas gift he'd picked up for her.

"It's been nice talking to you, Hezekiah. I'm going to go see what my *dochder* is doing," Caleb said, stepping toward the group of girls. He glanced at Irene and nodded. "*Frehlicher Grischtdaag*." He then stepped over to Susie. "What are you girls up to?"

Susie gestured toward the game. "It's Scrabble, *Dat*. Naomi gave it to me for Christmas."

"Want to play, *Onkel* Caleb?" Janie asked while putting letters on the letter stand.

"No, *danki*." Caleb nodded toward the door. "Have you seen Naomi?"

"No." Linda shook her head.

"She left a long time ago," Susie said.

"She left?" he asked.

"*Ya*, that's right," Susie said.

"A long time ago?" Caleb asked, glancing at the clock on the bookshelf. Could it really be close to seven? Disappointment coursed through him. How had he managed to miss Naomi? She was the one person he was truly looking forward to seeing tonight.

"*Ya*," Susie said. "She wasn't feeling well." She stood. "But she left me something to give you." Taking his hand, Susie pulled him toward the door. "Come upstairs with me." She glanced at her cousins. "Don't start the game without me. I'll be right back."

Susie and Caleb walked through the family room, and Caleb was surprised to see that nearly everyone had left. As he started up the stairs behind Susie, Lilly approached him.

"*Frehlicher Grischtdaag*," she said with a smile.

"Same to you," Caleb said with a nod. "Susie told me Naomi wasn't feeling well. I'm sorry that she left."

Lilly frowned. "*Ya.* It came on suddenly, and she said she had to leave. I tried to encourage her to stay, but she was determined to go."

Caleb pursed his lips. A feeling of suspicion rained down on him. Why would Naomi leave without speaking with him? Could she have been upset with him, and if so, why?

"Lilly," Miriam called, stepping into the family room. "Are you ready to go? Timothy said the snow looks pretty bad out there. We should get on the road." She looked toward the stairs. "Hi, Caleb. *Frehlicher Grischtdaag.*"

"Merry Christmas to you, too, Miriam," Caleb said with a nod before trotting up the stairs after Susie. He found her in her room sitting on the bed while holding a large bag.

"This is for you from Naomi." She held it up. "Open it! It's very heavy. I can't wait to see what it is."

He opened the bag and his eyes rounded as he pulled out the antique drill he'd shown her at the flea market on Wednesday.

"Oh, Naomi," he whispered. She'd gone back and bought him exactly what he'd wanted. He examined the antique drill, and his heart filled with warmth for the beautiful, soft-spoken young woman. A small piece of paper fell into his lap, and he read the words written with a flourish:

Dear Caleb,

Please accept this small gift as a token of our new friendship. I'm so glad that God saw fit to bring you and Susie into my life. I look forward to sharing the holidays with you and Susie, and I pray that with God's blessings we'll share many more together.

Frehlicher Grischtdaag!

Your new friend,

Naomi

Caleb stared at the note, reading it over and over again, committing it to memory. The note touched him deep in his soul, awakening feelings he thought he'd never feel again. He wondered why Naomi hadn't given this gift to him in person. Why would she write such a sweet, loving note and then give it to Susie to deliver?

Leaning over, Susie gave him a confused expression. "*Was iss letz?*"

"What did Naomi say when she gave you this bag?" he asked.

Susie shrugged. "She said she didn't feel well, and she asked me to give it to you."

"How was she acting when she gave you the bag?"

Susie shook her head. "I don't know. Upset, I guess."

"Upset?" He let the word roll through his mind as he tried to remember when he saw her. He'd been trapped in the sitting room listening to Hezekiah's monologue when he spotted Naomi chatting with and hugging Susie. He remembered thinking that Naomi looked like an angel as she smiled and spoke to his daughter. His heart had swelled when he observed the two of them talking together. Naomi was like no woman he'd met since he'd lost Barbara. He could tell that Naomi truly loved Susie, and Susie loved her as well.

And Caleb loved Naomi.

He shook his head at the realization. Yes, he did love her, and he needed to know why she'd left in such a rush. If she'd been ill, he would've been happy to take her home. Why did she rush out without even saying hello to him? Maybe there was something that had upset her. If Susie had been the last person to see her, maybe she would hold the key to finding out what had upset Naomi.

He turned to his daughter. "Did you say anything to Naomi before she left?"

Susie looked at him like he was crazy. "*Ya.* I said goodbye."

He shook his head. "No, that's not what I meant. Did you say anything that might have upset her?"

She shook her head. "I don't think so."

"Please, Susie." He placed his hand on her shoulder. "Can you try to think about everything you and Naomi discussed before she left?"

Deep in thought, she tapped her chin and looked up at the ceiling. "We talked about Christmas gifts. I gave her the little doll I bought her, and she gave me the game and a *schee* quilt that I love." She tapped a pretty quilt on her bed. "Then I asked her to play the game with me, and she said that she would play it with me every time I came to visit. So I told her we were moving here, and she was really surprised."

"You told her?" He'd hoped that he could get a

chance to speak with her alone and tell Naomi the news, but he wasn't surprised that Susie was excited to share it, especially with Naomi.

However, Caleb had hoped that the news would be something he and Naomi could celebrate. Why would that news cause her to leave without speaking to him? Had he been wrong about her feelings for him?

He studied his daughter's eyes, praying she held the key to what had upset Naomi. "What exactly did you tell her?"

Susie shrugged again. "I don't know. I said that you'd found us a house and that *Aenti* Sadie said you might work for Irene's *dat*."

"You told her that I'd be working with Hezekiah?"

"No, I said I didn't know." Looking confused, she hugged the blanket to her chest. "I said that *Aenti* Sadie said you might. I mentioned that I didn't think Irene liked me because she's not nice to me and she didn't want me to come to dinner with you and her. I also told her that I have a hard time using my manners when she's around and that Irene acted like she only wanted to be alone with you. I said that I could never be friends with Irene, but I was friends with Naomi." She paused, blushing a little. "And I also said that I wanted you to be with Naomi and not with Irene."

Caleb frowned. *This is not good.* "What did Naomi say?"

"She kind of looked sad," Susie said.

Caleb stood and placed the drill on the bureau while he considered Susie's story. It didn't make sense. Was Naomi upset that Caleb might be working with

Hezekiah? But why would that upset her—unless it had something to do with Irene? Was she jealous of Irene? Did she feel the same strong attraction to Caleb that he felt for her? If so, then being jealous of Irene might make sense—except that nothing was going on between him and Irene.

"Oh, there you are," Sadie said, stepping into the room.

"The girls are cleaning up the kitchen, Susie." Her eyes moved to the bureau. "What's that?"

"It's a Christmas gift from a friend," Caleb said, lifting up the drill and stepping toward the door. "Susan, please go down and help your cousins in the kitchen."

"Okay." Susie hopped down from the bed and skipped out of the room.

"What is it?" Sadie asked, her nose scrunched as she studied the drill.

"It's an antique drill," he said, holding the note from Naomi in his hand. He stuck it in his pocket for safekeeping.

"Oh." She smiled and clasped her hands together. "I saw you talking to Hezekiah and Irene. Have you decided to go into business with him?"

Caleb frowned. "No, I haven't. I've already told you what my plans are, and I need you to respect them. I'm tired of repeating myself over and over again, Sadie."

She blanched. "Well, it was *gut* to see you talking to Irene again. I think she would be a good *maedel* for you. I think she likes you."

He ran a hand down his chin and considered his response as his blood boiled with frustration. "I don't know how else to say this to you since you refuse to listen. Therefore, I'm going to say it the only way I know how. Sadie, I need you to mind your own business. I'm going to make the best decisions I can make for my *dochder* and me, and I need you to worry about your own family."

She winced. "Caleb, I only want what's best for you. It's my job to watch out for you since *Mamm* and *Dat* are gone."

He shook his head. "I'm a grown man, Sadie. Let me live my life the way I choose to live it." He held up the drill. "This gift is from a very special friend."

She raised her eyebrows, looking curious. "Who is this special friend?"

"Naomi King," he said with a smile. "That's who I—"

"Caleb!" A voice shouted from downstairs. "Caleb, come quick!"

Dropping the drill on the bed, Caleb rushed down the stairs, taking them two at a time, to where Robert stood next to Elam and Titus King, who were both frowning while holding their snowy hats.

"*Was iss letz*?" Caleb asked, his heart pounding in his chest as he looked between Elam and Robert.

"Naomi's missing," Elam said.

"What?" Caleb asked. "What do you mean?"

"She never made it home." Titus shook his head. "Lilly told Elam that Naomi didn't feel well and walked home alone, but she wasn't there when we arrived. We've searched our road and the surrounding area, but we haven't seen any sign of her."

"We need to look for her," Robert said, grabbing his

coat from the peg by the door. "I'll get my horse hitched to my buggy."

"What's going on?" Sadie asked.

"Naomi's missing," Caleb said, putting on his hat and gloves. "We're going to go look for her." He grabbed a flashlight from the table by the door.

Sadie gasped. "Oh no."

Caleb followed Elam and Robert to the door. He turned around one last time and faced Sadie. "Tell Susie I'll be home soon."

CHAPTER 15

"Which way do you think she went?" Caleb asked Elam as they stood by Elam's buggy in the driveway. The snow blew so hard that Caleb shivered and wiped the flakes from his face.

Elam shook his head. "I don't know. I thought she would've taken the main roads, but maybe she didn't."

Caleb turned in the direction of the pasture and remembered how he'd stood on the porch the night before and thought about how he could walk to her house. "Maybe she thought she'd take a shortcut?"

"Maybe," Elam said.

"I'll walk around the pasture, and you two go in the buggy and check the main roads again," Caleb said, holding up the flashlight, which gave a soft yellow glow reflecting off the snow. "Tell Robert to take his buggy farther up the road past your house in case she made a wrong turn."

"Sounds *gut*." Titus walked up to them. "I remember one time when Naomi was a teenager, she was out in a blizzard getting medicine and the buggy broke down not far from here. One of the wheels came clear off the hub." He gestured in the direction of the pasture.

"She walked home and she may have gone through this pasture."

"Oh no," Caleb said. "She's done this before?"

Titus nodded. "*Ya.* She made it home okay that time, but I'm not certain the wind was blowing like it is tonight."

Caleb shook his head as dread pooled in his gut. "I pray she's not hurt."

"I know." Titus looked grim. "Maybe you can find her footprints in the snow. Be careful."

"You too." Caleb set out across the pasture, his boots crunching as he trudged through the deep snow. He silently sent up prayers, begging God to lead him to Naomi. He hoped and prayed she was okay.

While he walked, he thought about her note in his pocket. Naomi had to be okay. They could have a future together, as a family, with Susie.

He couldn't imagine losing her. He'd just met her, and she already meant so much to him.

Losing another person he cared about would simply be too much . . .

As he moved through the snow, he lost his footing and nearly slipped. He righted himself again and then moved forward.

As he crossed the pasture, the visibility worsened, and he couldn't see the house behind him or the fence in front of him. Lifting the flashlight, he searched the surrounding snow, looking for footprints. He thought again of Titus's story about Naomi walking home in a blizzard, and he wondered if she'd taken this path. Was that why she thought she could make it home alone in this fierce storm?

Caleb spotted faint tracks that he thought might be her footprints, and he followed them, moving slowly despite the frigid wind. "Naomi?" he called. "Naomi, are you out there?" He trudged forward, following the tracks and shouting her name. Holding the flashlight up higher, he silently begged God to lead him to her. He needed to find her. He needed her in his life. Caleb continued on, marching through the snow and praying while he moved the flashlight back and forth and searched for any sign of her.

Suddenly, off in the distance, he thought he spotted something in the snow. Tenting his hand over his eyes, he tried to focus his eyes against the blowing flakes. The object looked like a black blanket peppered with snow.

Could that be her cloak?

His heart pounded against his rib cage as he quickened his steps.

"Naomi!" he shouted. "Naomi! Are you there?" As he approached, the black blanket came into view, resembling a person lying in the snow.

"Naomi?" he called, nearly running through the snow. "Is that you, Naomi?"

His heart beat faster when she didn't respond. Anxiety shot through him. *She's hurt!*

Caleb broke into a run, slipping and sliding over to the person. "Naomi?" he called. "Is that you?"

He found Naomi lying on her back with her eyes closed. Her cheeks were bright red, and her lips were a light shade of blue.

"Oh no," he moaned, praying softly. "Lord, please

don't let it be too late. Don't take her from me now. Please, don't!"

Placing the flashlight in the snow, he pulled her into his arms. "Naomi. Please answer me." When she didn't respond, panic gripped him, stealing his words for a moment. "I can't lose you, Naomi. Please answer me. Please, Naomi. I need you. Susie and I both need you." He sucked in a breath and silently prayed with all of the emotional strength he had left in him.

She moaned and stirred, causing him to release the breath he'd been holding.

"You hear me," he said. "It's okay if you can't answer. I'm going to get you home, and I'm going to take care of you." He liked the sound of that. He wanted to take care of her on a more permanent basis starting right now.

Slowly, he grabbed the flashlight and then lifted her into his arms. He heard the hum of a car and the *clip-clop* of hooves in the distance, and he knew that he would locate the road if he followed those sounds.

Holding Naomi close to his chest, Caleb managed to balance the flashlight in one of his hands. In a hurry to get her to safety, he moved as quickly as he could while trying his best not to lose his footing in the snow. He slipped twice and slowed his pace down slightly.

He marched through the snow, praying that he would find his way to the road and Naomi would be okay. The sounds of the cars and hooves grew louder, and he knew he was heading in the right direction.

"We're almost there, Naomi," he said. "I can hear road noise up ahead of us."

When she stirred again, he hoped she'd answer him.

"Naomi? Are you awake? You're going to be just fine. I promise I'll take *gut* care of you."

"Caleb?" she asked, her voice tired and hoarse. "Caleb?" She looked up at him. "Where am I?"

"I found you in the pasture," he said, still trudging through the snow. "I'm so thankful I located you in this horrendous storm. Are you hurt?"

"*Ya*. I think so." She sucked in a deep breath with her face red and tears spilling from her brown eyes. "It's my ankle. I fell and it twisted. It hurts so much." She wrapped her arms around his neck, and he relished the feeling of holding her so close.

"Don't worry," he said. "We're almost there. I promise I'll get you home safe."

"*Danki*." She rested her head on his shoulder.

Caleb felt a weight lift from his shoulders. He was thankful that she was awake and talking. Now he just had to get her home into the warmth and then have someone look at her ankle. She was lucky that only her ankle was hurt. A twinge of frustration nipped at him as he considered how much worse this situation could've turned out.

"What were you thinking trying to walk home alone in these conditions?" he asked.

"I thought I'd be okay," she said, holding tight to his neck. "I thought I could find my way. I've done it once before, and I found my house despite the snow."

"I don't think that would be possible in this blizzard." He spotted the fence in front of them. Relief flooded him. If they were close to the fence that meant they were almost to the road! "You're lucky I found you.

You could've been out there all night and wound up with pneumonia or worse."

"I know," she said with a sigh. "It wasn't very smart." Although the questions of why she left were still haunting him, Caleb carried her in silence while he concentrated on balancing her and the flashlight in his arms and continuing their trek through the blowing snow. She shivered against him, and he wished he had a blanket to shield her against the frigid weather.

When he stepped onto the road, he spotted a buggy bouncing toward them with lanterns blazing like a beacon. "I hope this is Elam," he said, picking up his pace.

The buggy approached, and Titus jumped out. "Naomi!" he called. "You found her!" He trotted over and took Naomi from his arms. "What were you thinking, *dochder*? You scared us to death."

"I'm sorry, *Dat*," she said, her voice breaking into a sob. Caleb hugged his arms to his chest. He could only imagine the fear Titus and Irma had felt for their daughter. He'd felt the same terror when he thought he'd lost Susie at the farmers market.

Titus looked at Caleb. "*Danki.*"

Caleb nodded. "*Gern gschehne.*"

Titus looked down at Naomi. "Let's get you home where it's warm and dry."

• • •

Caleb sat in Naomi's family room while he awaited the news on her injuries. Titus had carried her into her bedroom where her mother was going to examine her ankle and help her change into dry clothes. He'd spent the time drinking cocoa and talking with her siblings, but his mind had been focused on her, worrying and thinking of what he'd say when he finally got to talk to her again.

"Caleb," Irma called. "Naomi would like to see you."

He made his way to the bedroom located behind the kitchen and stood in the doorway.

Naomi gave a forced smile while she lay propped up on the bed with pillows. A quilt covered the length of her, and only her foot, wrapped in bandages, and the white sleeves of her nightgown were visible. Her cheeks and nose were still pink from the cold. She sipped from a mug of cocoa and then motioned for him to come in.

"I'll be right outside the door," Irma said as she stepped past Caleb.

"How are you feeling?" Caleb asked, moving to the end of the bed.

"I've been better," Naomi said. "The *gut* news is it's not broken." She nodded toward her foot. "It's a few pretty shades of red, but my *mamm* thinks it's just a real bad sprain. I was really cold, but there's no sign of frostbite. Cocoa helped warm me up right away."

"You're very lucky," Caleb said, sinking into a chair. "Everyone was worried about you. Robert was out looking in his buggy too. I'm glad I found you."

"I am too." She nodded. "*Danki.*"

"You're welcome." He smiled and then wagged a finger at her with feigned anger. "Don't you ever scare me like that again."

She laughed, revealing her adorable dimple. "I'll try not to."

"Now, tell me," he began, leaning against the bed-post, "why did you rush out of the party after you gave Susie her gifts?" He was certain her cheeks turned a deeper shade of pink.

"I didn't feel well," she said, fingering the ties on her prayer covering.

He raised an eyebrow with disbelief. "Then why didn't you ask Elam or me to take you home?"

She shrugged. "I didn't want to take anyone away from the party."

He snorted. "I would've been *froh* for you to steal me away from Hezekiah Wagler. That man held me captive with his boring stories for hours."

Naomi chuckled. "Did he?"

"I thought he would never stop talking." He raked his hand through his hair. "Why didn't you look for me?"

She frowned. "I'd thought you were busy with Hezekiah and Irene."

"Busy?"

"Talking business." She lifted her mug and took another sip.

He shook his head. "No, we weren't." She gave him a thoughtful expression. "*Danki* for the gift," he said. "It's perfect."

She cleared her throat. "*Gern gschehne.*"

He took a deep breath. It was time for him to be honest about his feelings. He pulled her note from his pocket. "I was touched to get this. It meant a lot to me."

Her cheeks flushed a deeper pink. "I'm glad to hear that."

"I wanted to tell you that I—" he began.

"I think it's time for you to get some rest, Naomi," Irma interrupted, stepping into the room. "It's very late and tomorrow is Christmas." She tapped Caleb's shoulder. "Robert is here. He stopped by to see if we'd found you. He's ready to take you home."

"Okay." Caleb stood. "Let me just say goodbye."

Irma gave him a stern expression. "Keep it short."

Feeling like a teenager, Caleb nodded and suppressed a grin. Did Irma truly think he was planning on misbehaving with her injured daughter?

Caleb waited until Irma stepped out to the kitchen and then walked around the bed to Naomi. Taking her hand in his, he looked deep into her eyes, which rounded with surprise.

"I'm glad you're okay," he said softly. "I was very worried about you."

She nodded, looking speechless.

"*Danki* again for the note you gave me with the drill," he said, holding the note up before putting it back into his pocket. "Your words touched me deeply. I, too, am looking forward to where our friendship takes us." He shook her hand. "*Frehlicher Grischtdaag, mei freind.*"

"*Frehlicher Grischtdaag,*" she echoed, her eyes still wide. He then stepped out into the kitchen.

"*Gut nacht,*" he said to Irma.

"*Danki,* Caleb," Irma said, shaking his hand. "We're so glad you rescued her."

. . .

Naomi adjusted herself in the bed. The pain from her ankle radiated up her leg in waves, stealing her breath.

However, the buzz in her mind affected her more deeply than the pain from her foot as she watched Caleb walk out into the kitchen. Her heart pounded and a smile spread on her lips as she remembered the look on his face as he'd held her hand. His words had left her both dizzy and speechless.

The note she'd written to him had touched him, and he looked forward to a future with her.

A future?

But what did that mean exactly? Did he only want to be friends or did he want something more?

"You're a very blessed *maedel*," Irma said, stepping back into the bedroom. "You could've been lost out there all night."

Naomi sighed. "I know." She tried to move her leg and sucked in a ragged breath when the discomfort shot through her ankle.

"*Ach*," her mother rushed over and took her hand. "Are you okay?"

Naomi nodded as the pain subsided a bit. "I think so."

"Do you want more painkiller?" Her mother's eyes were wide with worry.

"No, *danki*." Naomi forced a smile. "I'll be okay in a moment. The pain comes and goes."

Her mother pulled a chair up next to her. "Caleb is a *gut* man."

Naomi blinked, stunned by how direct her mother was.

Irma smiled. "I believe he may have feelings for you."

Naomi cleared her throat. "I'm not certain about that, but I hope so."

Irma raised an eyebrow. "I believe you know the answer to that."

Shaking her head, Naomi smoothed the quilt over her nightgown. "Susie told me that Caleb found a house and they're moving here, but I'm not certain of what that will mean for him and me. All I know is that I do care for him and Susie, and I hope to get to know them better."

"He cares for you, too, Naomi," Irma said with a knowing smile. "I believe he cares quite deeply for you. I wish you could've seen his face when your *dat* carried you in."

Naomi rubbed the back of her neck, which was stiff from the fall. "I don't understand."

Irma rubbed Naomi's arm. "He was worried sick about you. I was wrong to tell you not to consider him because he's a widower." She smiled. "My mother's favorite verse was from Romans. It went something like this: 'But if we hope for what we do not yet have, we wait for it patiently.'"

Naomi shook her head. "What are you trying to say, *Mamm*?"

"You've waited for your true love," Irma said, still smiling. "Now let God lead you and Caleb down the road."

"My true love?" Naomi whispered.

"I think so, but only time will tell. See where God leads you and Caleb. I think you're off to a *gut* start." Irma stood. "You need to get some sleep."

"What about the Christmas table?"

Irma kissed Naomi's head. "I'll take care of it."

"*Danki*," Naomi said, trying to find a comfortable position on the bed despite the discomfort in her ankle.

"You get better." Irma wagged a finger at her. "And don't you ever take off alone in the snow again. You hear me?"

Naomi smiled. "Yes, *Mamm*. I definitely learned my lesson. *Gut nacht*."

"*Gut nacht*." Her mother left, gently closing the door behind her.

Naomi stared up at the ceiling, ignoring her injury and thinking of Caleb. She fell asleep with a smile on her face, dreaming of her possible future with Caleb and Susie.

EPILOGUE

Naomi smiled, despite the pain in her ankle, while sitting at the kitchen table the following afternoon. Around her, all of her siblings laughed, ate candy, and played with their new toys.

"Naomi," her father said, tapping her on the shoulder. "You have visitors."

"I do?" She looked up at him, hoping that her prayers had come true. She'd been thinking of Caleb and Susie all morning.

"Let me help you into the *schtupp*." Taking her arm, Titus helped Naomi while she half hopped, half limped.

Moving to the doorway, she found Caleb and Susie standing in the room, and tears filled Naomi's eyes. Her prayers had been answered. She was going to spend Christmas with her new friends.

Caleb rushed over and took Naomi's other arm. "Let me help you."

"*Danki*," Naomi said, her cheeks burning with embarrassment.

"Are you in much pain?" he asked, his green eyes filling with concern.

"I'll be fine," she said.

They helped her to the sofa, and she sank onto the end cushion.

Susie rushed over and hugged Naomi. "*Frehlicher Grischtdaag!*"

"*Frehlicher Grischtdaag, mei liewe,*" Naomi said before kissing the little girl's head.

"Can I go see Levina and Sylvia?" Susie asked.

"Of course," Naomi said, gesturing toward the adjacent room. "Have fun."

Susie ran off toward the kitchen.

The sofa shifted beside Naomi as Caleb lowered himself down next to her. "*Frehlicher Grischtdaag.*" He handed her a bag.

"Oh, Caleb," Naomi said, taking the bag. "You didn't have to."

He laughed. "Of course I did. Please open it."

Naomi's heart fluttered as she opened the bag and pulled out the black Bible she'd longed to buy for herself. She ran her fingers over the cover. "Caleb," she whispered, meeting his intense stare. "You spent too much."

"No, I didn't." He nodded toward the Bible. "Please open it. There's something inside."

She opened the cover and found a note in neat handwriting:

Naomi,
I thought it was only fitting to give you this Bible for Christmas. I know how much it would mean to you to have a new Bible for your nightly devotions. I hope that you

realize how much you mean to both Susie and me.

Your friendship is precious to us, just like the precious verses contained in this holy book.

I'm so thankful that God led Susie and me back to my hometown for Christmas, and I'm even more thankful that He led me to you. You've taught me so much about finding joy in life again despite past heartaches. You've helped me remember what it means to be happy. I look forward to where God leads us on this journey together.

Frehlicher Grischtdaag!
        Caleb

She read the words over and over again, and she was both stunned and confused by the sentiment they contained. Questions swirled in her mind. She needed to know what the inscription truly meant, but she couldn't form the words to ask him.

Finally, with tears pooling in her eyes, Naomi looked up. "*Danki.* It's *schee.*"

He touched her hand, and her pulse skittered. "I need to know something. What did you mean last night when you said you thought I was discussing business with Hezekiah and Irene?"

"Susie said you were going into business with Hezekiah," Naomi said.

Caleb shook his head. "No, I'm not. I found a house that has a shop, and I'm going to open my own carriage shop."

Naomi smiled. "That's *wunderbaar*!"

"Hezekiah and Irene were talking my ear off last night, but it was nothing but idle conversation."

Naomi took a deep breath and glanced down at the Bible.

She needed to know the truth about him and Irene. "Are you courting Irene?" she asked while running her fingers over the cover of the Bible.

He snorted. "No. Why do you ask?"

She met his expression, not finding any sign of a lie. "I heard Sadie talking."

He frowned. "What did *mei schweschder* say now?"

"She was telling someone that you and Irene would be a *gut* couple. She made a point of saying that Susie needed a *mamm*, implying that Irene could be a *gut* candidate for that role."

Caleb rolled his eyes. "Sadie tries too hard to run my life. She means well, but she does more damage than good." His frown deepened. "And the last role that Irene would be *gut* for would be a *mamm*. She's terrible with Susie, and she's been nothing but rude to my precious *dochder*."

Naomi shook her head. "I can't imagine ever being rude or nasty to Susie. She's such a special girl. I'm sorry that Irene isn't nice to Susie, but I'm so glad Sadie was wrong."

"Sadie has been wrong about a lot of things," Caleb said. "Most of all, she was wrong about who I belong with. I definitely don't belong with Irene."

"Is that so?" Naomi's smile reappeared.

He nodded, his own smile growing. "She's not any fun to go shopping with."

"And I would imagine she doesn't like root beer." Naomi coyly tapped her chin. "I seem to remember that you promised me a root beer float."

He grinned. "I did. And I intend to keep that promise."

His smile faded. "But I must ask you one question first."

"What's that?"

He took her hands in his, and the feel of his warm skin caused her heart to beat at hyperspeed. "Naomi, that time we sat on the porch together, you asked me if I believed God gave second chances at true love. I told you yes, but I honestly wasn't sure." His eyes sparkled. "Since I've met you, I know that answer for certain. I think God has given me a second chance when He brought me to you. We would be a *gut* couple, and I would be honored to court you."

Tears filled her eyes. "After I had my heart broken twice, I was certain I'd never find love. Now I see that God had a plan all along for me. I think this is the Christmas miracle Susie wanted for you. It's also a miracle for me."

"She told me that she'd asked you if you believed in miracles," he said, running his finger down her jaw line.

She nodded, butterflies fluttering in her belly at the feel of his gentle touch.

"She also asked me if I believe in miracles, and I do

believe in them," he said. "And, *ya*, my little girl was right because you're my miracle. No, actually, you're a miracle for Susie and me. We both love you." He nodded toward the Bible. "There's a reason why I didn't have your name engraved on the Bible. I thought that you might change your name someday, and I wanted to be certain that I put the correct name on the cover."

Before she could respond, he leaned over and gently pressed his lips against hers, sending the pit of her stomach into a wild swirl.

"*Frehlicher Grischtdaag*, Naomi," he whispered against her lips.

"*Frehlicher Grischtdaag*," she whispered, leaning her head against his shoulder and closing her eyes.

DISCUSSION QUESTIONS

1. At the beginning of the story, Naomi feels that she's lost her chance to find true love. She thinks that after two failed relationships, God is telling her that she's meant to be her mother's helper instead of a wife. Have you ever felt as if God has given up on you, and you've lost your chance at happiness? Were your feelings validated, or did your experience change for the better? Share this with the group.

2. Naomi's mother quotes 2 Corinthians 1:7: "And our hope for you is firm, because we know that just as you share in our sufferings, so also you share in our comfort." What does this verse mean to you?

3. Sadie thinks she is helping Caleb by offering constant unsolicited advice, even though he frequently asks her to mind her own business. Think of a time when you may have had misguided intentions for a child or loved one. Share this with the group.

4. At the end of the story, Caleb and Naomi believe that their love is a Christmas miracle and God is giving them both a second chance at happiness. Have you ever experienced a second chance or a Christmas miracle? Share this with the group.

5. What did you learn about Amish holiday traditions? What is your opinion of their customs? Should we, as non-Amish, adopt more of their traditions of making Christmas more religious and less commercial? Share your thoughts with the group.

ACKNOWLEDGMENTS

As always, I'm thankful for my loving family, including my mother, Lola Goebelbecker; my husband, Joe; and my sons, Zac and Matt. Special thanks to Lauran Rodriguez for admiring the character of Naomi King and inspiring this book.

Thank you to my wonderful church family at Morning Star Lutheran in Matthews, North Carolina, for your encouragement, prayers, love, and friendship. You all mean so much to my family and me.

To my agent, Sue Brower—You are my own personal superhero! I can't thank you enough for your guidance, advice, and friendship. Thank you to my amazing editor, Becky Philpott for your friendship and guidance. I also would like to thank Kristen Golden for tirelessly working to promote my books. I'm grateful to each and every person at HarperCollins Christian Publishing who helped make this book a reality.

To my readers—thank you for choosing my novels. My books are a blessing in my life for many reasons, including the special friendships I've formed with my readers. Thank you for your email messages, Facebook notes, and letters.

Thank you most of all to God for giving me the inspiration and the words to glorify You. I'm grateful and humbled You've chosen this path for me.

Special thanks to Cathy and Dennis Zimmermann for their hospitality and research assistance in Lancaster County, Pennsylvania.

The author and publisher gratefully acknowledge the following resource that was used to research information for this book:

C. Richard Beam, *Revised Pennsylvania German Dictionary* (Lancaster: Brookshire Publications, Inc., 1991).

ABOUT THE AUTHOR

Amy Clipston is the award-winning and best-selling author of the Kauffman Amish Bakery, Hearts of Lancaster Grand Hotel, Amish Heirloom, and Amish Homestead series. Her novels have hit multiple bestseller lists including CBD, CBA, and ECPA. Amy holds a degree in communication from Virginia Wesleyan University and works full-time for the City of Charlotte, NC. Amy lives in North Carolina with her husband, two sons, and three spoiled rotten cats. Visit her online at AmyClipston.com; Facebook: AmyClipstonBooks; Twitter: @AmyClipston.

An Unexpected Joy

Ruth Reid

To Betty Reid (Memaw), my cherished mother-in-law. You're a blessing!

GLOSSARY OF PENNSYLVANIA DUTCH USED IN CENTRAL MICHIGAN DISTRICT

ach—oh
aenti—aunt
boppli—baby
bruder—brother
bu—boy
daed—dad
danki—thank you
Englisch or *Englischer*—a non-Amish person
fraa—wife
geh—go
guder mariye—good morning
gut—good
haus—house
hiya—a greeting
jah—yes
kaffi—coffee
kalt—cold
kapp—a prayer covering

kumm—come

maedel—young woman

mamm—mother

mammi—grandma

mariye—morning

mei—my

nacht—night

nau—now

nay—no

nett—not

onkel—uncle

Ordnung—the written and unwritten rules of the Amish

Pennsylvania *Deitsch*—the language most commonly used by the Amish. Although commonly known as Pennsylvania Dutch, the language is actually a form of German (*Deutsch*).

schul—school

sohn—son

wedder—weather

welkom—welcome

yummasetti—a traditional casserole common in Pennsylvania and Ohio Amish communities

CHAPTER 1

Abigail Kemp emptied her savings from the Mason jar onto her bed and began sorting the coins into piles. She counted her money each time she added to the jar and kept a detailed journal recording of each deposit—every cent—since last December. Once she realized she may never marry, she began selling baked goods and quilted potholders to save for a horse. In St. Joseph County, Michigan, an unmarried woman at twenty-two was more likely to get run over by a buggy than find a good man to marry—at least that was the joke at the youth singings. She met that milestone over a year ago, and now any offers to drive her home after the Sunday singings had dried up.

Footsteps clomped outside the bedroom. Her sister Elizabeth stormed into the room. "The next chicken that marks its territory on my dress sleeve is going in the fryer." She pulled the pins from her dress and slipped if off, letting the garment drop to the floor. "Do you want to trade chores this week?"

"Picking eggs for sweeping and mopping? Absolutely." Now that the weather had turned colder, the chickens weren't laying as many eggs. Besides, doing chores first thing in the morning offered more time to prepare and deliver her baked goods without interruptions. Orders for her fruitcakes were already coming in, and with Christmas only a few weeks away, she would be busy just trying to stay ahead.

Elizabeth scanned her side of the closet, pulled out a blue dress, looked it over, then exchanged it for the dark-green one.

"Are you going somewhere special?" Abigail had only seen her sister fuss over what dress to wear for Sunday singings.

"James is giving me a ride to work."

Elizabeth was two years younger and fell in love with James the first time he offered to drive her home from a singing. He was kindhearted and Father liked him. Elizabeth would get married first. Abigail pushed the thought aside. Jealousy would not rob her joy.

Abigail counted a stack of quarters and jotted the dollar amount on a piece of paper. "If you talked with the chickens more, they'd be less likely to perceive you as a threat."

"Change your mind about swapping chores?" Elizabeth fastened the front of her dress with pins.

"*Nett* at all. I talk to them all the time and they don't soil *mei* clothing."

"You're the only person I know who can carry a one-sided conversation. And with chickens, of all creatures." Elizabeth shook her head.

Abigail chuckled. "They're a trapped audience. They have to listen."

Elizabeth plopped down on the bed and motioned

to the jar. "You're always counting your money. If I didn't know better, I'd think you were worried Sadie or I were going to steal it."

"I'd never think that." She clutched her chest, pretending to be appalled by the suggestion, but a giggle erupted. "I would accuse one of the boys first."

"You should rethink leaving it in plain sight and tempting our *bruders*." Elizabeth smiled. "Unless you want to give someone an early Christmas gift, and if that's the case, let it be me."

Elizabeth had worked at the quilt store in town since last summer, and she spent all of her paychecks on fabric. She probably owned every shade of dress color acceptable in their district and was likely the only woman to own a half-dozen pairs of black shoes—unlike Abigail who owned one well-worn pair of everyday shoes and five dresses. Her two nicer dresses she saved for Sunday services and youth singings; the other three she wore the remainder of the week, saving the brown one for messy chores.

Abigail finished tallying her cash, then leaned against the pillow and smiled. "I almost have enough."

"You said that last month too."

Eight-year-old Sadie pushed open the bedroom door. "*Mamm* said it's time for breakfast." She continued down the hall, her shoes clacking against the wood floor. Her voice rang with the same announcement to the twins, Peter and Daniel.

Abigail scooped the money into her hand and deposited it in the jar. "I should have *mei* driver by the first of the year if *mei* baked goods keep selling the way they have."

"I don't know why a horse is so important," Elizabeth said. "If you concentrated on finding a *bu*, your transportation problems would be solved."

Abigail laughed, although even to her own ears, it sounded insincere. She had been dreadfully focused on securing a husband ever since she started attending the youth singings at seventeen. But for whatever reason, every bachelor who had driven her home never found the courage to ask to drive her again. *Don't dwell on it.* She prided herself on finding solutions rather than bemoaning her unfortunate situation. Buying the gelding from Mr. Troyer would allow more freedom, not to mention the time she would save walking to Centreville to sell her cookies. She wasn't sure her boots could handle another Michigan winter.

Abigail set the Mason jar on the chest of drawers and followed Elizabeth out of the room and down the stairs. The scent of bacon grew stronger as they neared the kitchen, and Abigail's stomach rumbled. *Mamm* and Sadie were busy at the stove, Sadie spooning oatmeal into the bowls and *Mamm* flipping eggs in the frying pan.

Abigail grabbed a stack of plates from the cabinet and placed them on the table while Elizabeth came behind her with the utensils.

The boys clamored down the stairs, cleaned up and ready for school. They took their places at the table as the back door opened. *Daed* and her older brother, David, entered the house.

Daed set the milk pail on the counter, then went to the sink and washed his hands. "Something smells *gut*." He smiled at *Mamm*.

"You say that every morning, Emery." She winked at him and brought the platter of eggs and bacon to the table.

Breakfast was Abigail's favorite time of the day. She enjoyed the playful banter between her parents and the lively chatter during the meal. The day wouldn't be the same if the boys didn't complain about having to go to school, or Sadie didn't prod them along to eat faster so they wouldn't be late. Her younger sister loved school while Peter and Daniel couldn't wait to finish their last year.

Daed took a sip of coffee and cringed.

"I should have warned you. We're out of sugar." *Mamm* turned her attention to Abigail and lifted her brows.

"I'm sorry. I made extra batches of oatmeal and more peanut-butter cookies to sell at the market."

Her mother's brows remained arched.

"And four apple pies, but I'll pick up more sugar when I'm in town today."

Mamm nodded. "Okay, but next time at least leave enough for your father's morning *kaffi*."

"I will." She glanced at her father's scowling face. "I promise." She waited a moment for the deep lines between his eyes to soften. "Can I borrow your horse and buggy to take *mei* cookies and pies into town? I won't be gone long, and I'll feed and brush Molly when I—" She glimpsed at her mother's stern expression. The one she made when Abigail started rambling. According to her mother, Abigail's mouth buzzed like bees. Lately *Mamm* had begun making buzzing noises whenever she thought Abigail was talking zealously. Abigail sucked in a breath and took a half-second to let her mother believe she was organizing her thoughts better, then opened her mouth to continue.

"I already asked to use it." David shoved a forkful of fried potatoes into his mouth.

Her father nodded toward her older brother.

Abigail sank lower in her chair. Ever since her brother's horse became pregnant, David had dominated her father's horse when it wasn't in use. Knowing David, he wasn't heading into town either. The entire family expected him to announce his engagement to Sally by Christmas.

"James is picking me up," Elizabeth said. "You can ride into town with us."

Normally she avoided being the third wheel, but carrying the extra pies would make the five-mile hike to town unbearable. "*Danki*," she said softly, demonstrating enough reserve to make her mother's lips stretch into a tight smile.

Abigail stood and collected the dirty dishes from the table. She wanted to clean the kitchen before James arrived.

A short time later, the washed dishes were drying on a dish towel, and Abigail was busy sweeping the floor when Elizabeth announced James's arrival. Abigail emptied the dirt from the dustpan into the trash can. "Can I mop later, *Mamm*?"

"*Jah*, *geh* on." *Mamm* made a shooing motion with her hand, dismissing her and Elizabeth.

Abigail put on her cloak and scarf, then grabbed the

basket of baked goods. "*Guder mariye*, James." Abigail climbed into the backseat.

He flicked his brows at Elizabeth seated beside him, then offered a polite but tight smile to Abigail. "Where are you off to today?"

"Gingerich's Market, please." Abigail hugged her basket. Perhaps if she increased the price of the fruitcakes, she would reach her goal faster and wouldn't have to tag along on rides. "Are you getting ready for Christmas?"

"Oh, I think so." This time when he glanced at Elizabeth, his face was flushed.

The trip into Centreville would have been silent had Abigail not kept the conversation going. She talked about the weather, the frozen pond where the youth gathered to skate, and how their town came to life during Christmastime with its lampposts decorated with wreaths and bows.

"Well, here you go." James stopped the buggy next to Gingerich's.

"*Danki* for the ride." Abigail climbed out. "I'll walk home. *Mei* basket will be empty." She also didn't want to wait in town until Elizabeth's shift was over at The Quilter's Square. She waved at her sister as the buggy jerked forward. If she read James's expression right, her younger sister would be engaged by Christmas. Abigail sighed. Next year would be a busy wedding season if her brother and sister both became engaged. Where had she gone wrong? She tapped her basket and proceeded into the building. At least she would have her own horse soon.

The bell above the door jingled as she entered the small country store. The woodsy scent of evergreen made her inhale appreciatively. Fran, the owner's daughter, loved changing the scented candles to match the season. The pumpkin spice during the fall was nice, but Abigail much preferred the evergreen. She approached the register, stood a moment, then proceeded toward the supply room at the back of the store, the wooden plank floor creaking under her feet. Abigail stopped midstep when she overheard Fran's voice coming from behind the row of dry goods.

"Maybe you should ask Elizabeth Kemp, Micah," Fran said. "I know she doesn't get too many hours at The Quilter's Square. She might be able to help you out."

Abigail's ears perked at the mention of her sister's name. She hurried around the corner and, not paying attention, ran into a wooden barrel of kidney beans. The nearly empty barrel wobbled, and Micah Zook grabbed it before it tipped.

"You okay?" He steadied the bin.

"*Jah*—I, ah . . ." Heat rushed to her face. *I overheard you talking about* mei *sister.* She pivoted and faced Fran. "I brought more cookies and four pies. They're all apple. Do you think they will sell? I figured everyone had their fill of pumpkin with Thanksgiving only a week ago."

Micah cleared his throat. "*Danki* for the suggestion, Fran." He took a few sideways steps toward the door. "I'll stop back later to pick up—"

Abigail covered the space between Micah and her in

a few quick steps and stared at her older brother's best friend. "Why were you talking about Elizabeth?"

Micah's gaze shifted to Fran, then dropped to the wooden floor. "I'm looking to hire a temporary caregiver for *mei* grandmother," he said. "*Mei* parents went out of town to stay with *mei* sister until she delivers her *boppli*, and I recently received some unexpected work." He looked toward the door. "But I have to go." Turning quickly, he practically knocked over a display of pine wreaths on his way to the door.

Abigail looked at Fran. "He's *nett* normally clumsy. Wonder why he's in such a hurry."

Fran shrugged. "Maybe it has something to do with his grandmother." She motioned to the basket Abigail was holding. "Yesterday, I was told that we can't sell any more of your baked goods."

"Why *nett*?"

Fran dropped eye contact and shook her head.

"I've been selling *mei* baked goods here for three years. You've even given me several fruitcake orders for next week. Do you still want them?"

Fran shrugged.

Abigail had never seen the store owner's daughter this apprehensive. "Fran, tell me what's changed?"

Fran leaned closer. "You've been seen at the Lambright farm," she whispered.

"Malinda's *mei* cousin. You know we're like sisters."

Fran nodded. "She was a *gut* friend of mine as well."

"*Was*?" Abigail stiffened her back.

"That's the way it is." Fran motioned to her basket. "I'm *nett* supposed to accept any more of your baked goods until you stop associating with the Lambrights. The family is on the verge of being shunned."

"The bishop hasn't made that official."

"But he did say the Lambrights are to be avoided until that decision is reached. Your defiance won't fare well. You'll be punished if you don't obey the rules." Fran bowed her head. "I'm really sorry, Abigail. I know a lot of our customers will be disappointed."

Nowhere near as disappointed as Abigail. She didn't agree with the bishop and elders' decision to isolate the entire Lambright family. They hadn't all disobeyed the *Ordnung.* But now that her income was cut off, how would she afford Cactus? Mr. Troyer wouldn't hold on to the horse forever. Clutching her basket close, Abigail chewed the inside of her cheek. Where could she sell her baked goods? The Quilter's Square? No, they would be under the same restrictions. Then remembering what Micah had said about hiring a caregiver, excitement bubbled within her. She raced to the door.

CHAPTER 2

Micah stood in the quilt shop next to the wall display of thread and waited for Elizabeth Kemp to finish helping a customer with her fabric selection. He tapped his boot against the hardwood floor. He should have brought his grandmother into town with him instead of leaving her at home alone. No telling what she might try to cook if she woke from her nap while he was gone.

The bell above the door jingled, and Abigail entered.

He stepped behind a bolt of fabric. As a close friend of her older brother, he'd known her for years. She hadn't changed much since school, still spindly with hair the color of milk chocolate and piercing green eyes. At twenty-three, she was still a sweet girl, but he didn't have time to get trapped in a long conversation. He peeked around the roll of green cotton material as Abigail breezed farther into the room, carrying a wicker basket.

She nodded at her sister, then pivoted around to scan the room.

Don't look this way. His heart beat faster. He dropped to one knee and retied his boot.

Footsteps grew closer, then stopped. "Micah, I'm so glad I caught you."

He forced a smile and looked up to face Abigail.

"Have you asked Elizabeth yet?"

He hesitated a moment. The twinkle in her green eyes was almost enchanting. Micah shook his head. "She's been busy with a customer." *Unfortunately.*

"I can do it," she blurted. Her head bobbed up and down like a horse trying to gain more rein.

His throat dried.

"You need someone to watch your *mammi, jah*?"

He nodded.

"I'm available." Her smile widened. "How long do you need someone? *Nett* that it matters. I don't have any plans. Will it be past Christmas?"

He glanced across the room at Elizabeth—the quieter Kemp sister. Another customer had stolen her away. He lost his opportunity and time was slipping away.

"So, do you need someone?"

Jah, someone compatible with Mammi. He glanced at the clock hanging on the far wall. He had to get back and he still had one more stop to make. Abigail stood patiently awaiting his answer. *Say something.* He had an overwhelming feeling he would regret this. Micah let out a breath. "I have an order to fill by Christmas Eve. It might be long hours."

"That's fine. I really want the job." She took a step closer and lifted her basket. "Do you like apple pie?"

Her eagerness was a bit daunting—unsuitable for a woman. If he had more time to call on someone else . . . but he didn't. Even taking time to ponder other possibilities when his grandmother was home alone was risky.

"Okay," he said, moving toward the door.

"Should I start today?"

He needed time to prepare *Mammi* and with the way this morning was going, he might never finish his business in town. "Tomorrow morning will be fine. *Kumm* by around eight."

She followed him out of the quilt shop and over to his parked buggy. "You never said if you liked apple pie."

"Sure." He untied Clover from the post and gathered the reins.

Abigail thrust a pie pan toward his chest. "Do you want one or two? Actually, I have four."

He eyed the sugar granules sprinkled over the golden crust. "One is plenty, *danki*."

She released the pie into his hands. "Tell your *mammi* I look forward to spending time with her. Maybe I'll bring a puzzle for us to put together."

Micah's insides wrenched. He still had to figure out a way to tell his grandmother that he hired a sitter to keep her company. Was it too much to hope for his parents to return early?

. . .

Elated to have a job, Abigail headed down the sidewalk with a skip in her step. She stopped at the grocery store and purchased a sack of sugar, then spent time gazing at the different Christmas displays in the store windows. Blinking lights framed the windows and fluffy, snow-like cotton decorated the display ledge. Shiny wrapped packages with big, fancy bows were placed under trees that were adorned with glittering ornaments. "I'll Be Home for Christmas" played as a shopper opened the door of the shoe store. Abigail had heard the song before in the grocery store and found herself humming along. She strolled down the sidewalk to more storefronts bedecked with Santa decorations. No doubt the owners were overlooking the real reason for the season. Three blocks later, she spotted a nativity display. Even then it shared a spot with an ice-skating snowman.

She lifted her face to the cloudless blue sky. She was thankful for the simple way her people celebrated Christmas. Sharing a large meal, exchanging practical, homemade gifts, and reflecting on our Savior's birth.

A woman and toddler exited a clothing store. The small boy stared at Abigail while his mother smiled apologetically, wished Abigail "Happy Holidays," then nudged the boy's shoulder to move him along.

"Merry Christmas," Abigail called as they walked away. She meandered farther down the sidewalk. It didn't feel like Christmas yet. Usually by this time in December, she and Malinda would be busy sewing or baking. Malinda had practically lived at their house while they were growing up. It wouldn't be Christmas if their families couldn't spend it together. A gust of wind nipped at her face. Abigail clutched the basket tighter against her chest and lowered her head to block the wind.

As she neared the old hardware store on the outskirts of town, a man dressed in tattered clothing and leaning against the side of the building stretched out his legs across the sidewalk just as she was about to pass. She stumbled but caught her balance before falling. "I didn't see you. I'm sorry."

He grumbled something about watching where she walked and pulled his knitted hat over his ears.

She took a few steps and pivoted around. Normally she didn't talk to strangers, not men anyway. But his face was gaunt and her conscience wouldn't let her continue without offering him something to eat. She reached into her basket and removed two large containers of cookies. "Would you like some cookies?"

He grabbed the containers and removed the lids. He consumed a peanut-butter cookie in a matter of seconds and then sank his hand into the tin for another one.

"Merry Christmas," she said, filled with the warmth of the season. Abigail waited a moment, then walked away. She hadn't made it to the next building before she heard footsteps behind her. She increased her pace. This end of town wasn't populated with shoppers. Her breath caught in her throat when something tugged the shoulder of her wool cloak.

"Hey, lady." The man pulled harder on her cloak.

She stopped and faced the tall stranger.

He swept the cookie crumbs from the front of his grungy shirt. "Merry Christmas, lady."

Abigail smiled, opening her mouth to return the greeting, but a strong hand clamped her arm and whisked her in the opposite direction.

Micah drew her closer. "*Mei* buggy is parked behind the hardware store."

Before she had a chance to register what was

happening, Micah took the basket by the handle and herded her away from the man.

"You should have said something at the quilt shop about needing a ride home," he said once they reached his buggy.

"I didn't need a ride." His concern was charming, but his curt reaction to the stranger was rude.

He opened the buggy door, set the basket on the bench, then nodded for her to get in.

She stilled herself. A gust of wind swept through the alley, lifting her prayer *kapp*.

"Abigail, I'm *nett* going to leave you with that stranger. Get in."

Her toes had turned numb and she'd lost the feeling in the tip of her nose. A ride would be nice. She climbed onto the buggy bench.

He untied his horse from a tree branch, then sat beside her.

"The man wished me a Merry Christmas. He was harmless."

"Maybe so." He clicked his tongue and the horse lurched forward onto East Main Street.

"I shared some of *mei* cookies with him."

"I saw you." He reined the horse, turning onto Nottawa Street, then turned to the right once he reached Market Street and headed out of town.

Abigail crossed her arms. She hadn't done anything wrong. Even Jesus fed the hungry. Yet he seemed annoyed by her kind gesture. The man on the street might have been unkempt, but Micah didn't need to shuttle her into the alley as if the man were a leper.

The rhythmic clip-clopping of the horse's hooves over the pavement filled the silence between them.

"The man's homeless," he finally said. "I'd feel horrible if something happened to *mei* best friend's little sister."

"Homeless and hungry. I couldn't pass by him without offering him something to eat."

"Did you walk into town?" Micah slowed the horse at the intersection and looked both ways even though he had the right-of-way.

"James was taking Elizabeth into town. They let me tag along." She picked at her nails. Admitting aloud she had to tag along made her sound like an old maid. One day she would have her own transportation. "Five miles isn't so far. I've walked to town plenty of times." She just hadn't planned on having to carry the basket loaded with baked goods.

"I know."

Of course he did. She had seen him outside many times either working in the fields or chopping wood when she passed his parents' home on her way into town.

He was silent over the next mile. Abigail studied his profile. Strong jaw, thick neck, wide shoulders, she liked how his dark hair flipped up at his ears.

He glanced at her briefly, but said nothing.

"Is there something wrong? You're awfully quiet," she said.

He shrugged. "Worried about *Mammi*."

"You should have brought your grandmother to town."

He nodded.

She pointed to the intersection up the road. "Drop me off at the corner, and I'll walk the rest of the way."

His forehead creased. "Abigail, it isn't that far out of *mei* way. I can take you home."

"I know. But I thought you were worried about your *mammi*."

He stared at her a moment before nodding. "*Jah.* She's probably wondering what's taking me so long."

"Then drop me off. I'll be all right."

"Are you sure?"

His thoughtfulness was sweet. Why he wasn't married puzzled her, but she reined in those thoughts. "I'm sure."

A few moments later, the buggy rolled to a stop. Abigail collected her basket. "I have more pies. They're all apple, but would you like another one to take home?"

"*Nay, danki.* The one you already gave me is plenty."

"Then I'll see you tomorrow," she said, stepping out of the buggy. "*Danki* for the ride."

"Any time."

She waited for him to pull away, then went the opposite direction. Malinda's house wasn't too far down the road. She hadn't seen her friend in almost a week and a short visit wouldn't hurt. She would still be home in time to help *Mamm* start supper.

Abigail hiked along the gravel road. The Lambright farm sat at the top of a hill surrounded by large oaks and maples. The bare tree limbs cast eerie shadows on the snow-covered lawn. Halfway up the driveway, she spotted an *Englischer* dressed in an olive-green T-shirt and jeans, tossing ashes from the woodstove over the garden area. He wore a baseball cap over a shaved head.

Abigail sucked in a deep breath when her cousin, Thomas, waved. No wonder the bishop and elders didn't approve of *Onkel* Titus allowing his son to return home. Anyone could see Thomas hadn't given up his worldly ways.

He set the ash pail on the ground and walked toward her.

"You'll be punished if you don't obey the rules." Fran's warning from earlier this morning returned. It was one thing to be seen with Malinda—she hadn't done anything wrong—but Thomas was different. She lowered her head. "Is Malinda home?"

"No. What's in the basket?"

"Pies." She glanced at the house. "I'll stop by another time to see her."

"What's your name?"

She eyed him closer. Did he really not remember her? "I'm Abigail Kemp . . . your cousin." His face held the same puzzled expression. "Our mothers are sisters." This was awkward. "Nice seeing you again, Thomas." Abigail turned.

"I like pie."

"Yes," she said over her shoulder. "I recall apple was your favorite."

"It was?"

She faced him again. This time, she took a hard look at him. His frame was as rugged as ever, but something was different about his eyes. They held a vacancy she hadn't seen before. "Yes, Thomas. I seem to remember you were always going back for seconds of apple pie."

He removed his hat and scratched his shaved head.

"You haven't been home in a long time." She wanted to ask why—why he hadn't written to his family, but she held her tongue. "Aren't you *kalt* dressed like that—I mean *nett* wearing a coat?"

Thomas glanced at his shirt, then pushed his sleeve up, exposing his tattooed arm. "See my tank?"

She gasped and looked away.

"Don't you like it?"

"Thomas Lambright, why would I like that? Why would anyone like tattoos?"

"It's a tank—" He puffed out his chest and patted it. "I'm tank." He pointed to her basket. "I like pies."

He wasn't the shy Thomas who spent most of his days driving a team of mules. She removed the sack of sugar, then handed him the basket. "I'll pick it up another day." She walked away while he was still searching the basket contents. Her heart weighed heavy in her chest, wondering what exactly had happened to him. She and Malinda might never be able to resume their friendship if her family continued to harbor this lost soul.

CHAPTER 3

Abigail Kemp wasn't my first choice." Micah pinched the bridge of his nose. He didn't have another option. Everyone, with the exception of Abigail, was busy this time of year with Christmas only three weeks away. Besides, Abigail Kemp was hard to say no to. She practically pounced on him yesterday at the fabric store, insisting she would do a good job.

His grandmother stopped knitting and glanced at him over her reading glasses. "I've never needed a caretaker before, and I don't know why you think I need one *nau*. Besides, I don't know anyone from this side of the district."

True, she hadn't attended any sewing get-togethers since she moved in with them last month, but had she forgotten about the grease fire two days ago or that she let the water overflow in the sink just this morning? At eighty-five, she was filled with vinegar, had a bounty of energy, and unfortunately, a mind that was slipping. A lethal combination if left alone. Despite what she believed, she did require more help than he could provide. Besides, how bad could it be to spend three weeks with Abigail—in a closed-up house? Micah cringed.

His best friend's sister was a bit overwhelming to say the least. But she was essential and her chatter would keep his grandmother busy.

"Abigail will keep you company," he said.

Mammi snorted.

"I'm going to be working long hours to get the glass orders finished before Christmas." He should be working now. Micah paced to the end of the room and peeked out the window facing the driveway. Snow was falling, but there wasn't any sign of Abigail. He walked back and turned. For someone who wanted the job so desperately, she could have at least shown up on time.

"You're going to wear the wax off those planks, pacing like you are." She pulled the end of the yarn, unraveling more from the ball.

He made another jaunt across the floor, this time leaving the room to look out the window in the foyer. Maybe he should get the woodstove fired up in the shop. It always took awhile before the kiln was hot enough to melt the glass. He pulled his coat off the hook and slipped his arm into the sleeve. Micah poked his head around the wall of the sitting room. "Abigail should be here shortly. I'm going to start the fire in the shop."

A knock sounded on the front door.

"That must be her." *Finally.* He went to the door and opened it.

Abigail looked up from stomping snow off her boots. Her green eyes held a twinkle, and her whimsical smile greeted him before she ever opened her mouth to speak. "*Hiya.*" She waved her blue mitted hand.

"*Kumm* in, Abigail." He moved aside so she could pass.

She breezed into the house, a brown shopping bag in hand. Moving toward the coat hooks, she thrust the sack at his chest. "It's snowing hard again. We probably had more inches fall last *nacht* than all of last week combined." She removed her mittens. "I just love this *wedder*. What about you, Micah, do you like it when it snows?"

"*Nett* so—"

"It's pure and I like catching it on my tongue. But it's cold . . ." Her assessment of the weather continued as she took off her wool cloak. "I think the horses like this *wedder* too. Don't you agree?"

He opened his mouth to speak, but not quick enough to get a word in.

"Horses grow such a thick coat of fur, which always makes for a lot of brushing in the spring, ain't so?"

He raised his brows. Horse grooming in their community was common knowledge. But she rattled on about how horses should be blanketed in the winter and given extra feed. A walking textbook. It struck him then that perhaps he was dense. All this talk about horses was probably her way of hinting that he should offer to unhitch her horse and put him in a stall. Still holding her bag, he went to the window and looked out. "Where's your buggy?"

"David was on his way to the hardware store so he offered to drop me off." She lined her snow-covered boots against the wall, then drew in a deep breath and clapped her hands together. "So, where's your grandmother?"

He motioned to the sitting room. "She's around the corner in the—"

Abigail went to the entrance of the sitting room and waved. "Hello."

Micah caught *Mammi's* grimace as he came up beside Abigail.

"You must be Abigail Kemp."

Mammi's lackluster tone didn't shy away Abigail; she beamed. "*Jah.* Should I call you Mrs. Zook?"

"*Edith* will be fine."

Micah tapped the paper sack. "Where do you want this?"

"On the kitchen table will be fine." She trailed him to the kitchen and started to unpack the bag. "I brought some puzzles for me and Edith to do. Does your grandmother like to put puzzles together?"

He shrugged, then nodded toward the door. "I should head out to the shop *nau*. Let me know if you need anything."

Abigail trailed him to the door. "How long did you say your folks will be away?"

"Until Christmas."

She nibbled on her bottom lip. "Three weeks?"

"Is there a problem with taking care of *mei mammi* that long?" He removed his hat from the wall hook.

"Nope." Her smile widened. "Just making conversation."

"Wasn't a conversation supposed to go two ways?" he muttered under his breath as he donned his hat and gloves.

She slipped into the sitting room. Within seconds,

the women were engaged in conversation—at least Abigail was. *Mammi* was being polite. Perhaps this arrangement would work out after all.

Micah went outside. A brisk wind lifted his hat, but he caught it and pushed it back into place. The temperature had dropped since he'd gone out to feed the horses earlier that morning. The tracks he'd made were barely visible now. He flipped his coat collar up and held it tighter against his neck. He sure didn't share Abigail's enthusiasm for the cold weather. Despite the festive Christmas season, this wasn't his favorite time of year.

The snow crunched under his boots as he trekked across the yard to the workshop. He should have hired Abigail last week when his parents first went out of town. He hadn't considered how much supervision his grandmother would require, nor had he expected his *Englisch* customers to make last-minute changes to their orders. Now, in addition to the wedding table centerpieces, he was commissioned to make the cake topper along with several hanging glass icicles and snowflake decorations.

Micah started the fire in the kiln and gathered the glassblowing pipe, metal crimpers, and the wooden shaping bowl. The sand, borax, and cullet mixture molted into a pliable mass of clear bubbles as the temperature rose. He slid the end of the blowing iron into the fiery liquid and slowly rotated the pipe, collecting the spongy material. Micah removed the pipe from the heat, rotating it so the molten glass didn't drip off the rod as he carried it to the steel table. Rolling it against the marver, he evened out the shape. The piece was cooling faster than he liked. He lifted the pipe and blew gently into the end.

The shop door opened and Abigail entered. "*Ach*," her eyes opened wide, "what are you making?"

He'd hired her to keep his grandmother busy, not bother him while he was working.

"Can't talk, can you?" She chuckled.

Micah withdrew his mouth from the pipe and capped the hole with his finger. "What do you need, Abigail?"

She pointed to the pipe. "It's . . . glowing—and growing."

He glanced at the glob of molten glass and groaned. The trapped air from closing off the hole had created a hollow bubble, as it should, but by not working the shape at the same time, the walls had overexpanded. The piece was too thin to develop any further.

"Is it supposed to do that?"

"*Nett* really." Another time he might have found her bright green eyes, wide with childlike wonder, attractive, but not today. He blew out a breath. "Is there something that you need?"

"You didn't say what time you wanted lunch. I found some jars of vegetables in the pantry. I thought I could make soup."

He used the pliers to snip the glass, then set the blowpipe on the steel worktable and moved toward her.

"Or I could make sandwiches. There's peanut butter and jelly or if you want—"

He reached for her elbow and turned her toward the door. "Anything you make will be fine with me." He opened the door. "I'm *nett* fussy," he said, guiding her outside the building.

She blinked several times in rapid succession, and for the first time, she said nothing when her mouth dropped open.

He closed the door. *That was rude. Apologize.* Guilt pricked his conscience, but he pushed it aside and returned to his workplace. He wasn't about to apologize. Doing so would only encourage the *maedel*.

. . .

Abigail touched her arm where Micah had cupped his hand over her elbow and shuttled her out. His simple gesture had generated a light tingling sensation that even now continued to circulate. She stared at the closed door. If he didn't want to be interrupted, he should have posted a sign.

She hesitated a moment, then yanked the workshop door open and reentered the building. Her eyes needed a second to adjust to the dimly lit room. Once they did, she spotted Micah hunched next to the furnace opening, feeding the blaze with more wood. Abigail approached the steel table.

"You never said what time you wanted to eat lunch," she said.

Micah jerked, then slowly facing her, his eyes narrowed.

She hadn't meant to surprise him. *Oh dear, he looks annoyed.* Her gaze traveled his six-foot frame as he stood. She swallowed hard.

He swept the wood bark off his knees, then wiped his hands of sawdust.

"Is there . . ." She straightened her shoulders and stood a little taller. "Is there a particular time you normally eat? *Mei daed* and *bruder* like to eat right at noon. But I thought I should find out from—"

His eyes closed for a brief second. "You're making cold sandwiches, right?"

"I don't have to. That was merely a suggestion. I could make something warm. Soup or macaroni and—"

"Abigail."

He stifled his stern tone with an extended groan, which sounded a lot like the bear she'd heard once while berry picking. That or the noise her father made when he tried to restrain his agitation with her mother's absentmindedness.

Abigail clamped her hand over her mouth before she said something stupid and then peered up. But the moment his hazel eyes met hers, a shudder cascaded down her spine. She looked away and focused on the pile of kindling stacked in the woodbox.

"Perhaps we should set some ground rules," he said. "I hired you to look after *mei mammi* so that I could work out here. Uninterrupted." He rubbed the back of his neck. "How about you make whatever *mei mammi* wants for lunch. If it's something hot, I'll warm it up myself when I come in, okay?"

Abigail nodded. Her attention skipped over to the flaming furnace, the bucket of water, and the long steel rod lying beside a glob of something green on the table. Her brother had said Micah worked with glass, making fancy things to sell in one of the downtown shops, but she'd never seen any of his products while window gazing. She scanned the nearby shelves lined with boxes labeled *molds*. Her curiosity rose, but she resisted asking about them. A wooden crate was marked *cullets* and he had various tools hanging from a pegboard over a workbench. The man kept his work area neat.

He cleared his throat.

"Oh, I suppose I should go." She headed toward the door. "I wouldn't want Edith to get worried about me being gone so long."

Abigail stepped outside. She clenched the opening of her cape at the neck and, with her free hand, caught the white flecks of snow. The last time it snowed this hard, she had been skating. Twirling in a tight circle with her head up, the mesmerizing snowflakes had made her dizzy. She'd only gone to the pond once this season. David had said the ice wasn't thick enough, but she'd tested it anyway and hadn't heard any cracks. Abigail slid her boot in long strides over the freshly fallen snow on the driveway. She hoped to have time before supper to skate.

Abigail removed her cloak at the door and hung it on the wall hook. Blowing warm air into her fisted hands, she crossed the room. "It's getting colder out there." She stopped in front of the woodstove, its radiating heat eased the winter chill from her bones.

"You need a hot cup of tea to warm your insides." Edith set her knitting aside and stood. "I'll put the kettle on to boil." She ambled toward the kitchen.

Abigail rubbed her arms a few minutes longer,

enjoying the warmth from the woodstove, then joined Edith in the kitchen.

Edith wasn't the frail, little woman Micah had made her out to be. She had climbed a footstool and was removing two cups from the cabinet.

"Let me help you with those." Abigail reached for the cups. An eighty-five-year-old woman shouldn't be climbing a stool. She might fall and break a hip. The cups rattled as Abigail set them on the counter. She took Edith's hand and helped her down.

"*Danki*, dear."

"I wish you would have waited for me to get them down." Abigail sniffed an awful metallic smell in the air. She glanced at the stove. It wasn't steam coming from the kettle's spout, but black smoke, and it was filling the room. She grabbed a potholder, lifted the empty kettle from the stove, and deposited it into the sink.

"Did I forget to put water in it?" Edith frowned.

"It's okay." She opened the window over the sink and waved the potholder, fanning the smoke outside. Icy air nipped at her nose and cheeks. "You might want to wait in the sitting room where it's warmer." Abigail glanced over her shoulder, but Edith had already left the kitchen.

A few moments later, the door flung open and Micah rushed into the kitchen, a bucket of water in his hand. "Where's the fire?"

"There isn't one." She stopped fanning the smoke.

He sniffed the air and grimaced. "What's that smell?"

"The tea kettle boiled dry."

"That's it?"

Abigail nodded.

He set the water bucket on the floor, then crossed his arms and glared at her. "That's the emergency? *Mammi* said the *haus* was on fire."

Edith came into the house, breathing hard and shivering. "Did you put the fire out, Micah?"

"Everything is fine, *Mammi*." He turned to Abigail. "I hope the next time you'll make sure there's enough water in the kettle before putting it on the stove."

"I—" Abigail bowed her head. Finger-pointing never gained favor. "I'll be more careful."

"I'm glad you're both okay," he said quietly.

"*Danki*." She forced a smile. He was probably thinking of a hundred different reasons to find someone else to care for Edith now. She'd better keep a closer eye on the elderly woman if she wanted to keep this job.

He picked up the water bucket. "I'll be out in the shop if you need me."

Abigail watched him walk to the door. His rolled-up shirtsleeves exposed muscular forearms. Carrying a full bucket of water, he never let a drop slosh over the side of the metal pail. He pushed his hat down, covering the tips of his ears before stepping outside. Abigail stared at his vacant spot at the door for a long moment.

"I thought I would make lentil soup for lunch," Edith said.

She closed her eyes and blew out a calming breath. "You're *nett* trying to take *mei* job, are you?" Without giving Edith time to answer, she continued. "I'm trying to save enough money to buy a buggy horse. Mr. Troyer has a gelding he plans to sell. He's a beautiful animal."

Abigail opened the lower kitchen cabinets and searched for a large pot and matching lid. If Edith wanted lentil soup, Abigail was going to make it. She filled the pot with tap water.

"What were we talking about? Oh, I remember. Mr. Troyer's gelding. I've been saving for a year. Mostly the money I made from selling *mei* baked goods at the—" She hushed herself. That wasn't a topic she wanted to discuss with anyone. She needed to learn to keep her mouth shut. Fran's words about Abigail's defiance replayed in her mind. If Fran was instructed not to sell Abigail's baked goods, Micah would probably be told he couldn't hire her to care for his grandmother. The ordeal would embarrass her parents, and the bishop may think her parents were unable to keep their daughter in line. Her thoughts flitted a dozen directions. She couldn't lose her job. Lose the chance to buy Cactus. All she had to do was keep her mouth shut for three weeks, and she would have her independence.

CHAPTER 4

The afternoon stole away from Micah. What he wasn't able to get done before lunchtime, he made up for later. He finished the first glass centerpiece. A green leafy wreath design with clusters of red berries. Micah held the lantern over it and admired the way the glass reflected the glow from the flame. He hoped the bride and groom would be pleased. They certainly paid a premium price for the artwork. When he met with the couple's wedding planner last week, she had mentioned the possibility of hiring him to make glassware for another wedding around Valentine's Day.

Micah had never been one to count his sales before delivering the product and getting the final nod of acceptance, but this account was different. If all went according to plan, he would be able to break ground on his own home come spring. His father had given him the back forty acres to build on. He had always assumed he wouldn't start building until he was married. His two brothers married and left home at twenty-one, his sister at twenty-two. At age twenty-four, Micah was ready to establish his own independence, even though he didn't plan to go far.

His stomach growled. The lentil soup he'd eaten at lunch hadn't filled him up. Micah cleaned up his work area and put the tools back in their proper places. He trekked across the yard, the snow crunching underfoot.

The scent of garlic bread and *yummasetti* met him at the door. He peeled off his coat and hung it on the wall hook. His mouth watered. Since his parents had left town, he'd eaten a few burned meals his grandmother made. Then deciding it'd be safer for her not to cook, he'd requested sandwiches.

He rounded the corner into the kitchen and paused. The sight of Abigail, standing at the stove, removing the tinfoil cover from the pan, made his heart skip a beat. Maybe there was something to that old saying about the way to a man's heart.

She motioned to the egg noodles and melted cheese. "I hope you're hungry."

"Starved." *And half-crazed.* His pulse hadn't been this erratic in years. Not that he wanted to relive that heartache. He would have been married now if Sue Ann's family hadn't moved.

Still, the sight of Abigail at the stove—seemingly at home—was enough to catch his breath. Why hadn't she married? It was no secret that she'd been driven home from every singing she attended. But he had never heard of any of the men asking again, and according to her older brother David, no one had asked to sit with her on his front porch either.

Mammi cleared her throat. "Are you going to gawk at the food all *nacht* or wash your hands and *kumm* to the table?"

Micah glanced at the dirt on his hands as he went to the sink.

Abigail carried the pan to the table, set it down, then backed away from the table. "I hope you like it."

He came up beside her and pulled out the chair next to *Mammi*. "You're going to stay and eat with us, aren't you?"

"I should probably go. It's getting late." She moved toward the door.

"Wait," he said, following her into the foyer. He reached for his coat. "I'll give you a ride home."

"*Danki*, but I'll be fine. You stay and eat while it's warm." She shoved her stockinged foot into her boot.

"*Nay*. It's snowing. And it's dark out. I'm *nett* going to let you walk home alone this late."

She nibbled on her bottom lip a half second, then kicked off her boots. "I suppose *mei* family won't miss me tonight at the supper table," she said, hanging her cloak back on the hook. Abigail returned to the table and sat beside *Mammi*.

The moment they finished silently blessing their food, Abigail began her report. "Edith and I had a *gut* day. We organized your pantry. It's alphabetical *nau*." She gave an hour-by-hour report of what she and *Mammi* had done since he'd seen them at noon. The partially assembled jigsaw puzzle on the other end of the table had already hinted to what kept them busy, but her chatter was somewhat amusing. He'd never known anyone not to take a breather between sentences.

His grandmother's eyes drooped. *Tired?* Listening to Abigail was a bit daunting. He would probably get an earful once Abigail went home.

Any thoughts he'd had earlier about finding Abigail attractive faded. He didn't know any man who would want to spend eternity with a woman who talked as much as she did. She had yet to take a bite of her food.

"The meal was *gut. Danki.*" He pushed away from the table and stood. "I'll hitch the buggy while you finish eating."

"I won't be long," she said.

"*Mammi*, would you like to ride along?" He hated the idea of leaving her alone, but he didn't want her to go out in the cold either.

Mammi shook her head. "I'm going to read for a while and then go to bed."

"Okay." He slipped on his coat, lit the lantern, and headed outside. Tomorrow he wouldn't work this late. Micah harnessed Clover and led him out of the stall. He had the buggy hitched and parked next to the porch when Abigail came outside.

She crawled up on the bench. "You didn't have to go to this trouble. I could have walked home. We only live a mile apart."

"I know." He snapped the reins and Clover lurched forward. Even so, he didn't want her to walk home in the dark on the snowy roads.

"You don't talk much, do you?"

He shrugged. "I say what's necessary."

"That's it? Just what's necessary?" She harrumphed as if that were a sin.

He clicked his tongue and Clover picked up speed.

She crossed her arms and slouched on the seat. "Must be lonely."

"*Nett* really. I don't need to come up with things to say just to hear myself talk."

She shifted on the bench to face him. "So, you wouldn't look up at the sky and say something about how bright the stars were?"

"Probably *nett*." He slowed Clover down before turning into her driveway. He stopped the buggy next to the house. "Do you make it a habit to talk about everything?"

She smiled. "It's a gift."

He chuckled. Only Abigail would consider prattle a gift.

"Don't laugh. God's given me a gift of gab and I intend to use it."

Gift of gab? He laughed harder. Maybe all the talking to herself had scrambled her senses.

"I'm glad you find that funny." She opened the buggy door and slipped down from the bench.

"Hey, Gabby Abby," he said as she was about to close the door. "If you had bothered to look up, you would have noticed the stars aren't out. It's snowing."

She lifted her gaze and stared into the darkness. "They're still there. Under cloud cover, but shining bright nonetheless. How else would the wildlife find their way around in the woods?"

"*Gut* point."

"So . . . should I still *kumm* tomorrow?"

She was a strange one. First she was overly eager to work, and now she sounded unsure. "Have you changed your mind about watching *Mammi*?"

"*Nay*, have you changed yours? I know today didn't go so well, but I promise tomorrow will be better. I'll make sure your grandmother stays away from the stove and—"

"Abigail, it's all right."

"I thought when you came into the *haus* with the bucket of water, I had lost the job. You weren't very pleased. I could see that in your eyes. I figured at the end of the day you'd tell me I was done."

He stared at her lips, which were drawn into a frown. "Is that why you were so anxious to leave?"

She nodded. "I thought if I left while you were eating, you might give me another chance. You are going to give me another chance, *jah*?"

Did she not listen to anything he said? How much more reassurance did she need?

She crossed her arms over her chest. "There you go, getting quiet again." She covered her mitted hand over her mouth. "Or . . . you don't want me to work tomorrow."

"Why do you want this job so badly?" Micah hoped her eagerness wasn't in hopes of something more developing between them. She was nice enough—attractive even—but she was also his best friend's little sister. He wasn't interested in courting her.

"I'm saving for a horse," she said.

"A horse?" He coughed into his fisted hand. Not many women in this district owned their own horses. Farmland was scarce and hay was expensive.

"I almost have enough money saved. So, are you going to give me another chance?"

He nodded. "I'll see you in the morning." He braced for a squeal that never came. Instead, she pursed her lips and exhaled.

"*Danki.*" Her smile returned wider and brighter than before. She bounded up the porch steps, paused to wave, then disappeared inside the house.

Micah chuckled to himself as he signaled Clover forward. Abigail Kemp's sunny disposition was as catchy as the common cold.

CHAPTER 5

The following morning Abigail woke before sunrise. She dressed in darkness so as not to awaken her sisters, sleeping in beds adjacent to hers, then tiptoed down the stairs and padded into the kitchen. While the others were still asleep, she filled a grocery sack with a few staples from the pantry: flour, yeast, uncooked noodles, rice, oatmeal, and two quarts of her mother's homemade tomato sauce. Abigail slipped on her boots and cloak, grabbed the basket, and headed outside.

The chickens flapped their wings and clucked as she entered the henhouse. "*Guder mariye*, ladies." She worked her way down the row of nesting boxes, collecting eggs and greeting each hen by name. Before leaving the coop, she fed and watered them. Once the eggs were washed, Abigail rolled a dozen eggs in the dish towel and placed them in the bag with the other items from the pantry.

"You're up early," *Mamm* said, entering the kitchen.

Abigail closed the bag and set it aside. "I promised Micah I would be early."

Mamm wadded up a few pieces of the newspaper,

placing it and some thin slabs of dry kindling in the cookstove. "Did he say if his sister had her *boppli* yet?"

"*Nay*, but I'll ask when I see him today."

Her mother filled the kettle with tap water and set it on the stove.

"*Mamm*, do you think we'll be able to have the whole family together for Christmas?"

"If you're wondering about the Lambrights . . . probably *nett* this year."

"It won't feel like Christmas," Abigail said softly.

Mamm's somber expression wasn't easily hidden behind her weak smile. "Keep the bishop and elders in your prayers as they decide if there will be a formal shunning."

"I will." Abigail hated to see her mother worried about *Aenti* Doreen's family. Her aunt had gone through so much having both her sons leave home. Over the years, Malinda had shared family secrets that Abigail had promised never to repeat. That wasn't to say rumors about Malinda's father's harsh discipline hadn't spread like fire in their district. He had driven both of his sons away with his well-worn leather strap.

Abigail cleared her throat. "Would it be all right if I skip breakfast?"

"You're in that big of a hurry?"

Abigail nodded. Her mother hadn't asked how many cookies and pies Gingerich's Market had ordered, and she wouldn't be pleased that Abigail had gone against the bishop's order and visited the Lambrights' home. Relatives weren't exempt, even in her mother's eyes.

"You have to eat something." *Mamm* motioned to

the pantry. "Make a peanut-butter sandwich to eat on your way."

She wasn't hungry, but she made a sandwich to take anyway. "I don't know what time I'll be home," she said over her shoulder. Taking the grocery bag, she headed out the door as the sun was coming up over the horizon. Clumps of snow collected on her boots as she trudged across the winter wheat field toward the Lambright farm.

Lamplight illuminated the kitchen as Abigail approached the farmhouse. She spotted her cousin standing in front of the window and waved. A few minutes later, Malinda came outside bundled up in her coat and scarf.

"I brought you a few things." Abigail handed Malinda the bag. "Be careful. I wrapped the eggs in a dish towel."

"Bless you." Her eyes glistened. "I was praying this morning that God would provide a miracle. I've made so many meals out of biscuits and gravy that we ran out of flour last *nacht*."

"How is your *mamm* doing?"

Malinda shook her head. "When she's *nett* crying, she's so quiet, it's . . . frightening. I've been doing all the cooking and cleaning, but . . ." Her words broke off as she gazed toward the house.

Aenti Doreen had slipped into a depression sixteen years ago when Boaz left home, then again when Thomas left six years later. Her husband refused to allow the boys' names to be spoken, and that deepened her despair.

Malinda's family had already suffered multiple

years of failed hay and corn crops along with several other families in this area. They relied heavily on the district's assistance, which made the threat of shunning that much harder.

Malinda swiped the tears away from her puffy eyes. "The apple pies you gave Thomas were delicious. You didn't have to bring so many. You could have sold them at Gingerich's."

"I thought your family might enjoy a treat. Besides, Thomas reminded me how much he liked apple pies."

"He remembered?" A ray of hope lit her friend's eyes.

"Sort of."

Malinda frowned. "He's changed a lot, hasn't he?"

"It's been ten years since he lived at home." Abigail stopped herself from adding how shocked she had been at Thomas's appearance.

"Did you talk with him much?" Malinda's eyes glazed. She blinked a few times, then tilted her head upward.

"I couldn't stay very long. I had to get home to help *Mamm* with supper."

"I wish he'd never left home to search for Boaz. Maybe then he wouldn't have joined the army."

Abigail's memory of her cousin Boaz was vague. She doubted Malinda remembered much either since she wasn't much older than seven when her eldest brother left home.

"Did you see the scar on Thomas's head?"

Abigail shook her head. "He was wearing a baseball hat."

"It's bad." Malinda ran her finger from the top of her head down to her ear to indicate the marking. "They had to do surgery to reduce the swelling on his brain. Now he has a metal plate in his head. His memory is spotty and he . . . just isn't the same."

"I never heard what happened."

"Apparently he was in Afghanistan when a bomb went off. The jeep he was in turned over." She wiped the tears from her face. "His memory is gone or at least most of the time it is. Even the doctor said it would take a miracle."

In the distance, horse hooves clapped the pavement.

"You better go before someone sees you. The bishop and elders think while Thomas was in the world, he partook in black magic."

Abigail gasped.

"Sometimes he randomly swears for no apparent reason. The doctor believes his head injury has something to do with that and the swearing might not stop." Malinda sighed. "It happened during one of the bishop's visits. He also has a tattoo now. No erasing that."

Abigail glanced at the fast-approaching buggy and turned her back to it. "What does your father say about everything?"

"At first *Daed* refused to talk to Thomas. He even said he had no *sohns*. But he's coming around. I think he regrets the pain he's put *Mamm* through for so many years."

"Perhaps the bishop will *kumm* around too."

Malinda nodded. "That's *mei* prayer."

"I should probably leave. Micah Zook hired me to watch his grandmother while his parents are out of town."

"I thought his grandmother lived in the west district."

"She moved in with them a few weeks ago. I don't think she can live alone anymore, which is *gut* for me. I should be able to buy Cactus soon."

"I suppose it's just as easy to make your fruitcakes and pies for the market while you're there. How is Micah to work for? I always thought he was standoffish at the youth singings."

Abigail held her tongue about not having orders to fill for the market. "He's even more so since he stopped attending."

"He never offered to drive you home from a singing, did he?"

Abigail shook her head. "Yesterday, he called me Gabby Abby."

Malinda smiled. "That's a fitting pet name."

"I wouldn't call it a pet name. He thinks I talk too much. Did you see whose buggy just passed?"

"I think it was Velda Schwartz."

Abigail exhausted a heavy breath. The bishop's sister-in-law had a tendency to weave her way into the heart of district happenings.

"You should go," Malinda said. "I don't want you to get in trouble."

"I should be able to drop off a few things to *mei* relatives. After all, I've always tried to share with others—including *Englischers*."

Malinda bowed her head. "Sometimes lately I've wished I wasn't Amish."

"Don't say that." Abigail reached for Malinda's

arm and gave it a gentle squeeze. "I can't lose *mei* best friend."

"Pray for me." The barn door opened and Malinda's father came out carrying a milk pail. "I have to go." She tapped the grocery sack. "*Danki* for this." She took a few steps away and then spoke over her shoulder. "Let me know how things work out between you and Micah. He might be a *gut* catch if you can get him to open up."

. . .

"Do all the young women on this side of the district talk a lot?" *Mammi* sipped her morning coffee. "I've never known someone to talk as much as Abigail."

A gift from God, Micah bit his tongue from saying aloud. He took a drink of his coffee and set the mug down. "Maybe she was nervous yesterday."

"A woman should be slow to speak."

Micah thought for a moment. Yes, Abigail talked a lot, but she also had many admirable qualities. She was kind, thoughtful, and had a sweet spirit. She could use some guidance. "Maybe you could mentor her."

Mammi's gray eyes sparked with purpose. "*Jah*," she said, nodding thoughtfully. "I could do that."

Micah smiled. *Mammi* hadn't had a chance to attend any get-togethers with his mother, but it wouldn't be long before she established new friendships with the widows on this side of the district. In the meantime, *Mammi* would have a project. His problem was solved. She would keep Abigail busy, and he would be able to work peacefully in his shop without more interruptions like yesterday.

A soft knock sounded at the door.

Micah glanced at the wall clock. Abigail was early. He opened the door.

"*Hiya*." A white fog escaped her mouth.

"Hello, Abigail." He opened the door wider and glanced outside. "Your *bruder* didn't bring you?"

"*Nay*, I walked." She moved past him and shed her wool cloak, mittens, and boots in the entry. She rubbed her arms.

Her rosy cheeks and the tip of her nose looked raw. He motioned to the sitting room. "Why don't you warm up by the woodstove while I make you a cup of *kaffi*."

"I c-can get it." Her teeth chattered.

"I insist. Go warm up."

"O-k-ay."

He didn't want her to get pneumonia—unless it was after Christmas. He shook his head. *Insensitive*, he chided as he removed a mug from the cabinet. He filled it with coffee, then walked back to the sitting room. "This should heat you up."

"*Danki*." She blew across the surface and took a sip.

Micah tipped his head toward the kitchen. "There's a pot of oatmeal on the cooling rack. You can reheat it if you like." He went to the entry and grabbed his coat and hat off the hook.

She came up beside him, holding her cup with both hands. "Anything special you want me to do or make?"

"I'm sure you and *Mammi* will figure out something." He slipped his arm into his coat sleeve. "You'll find packages of meat in the *icehaus* and canned vegetables down in the cellar." He donned his hat and gloves. "I'll see you sometime around noon for lunch."

"Maybe Edith and I will make a batch of sugar cookies. They were *mei* best"—her smile faded—"sellers at Gingerich's Market." She lowered her head and when she looked up again, her smile had returned.

"Sounds *gut*." Over the years, he'd sampled several of her cookies either at church functions or at the youth singings. He'd even bought a few dozen from the store once or twice.

"Customers liked *mei* oatmeal raisin ones too."

He reached for the door. "Make whichever ones you like." His mouth would water, whatever kind they were. Her baked goods were the first to go during the singings and probably why so many men vied to drive her home.

Micah went outside. Earlier, when he'd gone out to do barn chores, he'd shoveled the snow off the porch and steps and made a walkway to the barn. It was dark then and he hadn't noticed the snowdrifts that the wind pushed against the shop door. He grabbed the snow shovel from the tool shed and cleared the entrance to his shop. This might be a record-breaking year for snowfall. Hopefully it wouldn't hinder his parents' return. Sometimes the buses didn't run when the weather was bad.

Micah prepared the kiln, and as he waited for it to heat, he flipped through his sketchpad. The customers had requested different centerpieces for each of the twenty tables. He'd tried to tell them that every blown-glass piece was unique. Even if he wanted to make them identical, it would be next to impossible. One reason glassblowing never got old.

He studied the sketch for the bridal table. The groom wanted deer, the bride wanted doves, and they finally settled on both, leaving Micah to figure out the design. It proved to be a challenge trying to please them both. In just the short amount of time he'd spent with the couple, they had seemed polar opposites. His thoughts flitted to Abigail. The way her nose had wrinkled like she had smelled a skunk when he called her 'Gabby Abby' would be etched on his mind for some time to come. His thoughts shifted to the engaged *Englisch* couple and how they gazed into each other's eyes, then flitted back to Abigail. Her green eyes were vivid—lively when she talked. He found himself mesmerized by her animated expression when she described the starry sky. Not one star was visible, but somehow she managed to depict the perfect scene. She was right about God using the stars to direct the wildlife. He once watched a herd of white-tail deer follow a moonlit path over the pasture.

Maybe the stars will be out tonight, Gabby Abby.

Micah cringed. Stargazing was overrated. He hadn't wanted to think about a starry night since Sue Ann had moved. Abigail assumed he wasn't talkative when she mentioned the stars. Calling her 'Gabby Abby' changed that topic. He shouldn't have teased her. Although he'd meant it in fun, most women probably wouldn't find any humor in having that nickname. Perhaps *Mammi's* mentoring would help. It certainly couldn't hurt. With some help, Abigail might secure a husband. He smiled. Marriage probably wouldn't settle her down.

CHAPTER 6

Abigail selected a puzzle piece that looked like part of the sky and hunted for the spot where it would fit. "I love seeing puzzles come together, don't you? Especially puzzles of horses. This sorrel has the same coat color as the one I plan to buy."

"You talk an awful lot about wanting to own your own horse," Edith said, keeping her eyes on the puzzle piece she was about to place.

"You find that odd, don't you?" Abigail selected another piece of what was either a portion of the cloud or the white star between the horse's eyes.

"Just a word of warning. Unleashed desire for material possessions is a dangerous thing."

Abigail cringed. In her excitement, she probably had sounded obsessed. "I suppose I do sound overzealous. I've been saving since last December. Of course *mei* younger sister, Elizabeth, told me if I had a *bu*, I wouldn't need to save money for a horse."

"That's how it was in *mei* courting days." Edith joined two sections of the puzzle together. Now the galloping horse just missed its tail.

"I have to plan for the future. *Mei* courting days are over." A familiar pang gripped her heart. Sometimes the bitter truth was better left unspoken.

Edith looked up from the puzzle. The creases around her eyes softened. "It isn't too late for you."

Abigail forced a smile too difficult to hold. "What made you decide to move to this side of the district? You must miss your friends."

Edith nodded. "I do. But *mei sohn* and his *fraa* were concerned about me living alone, them being over ten miles away." She found where another piece of the puzzle belonged. "And they believe I'm losing *mei* mind."

Abigail's jaw dropped. Edith *had* forgotten to put water in the kettle yesterday.

"You find that hard to believe?"

"*Nay*—I mean—well, maybe a little forgetful."

Edith chuckled. "You're a sweet child. But it's true. *Mei* mind is slipping. Even Micah was worried about leaving me alone in the *haus* all day. He hired you."

"He knew he would be working long hours. I'm sure he didn't want you to get lonely."

Edith shook her head. "I left the water running in the sink and it spilled over. Trust me, he's worried."

"That doesn't necessarily mean he's worried. Once I left the tap open on the rain barrel, and it flooded a newly planted section of the garden. The next morning all *mei* starter plants were uprooted." Abigail shrugged. "I had gotten distracted and forgot. It happens all the time." She glanced up at the kitchen wall clock and bolted off the chair. "Micah must be getting hungry. I should start lunch. How does chili sound to you? Or

I can make sandwiches or—" She covered her mouth with her hand.

"Is something wrong, child?"

Abigail pulled her hand away from her mouth. "I'm talking too much, aren't I?"

"Cooking for Micah makes you nervous, I understand."

Abigail shook her head. "That's *nett* it. I naturally talk a lot. *Mei* mother makes the sound of bees buzzing when I start rambling." Her shoulders dropped. "I haven't had anyone to talk with in a while. *Mei* cousin, Malinda—"

Concern spread over Edith's face.

There she went again, talking too much. Edith probably didn't know about the Lambright's problems in the church or that they were about to be formally shunned. She went to the wall rack and plucked her cloak off the hook. "I'm going to check the *icehaus* for hamburger meat. I'll be right back."

"Why don't you take Micah a fresh cup of *kaffi* since you're going out?"

"I don't think he wants to be bothered." She'd learned that lesson yesterday.

"Nonsense, he's been out in his shop all morning. He'll enjoy the *kaffi*."

Edith was right. On a wintery day like today, Micah would probably appreciate something hot to drink. She went to the cabinet and removed a mug from the shelf.

• • •

Micah used the metal clippers to detach the glass from the blowpipe. The first satisfactory piece he'd made all morning. He let out a breath once it was safely cooling on the steel table. Light entered the doorway, and he looked up.

Abigail. He'd worked hard all morning to rid her from his thoughts and now here she was. "Apparently you forgot that I had asked *nett* to be bothered?"

"I remember." She inched forward anyway, her attention on the steaming mug in her hand. "This was full when I left the *haus*," she said, lowering it onto the table.

"*Danki*." His tone hinted of more aggravation than gratitude.

"No need to thank me." She clasped her hands behind her back and moved to the end of the table where he'd placed the glass poinsettia to cool.

In his experience, customers who viewed his work with their arms behind their backs were harsh appraisers. His jaw tightened.

She shot him a sideways glance, then returned to inspecting the piece. "Don't worry," she said as if reading his mind. "I'm *nett* staying."

He couldn't have these interruptions. He already had mental images of her embedded in his mind and they were jarring enough. "I'm *nett* worried," he said, evening out his tone.

She peered at him again, this time she narrowed her eyes.

He cracked a smile but made a slight gesture with his head toward the door hoping she would take the hint and he wouldn't have to escort her out like yesterday.

"I'm making chili and cornbread for lunch." She crossed the room, paused for half a second at the door, then yanked it open. "You're *welkom* for the *kaffi*."

Micah eyed the steaming mug. She had a servant's heart. But if he didn't put his foot down, the interruptions would be unending. She would smother him with questions. Questions she wouldn't even wait to have answered before blurting out the next one.

He picked up the blowpipe and went to the kiln, but the fire had died down. Perhaps God was trying to get his attention. Micah wasn't the most patient man, and it showed in his abruptness with Abigail. He tossed a few thin pieces of kindling on the bed of hot embers and watched them ignite as he recalled seeing Abigail give a tin of her delicious cookies to a man on the street.

Micah bowed his head. *Father, please forgive me for being rude. She has a good heart, but she talks too much. I'm nett sure she has a shut-off valve. Will You help her find it?* Heat from the kiln warmed Micah's face. *Father, please help me see her the way You do.*

Micah worked another hour and was able to get a few of the four-dozen ordered snowflakes finished. He'd hoped to get more done, but his stomach rumbled, telling him it was past time to eat. He needed to take a break soon or his scrap pile would be larger than the items to sell. Before leaving the shop, he added a thick log to the kiln to keep the fire from dying down completely.

He stomped the snow off his boots on the porch, then entered the house. The tantalizing aroma of cornbread filled the air. He removed his coat and hat, listening to Abigail talk about the Christmas gifts she had made for her family. Wool socks for her brothers and knitted scarves for her sisters. The house certainly felt more joyful with Abigail around.

He went to the sink to wash up. *Be nice*, he reminded himself when Abigail jumped topics and started talking about the cookies she planned to bake. *Mammi* stood at the stove stirring a pot of chili while Abigail stood at the counter next to the sink cutting cornbread.

"I'm only going to make a couple of fruitcakes this season because"—she interrupted herself to acknowledge his presence—"You're just in time, Micah"—then resumed her conversation with his grandmother, something about how expensive dates were this time of year.

When he finished washing up, Abigail handed him a dish towel. "*Danki*. Your cornbread smells *gut*." He smiled.

A rosy shade of pink spread over her cheeks. His smile appeared to take her by surprise. Abigail stared blankly at him a moment as if lost in thought, then returned his smile. She instructed him to take a seat, then grabbed the plate of cornbread and rushed it to the table. For the next several minutes, she created a whirlwind in the kitchen as she hurried to finish setting the table.

Mammi lifted the spoon from the pot and set it aside. "If you have a minute, Micah, I'd like you to look at the lantern on the table next to where I knit. I think the wick could use adjusting."

Lantern wicks were not difficult to adjust. The

meeting she'd called had to do with Abigail. *Mammi* was probably exhausted from listening to her all morning and would reiterate that she didn't need a sitter. But he rose from his chair and went into the sitting room. "The wick is fine," he said after a brief inspection.

"I want to talk with you about Abigail."

"I'll try to work faster."

Her forehead creased in puzzlement. "I don't know what was said this morning when Abigail brought you *kaffi*, but when she returned, I could tell that she was upset about something."

"I was a little short with her."

"Your parents didn't raise you to be harsh to women. She's a sweet child."

He nodded.

"I expect you to apologize."

Abigail poked her head into the room. "Lunch is ready."

"Okay," Edith replied.

Abigail took her place next to *Mammi* and bowed her head. If she had overheard *Mammi's* scolding, she never let on.

In his silent prayer, he asked God not only to bless the food, but to forgive him again. His sharp tone with Abigail earlier in the workshop probably had something to do with her nervousness around him now. Maybe he'd frightened her. *Forgive me if I have, Lord.*

He took a bite of cornbread. It melted in his mouth.

"You like it?" Abigail's eyes sparkled.

"Very much," he replied, then realized she had directed the question to *Mammi*.

Mammi took a nibble of the chili and smiled. "How do you make yours? I guess I wasn't watching."

"I put sugar in it." She motioned to her bowl. "I added some to the chili too."

"I used to add a chocolate bar to mine," *Mammi* said.

Abigail's eyes widened. "I'll have to try that next time."

Micah filled his spoon with chili and took a bite. He couldn't taste any sugar. The chili was as hot in spice as in temperature. His eyes watered. This was different, but he could get used to the spiciness with a larger glass of milk. Her cornbread on the other hand was perfect. He went back for seconds and thirds. He ate so much he wasn't sure he could get up from his chair when lunch was over.

He slowly pushed back from the table, then stood. "*Danki*. Lunch was *gut*."

"You're *welkom*." She followed him to the door. "Micah, I was wondering if it would be okay if Edith and I go for a drive. She hasn't been back to the other side of the district to visit her friends, and I thought it would be nice for her to do so before Christmas."

"Abigail." The moment he touched her arm, her mouth clamped shut. He released her arm and removed his coat from the hook. "It's a great idea."

"Oh, *gut*. I'll need to borrow your horse and buggy."

"That's fine. When do you plan to go?" He slid his arm into the coat sleeve.

She shrugged. "I was thinking maybe tomorrow, but I'll talk with Edith and let you know what we decide."

"Okay." He reached for the door handle, started to

open it, then stopped. "Abigail, I'd like to apologize." He turned and faced her. "I shouldn't have been abrupt with you this morning. I'm sorry."

A smile surfaced. "I understand. I won't bother you anymore."

Beneath her smile, he sensed sadness. Guilt gnawed at him. "I'm behind schedule. For some reason I haven't been able to keep the fire in the kiln hot, and the fluctuating temperatures have interfered with melting and molding the glass." He lowered his head and looked down at his boots. "I wasn't in the best mood when you brought me *kaffi*. I shouldn't have taken *mei* frustration out on you."

"I'll say a prayer that you can make your deadline."

"*Danki*." He smiled. "If I don't, I'll have an angry bride and groom on *mei* hands."

Her forehead wrinkled in confusion.

"I've been commissioned to make centerpieces for the reception tables, a cake topper, and different snowflake ornaments they plan to hang for decorations."

"Sounds like a fancy wedding."

"The woman who's planning the wedding said she has more customers who would like *mei* work too. I should have enough money to build a *haus* next spring."

"You better get back to work." She reached around him and opened the door. "No one wants to see a bride cry on her wedding day."

Again, he sensed sadness, but now wasn't the time to ask her about it.

CHAPTER 7

Three days of blizzard conditions forced Abigail and Edith to change their plans. Abigail wasn't sure they should venture out on the icy roads, and Edith agreed. Ten miles was a long trip when the weather was bad. Even Micah had made the statement more than once. Although he never said anything about their decision, he seemed relieved when they postponed the visit for another day.

"I don't think it's going to stop snowing." Abigail lowered a cup of tea onto the lampstand beside Edith. They had finished putting the puzzle together shortly after doing the lunch dishes, and now they planned to relax in the sitting room with a cup of tea and their knitting needles.

"I'd be happy if it never snowed," Edith said.

Abigail sat in the wooden rocking chair beside Edith and gazed out the window. "Snow is so much prettier than brown grass. Besides, it wouldn't feel like Christmas without snow."

"I suppose you're right." Edith took a sip of tea, then set her cup down.

Abigail picked up her knitting needles. She wasn't

sure what she wanted to make, but she had yarn left over from the scarves she'd made her sisters for Christmas.

Edith unraveled some yarn from the ball. "Are you going to make a potholder or something for your hope chest?"

"A potholder maybe, but probably nothing for *mei* hope chest." As it was, she had plenty of items tucked away for a wedding day that would never come. It wasn't like she had a suitor standing at her door, and she was getting older by the minute.

"You sound sad. Should I have *nett* mentioned your hope chest?"

Abigail studied her stitches. "I've *kumm* to terms with *nett* getting married."

"You're such a sweet girl. I have a hard time believing you haven't been asked home from any of the singings."

"I have. But . . ." Abigail had told herself so many times that she would never get married, she was convinced of that fact. So why was it so painful to admit it out loud? She bounded off the chair. "Would you like more tea?"

"*Nay, danki.*"

Abigail took her cup to the kitchen even though it still had tea in it. She stood at the sink, gazing at the big flakes of snow falling. Micah's workshop, painted white, blurred into the scenery. Except for the smoke curling up from the stovepipe, she wouldn't be able to make out the building at all. The thought of walking home at the end of the day made her shudder. Once she was back home, she would have to warm herself by the woodstove for hours just to thaw.

An image appeared outside the kitchen window, and she gasped. Standing on the wraparound porch, Micah was laughing, releasing white puffs of air. He went to the door, stomped his boots, and entered the house.

"I didn't mean to startle you," he said.

She dropped her hand from her chest. "I didn't see you leave your shop."

"I came from the barn. The weather is getting bad. I thought I should drive you home before it worsened."

"Oh, ah . . ." Abigail scanned the room. She had wanted to start supper and mop the floors before he ended his workday.

He went to the kitchen table and stopped in front of the puzzle. "I see you and *Mammi* finished it."

"*Jah*, after lunch." She admired the photographic image of the galloping horse.

Edith ambled into the kitchen with her cup. "I think I will have more tea." She eyed Micah. "Are you finished for the day already?"

"It's storming. I thought I'd better take Abigail home. I'm sure she doesn't want to get snowbound with us overnight."

"What do you think of the puzzle?" Edith pointed to the table with her free hand.

He nodded. "It's nice."

"Did Abigail tell you she's saving to buy a horse?"

"*Jah*, she mentioned it."

"I have one picked out." Abigail poured hot water into Edith's cup. In her district only those women who had jobs—and no prospects to marry—bought a buggy horse. Winter feed was expensive, and some considered it a luxury for a woman to own a horse. She set the kettle back on the stove. "Mr. Troyer is selling Cactus."

"*Cactus*?" Micah frowned. "That horse is called Cactus for a reason."

"You're sounding a little prickly yourself." She looked away from his bent brows. Sure, Cactus was green. Even Mr. Troyer said he needed more training, but Cactus was the only horse she could afford. She dunked a tea bag into the hot water, then went to hand it to Edith, but she had already left the room.

"Abigail, he isn't a horse for you."

She set the cup on the counter. "He's a little skittish, but I'll talk to him gently."

"That horse won't listen to you."

"I'm a *gut* driver."

"He's *nett* a *gut* horse." His tone hardened. "You're *nett . . .*"

"A man?" Her back stiffened.

He narrowed his eyes. "I was going to say strong enough—but obviously you're very strong-minded."

"Obviously." She picked up the cup of tea and headed into the sitting room where she handed it to Edith. "I'm going to leave *nau*, but I'll see you in the morning."

"Perhaps you should think about what Micah is saying," Edith said.

Abigail cocked her head.

"Just a suggestion, child." Edith leaned forward and lowered her voice. "Men like Micah are looking for submissiveness in their potential *fraas*."

Abigail stifled her laughter. Dear soul, Edith had

no idea how wrong she was to imply that Micah might have an interest in her.

Micah cleared his throat. "We should probably get going."

Abigail smiled warmly at Edith, then headed for the front door. "I won't be needing a ride." She pulled her cloak off the hook. "I'll walk."

"Don't be muleheaded."

"I'd rather think of myself as *strong-minded*." She shoved on her boots.

He shifted his stance, groaning under his breath. "Same thing."

She flung her scarf around her neck, then put on her mittens. "I'll see you tomorrow."

He stopped her from opening the door. "Let me take you home."

Looking into the warmth of his eyes, her heart said yes, but her pride said no. "I'd rather walk." She pulled the door open and stepped out into the cold.

. . .

Micah paced the floor. All he needed was someone to watch over his grandmother while his parents were away. Less than a month and his life could get back to normal. He wouldn't have to worry about what horse she was buying or if she made it home in this snowstorm. An image of her smiling crossed his mind. She was always so cheerful.

"Are you going to keep pacing or go after her?"

Micah left the sitting room and went into the

kitchen. He pulled the curtain back, but the whiteout conditions were such that he couldn't see the barn. She would find her way but probably freeze doing so. *Stubborn woman.*

His grandmother came into the kitchen. "I'll be all right if you want to check on her."

"Why would I want to do that!" He bowed his head. "I'm sorry. I don't know what's wrong with me. I didn't mean to snap at you."

"She sure does seem to get under your skin."

He rubbed the back of his neck. "More so every day. I'll be glad when I finish the order I'm working on."

"Did you get a lot done today?"

He shook his head. "I kept thinking about the weather getting worse and that I should take Abigail home."

"Then I suggest you go after her."

"She's probably almost home."

Mammi frowned. "You don't want her out in this weather."

Mammi was right. If Abigail caught a cold and couldn't watch his grandmother, the order might never get completed in time.

"She's been very *gut* company for me," *Mammi* added.

"I thought you said she talks too much."

"I'm beginning to understand her. Apparently, she hasn't had her cousin, Malinda, to talk with lately. Poor dear, I think she's lonely."

Lonely? Not likely. Abigail Kemp could keep herself company if she were the only person in the room. *Mammi* padded out of the room and returned with his straw hat.

He opened his mouth to object but closed it quickly. He should be grateful that *Mammi* and Abigail were getting along so well. He couldn't handle any more trouble.

CHAPTER 8

"He called me muleheaded." Abigail huffed to Malinda. Standing on the far side of her *onkel's* porch had blocked the snowy north wind, but the temperature was still freezing. She wiggled her stiff fingers inside her mittens, hoping to increase the circulation.

"Just ignore him. He can't tell you what horse to buy," Malinda said.

Jah, why was she letting Micah stir her up? He had no charge over her.

Malinda motioned to the door. "Are you sure you don't want to *kumm* inside and warm up by the woodstove a few minutes? I doubt anyone is out in this weather if you're worried about someone seeing you."

Abigail's legs had gone numb shortly after leaving Micah's farm. She couldn't feel her nose and her cheeks burned as if chapped by the wind.

"It's hot in the *haus*. Thomas is constantly putting logs on the fire."

"Okay, but I can't stay too long." She tapped her boots on the side of the house to knock the snow off.

A blast of warm air hit her the moment she stepped into the house. "Have you heard anything from Bishop Schwartz?"

Malinda shook her head. "Still the silent treatment. How long can this last? After *Daed's* crops failed, he'd been given a line of credit to buy livestock feed. Since the silent treatment started, Mr. Mast wants his money up front. I should be thankful that Thomas is home." Malinda swiped at a tear. "It's too late for him. He'll never be in the right frame of mind to repent of his waywardness."

"Don't lose hope. God knows his mind and his heart."

"I know." Malinda's voice cracked. When she looked up, tears were streaming down her face. "*Danki* for being *mei* friend."

Abigail smiled. "You're more like a sister than a cousin."

Thomas entered the kitchen. He walked to the sink and filled a glass of water, then set it on the counter and faced them. "*Hiya*, Abigail."

Abigail looked at Malinda, who seemed just as surprised to hear an Amish greeting.

"How are you, Thomas?"

He leaned against the counter and hiked up his T-shirt sleeve. "See my tank?"

Ignoring him, Abigail turned to Malinda. "I should head home." She would have liked to visit longer, but Thomas didn't look as if he was leaving the kitchen anytime soon.

He pushed off the counter. "You leaving?"

"I told you before, Thomas. I don't want to see that tattoo."

"You did?"

She caught Malinda's frown, then smiled patiently at Thomas. "You showed it to me on the day I gave you the basket of pies."

For a split second when he smiled, the old Thomas was present. God wasn't through with him. Head trauma couldn't stop God's spirit from reaching him. All Thomas needed was a chance to join in fellowship with the other men. He left the kitchen, spewing a curse word for no apparent reason, and hope disappeared like rain on parched soil.

"I'm sorry you had to hear that," Malinda said.

"At least he didn't use the Lord's name in vain."

"It's like he doesn't have any control of his speech—or maybe it's his thought pattern. One minute he's speaking Pennsylvania *Deitsch* and the next he's cursing."

"God can do all things." Abigail reached for Malinda's hands and gave them a gentle squeeze. "And He's given you the strength to do all things through Him."

"I just want things to go back to normal around here." Malinda squeezed Abigail's hands back.

"Me too. I want our families to be able to spend Christmas together and go skating on the pond like we do every winter."

"Have they started cutting the ice yet?"

"*Nett* the area I shoveled to make the rink." The men cut slabs of ice for the *icehaus* during the winter. Still being able to skate after that depended on how hard of a winter they were having. This year she should be able to skate all season.

"Is that Abigail's voice I hear?" The cellar door opened and a draft of cold air came into the room with *Aenti*. Her hopeful smile faded as she set the handful of red potatoes on the counter. "I thought maybe your *mamm* came with you."

Abigail shook her head. "She misses you, *Aenti*. We all do." She edged toward the front door. "I should go."

"Tell your *mamm* I said hello." The harsh shadows under *Aenti's* eyes made her face look gaunt.

Abigail wasn't sure how to respond. She would be punished if anyone found out about her visit.

Malinda pulled Abigail's cloak. "I'll walk you to the door."

Abigail stepped into the howling wind and waved, then spotting Thomas looking out the sitting-room window, waved at him too. A gust sent cold air down her cloak. She clasped the wool material tighter at the neck and plodded toward home. She could have taken a shortcut through the woods and made it home faster, but at least the longer route was plowed.

By the time she reached the house, Abigail was shaking, having been out in the cold so long. A buggy was parked next to the house. On closer inspection, she recognized the horse was Micah's. Had something happened to Edith?

Abigail hurried into the house. Micah was standing in the foyer talking with David. Micah's hat was in his hand and melted snow puddled on the floor around his boots. The men's conversation halted.

"We were getting ready to send out a search party for you," Micah said.

"Is something wrong with Edith?"

"*Mammi* is fine." He eyed her carefully. "You're winded. You should have a seat and catch your breath."

"I'm fine." She stepped aside as her brother reached for his coat, then told Micah he'd see him on church Sunday.

Abigail ignored her brother's leaving. "Did your parents *kumm* back early?"

Micah shook his head. "Are you sure you don't want to have a seat?"

"*Nay, danki*, I said I'm fine. Then what is it? Why are you here?"

He looked downward a half second, then lifted his head. "I was worried. I had to *kumm* by and make sure you made it home."

A smile creased her lips. *He cared enough to harness his horse and drive over.* Her heart thudded against her chest. She buried her smile. "*Danki* for your concern."

He shrugged. "Which way did you walk?"

"I took the road so I wouldn't have to plow through the snow in the fields." He didn't need to know she'd stopped at Malinda's house. Abigail removed her cloak and shivered. Their house wasn't nearly as hot as Malinda's.

"I don't know how I could have missed you."

Mamm came around the corner from the kitchen. "I thought I heard your voice, Abigail." She smiled at Micah. "Would you like a cup of *kaffi*?"

"*Nay, danki*, I can't stay."

"Any word about your sister?"

Micah shook his head. "*Nett* yet, but I expect to get a letter any day."

"If something comes up and they don't get back for Christmas, I want you and Edith to eat supper with us. There's no sense in the two of you spending it alone."

"I wouldn't want to invade your family time."

Mamm shooed the air. "You are like family, Micah."

"*Danki*, I'm sure *Mammi* will like your cooking better than mine."

The door flung open as Peter and Daniel rushed inside, a cold draft following them.

Mamm pointed her index finger toward the door, prompting them back outside to stomp the snow off their boots, then she disappeared into the kitchen.

"Do you have a few minutes to talk?" Micah said.

Abigail motioned to the sitting room. "Let's go in the other room where it's warmer."

Micah looked down at his boots, then toward the kitchen.

"It's okay, *Mamm* won't say anything to you."

"You sure?"

"The floors need mopping anyway." She waved and he followed her into the other room. The drafty wood floors sent a shiver up her legs. Wearing wet stockings didn't help. It would take forever to feel her toes again. She stopped before the woodstove and extended her palms toward the heat.

"It took you forever to get home," he said. "You must be freezing."

She nodded. "I keep thinking about that homeless

man on the street. His shoes had holes, and he wasn't wearing socks. He didn't have a coat on either. He'll freeze to death outside."

"He's a drifter. I'm sure he's already moved on."

Abigail frowned. While walking home, she couldn't stop thinking about the man, but maybe that was because he reminded her of Thomas. Thomas seemed so lost and yet he was home.

"You have a big heart," he said.

She smiled. "That's better than hearing I have a big mouth."

His face reddened.

"I know I talk a lot," she said.

He cracked a smile. "You have a gift of gab . . . Gabby Abby."

This time, his tone indicated he was teasing. *Gabby Abby.* She had a pet name.

"I should get going. Is there a chance you can *kumm* earlier tomorrow? I'm really behind and could use more time in the shop."

"Have you considered hiring someone to help?"

"*Jah*, I hired you, Abby."

"I mean in the shop."

"Without training, which I don't have the time or patience to do, there isn't much someone could do."

"What about stoking the stove? You said you couldn't keep up feeding the woodstove."

"I don't know anyone available. The younger boys are in *schul* and everyone else is working."

"But would you use someone, say an *Englischer*, if he was available?"

He cocked his head and raised his brow. "You're *nett* thinking about giving that homeless man a job, are you?"

She chewed the inside of her lip.

"Abigail?" His eyes narrowed.

"*Nay. Nett* him." *But someone just as lost and lonely.*

. . .

Micah slowed Clover when he came to the corner of Rambadt and Trukenmiller and looked down the road toward the house. He shouldn't leave his grandmother alone anymore. But he also had Abigail's voice in his head, and he couldn't ignore her concerns about the homeless man.

He continued toward town. The snow hadn't let up. No telling if cars would see his buggy. It was crazy going into town in this weather. He should be home preparing something for his and *Mammi's* supper.

Micah rolled into the city limits and stopped next to the hardware store. The store was closed, the street bare. *This is stupid.* He was about to pull away when he spotted movement in the alley, so he climbed out of the buggy. Slowly, he edged toward the side of the building. "Hello?"

A man coiled in the fetal position was lying next to the wall. Micah moved closer, and a hand grabbed his ankle and held it tight.

The stranger peered up at Micah. "Don't you know it's dangerous after dark around here, kid?"

"I, ah . . ."

The stranger released his hand. "Get lost."

"Don't you have any place to go?" Micah blurted.

The man was silent.

Micah took off his coat and lowered it over the man's shoulders. "The wool lining might itch at first, but you'll get used to it." He turned and took a few steps toward his buggy.

"There's a church a few blocks down the road," the man said. "They leave the door open to the youth center on cold nights. Sometimes they leave sandwiches out."

Micah pivoted around. "Wouldn't you rather sleep inside where it's warm?"

"I didn't think I could walk that far."

Micah swallowed hard. The man's shoes were ragged to the point that several of his toes were exposed. "I'll give you a ride." He'd ridden in *Englisch* cars before but had never offered one a ride in his buggy.

The man pushed off the ground, clutching Micah's coat in his hand.

"You better put that on. It's much colder outside this alley."

The man shoved his arms into the sleeves, the hem resting well past his wrists. A little snug, but at least he could close the front. The wind sent a shudder down Micah's spine, but doing something for a stranger warmed his heart. He pictured Abigail smiling approvingly and for a half second considered offering the man a job, but chose to pray about it and leave the outcome in God's hands.

CHAPTER 9

W hat were you thinking, Abigail! I couldn't possibly give him a job." Micah snorted and a cloudy patch hung in the air.

He resembled a bull. Any minute he would start pawing at the ground, ready to charge if she didn't calm him down. She glanced over her shoulder at Thomas, standing a few feet away from Micah's workshop, who seemed oblivious to the situation. Abigail returned her focus on Micah. "You need help. Thomas needs a job."

"It's *nett* that simple. The Lambrights are one step away from a formal shunning because of him. I don't need that kind of trouble." His index finger went from tapping his chest to pointing at her. "And neither do you."

"You and Thomas used to be friends. Aren't you at least curious where he's been? What's happened to him?"

He stared silently, taking deep breaths.

She glanced again at Thomas kicking at the snow. "Thomas could use a friend—a godly example." *Lord, I thought Micah had a heart like Yours. Was I wrong?*

He groaned under his breath.

"Did Jesus hang out with the religious folks or with the sinners who needed to see His love?"

"Abigail . . ."

"We're supposed to be Christlike. A light for the world."

The tension etched across Micah's face softened and his squared shoulders rounded. "All right."

"Thomas is *gut* at keeping the fire going." She grinned at Micah. "And he doesn't talk much."

"I already said yes. Are you going to delay me from working *nau* by talking?"

She slapped her hand over her mouth and shook her head.

"I hope I don't regret this."

"You won't, I promise. *Danki*, Micah."

"You're hard to say 'no' to." His lips curled into a tight smile, then he muttered something under his breath she couldn't decipher.

She waved Thomas over to them before Micah had time to change his mind.

Dressed in brown camouflaged pants and a dark sweatshirt, Thomas lumbered toward them.

"You remember Micah, don't you?"

Thomas nodded, although Abigail wasn't sure if he was just agreeing.

"He wants you to help him today." She caught a glimpse of Micah's glare and shifted her stance to avoid seeing him. "Do what he says, okay, Thomas?"

Thomas nodded.

She smiled at Micah, but it weakened when he didn't

return the same gesture. She leaned closer to him and whispered, "Please be patient."

"You have no idea how patient I'm being." He gave her a fake smile, then he and Thomas headed to the shop.

Abigail plodded behind their lengthy steps. When she came to the door, Micah held up his hand, stopping her from entering.

"He'll be fine." Micah went inside the building, Thomas at his heels.

She stood still a moment and stared at the closed door, then pivoted to leave. Abigail hadn't made it more than a few feet before the shop door opened. She glanced over her shoulder as Micah shot outside, a grueling expression on his face.

He stormed up to her, head wagging. "You said he didn't talk much."

She swallowed hard. "He doesn't."

"For someone who doesn't talk much, he's got a very *worldly* vocabulary."

Abigail cringed. "Oh, did he start cursing again?"

The muscles in Micah's neck corded. "You knew?"

"I can explain," she said. "He has a steel plate in his head. The head injury causes him to behave oddly . . . sometimes."

Micah rubbed the back of his neck.

"He also has something called post-traumatic . . . stress," she added, not quite sure the full extent of what that was.

"He's *nett* the only one under stress at the moment."

She took a few steps backward. "Remember"—*oh, please remember*—"you're a light into darkness."

"Abigail Kemp." He crossed the distance between them with a few long strides. "You better pray he doesn't use the Lord's name in vain. If he does—he's off *mei* property."

She liked it better when he called her Gabby Abby.

. . .

"No wonder the woman's *nett* married. She's either talking nonstop or trying to fix everyone's problems. It's enough to make a man run for the hills," he mumbled to himself as he reentered the shop.

Thomas stood next to his worktable, eyeing the glass pieces Micah had made yesterday.

Micah drew a deep breath as he approached the work area. Perhaps if he explained to Thomas why his word choice wasn't acceptable, maybe they could move forward. Thomas had changed over the last ten years and more than just the different style clothes he wore.

Micah motioned to the snowflakes. "They're fancy, *jah*?"

Thomas nodded.

"I'm making them for an *Englischer's* wedding." He slipped his work gloves on, deciding to wait until the need arose to talk with Thomas about his worldly language. Meanwhile, he would pray the occasion wouldn't arise. Micah went to the kiln and opened the wood-burner hatch. "This is what I want you to do." He used the fire poker to stir the ashes, then added pieces of kindling. "We need to keep it hot."

Thomas nodded.

Micah prepared a batch of sand, lime-ash, and cullet, then mixed the ingredients using a metal rod. While the mixture molted, he unrolled a tube of light-weight packaging paper. Before he started making the new pieces, he wanted to wrap and box the other items so they didn't break.

Thomas watched as Micah carefully bundled up the glassware and set the crate aside. He appeared just as interested in how Micah collected the mass of molten glass on the end of the blowpipe and then worked it into a recognizable object.

"A star," Thomas said as the glass took shape.

Micah tilted his head to view it from another angle. Perhaps the snowflake wasn't so recognizable. He clipped the pliable glass off the end of his pipe.

Thomas went to touch it, but Micah blocked his hand.

"Hot. Very hot." He grabbed the roll of brown paper and tore off a small section. "Watch this." He tossed it on the snowflake. Flames engulfed the paper.

Thomas jumped back, his eyes wide with curiosity.

Micah tasked Thomas with adding more wood to the kiln while he formed another snowflake.

It wasn't long before Thomas anticipated what tool Micah needed and would hand it to him. Within an hour, Micah admitted to himself that having Thomas to keep the kiln stocked with wood made the process go faster than he had expected.

. . .

Lunch sat on the table uneaten. Abigail craned her neck to look out the window. The only sign of activity was the smoke coiling into the air from the pipe.

"Stop fretting, child. Micah will *kumm* in when he's hungry." Edith tapped the chair next to her. "Let's eat."

Abigail wasn't sure her nervous stomach could handle food. She'd prayed all morning that Thomas would hold his tongue and that Micah would find it in his heart to accept Thomas's help. She sat down and bowed her head. *Lord, please grant Micah patience. Give him eyes to see Thomas as a lost and suffering soul who needs compassion. And Lord, please give Thomas a reconcilable heart, and the understanding needed to break free of the worldly bondage and ask for forgiveness. And Lord, please watch over the homeless man. I don't know why You've placed him on mei mind so much these past few days. Will You please bless him? Amen.*

Edith smiled. "You've been praying all morning. Is something wrong?"

Abigail's stomach roiled. She set her fork down. "Do you think I should go out to the shop and tell Micah it's time to eat?"

Edith chuckled. "You act like a newly wedded woman."

Heat erupted on Abigail's cheeks. A pleasant thought that Edith hadn't ruled her out of finding a husband, even if it would never come to pass.

Edith lowered her fork. "You haven't been yourself all day. Is something troubling you?"

"I've had a lot on *mei* mind." She chewed her bottom lip. "Christmas is almost here. I thought I would knit Micah a pair of socks. Do you think he would like socks? Maybe I should make him something less personal. A plate of brownies . . . that's *nett* much of a gift."

"You could give him both." Edith smiled. "I have some extra wool if you'd like to get started on them today."

Abigail rose from the table.

"Don't you want to eat first?"

"Maybe I'll be hungry later. But please, you eat." She wet a dishrag and wiped the counter, pausing every few seconds to glance out the window. Maybe Micah was avoiding her. Is that why he hadn't come inside for lunch? "I pray he isn't upset with me still," Abigail whispered.

"If he is," Edith said, coming up beside her and lowering her plate into the sink, "he won't stay that way long."

"You didn't see the look in his eyes."

Edith frowned. "Were you talking over him again?"

"*Nay*, I—I don't think I did."

"Too pushy?"

Abigail nodded. "Definitely that."

"*Tsk-tsk*." Edith shook her head.

"I know. Men don't like pushy women." Looking back at the men who had offered to drive her home after a singing, they were equally as eager to drop her off by the end of the ride. She must have sounded pushy or talked so much their ears burned from her nervous chatter.

"At his age, a man is looking for a *fraa*—even if he isn't willing to admit it."

"I'm sure he'll find the right *maedel*." A pang of despair weighed her words. "I think I'll get started on those socks," she said over her shoulder as she fled the kitchen. Abigail blew out a breath once she reached the sanctuary of the sitting room. She eyed the basket but wasn't sure which ball of wool, the black or gray, Edith had planned to give her to use.

Edith joined her, taking a seat by the basket of yarn. She fished the black ball of wool out of her basket and handed it to Abigail.

"*Danki*." Abigail looped the wool onto her knitting needles, focusing on her work more than she needed. She had learned to knit at age eleven and could do it with her eyes closed without missing stitches.

"Do the youth still have singings on Sunday evenings in this district?"

"They do, but if you're wondering about Micah, he stopped going to them a few years ago."

Edith smiled. "What about you?"

"I haven't attended one since last year."

"That's where I met *mei* Abraham." Edith stopped knitting. "We sat across from one another and each time he snuck a peek at me, his face turned red. I thought he might never ask to drive me home." Edith sighed.

"That's why I'm buying a horse," Abigail said. Edith frowned, but before she could express any pity, Abigail elaborated. "I'm very excited. I've even started making a quilted horse blanket to put over him in the winter." Abigail kept her head down, not wishing to see the pity in Edith's eyes. Over the years she'd seen her share of disappointment in her mother's expression. Her knitting needles clacked as she went faster.

"How often do the women have sewing get-togethers?" Edith asked.

"Usually once a month, but I think several of the widows get together more often." Abigail appreciated the changed topic. It wasn't long before she had the top portion of one sock knitted.

The door opened and Micah entered.

Abigail shoved her knitting aside and stood. "You must be starved." She crossed the room, alarms firing when she didn't see her cousin. "Where's Thomas?"

"Outside."

"I'm sure he's hungry too. He didn't pack a lunch." She pushed the curtain to one side and peeked out the window. Thomas's shoulders were hunched and he was standing with his back against the wind. Abigail grew more irritated by the second. She spun around to face Micah. "Would you leave a stray dog outside in that *wedder*?" Without waiting to hear his reply, she marched into the kitchen.

"Abigail," Micah said, tromping behind her. "We need to talk."

CHAPTER 10

Micah stormed into the kitchen behind Abigail. "You certainly are quick to talk and slow to listen. You—you disregard the rules. You're blatantly defiant, is what you are."

Abigail didn't so much as flinch at his words. She merely opened the cabinet drawer, removed the bread knife, and began slicing the loaf.

"The *Ordnung* clearly directs us *nett* to break bread or fellowship with shunned individuals. You know the rules and yet you expect me to invite him to *mei* table?"

She twisted toward him, wagging the knife. "I expect you to have compassion."

His jaw twitched. In other words, she expected him to bend over backward for a man who wasn't part of the fold.

"Your food is on the table," she said.

He leaned against the counter beside her and folded his arms over his chest. The woman was impossible. He was a fool to be mixed up with her. Before the week was over she would have him standing before the bishop, giving account for his involvement.

Abigail opened the jar of peanut butter, dipped the knife inside, and pulled out a glob, then slathered the slice of bread rather thickly.

He cleared his throat, which drew her attention. Micah eyed the sandwich she was making. "Thomas must love peanut butter."

"Even a horse that works all day in the field is fed extra oats," Abigail mumbled. She dipped the knife back into the jar and plopped another mound on the bread. "Jesus didn't send the multitude away when they were hungry. He fed them."

"*Jah*, I know."

"Do you think Jesus sat on the other side of the mountain so He didn't have to fellowship with the sinners?"

Micah clenched his jaw.

"Of course He didn't. He had a heart for the lost." She exaggerated a shrug. "Shouldn't our actions and *compassion* toward others reflect His?" Her piercing eyes held his gaze.

Micah turned his attention to the sandwich. "That's a lot of peanut butter for someone to—"

"I'll replace the jar tomorrow." She punctuated each syllable through clenched teeth.

Micah pushed away from the counter and went to the far cabinet. He removed his father's thermos from the shelf, then filled it with milk. "If you'd give someone else a chance to talk," he said, setting the thermos on the counter in front of her, "maybe you'd discover I'm *nett* as inconsiderate as you think." He motioned to the sandwich. "All that peanut butter will stick to the roof of his mouth if he doesn't have something to wash it down with."

The lines softened between her big green eyes.

"*Danki*." She quickly collected the sandwich and container of milk, then headed toward the foyer.

"Hey." He rushed after her. "I wanted to talk with you about tomorrow." He reached the door at the same time and grasped her hand when she went to turn the knob. Her face angled toward him at the same time he moved closer. For a half second, they were nose to nose. He stepped back and his gaze traveled to her parted lips.

The thermos landed on his foot with a thump. He sucked in a breath and held it.

"I'm sorry. It slipped out of *mei* hands."

Her face turned beet red, a perfect distraction. His pulsating big toe was a dull throb in the back of his mind.

"Are you all right? Can you stand on it?"

"It's nothing. I'm fine. See?" He hobbled a few steps until he caught sight of *Mammi* in his peripheral vision.

Mammi placed her hands on her hips. "What's all the commotion about?"

"I dropped the thermos on his foot." Abigail grimaced when she looked at him.

"It doesn't hurt as bad as when Clover stepped on me."

"I see you two have everything under control." *Mammi* ambled back into the sitting room.

"What did you want to say about tomorrow?" Abigail asked.

"I need to pick up a few things in town in the

morning. I might *nett* be here when you arrive. Do you think Thomas is capable of getting the stove going so we can get started right away? I asked him, but I'm *nett* sure he . . . comprehends everything."

"You want Thomas to start the fire?" Her brows arched.

Micah nodded. "I believe he still wants the job."

"But I thought . . . Yes, he's capable."

He removed her cloak from the wall hook. "You might want to put this on."

The red of her cheeks deepened. She handed him the sandwich and thermos to hold while she slipped on her cloak and mittens. "Same time then?"

"*Jah*." He opened the door. "I'll give you a ride."

She smiled. "And Thomas too?"

The muscles in Micah's neck stiffened.

Her smile faded. "Never mind, we'll walk."

"Abigail . . ." He exhaled a long sigh. At least when Thomas worked inside the shop, the likelihood of anyone finding out, especially this close to Christmas, was minimal. Driving him home was a risk. Besides, Thomas lived a quarter mile down the road. He could walk.

The door closed hard behind Abigail.

Micah groaned. Didn't she care if they were shunned? He looked forward to eating Christmas turkey and fellowshipping on Second Christmas with the members of the settlement. Being treated as if he were a fence-jumper wasn't his idea of a merry Christmas.

. . .

Abigail held her tongue when Micah stopped the buggy fifty feet from Thomas's driveway. *Be grateful. It's better than walking,* she reminded herself.

Thomas climbed out of the buggy. "Tomorrow, *jah*?"

Micah nodded. "*Danki* for your help today."

"Tell Malinda," her voice squeaked, "I said hello."

Thomas nodded. "You skate tonight?"

"I don't—" Her throat dry, she turned and coughed into her fisted hand. "I don't think so." The scratchiness made her cough again.

"Okay." Thomas waved.

Micah clicked his tongue, and the buggy lurched forward.

Abigail rocked back against the bench. "You could have waited until he was farther off the road before pulling away." Her hoarse voice was barely above a whisper.

"I have things to do at home." He stared straight ahead.

She gazed out the window. Gray sky. Bare trees. It couldn't get much gloomier. "Do you think it'll snow tonight?"

"It's December."

She shifted on the bench to face him. "Do you find it strange that the spruce trees stay green all year?"

"They're called *ever*greens."

She shrank back against the seat. "You don't have to be snippy."

He tapped the reins, nudging his horse faster.

Abigail gripped the edge of the bench. "You certainly are in a hurry to get home."

He glared in her direction, then resumed watching the road. "Perhaps you should conserve your voice and *nett* talk so much."

Nett talk so much. She harrumphed. Was it getting hot? She removed her mitten and touched her forehead. Moist. Her throat hurt when she swallowed, and her body was beginning to ache all over. She shifted on the bench. If she hadn't promised her mother she would help sew the boys' new clothes for Christmas, she would go straight to bed.

Micah pulled into her driveway and stopped the buggy next to the porch.

"*Danki* for the . . . ride." Her voice strained. She started to get out, but his hand caught her arm.

"Are you going skating tonight?"

She glanced at his hand, then looked into his eyes. He had a strange way of showing interest. Lousy time to feel feverish too. Perhaps she could skate for an hour. She hated to turn down an invitation. "Are you asking me to go?"

He released her arm. "*Nay.*"

Anger infused her fatigue as she swung around to face him. The motion roiled her stomach and caused Micah to blur before her eyes. "Then what were you doing? Just seeing if I'd say yes?"

"What? *Nay.*" He shook his head as if reinforcing his denial.

"Never mind." Abigail lowered her head, hoping to conceal her disappointment, and scooted out of the buggy.

She cringed. Why did she think Micah was different?

He wasn't interested in spending any more time with her than he had to. Well, Christmas was only a few days away. Other than seeing him at Sunday services, he would disappear from her life soon enough. As she hurried up the porch steps, Edith's words ran through her mind. *"Men his age are looking for a fraa."* Her throat tightened. His grandmother couldn't be more wrong.

. . .

The early-morning frost sparkled across the field of snow as Micah headed into town. His thoughts of Abigail had consumed him most of the night and early into the morning. She was like a wild vine that somehow, through sheer persistence, entwined her life with his. The mere thought of Abigail conjured an image of her lively wide smile and big green eyes.

She stole his breath like no other woman had. *Don't fall in love.*

A gust of wind sent a chill down his spine. He held the reins with one hand and used the other to rub his arm. He wouldn't be so cold if he had his other coat. The one he wore now was lightweight and all right for working in the barn. The animals and hay kept the barn somewhat insulated. His thoughts skidded to Abigail's plan to buy Cactus. Stubborn woman— stubborn horse—neither of them trainable. He made a mental note to talk with her brother and father after church service tomorrow.

Micah pulled into the back parking lot of the hardware store where the owner kept the barrel of broken pieces of glass for him to recycle. He set the buggy brake and climbed out. The barrel was nearly empty. He'd hoped there would be more, but he wasn't one to look a gift horse in the mouth. Micah dumped the contents of the barrel into the plastic bin he kept in the back of his buggy, then went inside the store.

"I hear we're in for another storm," the clerk said as Micah approached the counter. "Big one."

"How many inches?"

"Could drop as much as two feet according to the news this morning." He removed the two bags of sand from the back shelf that Micah had special ordered and placed them on the counter. "Can I get you anything else?"

With what sand he already had, the two bags should be plenty to finish this project. "That will do it." He paid for the supplies.

"Drive carefully. I see it's already starting to snow." The clerk handed Micah his change.

"*Jah*, thanks." Micah gathered the bags in his arms. He had one more stop to make before heading home. He glanced up at the snow coming down. Another hour and the roads would be covered. He rounded the corner of the building and slid to a stop. The man he'd given his coat to was standing next to Clover. Micah cleared his throat. "Can I help you?"

He looked Micah's direction and smiled. "I saw you pull up."

The man dropped his hand from the horse's neck and moved toward the rear of the buggy. "You save broken glass?"

Micah nodded. "I turn it into art." He kept his tone steady despite his veins pulsating with unease. A narrow alley joining the parking lot wasn't the same one where he'd found the homeless man the other night. Perhaps he wanted another ride to the church down the road.

A garbage truck rumbled into the parking area, its brakes screeching to a stop. The driver rolled down his window. "Mind moving your buggy? I need to get to those Dumpsters."

"Sure." Micah untied Clover from the tree branch and, when he turned around, the homeless man was gone. He climbed onto the bench and clicked his tongue. *Better not to get too friendly with the stranger.*

Micah stopped at Gingerich's Market.

Fran waved as he entered the store. "It's really snowing hard, isn't it Micah?"

"*Jah.* I heard we might get two feet." He pulled the supply list from his pocket and glanced over it. Thankfully, it wouldn't take long to gather the items his grandmother had jotted down. He grabbed a basket and moved down the aisle. He found everything except the cookies, for which his mouth had been watering.

Micah spotted Fran stocking a shelf of canned goods and went over to her. "Have you moved Abigail Kemp's baked goods to another area? I can't seem to find them *nau.*"

"Oh, Micah, haven't you heard?"

CHAPTER 11

Smoke curled up from the workshop's stovepipe as Micah pulled into the yard. After what Fran told him about Abigail, he had half a notion to send her and Thomas both home. He stopped Clover next to the barn and remained in the buggy while he contemplated what he should do.

I care a great deal for Abigail, Lord. But she's going to bring condemnation on both of us. He rubbed his palms on his pant legs. *Why am I so torn about this? I know what I have to do.* Micah climbed out of the buggy, tied Clover to the post, and headed to the workshop. He couldn't go against the *Ordnung* any longer. *Rules were developed to keep us on the straight path.* But the closer he got to the building, the more disheartened he became. He'd also given Thomas his word. What good was his word if he didn't keep it?

"*You're a light into darkness. Thomas needs to see Jesus through you.*" Her words were difficult to dismiss. He groaned. No doubt Abigail's voice would be in his head forever. Micah glanced at the kitchen window but didn't see any sign of her. A flurry of wind sent a chill down his neck. He tugged on his lightweight coat and crossed the yard. He would break the news to Thomas first.

The heat from the kiln struck Micah immediately as he entered the shop. Thomas had followed instructions and kept the fire blazing. Micah's eyes needed a moment to adjust to the dim light. When they did, he sucked in a sharp breath. The ornaments and centerpieces he'd made yesterday were not on the table where he'd left them to cool.

"What did you do with the glass pieces?" Panic infused Micah's tone as he scanned the shelves, the inside of the scrap barrel. Everything was gone. Acid rose to the back of his throat. "Thomas, they were sitting on the table this morning."

"I wrap." Thomas shifted his feet back and forth.

"You wrapped them? In what? Where did you put them?"

Thomas shied away from Micah like a dog who'd been kicked. He lowered his head and went to the far side of the room and picked up a wooden crate. He carefully brought it to the worktable and set it down, never looking Micah in the eye.

Micah looked inside the crate. Everything was bundled in brown packaging paper. Too much paper, probably the entire roll, but wrapped nonetheless. "It's very fragile. You didn't break anything, did you? You need to tell me *nau* if you did." Micah lifted one of the larger pieces from the crate and eased it out of the paper.

"I was careful," Thomas said.

"*Jah.*" Micah exhaled his pent-up anger. "So I see." He

made a quick inspection of the other pieces. Everything had been double, even triple wrapped.

Thomas beamed. "I thought it would save some time."

Micah nodded. "You could have—" *used less paper.*

Thomas's smile faded. Vacancy replaced his child-like expression.

"Have patience with him." Recalling what Abigail had said, Micah patted Thomas's shoulder. "I really appreciate your hard work, *danki.*"

"Welkom." His smile returned.

Micah silently tried to formulate what he would say to Thomas about not working for him anymore, but every time he came close, Abigail's words came to mind. *"You're a light into darkness."* Micah shook his head.

He would be eaten up with guilt if he sent Thomas away now. He whispered a prayer, asking God to speak to the bishop's heart regarding the matter, then turned to Thomas. "Let's get to work."

. . .

Abigail lifted the cool rag from her forehead and squinted at Edith. "I'm supposed to be the one taking care of you."

"Nonsense." Edith set another steaming cup of tree-bark tea on the lamp table beside Abigail. "Are you feeling any better?"

"I think so." She turned and coughed into her hand. Abigail had drunk a cupful of the bitter fluid earlier at Edith's insistence that it would ward off the flu-like symptoms, but her body hurt like she'd been kicked by a mule.

Edith placed her hand on Abigail's forehead. "You're still hot."

"I keep alternating between fever and chills." Now her stomach burned, but something told her that was from the tree bark.

"Take a sip of the tea. I think it'll help." Edith sat in the rocking chair and picked up her knitting needles. "I pray you're over this by Christmas. I'd hate for you to feel run-down during the holidays."

"Me too." Abigail groaned. "I have less than a week to finish Micah's socks."

Footsteps thumped on the porch outside the window, then the door opened. Abigail caught a glimpse of Micah as he went into the kitchen. She pushed off the sofa, a *whoosh* of dizziness staggering her first few steps.

Edith toddled behind her.

Abigail made it as far as the kitchen entryway and leaned against the trim molding, perspiration beading her forehead.

Micah stood at the kitchen sink, drinking a glass of water. His Adam's apple bobbed up and down as he drank. He set the glass down and glanced over at her.

"Abigail isn't feeling well," Edith volunteered.

"What's wrong?" His tone was flat with lack of interest. Something had changed since lunchtime, when he'd come inside long enough to grab food to take out to the shop.

Edith placed her palm over her own forehead. "I'm feeling a little faint myself."

. . .

Micah came up beside *Mammi* and wrapped his arm around her waist as Abigail supported her other side. "Are you okay?"

"Help me into the sitting room, please." *Mammi* sounded frail. She collapsed in the rocking chair with a heavy sigh.

"Micah, I could drink a cup of tree-bark tea. It's in the pot on the stove. Make Abigail one too."

He hadn't made it out of the room before he heard *Mammi* call him back.

"Micah, *kumm* quickly." *Mammi* motioned to Abigail who'd broken out in a sweat. "Help her, please."

"I'll be . . ."

Abigail teetered as Micah placed his hand on her back for support. Heat radiated through her dress. He guided her to the couch.

"I'm sorry. I don't know what happened."

"No need to apologize." *Not for being sick.* Omitting the fact the bishop had stopped her from selling baked goods at the market was another issue. He glanced over his shoulder at *Mammi.* Her eyes were closed. "I'll get the tea."

"I can do it."

"You're *nett* in any shape to do anything." He went to the kitchen, found the pot of amber liquid simmering on the stove, and poured two cups. Abigail's eyes were closed and she was slouched against a pillow. He placed one cup on the lamp table beside her and gave the other one to his grandmother.

Mammi took a sip, then handed the cup back to him. "I'll drink it after I take a short nap." She pushed off the chair. "Watch over Abigail." She pointed to the rag at the end of the couch. "I've been keeping a cool cloth on her forehead. Don't let her fever get out of control."

"Ah . . ."

"Micah, I won't be able to rest unless I know she's being cared for."

"Don't worry. I'll keep an eye on her." *I'll drive her home.*

"I thought you would." She ambled down the hall toward the bedroom.

He looked at Abigail sleeping peacefully. He should wake her. She'd be more comfortable at home in bed. The cherry-red hue gave her face a nice glow. He eased her into a more comfortable position and placed the pillow under her head. She was warm, her face boiling.

Micah re-wet the rag and returned to the sitting room. Kneeling down beside the couch, he placed the cloth on her forehead.

"I'm sorry," she muttered, her eyes still closed.

"Don't be." He watched her a moment, purring like a kitten, then sat in the rocking chair. A surge of protectiveness rose up inside him. He wanted to take care of her in sickness, in health, from buying a dangerous horse.

Two hours went by before she stirred. Abigail

removed the cloth from her forehead and squinted at him. "How long have you been sitting there?"

He shrugged.

"Where's Edith?"

"Lying down." He rose from the chair and came up beside her. "Are you feeling better?"

"I think so." She placed her hand on her forehead.

He picked up the cup. "I'll warm this up."

She shook her head, then cringed as if doing so gave her a headache. "I don't want anymore." She pushed into an upright position. "I didn't mean to keep you from working."

"It's okay."

"I'm sure Thomas is waiting for you. You should go back to work."

Micah shook his head. "I promised *Mammi* I'd look after you. Besides," he said, walking toward the kitchen with the cup, "I sent Thomas home awhile ago." He dumped the contents from the cup into the sink, then placed the pot on the stove to reheat. One whiff of the steaming contents brought back memories of when his grandmother had brewed the bitter concoction for him.

. . .

"Honestly, Micah, I can't drink that." Abigail held up her hand in refusal.

"I know it doesn't taste very *gut*, but it's *gut* for you." He stood before her, cup in hand and not budging.

She shook her head. The aroma roiled her stomach. If she drank anymore, she wouldn't hold it down. But he planted himself, feet shoulder width apart and as concrete as a pillar of stone. "Fine." Abigail took the cup and held it, warming her hands. She peered up at him when he didn't move away.

"Drink it," he said.

She sipped the tepid fluid and grimaced. "I think I'm feeling better."

Micah took a seat in the rocking chair, planting his elbows on his knees and studying her. "I can't figure you out," he said.

"I'm *nett* complicated. What are you trying to figure out?"

"I stopped at Gingerich's Market this morning. I tried to buy some of your cookies."

She swallowed hard. "I'll make you a batch when I'm feeling better."

"Why didn't you tell me?" His stare bored a hole through her heart.

Mammi entered the sitting room. "I think the nap helped. How are you feeling, Abigail?"

"She's feeling better." Micah stood and motioned for *Mammi* to take the rocking chair. "I'll hitch the buggy. I'm sure Abigail is anxious to get home."

Abigail felt the air leave her lungs. For a few short-lived minutes he'd treated her so tenderly. Fran must have told him why her baked goods were no longer for sale at their market. He didn't waste time hitching the buggy. Micah came back inside, plucked her cloak off the hook, and held it out for her.

Silence made the ride home seem longer than usual. Micah stopped the buggy next to the porch steps.

When she didn't immediately climb out, he shifted on the bench to face her. "Do you need assistance up the steps?"

"*Nay.*" Her throat tightened. "Would you have hired me if you knew the reason Mr. Gingerich wasn't accepting *mei* baked goods anymore?"

"*Nay.*" His jaw muscle twitched.

Tears burned her eyes. "I didn't mean for you to—"

"Find out?"

She bowed her head. "I just wanted to be able to buy *mei* horse. I shouldn't have involved you."

"You shouldn't have gotten involved yourself."

"Don't say that," she said. "Thomas is *mei* cousin. His family prayed many years for him to return." *God, please forgive Micah. He should understand that Thomas needs a bit more grace.*

Neither of them spoke for a few moments.

Micah was the first to break the silence. "You should probably go inside *nau.*"

. . .

Thirty people sat wedged, like a dozen cookies in a box too small, in the bishop's sitting room for Sunday service. Abigail liked the summer months better when they could fellowship outside. She missed Malinda. The two of them always sat together in the back row along with the other unmarried women. Abigail looked beyond her sister Elizabeth and stole a glance at Micah, seated across the aisle. His solemn face tore at her heart.

She hung her head and closed her eyes. *Forgive me, God. I should be paying attention to the Scripture reading.*

The bishop would probably call her name at any moment and ask her to stand. She would have to give account to her actions. Abigail wasn't sure she could repent for helping the lost, feeding the hungry—despite breaking the rules of the *Ordnung*. Even under the weight of Micah's disappointment in her.

The service ended with a prayer.

Chatter about Christmas filled the room as the women made their way into the kitchen. Abigail rose from the bench. If she could go home without bringing attention to herself, she would.

Edith ambled toward her. "How are you feeling?"

Abigail forced a smile. "Better. And you?"

"I'm full of energy. Shall we go help the others prepare the meal?"

Apparently, the tea worked for her new friend; Edith was already heading toward the kitchen. Abigail trailed behind. Although once the meal was served, she planned to make an excuse to go home. Rounding the corner of the kitchen, she glanced over her shoulder at Micah. He stood near the woodstove talking with David and her father.

Micah stopped and looked her way a brief moment, as did her father and brother. Something in their riffled expressions told her they were discussing Cactus.

She lowered her head and continued into the kitchen. She had a suspicion that her dreams were about to be shattered.

. . .

That night at the supper table, her father finished the last bite of his cherry cobbler, set his fork down, and cleared his throat. "Peter, Daniel, if you two are finished, I'd like you to start the barn chores."

They pushed off their chairs at the same time and scampered out of the kitchen.

"Sadie, why don't you help your *bruders* tonight." *Daed* nodded toward the door, and she scurried out of the room.

With Elizabeth and David at the singing, it left Abigail alone with her parents. She stood and began gathering the dirty dishes.

"Have a seat, Abigail," *Daed* said.

She eased back onto the wooden chair.

"I understand you've been talking to Mr. Troyer about buying his horse."

Abigail nodded. "I've been saving for a year."

"She has, Emery," *Mamm* added.

"I don't want you buying that horse. He isn't the right one for you." *Daed* took a drink of coffee.

"Mr. Troyer has several horses for sale." Not that she could afford a different one.

"I'm referring to the one named Cactus. I'm *nett* familiar with the horse, but Micah tells me he's too high-spirited for you."

She chewed the inside of her cheek. Micah probably gave him an earful of other news too. "I'm *gut* with horses. You know that. I'll have Cactus trained in no time."

Her father shook his head. "I have to agree with Micah. He knows a lot about horses, and he claims that one has a bad disposition."

Mamm reached for her hand and gave it a gentle squeeze. "You'll find another horse—a better one."

Abigail nodded, but she found it difficult to believe. She never should have told Micah about Cactus. She wheezed.

"Are you feeling sick again?" her mother asked.

"*Jah*—" Her dry, scratchy throat made it difficult to talk. She turned her head and coughed, but it was more for a reason to be excused.

"I'll *reddy-up* the kitchen," *Mamm* said. "Go upstairs to bed."

Abigail looked at her father, then seeing his nod of dismissal, rose from her chair. She hurried out of the room before he could call her back and ask about her baked goods.

The Mason jar of money caught her eye the moment she entered her bedroom. It would take another year—maybe two—to save for a better horse. That's if she found another job. Micah wouldn't need her after . . . She dropped on her bed, buried her face in her pillow, and sobbed.

Several hours later, something hit Abigail's window with a thud. She squinted in the darkness. Another thud. This time Abigail could see the imprint of the snowball. Her sisters were fast asleep in their own beds on either side of her. She went to the window, spotted a flicker of lantern light, and lumbered downstairs to check out who it was. The last person to wake her up was James. Last spring he'd thrown pebbles at the window trying to get Elizabeth's attention.

Abigail slipped her bare feet into her boots and put on her cloak.

"*Psst.* Over here," Malinda whispered.

Abigail scurried across the lawn to the large maple tree. "What's wrong?"

"I had to talk to you." She sniffled. "I overheard *mei* parents talking about moving."

"Oh no. That's horrible news." Abigail wrapped her cousin in a tight hug.

"We're going to go live with *mei daed's* parents . . . in Lancaster." Her breath hitched.

"Because of Thomas?"

"I heard *mei daed* tell *mei mamm* we won't make it through the winter."

"Has he tried to talk to the bishop? What about *mei daed*? I'm sure someone would loan him money to get through the winter."

Malinda shook her head. "He's hardheaded, and he refuses to let *Mamm* ask your *mamm*." She wiped her face on her coat sleeve. "Do you know when Thomas will get paid?"

Abigail didn't even know if he still had a job. Micah had sent him home early. "Wait here." She retraced her steps back to the house, tapped her boots against the porch railing, and brushed the snow off the hem of her nightdress, then tiptoed inside and up the steps. She grabbed the Mason jar from the top of the dresser and made her way back outside.

Malinda shook her head when Abigail tried to hand

her the jar. "I can't take your savings. What about Cactus?"

"Your family needs it more than I do. Besides," she said with a winded sigh, "I'd like to think this was the reason God had Micah crush *mei* plans to buy Cactus."

"How did he do that?"

"He told *mei daed* that Cactus wasn't a *gut* horse for me, and *mei daed* listened."

"I'm sorry." Malinda patted Abigail's arm.

"So you can't move—unless you take me too. You're *mei* cousin, *mei* best friend."

Malinda hugged Abigail. "I don't know when we can repay you."

"It's a gift." Abigail smiled. "It's better to give than receive." She couldn't explain the warmth—the peace she was experiencing.

"I don't know how to thank you. You've blessed us more than I—"

"God blessed you. The gift is from Him."

CHAPTER 12

M icah paced to the end of his workshop and gazed out the window overlooking the house. He and Thomas had been hard at work over an hour and still there was no sign of Abigail. It wasn't like her not to show up.

Just then, a buggy pulled into his driveway. "I'll be back in a few minutes," he told Thomas, who was adding more wood to the kiln. Micah jogged up to the driver's side of the buggy and stopped short at the sight of Abigail's brother, David.

"*Guder mariye*," David said.

Elizabeth climbed out from the passenger side.

"*Mariye*," he muttered, turning toward Elizabeth. "Is something wrong with Abigail?" She'd appeared fine at church yesterday, although he never had a chance to ask if she was feeling better from her bout with the flu.

"*Nett* that I know of," she replied with a shrug. "She asked me to sit with your grandmother today. You do still need someone, right?"

"*Jah*." Micah had hoped to get the bulk of the work done by the end of the day.

"I have a few errands to run, so I'll catch up with you later," David said.

Micah nodded. He turned to Elizabeth as David's buggy pulled away. "Abigail didn't say why she couldn't come today?"

Elizabeth shrugged again. "She pulled the unfinished horse blanket out of the closet and asked if I had any unused material or an old dress she could have."

"I thought maybe since she was sick the other day . . ."

"I don't know, maybe she is. She moped most of yesterday."

Moped? That wasn't like Abigail. Perhaps she'd overdone it by attending services and she'd relapsed. She certainly wasn't someone to shirk work obligations. After all, she had sent Elizabeth in her place. But something Elizabeth said about Abigail wanting to work on an unfinished horse blanket niggled at him. Maybe she wasn't sick after all but was planning to follow through with purchasing Cactus. Would she ignore her father's wishes?

He went inside with Elizabeth and introduced her to *Mammi*, who had many of the same questions about Abigail's whereabouts. Then he tracked along the snowy path back to the shop. Maybe if he worked fast, he could visit her later this evening and get to the bottom of things.

· · ·

Abigail cut the dress Elizabeth had given her into strips. She'd never used a dress to make quilt binding, but she didn't have much choice. With only a few dollars to her name, she couldn't afford new material. Abigail spread the horse quilt out on the floor. It was larger than a full-size bed. She threaded the needle.

Her little sister Sadie poked her head into the room. "Do you have a pencil I could use? I've worn mine down to the nub and I need one for *schul*."

Abigail motioned to the table beside the bed. "There should be one in the drawer."

Sadie skirted the material on the floor so she didn't step on it. "Your blanket is big."

"*Jah*. Even looks big for a horse, doesn't it?"

Peter called for Sadie to hurry, a first for one of the boys to be eager to go to school. Sadie grabbed a pencil from the drawer and rushed out the door.

Abigail began sewing the strips of material together. She jabbed her finger with the needle several times trying to hurry. God had given her a purpose for the quilt—or so she believed after the dream she had last night.

Abigail steadily stitched the material in place, turning the strip just right to miter the corners. Without having anyone to talk to, she progressed quickly. She stitched the two ends together.

Hours later, she rubbed the kinks in her neck muscles. "Lord, if this is Your will, please give me favor for borrowing *Daed's* buggy." She stood, folded the quilt, then went downstairs.

Seated at the kitchen table, *Mamm* looked up from darning socks. "Are you feeling better?"

Abigail nodded.

"I have a pot of stew and biscuits ready for lunch." *Mamm* glanced at the wall clock. "Your father and David should be in any minute. They're working on something *privately* out in the barn. I think I might be getting a new rocking chair for Christmas."

Her mother had hinted ever since the leg on the old one cracked. Their family made most of their gifts for each other and had fun teasing one another about the surprise. *Don't lament over what's already done*, she chided. Needs must always come before wants, even if it's another person's need. And Malinda's family needed the money.

Lord, You gave me peace last night about giving the money away. I don't want to grumble or have any regrets about it now. I did the right thing.

"I think your *daed* is trying his best to cheer me up. This will be the first Christmas without *mei* sister and her family."

"Have you talked with *Aenti* Doreen lately?"

Mamm frowned. "You know I haven't."

"I just thought with Christmas a few days from *nau* maybe . . ."

Daed and David were in the midst of a friendly debate over fertilizers when they came in from the barn.

Mamm set her sewing aside and went to the stove.

Abigail loitered by the kitchen entry, listening to her *daed* and brother's conversation as they removed their coats and hats. *Daed* chuckled over something David said. Abigail smiled. Asking to borrow his horse and buggy was easier when he was in a jovial mood. She scooted over to the counter beside her mother as they approached the kitchen.

Daed tilted his head and drew in a breath through his nose, as he always did. "Something smells *gut*."

Abigail recalled Micah's expression the first day she had worked for him. She had pretended not to notice how long he'd looked at her. She pushed the thought aside. If he'd been interested in her, he would have never shot down her dream to own Cactus.

"Place the biscuits and butter on the table please," *Mamm* said.

Abigail did as her mother requested. Once they were all seated and prayers were said, she turned toward her dad. "Would it be possible for me to borrow the buggy?"

David groaned. "I wanted to use it to go—"

Daed lifted his hand, cutting David off. *Daed* gave Abigail his attention. "Where do you plan to go?"

"Into town." *Daed's* scrutiny was difficult to avoid. She shifted on the chair. Did he know something about Gingerich's?

Mamm broke the tension. "Don't you think you should stay home and rest? You haven't been feeling well lately."

"I don't have a fever." Abigail briefly placed her hand on her forehead. "It's just a sore throat," she rasped.

"That sounds like laryngitis to me." *Mamm* took a sip of tea.

David lifted his fork and paused before it reached his mouth. "Well, if she's *nett* going to use the buggy, can I?"

Daed shook his head at David, then turned to her. "Abigail, you can use it."

"*Danki*, I won't be long," she said, more for her brother's benefit. She soaked the corner of a biscuit in the stew gravy, then took a bite. She loved the flavor of the beef and the fresh vegetables they had canned from the garden last summer.

Daed and David's conversation about farming continued. *Mamm* talked about a new recipe for turkey stuffing she planned to make for Christmas, and Abigail offered to make the sweet-potato casserole since everyone liked it last year. In a short time, the Christmas menu was planned as well as what they would bring to the district fellowship on Second Christmas. Abigail had always looked forward to the district fellowship on the day after Christmas, but this year, without Malinda, Abigail wasn't sure she wanted to go.

"I'll harness Molly," *Daed* said after he finished eating. He and David returned to their project in the barn while Abigail and *Mamm* cleaned the dishes.

"I've started a list of things we'll need," her mother said. "I thought you could stop by Gingerich's Market while you're in town."

"All right." Abigail hadn't planned on going to the market. She scanned the list. This wasn't too bad. She should be able to get in and out quickly.

• • •

The pungent aroma of evergreen filled her senses as Abigail entered Gingerich's Market. She hurried through the aisles, collecting the items on the list, then sucked in a breath when she approached the register.

"Abigail, I'm glad you came in." Fran held up her index finger. "Wait here a minute." She disappeared into the back room and returned a moment later with an envelope. "You left so suddenly the last time you were here that I didn't have a chance to pay you for your baked goods." She handed Abigail the envelope.

"*Danki.*" Abigail smiled. She still had a few Christmas gifts to buy.

"I've had several customers ask about your cookies and pies," Fran said.

Abigail bit her tongue. She wanted to believe Fran was her friend and wouldn't spread gossip, but she'd told Micah everything.

Fran rang up the items on the counter. "Hopefully, you'll be able to sell your baked goods again soon."

"*Jah*, maybe." Christmas had always been her busiest time of the year. She missed those sales. Abigail paid for the grocery items. "I hope you have a merry Christmas."

"You too. I'll see you at the fellowship on Second Christmas."

Abigail forced a smile and held it until she was out the door. This year wouldn't be the normal joyful occasion. How could it be without a *bu*, a horse, or her cousin? She had nothing to be joyous about. She placed the sacks of groceries into the back of the buggy. After stopping to buy a new lantern for her mother and puzzles for Edith for Christmas, she searched for the homeless man.

Her gaze landed on a man slumped against the

hardware store. He was wearing what looked like an Amish-made coat. Abigail grabbed the quilt from the bench and a few bananas from the bunch.

"Hello again," she said, walking up to him.

He grumbled something undecipherable when she repeated the greeting. When he turned, she got a better look at the coat. Wool-lined, hand-sewn stitches. It was Amish made. She held up the bananas. "I thought you might like these."

He peeled one and took a large bite.

She debated whether she should ask about the coat. It certainly wasn't something he would have found in a Dumpster. "I thought you might need a blanket." She set it down next to him. "I made it."

He continued chewing.

She stood there a moment. "I should probably go. Nice visiting with you." She turned away.

"Why are you doing this?" His words slurred. "Strangers go by me every day. They step over me and don't acknowledge me, but you . . . you not only acknowledge me, you give me stuff."

"God placed you on *mei* heart," she answered.

"Why? I'm no one."

"Jesus loves you."

The man huffed. "I don't know why He would."

"His love is unconditional."

"I heard that before." He flung the banana peel across the alley, draped the quilt over his shoulders, then slumped against the brick building and closed his eyes.

Her shoulders slumped. *Lord, why did You place him on mei heart if what I say makes no difference?*

CHAPTER 13

"Did Elizabeth mention anything about Abigail?" Micah asked nonchalantly as he added a log to the woodstove in the sitting room.

"She said plenty." *Mammi* continued to knit.

He tossed in another log. "Did she say why Abigail didn't come today?" He closed the firebox hatch and adjusted the flue.

His grandmother furrowed her brows at him. "She was upset about a horse. Apparently someone told her father the horse was no good, and he stopped the sale."

"It isn't a *gut* horse."

"You don't understand. Buying that horse represented independence for her."

"A headstrong woman with independence isn't a *gut* combination." He stormed into the kitchen. Someone needed to stop her from buying that horse. He'd done the right thing.

Mammi lumbered into the kitchen. "She's of the marrying age . . ."

His eyes widened. And she was telling him, why? Micah filled a glass with water and took a drink.

"When a woman reaches a certain age . . ." She

touched his arm with her frail hand. "She starts planning her future. For Abigail, it's buying a horse."

He eyed her closely. She cared a great deal for Abigail. "Why are you telling me this, *Mammi*?"

"Be her friend, Micah. If that horse isn't the one she should buy, help her find the right one."

"I'm *nett* sure that's a *gut* idea." The past two weeks he spent with her had sent him into a tailspin. He hadn't sorted his feelings out yet. He only spoke up about the horse because . . . he cared for her. "I wouldn't want her to get the wrong idea."

Mammi chuckled. "If she were interested in you, she wouldn't be looking to buy a horse. She'd be pampering you with cookies and pies." She patted his arm. "I think you're safe."

Safe. That should have pleased him, rather than knot up his insides.

. . .

Abigail skated to the center of the rink and spun in a tight circle. She liked to skate while the younger children were in school and she had the rink to herself. Abigail glided with her hands behind her back, making long, graceful strides. The air was cold on her face and white puffs of foggy breaths escaped her mouth when she increased her speed. After baking Christmas cookies all morning, it felt good to spend time outside.

She circled the rink several times, relaxing to the sound of blue jays chirping nearby. The two-acre man-made pond was a natural resource for wildlife and a place to harvest ice for their settlement's *icehauses* in the winter, but to her, it was a slice of heaven.

"I thought you were sick," Micah called out.

Abigail's blades went out from under her and she landed on her rump. She caught a glimpse of him shuffling over the ice toward her and pushed to her feet.

"You okay?"

"I'm fine." If she didn't think about how painful it was to land on her tailbone. Her ankles wobbled. Sometimes standing still on ice was more difficult than moving. "How long were you standing there?"

"Long enough to know you're *nett* sick."

"Who said I was?"

He shrugged. "I guess I was hoping you were."

She snorted. "Gee, thanks." She swiped at the snow on her dress skirt.

"That came out wrong." He kicked at a clump of snow. "I was hoping you weren't upset with me."

"So you're sorry you told *mei* father about Cactus?"

"*Nay.* I had to."

Abigail skated past him, the blades scraping against the ice. Nearing the edge of the pond, she dragged the tip of her blade over the ice to slow down. She stormed off the rink, trekked through the snow to where she'd left her boots next to the old oak tree, and plopped down.

He came up beside her, breathing heavy. "Don't be angry. That horse is trouble. He requires a strong hand."

"*Jah*, so I heard." She unlaced her skate and jerked it off her foot.

He handed her boot to her. "There are other horses for sale. Better ones. Safer ones."

It didn't matter now. Even if she found one for the same price as Cactus, it would take another year to save up. She slid her foot into her other boot, tied the laces of the two skates together, and stood.

"I didn't want you to get hurt . . . I care about you."

She allowed his words to register.

Micah broke eye contact and glanced at the ground.

He must mean like one of her brothers. She dismissed the glint of hope that his words could mean something more and turned toward the path home.

. . .

Micah raced to catch up to Abigail. "I'll help you buy a better horse."

She stopped, her brows crinkled with puzzlement. "Why would you do that?"

Micah cupped his hands on her shoulders. "I told you . . . I care about you." Saying it the second time was easier. "I'll carry these." He lifted the skates off her shoulder.

Except for the snow crunching under their feet and the occasional branch snapping under the weight of heavy snow, they walked in silence.

And he couldn't stand it.

"There's only three days until Christmas," he said, breaking the silence.

"Are you going to complete your order on time?" Flecks of snow glistened on her face.

"I think so. The cake topper and centerpieces are finished. Tomorrow I'll make the remaining snowflakes."

Abigail smiled. "I'm happy for you."

The Kemp's barn was in the distance. The trail would end soon. Micah moved ahead of Abigail and stopped her. "*Mammi* would like you to *kumm* back. She wanted me to remind you that your knitting project is at the *haus*."

Abigail bowed her head.

"Can I tell *Mammi* you'll be there tomorrow?" *Please.*

She shrugged without looking up.

He lifted her chin and swallowed hard when their eyes met. His focus shifted to her lips. "I'd like to see you tomorrow too," he said, leaning closer.

"You would?" She jerked her head back.

Stupid move. He'd almost kissed her. Now she was blushing.

"I, ah . . . I didn't mean to . . ." He hadn't felt this foolish in a long time.

"I'll be there bright and early." She stepped away, then smiling awkwardly said, "I should probably get home."

He nodded.

They plowed through the snow at a quick pace. Minutes later, they'd reached her yard and his buggy. "See you tomorrow." He nervously untied Clover from the post.

"Tell your *mammi* I said hello." She hurried up the porch steps and shot him a wave before disappearing inside the house.

Micah grimaced at the sight of her skates still draped over his shoulder. He climbed the steps two at a time and knocked on the door.

Abigail answered. "Did you forget—" She noticed the skates he was holding.

Abigail's mother came around the corner of the kitchen. "I intended to tell you earlier, Micah. We'll be eating Christmas dinner around four." She glanced at Abigail. "Did Micah tell you? He and his grandmother will be spending Christmas with us."

Abigail faced him. "You heard from your parents?"

"*Mei* sister had her *boppli* last Friday, but he's still in the hospital."

"What's wrong?"

"He had breathing problems. *Mei mamm* doesn't want to leave Lancaster until they know more about his condition."

"I insisted he and Edith spend the holiday with us," Mrs. Kemp said.

Abigail smiled. "The more the merrier."

He handed her the skates. "I'll see you tomorrow." Micah left, repeating her words to himself. *"The more the merrier."*

Was that sarcasm?

. . .

After hearing that Micah and Edith would be spending Christmas with them, Abigail worked herself into a frazzle scrubbing the floors and washing windows. With only two days until Christmas, she worked well into the night. Cleaning helped burn off pent-up energy, and she was exhausted by the time she dropped into bed.

Her thoughts flitted between what still needed to be done before Christmas to the shudder that went through her when Micah had lifted her chin. Her breath caught in her chest just as it had when they were standing so close and he'd leaned toward her. He would have kissed her if she hadn't interrupted him. Now she might never know what that would feel like.

Abigail covered her mouth to stifle her groan. She'd ruined the moment. He'd joked that she had a gift of gab—now it felt more like a curse.

CHAPTER 14

The following morning Abigail stood on Micah's front porch, her nerves jittering as if she'd consumed a whole pot of coffee by herself. She brushed the snowflakes off the front of her cloak, drew in a deep breath, and exhaled slowly. "Relax," she told herself. "It's just Micah." *Just Micah.* She shuffled her feet, unable to stand still. "Why am I nervous? I'm *nett* normally nervous. He's just—"

Footsteps clomped on the steps behind her. "He's just what?"

Abigail twirled at the sound of Micah's voice. Heat spread over her face.

"So why are you so nervous?" He grinned. "Is Miss Gabby Abby tongue-tied?"

"I, ah . . . Have I ever been tongue-tied?" She shook her head. "I'm *kalt.*"

"Hmm . . . I thought those rosy cheeks meant something else." He reached for the doorknob and held it. "I am glad you came today."

She brushed imaginary flecks of snow off her cloak. "Two more days, *jah*?"

He shrugged. "I'm hoping to complete the order today."

"Then this will be *mei* last day." She tried to mask her disappointment with a smile.

He opened the door and motioned for her to go ahead of him.

Edith greeted her at the door with a wide smile that reached her eyes and deepened the lines around them. "It's *gut* to see you, Abigail. I missed you." She shrouded her in a warm hug.

Micah moved past them, went into the kitchen, and returned with a cup of coffee as Abigail removed her cloak. "I'll be out in the workshop if you need me."

Edith shuttled Abigail into the kitchen. "We'll fill our cups with *kaffi* and take it into the sitting room. I'm sure you'll want to work on those socks for Micah."

Abigail picked up the cups and carried them into the sitting room.

Edith settled into her chair and began knitting. "Micah mentioned your mother invited us to spend Christmas at your *haus*." Edith glanced up and smiled. "I think Micah is looking forward to it."

"You think so? I mean"—she gulped a breath—"did he say that he was?"

"Oh, sweet child, it's what he doesn't say that's important."

Abigail crinkled her nose. "I'd rather him speak his mind than have to decipher what he isn't saying."

"Perhaps you should just practice being a bit more quick to listen and slower to speak."

"*Jah*." Abigail resumed knitting. Her situation was

hopeless. She would be an old maid before she developed the traits Micah wanted in a *fraa*. She wouldn't dwell on it. God never promised her a husband.

"Do you like to garden? I used to put in a large garden every year," Edith said.

Abigail appreciated Edith changing the subject. "I love working in the garden. Did you have problems with aphids? Last year they destroyed *mei* cucumbers."

"Ah, you can rid them with a mixture using the rinds of lemon and oranges. Just spray the plant leaves every few days."

"I'll have to try that this summer."

The two women continued to chat while they knitted. A few hours later, Abigail tied off the end stitch on the wool sock. She lifted it up to show Edith. "This one's done. *Nau*, I just need to make its mate."

"That's *wunderbaar*."

Abigail examined the sock closer. "It's too long, isn't it?"

"Is it a knee sock?" Edith chuckled.

"*Nay*." Her eyes widened at the thought.

"Don't fret. It'll shrink."

"*Jah*, after a few washings." Abigail laughed as she reloaded the wool yarn on her empty needle.

Micah poked his head around the wall of the sitting room. "Sounds like a *frolic* in here."

Abigail shoved her knitting aside. "Is it lunchtime already?" She bounded out of the chair, bolted past him to the kitchen, then grabbed a knife from the drawer to slice the bread. She had planned to make macaroni and cheese, but sandwiches would have to do.

He entered the kitchen. "I'm early."

She glanced at the wall clock. "*Jah*, you are. It's half past ten. You must *nett* have eaten a big breakfast."

"Thomas didn't show up today. I was hoping you might have a few minutes to help me."

"Abigail would love to help," Edith interjected. She smiled at Abigail. "Wouldn't you, dear?"

"Ah . . ."

"Don't worry about me," *Mammi* said, holding up her hands. "I won't touch the stove."

Abigail set the knife on the counter. "Let me get *mei* cloak." The way the wind had howled all morning, it must have been difficult to keep the fire going without Thomas.

Edith came to the door with a plate of cookies as they were leaving. "In case you get hungry."

Micah took them. "*Danki, mei* stomach is already growling."

The wind was stronger than Abigail anticipated. Her bonnet lifted off her head and would have blown away had she not held the strings.

Micah went ahead, opened the door, and ushered her into the warm building. He set the plate of cookies on the bench next to the wall of shelves.

Abigail's gaze fell on the shiny glass doves sitting on the steel table. "You've put a lot of details in the doves' wings. They're beautiful."

He came up beside her. "This is the cake topper."

"It must be a fancy wedding."

"Much fancier than any Amish wedding I've been to." He went to the kiln and opened the fire hatch.

She focused on the other glass pieces, admiring the intricate details. "You're very talented. Are the snowflakes hard to make?"

"*Nay.* I can make them in *mei* sleep." He tossed a chunk of wood into the furnace, closed the hatch, then swept his hands of bark. "It'll take a minute or two to melt the glass."

She smiled nervously. "So, what would you like me to work on?"

He went to the shelf and removed a roll of brown paper, then looked it over. "Hopefully there's enough paper. Thomas got a little carried away with wrapping the other pieces."

Abigail took the roll from Micah. "I prayed every day that you and Thomas would work well together, and that Thomas would want to return to the church."

"He lived in the world a long time. He's changed a lot."

Abigail spread the paper over the table next to the glasswork. "I know you're right. But I still believe that God can restore his mind so that he has the ability to know right from wrong and can repent." She picked up the smallest piece and wrapped it in the paper first.

"I only heard him curse the first day," Micah said with a shrug. "That must mean something."

"I hope so."

Micah set a wooden crate beside her. "Try not to pack them too tight."

He returned to the stove and added more wood. A few minutes later, he dipped the end of the pipe into the molten glass and twirled it slowly.

Abigail watched in awe as he shaped the glass into a deer. "You make that look easy."

"Just takes practice." He smoothed the hooves of the deer with a flat piece of wood, then eased it into a standing position on the table.

"I'm amazed at your talent."

He looked down, a humble gesture.

"I'm sorry. I didn't mean to embarrass you. I joke about God giving me a gift of gab, but He's clearly given you a *real* gift."

"*Danki*," he said softly. "I view it as a means to one day . . ." He moved in front of the kiln, then dipped the end of the pipe into the molten glass and began twirling.

"One day what?"

"Support a family," he replied, keeping his focus on the end of the pipe. Then, as if cutting off further discussion, he removed the pipe, twirled it a few times, and lifted the end to his mouth. He made another deer, this one with antlers.

Abigail stared at the glowing glass. "It's perfect."

He set the pipe down and eyed his work. "They can be better." His gaze traveled to the end of the table where the snowflakes sat that hadn't been wrapped.

Abigail ripped a section of paper off the roll. "Sorry, I guess I was distracted." She picked up an ornament and gently wrapped it in the paper. "I like that you made each of the snowflakes different."

"It wasn't intentional."

She folded the paper over another piece. "God makes each snowflake different, yet it all blends into a beautiful landscape of snow." She placed the glass ornament into the crate, catching a glimpse of his smile. "It's one reason I like winter."

"Each person is unique too." His gaze met hers.

"*Jah*," she muttered, mesmerized by his eyes. "Why aren't you married?" It wasn't until his smile dropped that her words registered. She hurried and wrapped the last piece, then added it to the crate with the others. "Should I add more wood to the kiln?"

"It doesn't need any."

She reached for the crate. "I can move this out of the way. Where should I put it?" She grasped the wooden handles and lifted it. Her muscles strained under the weight, but Micah lunged forward and supported the container.

"I have it," he said calmly. "You can let go of it *nau*."

Abigail released her hold.

"I've been loading the crates in the back of the buggy." He headed to the door.

She raced around the other end of the table and held the door open. Abigail followed him outside. "I'm sorry if I embarrassed you."

"You didn't." He stepped cautiously through the snow.

"Well, I shouldn't have asked that."

His foot slipped, and the glass rattled inside the box.

Abigail reached for the container, placing her hand on the bottom of the wooden slats.

"*Danki*. I think with your help keeping it steady, we'll make it." He smiled.

She kept her hand in place and stepped backward.

"Why don't you have a *bu*?"

"Do you really need to ask?" Her foot landed on an icy patch and she lost her balance. Somehow, her feet tangled with his and they both crashed to the ground.

He closed his eyes and held them shut for several seconds, grimacing.

"Are you okay?" she asked.

"I am. Are you?" He pushed to his knees and began collecting the scattered pieces.

"I'm sorry. I must have stepped on a patch of ice." She should have paid closer attention to where she was walking.

"Are you hurt?"

She shook her head. "But your glass. Oh, Micah, I'm sorry."

"It was an accident. It's *nett* your fault. I'm glad you didn't get hurt." He reached for her hand, helped her up, then gathered the last few items and placed them in the crate.

"Do you think they all broke?" She bit her bottom lip.

"We'll know in a few minutes." He carried the container back into the shop.

Abigail held her breath, watching him carefully remove each piece and unwrap it. So far, three snowflakes had chipped glass.

He peeled back the paper on a dove and sighed.

The wing had broken off.

Tears pricked her eyes. He wouldn't have fallen if she hadn't slipped. Now his hard work lay in shambles.

Micah inventoried the pieces and blew out a breath. "Nothing broke that Thomas wrapped." He shook his head as if in disbelief. "I kept telling him *nett* to use so much paper . . ." He smiled. "I'm glad he didn't listen to me."

"I am too." She sniffled.

His expression sobered. "Don't cry, Abby."

She cracked a smile. "You forgot Gabby."

He cupped her face in his hands and brushed away her tears with his thumbs. "Don't cry, Gabby Abby. We have time to remake what broke."

"Are you sure?"

He smiled. "If you're still willing to help."

Light flooded the room. Micah dropped his hands, and his face paled.

The door closed and Abigail recognized Bishop Schwartz's shadowy figure before he spoke.

"Micah, I'd like to speak with you about a matter that's *kumm* to *mei* attention." His stern glare fell on Abigail as he approached them.

She swallowed hard. The bishop's sister Velda must have filled his ears. *Say something.* Her throat tightened.

Micah turned to her. "Will you go into the *haus* and check on *Mammi*?"

No, she had to set things straight.

"Please," Micah said.

Abigail nodded. She hurried to the door without looking back. *Lord, I never meant to get Micah into trouble.* This was all her fault. *Please forgive me, Lord.*

Tears streamed down her face as she crossed the yard to the house.

Edith glanced up from her knitting when Abigail entered the sitting room. "Is everything all right?"

"*Jah*." She hesitated, then blurted, "*Nay*, I don't think it is." Abigail went to the window and looked toward the workshop.

"What is it, dear?"

Abigail closed her eyes. "I made a mess of things."

"Was Micah short with you again? I'll have another talk with him."

"*Nay*." Abigail moved away from the window. "The bishop's here to have a word with Micah."

"Perhaps he's inquiring about Micah's sister's new *boppli* or when his parents are expected home."

Abigail picked at her nails. "It's something else. I'm afraid I've gotten him into trouble."

Edith's expression sobered. "Why do you say that?"

"Thomas, the man who helped Micah the past two weeks, is a fence-jumper. He left the faith several years ago. He's Malinda's *bruder—mei cousin*, and . . . and her family has been given the silent treatment ever since they took Thomas back into their home. They'll be formally shunned any day. The bishop was lenient, but Thomas hasn't shown any interest in returning to the church." She pointed to her head. "He has a brain injury. I don't think he's capable of repenting."

Edith was silent several seconds. The lines in her forehead deepened. "I suppose that is a lesson for us all. We must remain close with God at all times. We don't know what tomorrow holds."

"*Jah*, that is true."

"Another reason we must separate ourselves from the world."

From Thomas. Abigail's heart grew heavy. *God,*

Your word says You are faithful even when we are nett. Why would Jesus tell the story about the prodigal *sohn* if it wasn't a message of forgiveness?

Abigail turned to look out the window and gasped. Thomas was traipsing across the yard. "I have to stop him." She rushed out the door without taking time to put on her cloak and met Thomas at the corner of the shop.

"Thomas."

A smile lit his face. "*Hiya.*"

"Hello." She hugged herself, trying to get control over her shivering. "Would you bring an armload of firewood into the *haus*, please?" She reached for his arm and turned him toward the woodshed. "I'll show you where the wood is kept."

CHAPTER 15

Micah's heart thudded against his chest as Bishop Schwartz quietly surveyed the glasswork on the table.

Bishop Schwartz rounded the corner of the work area, his attention still on the glass. "You do nice work, Micah."

"*Danki.*"

The bishop shifted his gaze to Micah. "I understand Thomas Lambright has been helping you."

Micah cleared his throat. "*Jah*, he's been loading the kiln with wood. I received a large order that's due tomorrow, and I needed to hire temporary help."

"I see." Bishop Schwartz glanced over his shoulder at the kiln. "I've never seen a stove like yours."

"Would you like to see it in operation? As you can see by the broken pieces, I have some things to remake." Micah went to the stove and opened the fire hatch. Perhaps if the bishop observed the glassblowing process, he would understand the importance of maintaining the fire and the need to hire Thomas.

"*Mei* kiln is small and doesn't hold a lot of wood."
Micah added a few slabs of wood. "The advantage is
it doesn't use much space, but the disadvantage is that
it requires constant wood." He gathered the raw products necessary, mixed a small batch, and within a short
time, the molten glass bubbled to the surface.

Bishop Schwartz stepped back. "Is it as difficult to
manage as it looks?"

"Once you get into the rhythm, it's like milk-
ing a cow." Micah rotated the pipe in the hot glass.
Manipulating the molten glass was easier than looking the bishop in the eye. He needed additional time to
gather his thoughts. As it was, he couldn't keep Abigail's
voice from invading his mind. *"Thomas needs to see
Christ's love through us—the members of our district."*
Micah blew gently into the end of the pipe, rotated it a
few times, then blew again. He formed the body of the
dove within a few minutes, adding the feather details
with a metal blade.

Bishop Schwartz cleared his throat. "I'm sure you
heard that after Thomas left the faith, he joined the
armed service."

"*Jah*, I did." Micah snipped the end of the dove,
releasing it from the pipe, then gently lowered it to the
table. "But he came home."

"So he did." The bishop crossed his arms over his
chest. "I'm *nett* convinced he's given up the world.
Wouldn't you agree he's still worldly in many ways?"

Micah shrugged. "If I judged him solely on his
actions the first day, then yes, I would agree. But the
longer I worked with Thomas the more I could see he

was trying." Micah paused, then added, "In the Bible, the father prayed for the prodigal *sohn* to return. Do you think he came covered in pig slop or cleaned up?"

Bishop Schwartz let out a long breath.

"Thomas might have returned because of a head injury, but I believe it was God's will for him to come home," Micah said. "Perhaps this is a test for the church members. Do we forgive?"

"Thomas hasn't asked to be reconciled with the church—with God."

"Jesus loved us when we were yet sinners," Micah said softly, adding, "He also said, 'Let the children come unto me.' In some ways, Thomas has reverted back to being a child, because of the injuries he sustained. Perhaps if we accepted him . . . as he is *nau*, he might see the light of Christ through us."

Bishop Schwartz stared at the floor several seconds, then looked up. "I understand your parents have been delayed in Lancaster."

Micah nodded. "*Mei* sister's *boppli* was born with breathing problems, but I expect them home the week after next."

"Do you and Edith have plans for Christmas?"

Micah smiled. "*Jah*, we've been invited to the Kemps'."

"Hmm . . . Just how much time has Abigail Kemp been spending here while your parents are away?"

• • •

Micah had barely opened the door and stepped inside the house when Abigail pounced on him.

"How upset is Bishop Schwartz? Is he going to bring us before the church?"

Micah caught a glimpse of Thomas in the sitting room next to the woodstove. "When did he *kumm*?"

"A few minutes after the bishop arrived. Oh, please don't be upset with me for bringing him in the *haus*."

Micah moved past her. "We'll talk about it later." He walked into the sitting room. He nodded at *Mammi*, sitting in the rocking chair knitting, and went over to Thomas who was adding another log to an already-roaring fire. "I wasn't sure you were going to make it today."

"I bring in wood." Thomas smiled proudly and pointed to the full woodbox. "See?"

"*Jah, danki.*" Thomas was simple-minded. Hopefully the bishop would take his brain injury into consideration. "I could use your help in the shop."

Abigail came up behind Micah. "You want him to help you?"

He nodded. "I still have some things to make before tomorrow."

"But I thought—"

Micah winked and enjoyed watching her face turn the shade of holly berries. "I'm sorry I had to replace you."

"That's quite all right." She leaned closer and whispered, "What did the bishop say?"

"We'll talk about it later." He headed to the door with Thomas trailing. Once they were in the shop, Thomas filled the kiln while Micah mixed another batch of material. Micah wasn't sure what the bishop would say about continuing the same work arrangement, but he whispered a short prayer and left the outcome in the Lord's hands.

It was getting late and the lack of window light made the last few pieces a bit more challenging. Micah clipped the end of the glass, but the piece rolled off the table and shattered on the cement floor. "Will you grab the broom, Thomas? It's in the corner."

No answer.

Micah looked over his shoulder, then turned completely, not seeing him. "Thomas?"

A soft whimper came from behind a barrel of broken glass. Micah found Thomas hunched down, head tucked between his knees, arms shielding his head, and wracked with tremors. "It's okay, Thomas."

He cowered, shaking uncontrollably and gasping.

"I didn't mean to frighten you." Micah patted Thomas's shoulder. Suddenly Thomas's arms began flailing. He lunged at Micah, sending him several feet back and landing him hard on the floor.

Then Thomas leapt to his feet and fled the building.

Micah shook his head, feeling stunned. He pushed off the floor. He had to find Thomas and calm him down. In his current state, he may be a danger to himself and anyone he encountered.

• • •

Abigail had a pot of beef stew simmering on the stove and was taking a pan of cornbread out of the oven when Micah barged into the kitchen.

"Have you seen Thomas?"

"I thought he was still working with you." Abigail set the pan on the cooling rack.

"*Nay.* He left. I've searched the area. He's gone."

His sharp breaths and movements from one window to the next frightened Abigail. "What do mean, you've searched the area?"

"He's gone—I broke a piece of glass and it sent him into some sort of . . . panic mode."

"I'll get *mei* cloak." She headed for the door despite his warning to stay. "He probably went home," she said, tying the ribbons of her winter bonnet under her chin.

"*Mammi*, will you be okay alone? I'm going to take Abigail home, then check on Thomas."

"I'll be fine. I lived alone up until a few weeks ago."

"I'll try *nett* to be late."

Abigail waited until they were outside. "We're going to check on Thomas first, right?"

He walked faster to the barn, hitched the horse in mere minutes, and shuttled her into the buggy.

"Micah, you're *nett* telling me something. What is it?"

"That glass shattering triggered something. One minute he's convulsing in fear, the next he's tackling me to the ground."

"He attacked you?"

"He didn't take a swing and he had plenty of opportunity." Micah stopped at the intersection of Trukenmiller Road and Rambadt and waited for a car to pass.

"Don't turn. I have to know if he went home. Besides, it'll be easier for me to explain what happened. *Mei aenti* will want to know why he's agitated."

He hesitated a moment, then nodded.

A few moments later, they pulled into Thomas's driveway. They both climbed out of the buggy.

Malinda answered the door. She looked at Abigail, then Micah, then steadied her puzzling gaze back on Abigail. "It's *gut* to see you." She looked beyond them with growing concern. "You didn't bring Thomas with you?"

"He isn't home?"

"*Nay*, why?"

"We better *kumm* in and talk with your parents," Micah said.

Malinda teared up before hearing the news. Abigail wrapped her cousin in a tight hug as Micah told her *aenti* and *onkel* what had transpired. Arrangements were quickly made to form a search group, with Micah saying he would pass the word along to Abigail's father and brothers.

Abigail protested the moment they were outside. "I'm going with you."

Micah didn't respond.

"He trusts me. I can convince him—"

"You can't. *Nett* in the mental state he was in."

But Micah's warning didn't stop her from voicing her request to her father once they reached the house.

Daed looked at *Mamm*. "What do you think about her going?"

"She can ride with me," Micah said.

"It might be easier having two sets of eyes," her *mamm* replied.

Daed nodded. "Okay, but when we get home, you're

explaining that." He pointed to her empty money jar.
"And I better *nett* hear you bought Mr. Troyer's horse."
He grabbed his hat from the hook. "I'll stop at the bishop's *haus* and let him know what's happening. He can
help spread the word for everyone to check their barns
and outbuildings. Why don't you take the road into
town, Micah?"

"Okay." He motioned to Abigail and they left the
house, picking up an extra lantern from the porch on
their way to the buggy.

Micah turned the horse toward town. He kept a
tight rein, pacing him slow enough that they could
scan the roadside ditches. "Why does your *daed* think
you may have bought Cactus?" His question held a
sharp irritation.

"I was saving *mei* money in that Mason jar."

"I figured that much by the 'Horse Fund' label." He
swept the area with his gaze. "Why were you finishing
your horse quilt?"

"How do you know about that?" An approaching
car's headlights lit the shoulder of the road, reaching
farther than their lantern glow. The heaped banks of
snow from where the snowplow had cleared the highway made it difficult to see the moonlit field.

"You bought him, didn't you?" Micah's tone sharp-
ened. "You went against your father's wishes and did it
anyway. How are you going to feed that horse if your
father disapproves?"

She squared her shoulders and turned to him, but his
attention was outside the buggy, searching. She should
be searching. "Why does it matter to you anyway?"

He was quiet a long while. They reached the edge of town, the stores were closed, the streets deserted. Micah made a quick pass down Main Street and covered the block around the hardware store, then drove a few blocks down the road and stopped in front of Community Fellowship Church. Micah set the brake, then shifted on the bench to face her. "It matters," he said. "There isn't an Amish man who wants a *fraa* who's as . . . as disobedient as you."

She flinched at his words. "Or as talkative," she said. "I know that isn't a trait anyone wants either."

"Stay here," Micah grunted as he slipped out of the buggy.

She watched him take the sidewalk to the side entrance and go inside. Abigail slouched on the bench. Micah was the last person she wanted to hear a lecture from on what a man wants in a wife. *"There isn't an Amish man . . ."*

. . .

A lanky forty-something man introduced himself to Micah as the pastor and offered to show him around the fellowship hall once Micah had explained who he was looking for. The converted gym had a long table in the center where several homeless men were eating. "We open our doors on the really cold nights, which in the winter is daily," the pastor explained. "We don't ask questions. We simply offer a roof over their head, something warm to eat, and the Word of God to feed their soul."

"That's very generous," Micah said.

"You'd be surprised how many drifters we have around Christmas."

Micah frowned. "That's sad."

"I like to believe God is calling them closer."

Micah spotted a man at the far end of the gym, lying on the floor wrapped in what looked like an Amish patterned quilt. "That might be him."

"He's one of our regulars."

As Micah approached, he recognized the raggedy shoes before he saw the man's face.

"I'm trying to sleep," he grumbled.

"I noticed the Amish quilt and thought you were someone else."

The man sat up and gripped the blanket tighter. "It's mine. An angel gave me this to keep warm—she gave me cookies too."

Cookies? Micah smiled. "I'm *nett* interested in your blanket. I'm looking for a friend of mine. I thought maybe he came into town."

"A young fellow? Wild look in his eyes?"

That described most of the homeless in the room, but Micah nodded. "He was wearing a brown—maybe military shirt."

The man stretched his neck out from under the blanket like a turtle out of its shell. "Saw him awhile ago. Torn up with the shakes. You need to take him to the VA before he goes insane. Like some of us," he mumbled. Something clanged like a metal pot hitting the floor, and the man disappeared under the blanket.

Hope rose up within Micah. Thomas was here. He

walked the length of the gym, trying not to stare, but not wanting to miss Thomas if he was one of the many lying on the floor. He came to the end of the row, his hope depleted. Then a worker called out to someone who had crawled under the long table.

"Don't you want to come out and get something to eat?" the worker said.

Micah knelt down beside the table. "Thomas, it's Micah."

Thomas lifted his head and looked Micah's direction.

"I've *kumm* to take you home. Your family is worried about you."

He shook his head.

"It's true, Thomas," Abigail said, squatting down beside Micah. "Please, *kumm* back with us."

Thomas didn't move.

Abigail sat back on her heels for a moment. "I was thinking about going ice-skating," she said.

"Me too," Micah added.

A few seconds went by, then Thomas crawled out from under the table. "Do I like to skate?"

"You love to skate, Thomas." Abigail's smile reached her eyes.

CHAPTER 16

Christmas morning Abigail woke to the tantalizing scent of cinnamon buns. A family tradition ever since she could remember, only she normally took part in preparing them. She glanced at Elizabeth's made bed, then over to Sadie's, and bounded out of bed. How could she have slept so hard that she missed Christmas?

She dressed in a hurry and as she tromped down the stairs, laughter rang out from the kitchen. She hadn't heard her mother's lighthearted laugh since Thomas had returned and *Mamm's* sister's family had been issued the cold treatment. It sounded like music to Abigail's ears.

"What's the excitement about?" Abigail looked from her mother to Elizabeth and over to young Sadie, with her hands covered in flour and white powder on the counter, the floor, the wall, everywhere.

"I patted the mound of bread dough too hard and flour went all over," Sadie said.

And *Mamm* was laughing—hysterically. She lifted her brows at *Mamm* who merely shrugged. "It's Christmas!"

Abigail wished she shared the same joyfulness.

Micah had dropped her off the night before last before taking Thomas home. Micah hadn't wanted to spend a few minutes more alone with her, or he would have driven Thomas home first. He had told her to stay in the buggy, and she had gone inside the church after a while because Micah was taking so long and she was getting cold. Although he didn't say anything about her not doing as she was told, he certainly hadn't knocked on her door to see her either. Yesterday he wouldn't have driven the glassware into town. Who'd sat with Edith?

"You must have been tired," her mother said.

"*Jah*, must've been." She yawned.

"*Daed* said we're opening gifts early since we have so many coming for Christmas dinner," Elizabeth said.

Abigail shifted her attention to *Mamm* who was tearing up and giggling at the same time. "The Lambrights will be spending Christmas with us after all," she said, dabbing her eyes with the corner of her sleeve.

"Even Thomas?" Abigail asked.

Mamm nodded. "Doreen didn't have time this morning to tell me everything, but she said Micah had talked to them and Bishop Schwartz about getting treatment for Thomas. Apparently there are doctors who specialize in treating people returning from war. His stress syndrome might just be manageable, and there's a new study being done to help retrain the brain after injury, so maybe he can learn to control his cussing. Isn't that the best Christmas gift ever?" Tears of joy streamed down her face. "I'm so happy for *mei* sister."

Abigail hugged her mother. "That is *wunderbaar* news." *Lord, let it be so.* She released her mother. "Do

I have time to make a fruitcake before we open gifts?"
Malinda always said fruitcake was the best part of the
holidays, and Abigail wanted to make a special one
for her.

"Let's get it started *nau*," *Mamm* said. "It can be baking while we open gifts."

Abigail hadn't heard this much excitement in the
kitchen in a long time. She could hardly keep her emotions about Micah intact. She would thank him first
thing when he arrived later today for the meal. That is,
if he would listen to her.

Daed called everyone into the sitting room just as
Abigail slipped the fruitcake into the oven. It seemed
odd opening presents this early in the day, but the
twins and Sadie were certainly excited.

Abigail untied the piece of yarn from around the
package Elizabeth had given her. She unwrapped a
beautiful royal-blue dress and matching apron. "I love
it, *danki*." She rose from her chair and hugged her sister. "I didn't even see you working on this."

"I'm glad you like it."

"I'm going to wear it to dinner tonight." She sat
down, barely paying attention to what everyone else
unwrapped. She ran her hand over the fine stitches.
Would Micah like this color on her? She hoped her
stockings without the holes were clean. She touched the
strings on her prayer *kapp*. She would replace it with
the one she saved for Sundays. It wasn't tattered.

Daed placed a brown paper-wrapped package on
her lap.

"I have another one?" Abigail thought she'd

unwrapped everything. Opening the box, her eyes misted as she stared at the leather halter. "It's beautiful."

Daed smiled. "I think you'll have use for it one day— when you find the right horse."

"This will give me incentive to start saving again."

"*Nett* Cactus," *Daed* said, then cleared his throat. "I want you to know how pleased I am that you were willing to sacrifice something that meant so much to you. You responded to others' needs as Jesus would want, and I'm proud of you." He looked at *Mamm* and winked. "I need to get something from the barn. I have one more gift to bring in."

"I'll help." David followed him outside.

A few minutes later, they returned with a wooden rocker for *Mamm*. Her face glowed as she eased into the chair. "It's perfect," she said, running her hands along the armrests.

Elizabeth leaned closer to Abigail. "You better go change. Micah will be here soon." Her sister was already a vision of beauty wearing her forest-green dress. James was also due to arrive for their family dinner. "I'll help get dinner ready, you go."

Abigail gathered the dress into her arms and scooted upstairs. She hadn't felt this nervous—ever. The dress was a perfect fit. Abigail twirled around in a tight circle. She hadn't worn a new dress in a long time. She removed her prayer *kapp*, letting her hair fall over her shoulder. She heard a buggy pull into the driveway and rushed to the window. James was the first to arrive. Abigail brushed her hair and secured her Sunday *kapp* in place. More voices filtered upstairs as other guests arrived.

Abigail padded down the steps. She greeted Edith who, with *Mamm's* help, was removing her cloak at the door. Abigail's gaze automatically traveled the room for Micah. He wasn't in the sitting room with David, James, and *Daed*. She eased over to the window and glanced outside. His horse and buggy was tied to the post next to the barn. Her shoulders dropped. Had he changed his mind about dinner?

"He had to run back home," Edith said as though reading her mind.

"But he's still coming for dinner?"

"Yes, dear." Edith smiled warmly. "Is that a new dress you're wearing?"

Abigail nodded. "Elizabeth made it."

"That blue is a *gut* color on you."

"*Danki.*" She hoped Micah thought the same.

"Can I make you a cup of tea, Edith?" *Mamm* motioned toward the kitchen and Edith joined her, commenting on how good the turkey smelled.

Abigail glanced out the window again. Why wouldn't Micah have taken his buggy? She meandered into the kitchen. "Is there anything you'd like me to do?" she asked her mother.

"We're just waiting on the turkey," *Mamm* said.

She wouldn't be able to eat a bite if Micah wasn't back. She removed a glass from the cupboard, filled it with water, and took a drink. A knock sounded at the door and she spilled water down the front of her dress.

• • •

Micah greeted Abigail's father, brothers, and James in the sitting room, then made his way to the kitchen. Falling in love had set his nerves on edge, and he wouldn't be able to sit through dinner without talking to her first.

"Abigail, do you have a minute?"

She stopped blotting a wet spot on her dress and tossed the dish towel on the counter. "Oh, hello, Micah."

He rubbed his moist hands on his pant legs, glanced at his grandmother and Mrs. Kemp, and nervously smiled. "Merry Christmas."

Abigail's mother bounded off the chair. "Merry Christmas, Micah. Can I make you a cup of *kaffi* or tea?"

"Maybe later. If you don't mind, I'd like to take Abigail on a short ride."

"*Nau*?" Abigail interrupted. "The turkey is almost done."

"I won't keep her long," he said.

Mamm exchanged glances with Edith, then nodded. "Dinner won't be ready for a while."

Abigail was fussing with the spot on her dress again when he removed her cloak from the hook and handed it to her.

"*Mamm* will pluck you like a turkey if we're late for dinner," Abigail warned as they left the house. She glanced upward and smiled. "It's snowing. Of course, I don't have to point that out to you."

He reached for her elbow, then guided her to the sleigh parked next to his buggy. "Would you like to go for a ride?"

"*Jah*." Her eyes lit with excitement. "*Daed* puts the

runners on the buggy when the snow gets too deep, but I've never ridden in an open sleigh."

He untied the mare's reins from the post. "This here is *Mammi's* old horse, Sugarplum."

"She's beautiful." Abigail patted the horse's neck. "Hello, Sugarplum."

Micah brushed the light dusting of snow off the bench, then helped Abigail into the sleigh. "I thought we would take a ride down to the pond," he said, signaling the horse.

Hearing her teeth chatter, he reached behind the seat for the blanket. "This should keep you warm."

"*Danki.*"

Sugarplum plodded along the snow-covered trail. He stopped the sleigh at the edge of the pond and they sat quietly for a couple minutes. "I'm going to miss *nett* seeing you at the *haus*."

"I promised Edith I would stop by and visit."

"Just *Mammi*?"

"And you . . . if you're *nett* in your shop. We both know how you don't like to be bothered when you're—"

He brushed his hand over her cheek.

"Working," she said, breathlessly. "I, ah . . . I wouldn't inter . . . fere."

He leaned closer, his attention focused on her lips. "Are you going to keep talking?"

"It is a problem . . . I have . . . sometimes."

He captured her mouth with a long kiss. Her lips were soft and moved with his. Placing his hand around her back, he pressed her closer. He trailed kisses across her cheek.

"What was . . . I saying?" Her voice broke.

"That you talk a lot," he whispered in her ear.

"Is that a problem?"

"*Nett* anymore." He kissed her temple. "I know how to quiet you *nau*." He kissed her on the lips, this time possessively.

"I think I might talk all the time."

"*Jah*, you do that." His lips found hers once again, and when he had kissed her so much that his lips tingled, he placed his arm around her shoulder and she nestled in the crook of his arm. "Are you *kalt*?" he asked, squeezing her a little tighter.

"*Nay.*"

He pointed to left. "You see that hill in the distance?"

"It's your father's land, I know."

"He gave it to me. I'm going to build a *haus* on it this spring, so I can look out *mei* window and watch you skate in the winter."

"You're welcome to skate with me."

He shifted slightly in order to gaze into her eyes. "In the summer you can look out your window and watch me fish."

"*Mei* window?" Her brows lifted.

He nodded. "Unless you'd like to go fishing, but I'll warn you, I get up early."

She sat up straight. "What are you saying?"

"I love you, Gabby Abby. I want you to be *mei fraa*."

Her eyes glistened with tears. "But you said just the other *nacht* there wasn't an Amish man who would want—"

He kissed her hard, convincingly. "I was wrong." He

kissed the tip of her cold nose. "Tell me you love me. That you will be *mei fraa*."

"Yes, yes, yes, yes. Should I go on?"

He wrapped her in a tight embrace. "Yes, go on. I love hearing those words." He held her a few minutes longer before releasing her. "We should probably get back to the *haus*. I don't want *mei* future *fraa's mamm* upset with me."

"After what you did for Thomas, there's no chance of that."

Micah extended the reins to her. "Would you like to drive home?"

"I've never driven a sleigh."

"She's a *gut* horse, as sweet as her name," he said. "As sweet as her new owner."

Abigail crinkled her brows.

"I attached a bow to her harness, but it fell off on the way here." He shrugged. "She's a bit awkward to wrap in brown paper, but I hope you like her."

"You bought me a horse?" Abigail gasped.

He nodded. "*Mammi* mentioned you wanted a horse more than anything. Something about your independence . . ." He placed his hand over hers. "I hope this makes you happy, Gabby Abby."

"I've never been happier." She placed her free hand on her chest, breathing heavily. "I might burst!"

Micah chuckled. "Does that mean you'll still want to marry me? I mean—*nau* that you have your independence."

She blinked and tears rolled down her face. "I'll marry you today, Micah Zook. Today! Well, maybe *nett* today. Your parents are *nett* back in town. Oh . . ." Her eyes widened. "I only made you a pair of socks for Christmas."

He grinned. "But you've shared your gift of gab with me throughout this entire Christmas season." A chuckle erupted he couldn't contain.

She pulled back. "Are you making fun of me again?"

He brought her back into his arms. "I don't ever want you to change," he said, pulling her closer. "I love you just the way you are."

DISCUSSION QUESTIONS

1. Abigail admittedly talked too much, and even claimed God had given her a gift of gab. Do you think she used her gift to edify and encourage people with positive talk? There are a lot of hurting people around us; what might you say to uplift someone today?

2. How did Micah's grandmother play a part in getting Abigail and Micah together? Did Abigail take Edith's advice?

3. Why was it so important to Abigail to own her own horse? Did owning the horse represent something other than transportation?

4. Thomas suffered a brain injury while in the service, which altered his behavior. Do you think he was treated like a prodigal child who had returned home?

ACKNOWLEDGMENTS

As always, I want to thank my family for their continued support. To Dan, who demonstrates unconditional love when it comes to my spending long hours in the office writing, I love you for your understanding and support. To my daughter Lexie, who used my Amish characters in her stand-up comedy routine. I'm glad the comedy-club audience got a kick out of your "plain" humor. To Danny, the new licensed driver in the family, I'll be expecting you to do the post office runs to mail out books. To Sarah, you're an awesome cheerleader—not just for PHS. You are a constant source of encouragement, and I am so thankful to have you as a prayer partner.

To my parents, Paul Droste and Ella Roberts, thank you for your unconditional love and support. For those of you who don't know my mother, she's got the gift of gab. Mom has always said that God gave her the gift of gab and she was going to use it. And she does! You spread sunshine wherever you are. ☺

To my editors, Becky Philpott and Natalie Hanemann, you two are the best! Your skills brought this book to life. To my agent, Susan Brower, I look forward to churning out many more books with you. I'd like to also thank Daisy Hutton, Vice President and Publisher for HarperCollins, and the entire publishing team for believing in me and making this story possible.

A big thank you, dear readers, for your encouraging notes and comments on Facebook.

Above all, thanks be to God, the almighty author of my life!

ABOUT THE AUTHOR

Ruth Reid is a CBA and ECPA bestselling author of the Heaven on Earth, the Amish Wonders, and the Amish Mercies series. She's a full-time pharmacist who lives in Florida with her husband and three children. When attending Ferris State University School of Pharmacy in Big Rapids, Michigan, she lived on the outskirts of an Amish community and had several occasions to visit the Amish farms. Her interest grew into love as she saw the beauty in living a simple life. Visit Ruth online at RuthReid.com; Facebook: AuthorRuth-Reid; Twitter: @AuthorRuthReid.

A Christmas Visitor

Kelly Irvin

To my husband, Tim. I consider every day with you in my life a gift from God. Love always.

GLOSSARY OF PENNSYLVANIA DUTCH WORDS USED IN BEE COUNTY, TEXAS

aenti—aunt
Ausbund—hymnal
boplin—baby
bruder—brother
daed—dad
danki—thank you
Deutsch—Pennsylvania Dutch
dochder—daughter
Englisch—English
Englischer—a non-Amish person
fraa—wife
galluses—suspenders
Gelassenheit—yielding to God's will and forsaking
    selfishness
Gott—God
groossmammi—grandmother
jah—yes
kaffi—coffee

kapp—white head covering
kinner—children
mann—man
mudder—mother
nee—no
onkel—uncle
Ordnung—the written and unwritten rules that guide the Amish way of life
rumspringa—the running-around period
schtinkich—stink

CHAPTER 1

They meant well. All of them. Frannie Mast ladled another spoonful of steaming okra gumbo into her bowl. The spicy aroma tickling her nose did nothing to calm the willies in her stomach. She couldn't help herself, her gaze wandered down the crowded table past *Aenti* Abigail and her self-satisfied smile to Joseph Glick sitting on the other side with Caleb and her cousins. A giggle burbled in her throat. *Stop it. Be kind.* Did Joseph know he had a smear of butter on his upper lip? Did he know her aunt and uncle were doing a little matchmaking? Not that they would admit it. Plain boys and girls were to find their own mates during their *rumspringas* with no interference from their elders.

Apparently her situation had been deemed an exception to the rule.

Joseph flashed Frannie a smile. A chunk of venison had found a home in a gap between his lower front teeth. She suppressed a sigh and forced a smile. None of this could be construed as his fault. She remembered Joseph from school. He had been a so-so student, but a good softball player and a hard worker. He was easy to look at, with toast-colored hair, green eyes, and tanned skin. He was also the third single man *Aenti* Abigail and *Onkel* Mordecai had invited to supper since her return to Bee County, Texas, three weeks earlier.

It seemed more like two years had passed since her arrival in her childhood community after three years in Missouri.

They meant well, but what were they thinking? Joseph was Leroy Glick's son. Leroy, the bishop. Did they think Joseph would keep an eye on her, too, and report back to his father and to Mordecai, the district's deacon? Would he keep her from going astray?

She wouldn't do that. If they'd give her half a chance, she'd show them.

A fierce burning sensation assailed Frannie's fingers. She glanced down. Gumbo dripped on her hand. The burning blush scurrying across her face had nothing to do with the soup's heat. She dropped the ladle and grabbed her napkin, attempting to wipe the hot liquid from her fingers.

"Ouch!" She stood. Her pine chair rocked on spindly legs, then tumbled back. "Sorry. I'm sorry."

"Child, you're always spilling something." *Aenti* Abigail's fierce blue eyes matched the frown lurking below her high cheekbones and long, thin nose. "Get it cleaned up."

"It's fine. No harm done." Deborah King leaned over and wiped up the soup with her own napkin. Something in her tone reminded Frannie of the way her favorite cousin talked to her two-year-old son, Timothy. "Stick it in some water."

"Rub some butter on it. It stops the sting and helps it heal." Joseph held out the saucer with the puddle of half-melted butter that remained, still unaware it seemed of the smear on his own lip. He grinned. The venison hadn't dislodged from his teeth. "That's what my *groossmammi* used to say."

"Old wives' tale." *Onkel* Mordecai shook his head. His shaggy black beard, streaked with silver, bobbed. Mordecai mostly knew everything. "Water is best since we have no ice. Go on to the kitchen then."

Relief washed over Frannie. Escape. She whirled, stumbled over a chair leg, righted herself, and rushed into the kitchen. A tub of water sat on the counter in anticipation of the dirty dishes. She shoved her hand into it, barely aware of the stinging skin on her fingers. Gumbo stained her apron. Tomato juice from the canning frolic earlier in the day provided background color. Without looking, she knew sweat stains adorned the neck of her gray dress, like jewelry she would never wear. She was a mess as usual.

Why did *Aenti* Abigail insist on having gumbo in this weather? Something about soup cooling a person off because it caused him to sweat. This had to be an *Onkel* Mordecai theory. He had tons of them, each stranger or funnier or more interesting than the last. At least life with him would not be boring. Which was good, because Frannie likely would spend the rest of her life in his house if she behaved like that in front of every man in the district. She wanted to marry and have babies like her cousins and her friends. Like every Plain woman.

Why did that seem so hard for her?

She swished both hands in the lukewarm water and stared out the window at the brown grass, wiry mesquite, live oak trees, and a huge cluster of nopals. No breeze flapped the frayed white curtains. September weather in Bee County hadn't changed, just as nothing else had. No one who grew up here minded hot weather. They embraced it. Still, Frannie would savor her memories of evenings in Missouri this time of year. The air steamed with heat and humidity, but huge elm, oak, hickory, and red mulberry trees populated the countryside. A breeze often kicked up the leaves in the evening hours, making it a perfect time to sit in the lawn chairs and watch the sun dip below the horizon.

Nee, she wouldn't think of that. Thinking of those long summer nights made her think of him.

Rocky.

She swallowed hard against tears that surprised her. Rocky was only a friend. He couldn't be any more than that. Not for a faithful Plain woman such as herself. She understood what that meant even if her parents didn't trust her to make the right choices.

Gott, help me be good.

"Frannie, come out here."

Clear notes of disapproval danced with surprise in *Onkel* Mordecai's gruff voice. What had she done now? Drying her hands on a dish towel, Frannie trudged from the kitchen to the front room where her family sat, scrunched together like peas in long pods at two rough-hewn pine tables shoved together. No one looked at her when she entered the room. They all sat, not moving, staring toward the door as if mesmerized by a hideous rattlesnake coiled and ready to strike a venomous blow.

She plowed to a stop.

Nee. It couldn't be.

CHAPTER 2

Frannie managed to clamp her mouth shut without biting her tongue. All six foot two, two hundred pounds of muscle known as Richard "Rocky" Sanders towered in the doorway. He waved his St. Louis Cardinals ball cap at her with a hand the size of a feed bucket. Acutely aware of the gazes of a dozen pairs of eyes drilling her in the back, Frannie waved a tiny half wave. Her burned fingers complained.

Rocky cleared his throat and shuffled work boots in the size-fourteen range. "Hey, Frannie."

"Hey." Her voice came out in an unfamiliar squeak that reminded her of the stray cat out by the shed when she fed him table scraps and accidentally stepped on his tail. A drop of sweat ran down her nose and dripped onto her upper lip. She fought the urge to scratch the spot. "Rocky."

No one spoke for several long seconds. Rocky shifted his feet again. His dark brown almost black curls hung damp around his ears. His blue eyes, so like the color of Missouri sky in summer, implored her. She took another step forward.

"Introduce your guest, Frannie." *Onkel* Mordecai's

disapproval had been displaced by the politeness they all were taught from childhood to show guests. "Invite him in."

"This here's Rocky Sanders from Jamesport. I . . . knew him up yonder." Frannie couldn't help herself. She glanced at Joseph. He studied his bowl as if gumbo were the most interesting food he'd ever tasted. "He used to come into the restaurant where I was a waitress."

She kept to herself the longer version, how Rocky began to make an appearance at Callie's Restaurant and Bakery two or three times a week. How he left big tips on small meals and complimented the food as if she'd cooked it herself. How he showed up at the school fund-raiser on July Fourth and spent too much on a treadle sewing machine he said his mother wanted to use as a "conversation piece" in their living room. Her throat tightened at the memories. *Breathe.*

Mordecai nodded. "We're having gumbo if you want to pull up a seat."

"No, no, I can see you're having dinner. I don't want to barge in on you." Rocky edged toward the door, but his gaze remained on Frannie. "I'm sorry to drop in without letting you know I was coming. Being you don't have a phone—not that there's anything wrong with that. No calls from those pesky salespeople at dinnertime. I was . . . in the neighborhood."

After that preposterous statement, he tugged a red bandanna from the back pocket of his faded blue jeans and swiped the sweat dampening his face. "Begging your pardon, but could I have a quick word with your niece . . . on the porch? I won't keep her long."

Frannie's breathing did that same strange disappearing act it did when she jumped into the cold water at Choke Canyon Lake. She dared to hazard a glance at *Aenti* Abigail. Her lips were drawn down so far it was a wonder they didn't fall from her face onto the planks of the wood floor. The blue-green of *Onkel* Mordecai's eyes had turned frosty. "Go on, but make it quick. There's dishes to wash and chores to do."

Frannie whipped past Rocky, catching the familiar, inviting scent of his woodsy aftershave and Irish Spring soap—what she'd come to think of as Rocky smell—as she opened the screen door and led the way outside. To her relief he followed without another word. On the porch, she drank in the sight of him, now that they had no audience. Same tanned face, same little scar on his chin where he fell from a swing in the second grade, same little twist to his nose where he took a punch in a boxing match. "What are you doing here?"

The words sounded inhospitable. She wanted them back as soon as they fell on the early-evening air. Rocky's smile faded. His Adam's apple bobbed. He ducked his head and smoothed the cap in his hands. "Like I told you before, I have a bit of a wanderlust. You talked about this place so much, I figured I'd come see it for myself."

A wisp of disappointment curled itself around the relief that rolled over her. He simply wanted to travel. He knew her so he stopped by. Like stopping by Bee County in the far reaches of south Texas was an easy feat. Most folks couldn't find it with a map. "Are you staying long in the area—*where* are you staying?"

"I just got here." An emotion Frannie recognized—disappointment—soaked the words. "You want me to leave?"

Nee. *Not at all. Stay. Please stay.* She swallowed the words before they could spring forward and betray her. "It's just . . . surprising."

"My Uncle Richard passed."

"Oh, Rocky." With no thought for appearances, Frannie touched his hand. Richard had been the only true father Rocky had ever known. His eyes blazed with sudden emotion as his long fingers turned and wrapped around hers. His strong grip seemed to embrace her. A slow heat warmed her from head to toe. "I'm so sorry. What happened?"

"Heart attack. Sudden. He left me a small nest egg."

She itched to give this bear of a man the hug he deserved. That he needed. She kept her gaze on their entwined hands. "That was nice of him."

"He was a nice man. He was a good man." Rocky's voice had a sandpaper roughness about it she'd never heard before. "Anyway, he gave me the chance to have a fresh start if I want."

The last sentence seemed more of a question than a statement. A fresh start. Was Bee County his fresh start? Was Frannie his fresh start?

The screen door slammed. Frannie tugged her hand back, fingers burning worse than when she'd spilled the gumbo. Joseph clomped past them, a painful smile plastered across his face. "Mordecai said to tell you there's plenty of leftovers if your friend has a hankering." He tossed the words over his shoulder without looking back. "I'm headed home. Chores won't wait. I imagine those dishes won't either."

"Be safe." Now what a thing to say. Like Joseph couldn't take care of himself. Like he hadn't grown up with the javelinas, the bobcats, the rattlesnakes, and the occasional escapee from the prison outside Beeville. "Bye."

"You too." This time Joseph looked back. His gaze skittered from Frannie to Rocky. "You never know where danger lurks."

CHAPTER 3

Rocky smoothed the folds in the tattered road map. He'd found the King farm once, he could do it again. Even though it had been by sheer beginner's luck the first time. He would find it and he would take Frannie for a ride, like he'd done in Jamesport. He liked the idea of shining a flashlight in her window. It was sweet, like Frannie. Her uncle might be stern-looking, but he was a pacifist. All the Amish were. Frannie had assured him of that the first time he picked her up for a ride after her parents went to bed that momentous evening six months earlier. The night he'd fallen in love.

Best get to it or she'd be asleep. He studied the map. His scribbles on the margins had been gathered from a convenience-store clerk, a guy at the Dairy Queen, and the librarian in Beeville. Did the Bee County Amish District go out of its way not to be found? Surely not, considering their store, the honey sales, horse training, and saddle-making businesses. They needed outsiders to survive. What Rocky needed was a GPS. He patted the steering wheel as if the old Dodge Ram with a hundred-fifty thousand miles on its odometer had heard the traitorous thought and taken umbrage.

"We made it this far, we're doing fine," he muttered. To himself, not the truck. He'd replaced the battery in Oklahoma City and the water pump outside Dallas. Blown a tire in Killeen. What else could go wrong? "We should hold off a day or two anyway, let them get used to the idea."

Let Frannie get used to the idea. She'd looked as surprised and horrified as her family at his sudden appearance. Her relief had been abundantly clear when he'd taken his leave of the porch shortly after the surly-looking man named Joseph the previous evening. Somehow he'd seen their reunion going differently than that. Her face would light up with that trademark Frannie Mast grin that spread across her face so wide her freckles nearly popped off her nose and cheeks. She'd run to meet him like those cheesy commercials on TV.

They'd kiss.

As if they'd done that before. He respected the line Frannie had drawn, even if he longed for so much more. He'd settle for a handshake at this point.

Frannie wasn't a beauty by most standards. Rocky's friends went so far as to call her scrawny when he announced his plans to follow her to Texas. They pointed out he'd never seen her legs, what with the long skirt, or her hair, hidden under that cap, even on the hottest day of the year. He liked her modesty and the thought that she guarded those secrets for the one she would love for the rest of her life. In his eyes, her beauty was unquestionable. The south Texas drawl with the strange German—*Deutsch* words, as she called them—sprinkled in. From the prayer *kapp* setting askew on hair the color of carrots to the sea of freckles to the black sneakers she wore everywhere, even to church, she captivated him. Even with tomato stains on her apron and sweat on her dress.

And she had feelings for him. He had no doubt of that. No matter what lines she drew or how she'd acted the evening before. No waiting. Time to put up or shut up. He shoved his hat back on his head, turned the key in the ignition, and pulled out from the motel where, in a moment of eternal optimism, he'd plopped down a month's worth of rent up front. It took a chunk from his nest egg. He'd have to find a job soon or stick to eating ramen noodles like he had during his college days.

Thirty minutes later he saw the SUPPORT BEEVILLE BEES, BUY LOCAL HONEY sign on Tynan Road. *Score.* Three minutes later, the Combination Store, a long, dirty white building with rusted siding and a tin roof, came into sight with its adjacent junk graveyard of buggy parts and farm equipment. They weren't much for sprucing up around here.

Close. He was very close. The King farm was a few miles from here. The sun had begun its descent in the western sky. That would make it harder to find the turnoff. Maybe someone at the store could point him in the right direction for one last turn.

Likely the store was closed. Still, a wagon with a weary-looking Morgan hitched to it stood near the door alongside a shabby black buggy that sported an orange triangle dangling from the back along with a FOR SALE sign. It couldn't hurt to try.

Rocky hopped from the truck and strode to the door. To his relief it opened. After a few seconds his eyes adjusted to the dusky interior. Jars of honey, baskets of fresh produce, stacks of straw hats, candles, cookbooks, a quilt, dusty saddles, a couple of handmade rocking chairs, even lip balm made from beeswax. A veritable collection of unrelated stuff. No customers perused the aisles. Nor a salesman.

Someone had to be here. "Hello?" His voice sounded weak in his own ears. "Hello, anyone here?"

A man nearly Rocky's height, beginning to stoop with age in his broad shoulders, strode through a door behind a streaked glass counter. His long beard was snow white. That and the round, wire-rimmed glasses made him a Santa Claus look-alike, or it would have if the beard hadn't lacked a mustache. "Hello yourself. I'm closed. Just doing some recordkeeping. What can I do you for?"

"I was wanting some directions to the King farm. I found it yesterday, but I think it was beginner's luck. I think I've gotten turned around or something."

"Mordecai or Phineas?"

"Pardon me?"

"We have father and son Kings in these parts."

Of course. When Frannie spoke of her favorite cousin, Deborah, she'd also mentioned her husband, Phineas, the younger part of the beekeeping father-and-son duo who tended an apiary of more than three hundred hives in this small patch of south Texas. "Mordecai."

The man's genial smile disappeared. His wrinkled hands dotted with brown age spots grasped at suspenders as his steely-blue eyes did a once-over that left Rocky feeling as if he'd just been thoroughly frisked. "You must be Frannie's Rocky."

Frannie's Rocky. The words had a sweet ring to them. He'd like to be Frannie's Rocky. He swallowed. "So to speak, sir."

"No need to 'sir' me. The name's Leroy."

Leroy. Rocky did a quick check on his mental Rolodex. *Leroy. Leroy Glick.* Frannie had mentioned him during her rambling explanation of the Amish faith and how their communities were structured.

The bishop.

Lord, have mercy or shoot me now and put me out of misery.

"It's good to meet you, sir, I mean Leroy. You're the bishop."

"I am. Among other things. I reckon Frannie explained what that means."

Rocky slipped his ball cap from his head and fanned his face. Sweat slid between his shoulder blades and dampened the back of his best checkered, western-style shirt with its pearl-covered snaps. So much for looking fresh when he visited with Frannie. *God, don't let my deodorant fail.* His mama's preacher said a person could take everything to the good Lord in prayer. Surely he knew what he was talking about. "You make the rules."

Leroy shook his head, causing his beard to sway ever so slightly. "The district makes the rules. The *Ordnung*.

We all meet twice a year and decide on them, whether they need changing. I help make sure folks follow the rules."

"Right."

"Frannie's on her *rumspringa*. You know what that is?"

"Yes, sir—I mean, yes, she explained the running-around thing."

"She explain how she has this time to find a proper husband, then she has to decide if she wants to join the church and be Plain for the rest of her life?"

She did. When she told Rocky she could never yoke herself to an English man. That's what she called him. An English man. Now it didn't seem so funny. "I know that."

"Then you know coming here isn't helping her. If you care for her, you'll go on home."

Rocky thought about moving closer to the counter. His feet seemed stuck to the rug in front of the door. "I didn't come just for Frannie."

Leroy's expression could only be described as skeptical. He leaned forward and planted his elbows on the counter. "We have a phone there in the back. The only one in the district. It's for business and emergencies." He cocked his head toward the door through which he had appeared. "Frannie's *mudder* and *daed* call me every day to see how their *dochder* is. They think this is an emergency. They sent her here to get her away from you. You know that. Yet, here you are."

"I know that's how it looks."

"Then most likely that's how it is."

How could he explain? Yes, all he could think of every night when he laid his head on his pillow was Frannie. Her image danced in his mind's eye, and he fell asleep imagining what their life could be like if it weren't for this one thing that separated them. This one big thing.

He went to church every Sunday morning. He slapped a twenty in the basket when it came down his row. All the while wondering how they could talk about this God as the Father, *Abba*. His own experience with fathers hadn't amounted to much. The man left his mama—and his ten-year-old son—for the daughter of the feed-store owner. So Rocky bowed to Mama's demands that he attend church. Then he went home and inhaled her fried chicken, mashed potatoes, gravy, and biscuits, determined not to give the Father thing another thought. His emptiness had been filled by college, coaching, and by helping his uncle. Now Uncle Richard was gone too. "I came to see what all the fuss is about."

"Fuss?" Leroy straightened, his white caterpillar eyebrows doing a quick push-up. "If you don't know what the fuss is about, you truly don't belong here. You'll only cause her heartache."

"I want to know. Isn't that worth something? I came all this way to find out . . ." He didn't know Leroy well enough to explain his reservations, so he stopped. Forcing himself to move, he trudged to the first aisle and picked up a large jar of honey the color of amber. It had a bit of honeycomb in it. "The honey looks good. I'll take a jar of it."

He turned and strode to the counter, jar in one hand, the other reaching for the billfold in his back pocket.

"It's on the house." Leroy waved one hand, his expression dismissive. "Consider it a going-away gift."

Rocky was not a quitter. "How do I get to Mordecai's farm?"

Leroy walked around the counter, his work boots making a *thump-thump* sound. He tapped the glass in the door. "Head east and make a right turn at the first four-way stop. Follow the dirt road." He let his hand drop and turned to face Rocky. "What kind of name is Rocky?"

"I'm named for my Uncle Richard. He was a professional boxer." He let his voice trail away. Leroy would never understand. Not having a father who stuck around, Rocky had treasured his relationship with his uncle. "He went by Rocky in the ring. So did I."

"You hit people for money?"

"No, I was an amateur." The words caused a fiery burn to engulf Rocky's face. He shuffled his feet, working to keep emotion from his voice. "But my uncle did. That's how he helped my mom out and raised me, so I don't turn up my nose at what he did for his family. After he retired, he went back to farming. I helped him—until recently."

"Reckon you got a point there." Leroy's tone was a tad more conciliatory. "So you're a farmer."

"I'm a high school coach now. My mom sold our acreage after my dad left us." At least Rocky would've been if he'd signed the new contract offered by the school district instead of coming to Texas. Somehow the idea of coaching his own basketball and baseball teams at a small Missouri high school didn't light a fire under him the way it had all through college. "I liked helping my uncle whenever I could. It felt good to be outside working the land."

The older man pursed his thin lips, his expression grim. The silence held for a good ninety seconds. "You want to know what the fuss is about? Come see for yourself. Church is at my place Sunday morning in two weeks. Three hours. In German. You'll see and then you'll go. In the meantime, give Frannie a wide berth."

Leroy Glick did not know Rocky. He only needed a foot in the door. After a quick thanks, Rocky shut the store door behind him, pumped his fist, and whispered, "Yes." He almost ran to the truck, whistling under his breath.

All he needed was a foot in the door.

CHAPTER 4

Frannie stared at the bedroom ceiling. As it had so many nights since her return to Bee County, sleep eluded her. The sweltering heat, *Aenti* Abigail's constant vigilance, the curious side glances of her cousins, the feeling that something was about to happen over which she had no control—all these things conspired to keep her eyes open and her stomach swirling with a mixture of excitement and dread that seemed to be trying to outdo each other. Sweat trickled from her temple into her hair and tickled her ear. Desperate for a breath of air, she eased from the bed, careful not to rock the thin mattress laid over a box spring that squeaked worse than a herd of mice. Hazel muttered in her sleep, turned over, and smacked Rebekah with her chubby hand. Rebekah shushed her sister without opening her eyes.

Holding her breath, Frannie waited for her cousins to settle, then tiptoed to the room's only window. No breeze stirred the tattered white curtains. Sounds were muted and distant. The sad coo of a mourning dove carried in the still night air. A barn owl hooted. A dog barked. An eighteen-wheeler changed gears on the highway. A multitude of stars lit the cloudless sky. *Gott, what is the plan? Why do I feel this way? Like I have a hole in my heart the size of Texas only Rocky can fill? I know it's wrong. I want to do the right thing. Help me do the right thing. Send Rocky home. Thy will be done.*

Tears formed. She forced them back. To never see Rocky again. The ache where her heart should be took her breath. God's plan surely did not include an *Englisch* man. Doing the right thing wasn't always easy. *Daed* taught her that. The memory of her parents' anxious faces as *Daed* handed the ticket to the Greyhound bus driver kept her company every day. *Daed* had clapped his arms around her in a rib-crushing hug. She couldn't remember him hugging her since she was old enough to sit on his roomy lap and braid his beard. *I'm trying,* Daed. *I'm trying not to disappoint you.*

How Rocky must've hurt when his *onkel* passed. He would've been so heartbroken. The little boy who needed a father would still be heartbroken. She peered up at the stars, seeking the constellations her *daed* had pointed out to her on the long evenings under the Missouri sky. *Let Rocky find peace and comfort even if it doesn't come from me. Give me the strength to do Your will.*

The unmistakable *clip-clop* of horse's hooves thudding against sun-hardened dirt rang in the distance. Who would arrive at the King house at this late hour? Everyone slept. Except her. A suitor for Rebekah? It seemed unlikely. Abigail employed the same vigilance over her third daughter as she did Frannie, given cousin Leila's decision to leave the district to marry outside her faith.

The buggy came into sight. The darkness hid the driver. The buggy stopped and a shadowy figure hopped out. Butch barked once, twice, then stopped. The dog always welcomed folks he knew. A minute later the flashlight's beam bounced and found her second-story window. She shaded her eyes and forced herself to keep her voice down. "Who is it?"

"Who were you expecting?"

Joseph.

Frannie drew back from the window, suddenly aware of her thin nightgown. "It's late. Why are you here?"

"I reckon that's obvious." His hoarse whisper mingled with the night sounds. "Come down. We'll take a ride."

Gott's answer to her prayer? The tightness in her throat told Frannie it wasn't the answer for which she'd hoped. A person didn't always get the answer she wanted. *Gott's* plan was bigger than her. She swallowed the lump. So be it. She dressed quickly in the dark, comforted by the steady breathing of her two cousins. Sneakers in her hand, she padded barefoot from the bedroom, down the stairs, and out to the porch where Joseph sat on the steps, one hand scratching Butch's bony back, staring at the sky as she had done only minutes earlier. Butch, with his black patch of fur around one eye that made him look like a pirate, scrambled to greet her, tail wagging. "No barking, Butch. You'll wake *Onkel* Mordecai and he needs his rest."

"He's a good watchdog." Joseph waited while she tugged on her shoes and then stood. "It'll be cooler in the buggy. We'll whip up a breeze."

Something about his clear assumption that she

would go with him irked her. *Aenti* Abigail's stern face loomed in her mind's eye followed by *Mudder's* worried one. "Sounds good."

She lifted her chin and offered him her hand to help her up. His fingers were warm and damp. When he trotted around to the other side, she wiped her hand on her dress. She couldn't blame him. Hers was surely damp too.

"Here we go." Joseph clucked and snapped the reins. The buggy jolted forward. "So, I reckon you were expecting your *Englisch* man."

"Rocky doesn't drive a buggy." Nor was he her *Englisch* man.

"True."

How so much could be said with one word amazed Frannie. "Is that what you came out here to talk to me about? If it is, you should get on home because I get plenty of that from *Aenti* Abigail."

"*Nee.*" He paused. The pause grew and grew. Joseph snapped the reins again. The buggy picked up speed. "I heard you might help out at the school, now that you're back."

As good a topic as any. She wouldn't think of the silly jokes and funny stories with which Rocky regaled her about his childhood with a boxing farmer uncle. He knew how to laugh despite the sadness that lurked behind those enormous blue eyes. "My aunt's idea. Susan has been doing it for years. She doesn't need help. And if she does, Rebekah fills in." *Aenti* Abigail didn't need Frannie's help either. She had Hazel to help with cooking and cleaning. Frannie's role remained to be seen in this tiny district with only a handful of young single men, most of whom had already set their sights on their future *fraas*. "I worked as a waitress in Jamesport. The money helped out a lot. I liked it."

"Ain't likely *Daed* will allow that, after what happened with my brother and Leila. No one is working in town anymore."

His tone was matter of fact, but losing a *bruder* to the outside world surely caused Joseph pain. Leila and Jesse had left the district so Jesse could be a minister and they could practice a different form of faith. Frannie often caught sadness settling on her aunt's face in the midst of baking a pie or canning or washing clothes. She never wanted to cause such pain for her own *mudder*. Surely Joseph, having lost a *bruder*, felt the same about his *mudder* and *daed*. "That's understandable. What about you? Working in your *daed's* store then?"

"*Nee*. My cousin Will does most of that. I'm helping *Daed* break horses and build buggies. I like being outdoors more. I don't abide with spending time with the *Englisch* folks who come into the store itching to take pictures and wanting to know why we don't have more quilts for sale."

The disdain in his voice made Frannie squirm. She'd enjoyed working as a waitress. Maybe too much. Rocky's visits became the highlight of her days even as she knew they could lead nowhere. The other *Englisch* folks might have been curious, but they tipped generously, and their questions were born of a desire to know and understand. Most showed the courtesy of waiting until she turned away to snap a photo. "It will all work out for the best, I reckon."

"There's been lots of talking. Working at the school would shut the grapevine down."

Undoubtedly. "Folks should mind their own p's and q's."

"That's for certain."

"I came back to Bee County to honor my parents' wishes."

"*Jah*, but the look on your face yesterday when that *Englischer* showed up said it all."

"You're wrong." *Nee*, he surely wasn't. "Then why did you come to fetch me tonight?"

A molted red crept across his whiskerless cheeks. "Your *aenti* Abigail . . . she made it sound like you might have an interest. I realize now that was her way of steering you from your *Englisch* man. "

Heat burned Frannie's face. She hadn't known until right this moment of Joseph's feelings. "Rocky's not my *Englisch* man."

Joseph cleared his throat. "Remember school? You learned *Englisch* faster than any of the rest of us, and you were the best at kickball and volleyball—for a girl."

"I was okay. No better or worse than the rest." Surely he thought of how *Englisch* would be helpful if she courted an *Englisch* man. "Anyway, not skills likely to help me be a good *fraa* and *mudder* now."

"Maybe, maybe not."

Nothing to say to that. Silence again.

Twin bright lights lightened the darkness on the road ahead, blinding Frannie. The deep rumble of an engine filled the air. A truck engine. The horse whinnied, an uneasy sound that matched the feeling in the pit of Frannie's stomach. She recognized that rumble. She'd spent more than her share of evenings in that truck, rambling on about her family and her faith and trying to make a man understand why Amish didn't mix with *Englisch*.

A man trying to rebuild a faith shattered by circumstances beyond a young boy's control. Could Leroy understand such a situation? Surely *Onkel* Mordecai could after losing his first wife in a van accident that scarred his son for life. Frannie understood it, and the worst thing that had ever happened to her was the loss of their house and everything down to their last bit of clothing in a fire caused by a lightning strike. Life was hard. People like Rocky deserved a chance.

She shouldn't be sitting next to Joseph and thinking about Rocky.

Illuminated in the buggy's battery-operated lights, the black-and-silver truck drew even with them. The driver's-side window was down. The AC must be out again. His expression hidden in the shadows, Rocky waved and gunned the engine. The truck rocketed past them. Exhaust fumes filled the night air, a *schtinkich* that reminded Frannie of the enormous chasm that existed between her buggy-paced world and the man driving the truck.

As if she didn't already know. *No need to rub it in,* Gott.

Joseph jerked on the reins as if to stop the buggy.

"*Nee, nee,* keep going." Frannie stuck her hand on

the reins. He couldn't stop. Nothing good would come of it. "Don't stop."

Joseph pushed her hand away, a gentle, warning motion. "Are you sure?"

Nee.

"*Jah.* Very sure." She took a deep breath and focused on the road ahead. Joseph had come for her. She owed him the courtesy of paying attention to his conversation. "Breaking horses must get exciting. Ever had one throw you?"

. . .

Murphy's Law. Rocky glanced at the dashboard and groaned. The CHECK ENGINE light shone brilliantly in the dark, like a big stop sign. A headache gathered strength behind his temples. He should turn the truck around and head to Beeville now. That way he'd be close to an auto repair store and mechanic's shop come daylight. The engine temperature continued to climb. No sense driving on to Mordecai's house.

Rocky knew all this, but he couldn't help himself. If he turned around now, he would simply overtake the buggy and then have to pass them again. To see Frannie in there with that Amish man, snug as a bug. He knew all about the courting rituals. He'd shared them with Frannie while her parents—her *mudder* and *daed*—had slept blissfully unaware. The *mudder* and *daed*. She laughed at how he pronounced the *Deutsch* words.

No one laughed now. Rocky rolled in to the Kings'

front yard with its withered grass and weeds trying valiantly to survive in a sea of brown dirt. He switched off the lights and the truck. His hands gripped the wheel until his fingers hurt. He forced himself to ease his grip. *No. No.* He smacked his fist on the wheel. "Ouch."

He needed to do a hundred push-ups, fifty sit-ups, then run ten miles. Maybe then the ache in his chest would ease enough to allow him to turn around and drive home. All the way to Missouri.

The silence pressed on him. He'd driven nearly a thousand miles and almost twenty hours with stops for repairs to get to Bee County. And for what? Thinking that for once God would answer his prayers. He hadn't brought Rocky's dad back. He hadn't saved Uncle Richard. What made him think God would see fit to give him this happiness?

"Who's out there?" A light blinded Rocky, then danced away. A flashlight. "I said, who's there?"

Had to be Mordecai. Rocky took a breath and pushed his door open. "Me. Rocky. Rocky Sanders."

Mordecai lowered the flashlight. As his eyes adjusted to the dark, Rocky could see that the tall, muscle-bound man seemingly unfazed by middle age stood on the porch, his shirttail out, no suspenders, head and feet bare. His hair, usually covered by a straw hat, looked like he'd stuck his finger into an electric socket. If he had one. Most days, Rocky could say the same about his own. "Figured as much."

"Sorry. I didn't mean to wake you."

"I keep telling my *fraa*—my wife—that it's none of

our business." He moved down the steps, his bare feet slapping on the wood. "*Rumspringa* and all."

"Nothing to worry about. Your wife—your *fraa*— will be pleased to know I just saw Frannie on the road in a buggy with that Amish man who was eating dinner with you last night."

"That would be Joseph." Mordecai sniffed. "That was Abigail's idea. We don't abide much by matchmaking."

Rocky leaned against the truck's bumper. His legs waffled under him. An exhaustion the likes of which he'd never experienced before invaded his muscles, head to toe. The hood steamed against the back of his shirt. A faint burned smell wafted around him. "Why not?"

"Because *Gott* knows what's best for each one of us. He'll provide. He has a plan. We need only obey and try to stay out of His way."

"You really believe that?"

"I do."

"Your bishop is allowing me to come to church next service. He thinks once I see how you worship, I'll get the picture and leave."

If this news surprised Mordecai, Rocky couldn't tell in the darkness. The man plopped down on the step and leaned back on his elbows as if it weren't the strangest thing in the world to be having this conversation with an *Englisch* man—a virtual stranger—in the dark of night. "Leroy has been bishop for many years. He's a wise man."

"You think I don't know there's a mountain separating Frannie and me right now." Rocky did know, but couldn't every mountain be climbed with the right amount of persistence, perseverance, and dedication? Olympic athletes knew it. Folks who climbed Mount Everest knew it. Triathlon athletes knew it. "It's not in me to be a quitter."

"I wouldn't be so prideful as to claim I know what *Gott's* plan is for Frannie or for you." Mordecai rolled the flashlight from one hand to the other and back. "But it's my job to hold her close and pray that she makes choices that are pleasing and obedient to Him."

Choices that couldn't include an outsider named Rocky Sanders. "I best get home and let you get back to sleep." Rocky trudged to the truck door and slid onto the ragged cloth seat. It seemed he'd spent the better part of the last year in this truck that looked as weather-beaten as its owner. "Sorry to have bothered you."

"No bother. I hope you find what you're looking for."

He had. Or so he thought. No sense in trying to make sense of it. "Thanks."

He turned the key. The engine cranked, coughed, then fell silent. He tried again. More coughing. Smoke seeped from the front end and dissipated in the late-night breeze. Rocky bowed his head, fighting the urge to smash his fist against the wheel again. "Come on, don't do this to me. Not now."

He cranked again. Nothing except more smoke.

"Looks like you're having some trouble there." Mordecai stood outside the truck passenger window. His big hand rested on the frame. "You know about fixing these things?"

"A little." Rocky dug his flashlight from the glove

compartment and slid from the truck. "Thing is I don't have the tools or the parts I'll surely need."

Mordecai rounded the front end and stood there as if offering silent commiseration.

Rocky shoved open the hood. Smoke billowed out. He staggered back, doing his own coughing. "Great. Perfect."

Mordecai crossed his arms over his chest. "Something you can fix?"

An oil leak, most likely. It had expensive written all over it. "No."

"I reckon you have one of those cell phones to call for help?"

"I do." He only kept it for his mother's sake. He wasn't much for talking on the phone or for electronics in general, though they came in handy for emergencies. Like this. Rocky glanced at his watch. "It's late, and I don't know if they'll be able to find us out here in the dark."

"It's not like the auto fix-it folks have to come to our place much." Mordecai's dry chuckle eased Rocky's discomfort. "I have a stall in the barn with your name on it. You'd be surprised how comfy a bed of straw can be. I reckon we have a few horse blankets out there as well."

"I don't know. What about your wife?" Not to mention Frannie. She would come back with her date to find his truck parked in front of the house. "I don't want to upset anyone."

Mordecai cocked his head toward the house. "My *fraa* puts out a good spread for breakfast. Stop in and eat while you're waiting for the tow truck."

A strange sense of unreality settled on Rocky. He was too tired to do anything else but wait for Mordecai to show the way. He slipped into the house and returned a few seconds later with a lit kerosene lamp. He led the way to the barn where he dropped a pile of blankets in a stall next to three others occupied by some decent-looking horses. "Don't be surprised if a mama cat joins you. I think she's about to have a litter, and she's already staked out her territory."

"There's plenty of room." Rocky squatted and smoothed the blankets, folding one at the top to serve as a pillow. "Thanks for the hospitality. I hope it doesn't get you into trouble."

"Kindness and hospitality don't count as trouble in our book." Mordecai shoved the stall gate closed. "I don't know what you're looking for, but it don't seem likely you'll find it here. Frannie is a good girl with a good heart. Pursuing her can only cause her misery. Yourself too."

"I'm getting that." Rocky turned his back and rearranged the blankets. Heat burned behind his eyes. He heaved a breath and turned to face Mordecai again. "I don't know what I was thinking when I got in my truck and drove down here. It seemed like the only thing I could do. Nothing else made sense. Haven't you ever felt that way?"

"Yep, I have, but we don't know each other well enough for that story. In my case, a girl's life with her family and her community—her church—wasn't at stake."

"But what about that plan you were talking about. God's plan. You claim to know what that is?"

"*Nee*. I am *Gott's* humble, obedient servant." Mordecai's expression was kind, but his tone stern. "I would never be so arrogant as to say or think such a thing. We believe in what's called *Gelassenheit*."

Rocky shook his head. "Gela-what?"

"*Gelassenheit*. Yielding to God's will and forsaking selfishness. Thy will be done."

"So you think me coming here for Frannie is selfishness?"

"That's something only you can know. Ask yourself, whose will is being done here?"

Could love and selfishness come in the same prettily wrapped gift? "Then maybe we should just see how it plays out."

Mordecai's head bobbed. He strode to the barn door, tugged it open, and looked back. "We also value the virtue of patience. We wait on God's plan instead of rushing to judgment or conclusion."

"Exactly."

"Godspeed, son, and sweet dreams." He shoved the door shut. The barn went dark and sweet silence like a soft blanket fell over Rocky.

Son. He closed his eyes against the pain of that one word. No one had called him 'son' in a long time. He inhaled the scent of hay and manure and dust, familiar smells that had grounded him his entire life. Working on the land, sowing and reaping. God's work. That's what his uncle always said. He never understood Rocky's desire to leave home and teach sports to kids. "You want to play games for a living? That's almost as bad as hitting guys for money." He'd shove back his white, sweat-stained cowboy hat and shake his head. "Putting food on people's tables, now there's an honorable living."

Hard work, honest work. Close to the land. Close to God. That was Uncle Richard's life. Could it be Rocky's too? *God, if You're really there, help me. I'm too stupid to figure this out. I need a hint.*

The answer was as clear as the night sky. A broken-down truck sitting in front of Frannie Mast's uncle's house despite every attempt to drive him away. What more direction did he need?

He closed his eyes and slept.

CHAPTER 5

Frannie's hands shook. She smoothed her apron. Ridiculous. Her stomach roiled at the mingled aromas of *kaffi* and baking bread, normally two of her favorite smells. She hadn't done anything wrong. She wavered at the end of the hallway that led to the stairs that would take her to the front room. No point in procrastinating. A quick peek from the window had confirmed the worst. Rocky's battered two-tone black-and-silver pickup truck still took up space in the front yard, just as it had when she returned from her ride with Joseph. No way Joseph had missed it. He simply doffed his hat and snapped the reins, his disapproval apparent in the rigid set of his broad shoulders.

She didn't invite Rocky to come. Yet she could think of nothing else now but seeing him.

What would *Onkel* Mordecai think? And *Aenti* Abigail? She must be having a cow or even two.

Frannie closed her eyes, breathed a quick prayer, and opened them. Squaring her shoulders, she marched into the front room. She plowed to a stop. There he sat. Eating a pancake slathered in butter and dripping with syrup. Across the table from her uncle, who sipped *kaffi* from his usual chipped blue mug. He smiled at something Rocky said.

Not so with her aunt. She plopped a pan of corn mush on the table and turned. From the expression on her face, she'd apparently eaten an entire jalapeño, seeds and all. "It's about time you got out of bed. I've already made breakfast. I reckon you can clean up."

With that, she flounced from the room.

Rocky turned to stare. He had bits of hay in his ruffled hair. His khaki pants and gray checkered western shirt were wrinkled. Lines around his eyes spoke of a restless night. He smiled. "Hey."

How dare he "hey" her? Any minute the women would start showing up for the sewing frolic. Their tongues would wag until they fell off over that pickup truck sitting in the yard at the crack of dawn. *Had it been there all night? How could her uncle allow it? What would Leroy say?* They'd be gobbling like a rafter of turkey hens. "What are you doing here?"

"He had some trouble with his truck last night." *Onkel* Mordecai set the cup on the table and burped gently. "He's already called for a tow truck."

"I'll be out of your way soon as they get here." Rocky rose and dropped his napkin by his plate, his smile gone. "Thank you for the hospitality, Mordecai."

"I'll expect you back tomorrow then." *Onkel* Mordecai stood as well. He settled his straw hat on his head. "We'll get that cement poured for the honey house in no time. I reckon we can finish up Albert's milk barn and milk house combo at the same time.

We've got cabbage, broccoli, and onions to plant. Lots of work for willing hands and a strong back."

"You're working here?" How was she supposed to move on if he kept showing up? "Why?"

"Rocky here says he did construction work to put himself through college. He's handy with tools and such." Her uncle seemed unperturbed by her distress. "And he's a farmer. Not a combination you find all the time. He offered to help, and we can use all the help we can get."

Frannie didn't ask permission this time. "On the porch."

Rocky led the way, holding the screen door for her in such a polite way she wanted to kick someone in the shins, something she'd never done in her entire life. "Why are you here?"

His gaze bounced from her to Caleb, who kicked a half-deflated, gray soccer ball as he made his way out of the yard, headed to school. "Has he ever played basketball?"

"What?"

"You know, not everything is about you."

It took Frannie a second to realize her mouth had dropped open. She shut it. *Breathe.* "What is that supposed to mean?"

"Sure, I came down here because of you, but the more I see, the more I realize something else brought me to Bee County."

"Like what?"

"I'm not sure, but I aim to find out." He slapped his ball cap on his tousled hair. "I see a line of dirt blowing on the road out there. I imagine it's the tow truck. I better go wave them down or they'll miss the turn in."

He stalked down the steps without looking back.

"Rocky."

"Don't worry about it."

"I'm sorry about last night." Even in wrinkled clothes, hair a mess, sleepers around his eyes, he looked like the best, most wonderful specimen of a man she'd ever seen. "I didn't mean to cause you hurt. I don't want to ever cause you hurt."

He turned and lifted his huge hand to shade his eyes from the morning sun. "I know you're between a rock and a hard place here. I'm sorry I'm making it harder for you. But I'm not giving up on us. I have to figure some things out first, but in the meantime, I'm asking you, don't make any rash promises to someone else. Please."

He spun around and marched away, leaving Frannie standing on the porch, her mouth open once again. "I don't make rash promises," she sputtered. "I only make promises I can keep."

"Promise me you'll wait, then." He kept walking. "First I need to fix my truck. Then I need to get me a job. Then I need to see a man about a horse. Then we'll talk."

"Or we could talk now."

"*Nee.*" *Aenti* Abigail let the screen door slam behind her. "You can't."

Frannie faced her aunt. "I know. I know, but I just—"

"You can't help but think with your heart instead of your head? Don't do it. You'll only be hurt or hurt others."

"Doesn't love come from the heart?"

"It does, but that doesn't mean you rule out all reason when you make your decisions." *Aenti* Abigail smoothed an errant blond hair back under her *kapp*, her blue eyes pensive. "I know how hard it can be. I moved to Bee County thinking I would marry one man and ended up marrying Mordecai. I hurt a good man in the process. I'll always regret that."

"But you married for love."

"The difference is my faith wasn't at stake. I didn't stand to lose my family and my church if I made the wrong decision."

"I would never marry outside the church." As much as the words pained her, Frannie knew they were true. She might never marry as a result, but her faith would stand the test. Gott, *is this some kind of test? If it is, it stinks.* "I plan to be baptized in the spring."

"I'm glad to hear that." Her aunt's hand rubbed Frannie's shoulder for a brief second. "I'll get the sewing supplies out while you finish the dishes. I see the women coming down the road."

Indeed they were. Frannie lingered on the porch, watching the two wagons that carried almost a dozen women, girls, and babies pull in next to Rocky's truck.

They hopped out in a melee of laughter and high voices that carried on the soft breeze that spoke of autumn just around the corner. Every one of them gave a second look at the truck. Even the little girls.

"Nice truck." Deborah padded up the steps first, little Timothy toddling behind her. "That the same one that was here the other night?"

Frannie breathed and lifted her chin. "It is indeed a nice truck. It's a classic. Needs a little work, though."

Nodding as if she didn't know what else to do, Deborah moved on. Leroy's wife, Naomi, was next. She said nothing, but her expression conveyed a passel of disapproval. Leroy would get an earful at the supper table.

The others didn't ask Frannie directly, but their faces were full of curiosity and concern as they chattered among themselves. The words *Englischer* and *truck* and *early* floated on the air as they bustled into the house, their bags of sewing supplies hoisted on their shoulders, their bare feet slapping against the wood. A few looked as if they might burst before they could tell someone. Frannie's *Englischer* had his truck parked at the King house at the crack of dawn.

Tongues would wag until they fell off. Let them. It would be hard to eat beans without tongues.

CHAPTER 6

Frannie inhaled the sweet, fresh smell of fall weather. October had brought with it cooler temperatures and the promise of rain soon. She wiggled, trying to get comfortable on the bench between Rebekah and Hazel. Her gaze wandered to the windows beyond the men's side. Leroy's house had more windows than *Onkel* Mordecai's. More opportunity for a breeze. She liked that. Everything in the front room looked scrubbed and freshly cleaned. The Glicks knew how to prepare for service. The last sermon was drawing to a close. She could tell by the way Leroy had ceased to pace and his thunderous voice had lost volume. As if he'd worn himself out. Soon they would sing, pray, and then eat.

A bang resonated through the room, causing more than one young girl to gasp as if jolted awake. Clutching her *Ausbund* hymnal to her chest, Frannie pivoted and craned her neck. The screen door stood open. And there, like the proverbial prodigal son, stood Rocky. Once again towering in the doorway.

"Sorry, sorry!" Off came the ball cap once again, revealing damp ringlets of hair. "I still don't have the hang of how long it takes to get around in a buggy." He laughed, a low, embarrassed laugh, not like the ones she remembered from their drives. "I'll just grab a seat."

He plopped down in an empty space on the last bench, right next to the young boys, who, by age, sat in the back.

Grab a seat? Buggy? She turned to Deborah, who shrugged, her eyebrows popped up so high they might touch her hairline. "Did he say 'buggy'?"

Deborah put a finger to her lips. "Hush!" She tugged Frannie's arm and they both sank to their knees for prayer. Frannie couldn't help herself. She looked back. Even on his knees Rocky towered over the boys. He looked as if he needed his handy-dandy playbook from his basketball-playing days to know what was going on.

How could she possibly concentrate knowing his eyes gazed on her back? She hadn't seen hide nor hair of him in the two weeks since he'd helped *Onkel* Mordecai and the other men build the honey storage shack and put up the milk house. They'd planted the winter vegetables and then he'd left without staying for supper or saying a proper good-bye.

Nothing. It was as if he'd picked up and gone home. That thought had made it nearly impossible for her to sleep most nights since.

Now he sat in her church in his Sunday-best black pants and white long-sleeved shirt with a button-down collar, the most agreeable-looking man she'd ever seen. Her throat went dry at the thought. Heat crept up her neck and scurried across her cheeks. *You're in church, Frannie Mast, in church. Gott, help me.*

They stood for the benediction. She breathed a sigh

of relief. *Almost done. Almost.* The closing hymn, slow and steady, calmed her. At the tail end of the last endless note, she skirted Deborah and the others on her row, intent on getting to the kitchen. A safe haven. Much as every fiber of her being ached to rush back and ask Rocky what all this meant, she would do the right thing. She would serve the fellowship meal, keep her mind and her hands busy. She would not give the women who stared at her, expressions ranging from curious to disapproving, more to talk about. No one could fault her for this.

"Frannie."

Rocky blocked her path. He smiled from ear to ear as if he had no clue as to the predicament he represented for her. He knew. He was no fool. He had a college education and a good head on his shoulders. "Rocky."

"We need to talk."

Talking would only lead to other things. She inhaled his scent. If only she could bottle it and hold it close. "I have to help with the meal."

"After, then."

"It's not done."

"Only for a minute. I want to show you something."

"I have to go home after."

"I have something for the *kinner*. I'll bring it by then."

He did *not* just use a *Deutsch* word in a sentence as if it were the most natural thing in the world.

"That's between you and *Onkel* Mordecai, then."

He grinned like a boy who'd just caught his first fish. "See you in a bit."

Frannie couldn't help it. Her smile escaped like a

kitten from a cardboard box. She would see him again, even if only for a few minutes. She would inhale his scent and memorize his smile. "See you."

It sounded like a promise. She scurried into the kitchen, not at all sure it was one she could or should keep.

. . .

Rocky tied the reins to the hitching post near the Kings' barn. The spot above the long sliding doors would be perfect. He sauntered to the back of the buggy, at peace for the moment. For once, he was doing something he knew how to do. After pushing back the basketballs rolling around, he slid out the basketball hoop. He hoisted it to his shoulder, grabbed his tool bag with his other hand, and headed to the barn. Caleb, Mordecai's youngest stepchild, who looked to be about eleven or twelve, sped across the yard toward him, gangly legs flailing. "Hey, Rocky, what's that you got?"

The boy knew his name and who he was. That made Rocky feel good. Acceptance came easier to the younger folks. Now if he could get Frannie to understand his intentions. "It's a basketball hoop."

Caleb double-stepped to keep up. "Whatcha gonna do with it?"

"You got a ladder?"

"Sure we do."

"Haul it out here."

Caleb grinned and disappeared into the barn. He reemerged a few minutes later with the ladder on his back, dragging the end behind him. Together they positioned it against the barn. Rocky started up, Caleb holding on at the bottom, just for good measure. Seconds later, Rocky stood on the top rung, his tool belt slung over his shoulder. He'd hung plenty of hoops in his day. Pickup basketball games kept boys—and girls—out of trouble. Even if it was a freestanding hoop in a paved cul-de-sac, it was an invitation to play, to work off excess energy, to stay out of trouble, to get away from computers and video games and TV programming that turned young brains to mush.

Not that these kiddos—a half dozen had gathered around since he started screwing in the bolts—had access to any of those things. The curiosity and wide grins on their faces told him they were like other kids in more ways than one. They liked to play games and have fun.

"You know, you might have asked *Onkel* Mordecai before you started hanging things on his barn." Frannie's voice wafted over the chatter of the *kinner*, as he had learned from Leroy to call them in the two meetings he'd had with the bishop and Mordecai in his role as deacon. Leroy was concerned about the influence Rocky's presence might have, especially on the boys. He would show the bishop the good he could do, for all of them. "You're banging on someone else's property, you know."

Funny thing was, she didn't sound all that upset.

He clopped down the ladder and gathered up his tools. "You can put it away." He nodded to Caleb and a boy about the same size who stood next to him. "I'll be right back."

He strode past Frannie, with her tantalizing scent of

vanilla and soap, without giving her a look. He knew what he'd see. Hands on her hips, her cheeks pink, her mouth open to scold him some more. She would look so pretty he'd forget what he planned to do next. "Help me get the balls from my buggy."

"Your buggy?"

He'd set the trap and she'd fallen right in. "Yep."

She strode after him. "What are you doing here?"

"Seems like you ask me that every time I come around." He opened the back door on the buggy and tossed her a clean, fresh orange ball. He loved new basketballs. The smell of rubber. "By the way, I did talk to Mordecai. He graciously accepted my gift. Surely, you can do the same. Or hush up. One or the other."

Her mouth closed, but he could see her brain turning, *clickity-clack*, a hundred miles an hour. That was his Frannie.

His Frannie. Gott, *please*.

Gott. Another word he'd picked up in his visits with Leroy and Mordecai. Not just God the Father, as he had once thought. But God of all. He spent most of his daily morning runs contemplating this concept. One of the Hostetler boys nearly hit him with a buggy when, deep in thought, he meandered into the road. This God with a plan so big, no man or woman could understand it with their little pea brains. He certainly couldn't. Neither man approved of his intentions with Frannie, and neither would give an inch, but their tradition gave them no choice but to hear him out. If he truly had an interest in their faith, they had to see it through. Bless both of them for being so honorable.

For giving him a chance when disapproval oozed from their pores.

Frannie sauntered to the front of the buggy and began to stroke the Morgan's thick mane. "He's a beaut. Where'd you get him?"

How did he afford the horse? That's what she really meant.

"Belongs to Seth Cotter. I took a job with him. He has that big farm right there where you turn off the highway. He's getting up there in years, and there's a lot of work he can't do himself anymore, even in fall and winter. I'm staying in his bunkhouse now."

Contemplating how she'd react to this news, Rocky motioned with the first basketball. She held out her hands. He tossed it to her. Grinning like he'd just given her the keys to his old truck, she caught it. The ball smacked against her long, thin fingers. Giggling, she tossed it up and down. Another thing among the multitude of attributes he liked about Frannie. She had a natural-born aptitude for sports. Not only that, she liked them. Under different circumstances, she would've been an athlete.

She shook her head so hard her *kapp* slid a little more cockeyed than usual. "You're thinking of buying a horse to go with the buggy. When you have the money. I don't understand. I truly don't."

"When I said it wasn't just about you, I meant it." He snagged two more balls. "I've been doing a lot of reading and thinking. I visited with Leroy and Mordecai a couple of times."

Her full lips were shaped in an *O*, but no sound came out.

"I got rid of my cell phone and iPad. I never turn on the radio or the TV in the bunkhouse. I heat my ramen noodles on the woodstove."

"How will you stay in touch with your mother?"

That's what she chose to latch onto? "I write her letters." He gave her his best grin. "Isn't that how you stay in touch? And if there's an emergency, she has Seth's number."

Frannie nodded, but she didn't meet his gaze, instead studying the lines on the basketball as if memorizing them.

"I sold my truck. That's where I got the money for the buggy."

"You sold your truck?" The words came out in a squeak. She stared up at him. "You loved that truck. It's a classic."

"I'll love this buggy too." He started toward the barn. She trailed after him, still tossing the ball from one hand to the other. "Leastways I will once I get used to driving it on the highway with all those eighteen-wheelers whizzing past me."

"It's five to eight miles an hour."

Rocky glanced back at her. "What?"

"Horse-drawn buggies travel about five to eight miles an hour. That's what *Onkel* Mordecai says and he knows everything." She smiled. His heart catapulted to a spot by his collarbone in a spectacular jump shot, then plummeted back to its normal resting spot. "Keep that in mind. Leroy doesn't like folks to be late to church."

She was warming up to the idea. Leastways, Rocky could hope. He tossed a ball to Caleb and another to a boy half his size. "Hold these, while I mark the out-of-bounds lines."

"Out-of-bounds?"

Frannie let her ball sail. It smacked against the backboard and slid around the hoop's rim before falling through the net for a neat two points. The kids dived for the ball and tussled over it, laughing and cheering.

All was right in the world when a pickup basketball game took off.

"Beginner's luck." Rocky took the ball from Caleb, raced toward the basket, jumped, and jammed the ball through it. "Wahoo, nothing but net!"

Frannie wrestled Caleb for the rebound, but her cousin had more strength. In a flash, he made another basket. "That's two points, right? Are we having teams?"

"Teams. It's more fun if you keep score. I'll be on one team, Frannie on the other, since we're the grown-ups." Grown-ups, of a sort. Rocky grabbed a stick and began marking the out of-bounds lines and the free-throw line in the hard-packed dirt that passed for a yard. "We'll do a half-court game. I reckon you don't know what that means."

Frannie snorted, a very unladylike sound that only served to endear her more to Rocky. "Sure I do. They had games on the TV in the restaurant."

"And you watched? Shame on you."

"*Nee*, I heard. Who could help, the way they yell and scream over a game?" Frannie snatched the ball from Caleb. She scampered past Rocky, her long dress flapping behind her. "Hurry up. We're playing basketball."

Indeed, they were.

. . .

"What is wrong with you?"

Frannie whirled. She hadn't heard *Aenti* Abigail enter the room she shared with Rebekah and Hazel. She smoothed her straggling hair with both hands. Her *kapp* hung by a hairpin. Dirt and sweat marred her apron from top to bottom. "What do you mean?"

"Don't act all innocent with me." Her aunt crossed her arms over her chest. "Everyone saw you out there playing games with him."

"Him" had a name. Rocky. "Having fun. There's no rule in the *Ordnung* that says we can't have fun."

"Don't make me the bad person here. There's fun and then there's *fun* and you know it."

Frannie did know it. She'd had more fun playing basketball with Rocky and the *kinner* than she'd had in all the days since she returned to Bee County. Running and shooting and scuffling over the ball. Rocky towered over her and the other players, making it easy for him to block shots. Sometimes he took pity and let her make a shot here and there. Two-pointers, as he called them. She'd learned to defend the basket and what a foul was. Her specialty seemed to be free throws. With no one defending the basket, she couldn't miss. Her arms ached and her legs shuffled like wet noodles, but she felt . . . happy.

"It's just a game."

"A game everyone saw you playing with a full-grown man."

"There were a bunch of us."

"You were the only woman."

Frannie sank onto the bed. *Aenti* Abigail joined her. She patted Frannie's dirty hands. "I don't want you to think I don't understand what you're going through, but you told me you would never marry outside the church. I took you at your word."

"I meant it."

"That's not what it looked like today."

"We had fun, that's all."

"Joseph is coming for supper tonight."

"Joseph isn't interested in me. He just likes your casserole." Frannie went to the window. Dark clouds hung close to the earth, heavy and damp. Rain had finally begun to fall, heralding the end of a long, hot summer. For everyone. She breathed in the scent of moist dirt, fighting the urge to bawl. Plain women didn't bawl. Inhaling, she faced her aunt. "You didn't marry Stephen because you knew you didn't love him."

"I gave him a chance before I made that decision." Aunt Abigail plucked at a thread on her apron, her expression distant, remembering. "I told your *mudder* I would watch out for you and I am."

"My *mudder* would like a good game of basketball."

"She wouldn't like it if her child left the district and she couldn't see her anymore, ever. That's what's at stake here." Her aunt's voice trembled. Surely she thought of her own daughter, Leila. "You know that. Do you want to give up everything and everyone you love for a man?"

"I'm not Leila. I will never do that. I'm Plain through and through."

"So was Leila. Or so I thought."

"If you believe in *Gott's* will, wasn't leaving here *Gott's* plan for Leila and Jesse?"

"I'm not smart enough or prideful enough to think I know what *Gott's* plan is. It will unfold on *Gott's* time, not ours." Aunt Abigail sounded so sure of herself. Even the loss of her daughter didn't shake her faith. "*Gott* is good. What we see today or tomorrow is not the end. We have to have patience and wait on the Lord."

Patience had never been one of Frannie's strong suits. "I'm sorry. I have trouble seeing my life without Rocky in it."

There, she'd said it. Her aunt's arms came out and Frannie found herself embraced in a warm, sure hug. Surprise overcame her. Tears formed. She sniffed. *Aenti* Abigail did the same and sat back.

"Did you know I have a new granddaughter whom I haven't seen? Deborah received a letter from Leila." She wiped at her face with her sleeve. "Her name is Grace. You'd be surprised at what you can get through. I know I am."

"There have been times when people have joined our faith and become members of the district, haven't there?"

Aenti Abigail sighed. "Wishful thinking, child."

"Why? He bought a buggy."

"He's thinking with his heart too. A buggy doesn't a Plain man make."

"Doesn't it count for something?"

"It's true that it's happened in other districts. I've heard." Aunt Abigail smoothed her apron, leaving the loose thread to its own devices. "Different districts do it differently, but usually the person who joins spends at least a year getting used to the idea of giving up all those luxuries like electricity and cars and such. The bishop interviews the person to see if his heart is really in it. Sometimes the whole church votes. I don't know how Leroy would do it."

"So it is possible?"

"But not likely." Her aunt stood. "Get cleaned up. I need to warm up the enchilada casserole. You can set the table. Put out the pickled jalapeños. You know how Mordecai likes those with his enchiladas. And don't forget to set a place for Joseph."

Her aunt disappeared through the door.

A pain pierced Frannie's chest so sharp she doubled over. The happiness of only a few minutes earlier dissipated like dew in the rising sun on an August morning. She closed her eyes and rocked, willing the pain to subside. *Gott? Gott!*

Nothing.

She jerked off her apron, wadded it up, and slung it across the room. "Thy will be done?" She spoke the words aloud in the still silence of her room. She'd heard them a million times it seemed, and she still couldn't understand how a person knew. How did she know?

Gott?

Silence. Heart as heavy as a year's supply of firewood, she trudged across the room to pick up the apron.

Thy will be done, but please let it include Rocky. Somehow. Some way.

Some kind of prayer that was. Trying to say, "Lord, have it Your way, but first, Lord, have it my way."

Lord, have mercy on my rebellious soul.

Worn to a frazzle, she combed her hair, replaced her *kapp*, and slipped on a clean apron.

Time to set a place for Joseph.

CHAPTER 7

The horsey smell mixed with the rank odor of manure should be considered for a man's cologne. Rocky smiled to himself. Women might not think so, but any cowboy worth his salt would wear it. The rhythm of his strokes across Chocolate's wide back and flanks was almost as calming to him as it was to the horse. He leaned his head against Chocolate's long neck for a second and heaved a sigh. Take away everything going on in his life right now, capture the soft evening glow of sunset, a mourning dove cooing in the distance, two calico kittens chasing each other in a rough-and-tumble race across the yard outside the corral, and this moment could be almost perfect.

Almost.

The distant *clip-clop* of horse's hooves and the *squeak-squeak* of wheels traversing the rough terrain of the dirt road that led to the Cotters' homestead forced him to raise his head and squint into the setting sun. A buggy. Too soon to say whose. Chocolate raised his head and nickered.

"You and me both, sweet thing, you and me both." Rocky gathered the harness and led the horse toward the fence. "Well, I'll be a monkey's uncle. That there is the bishop, Chocolate. What do you think he wants?"

To tell Rocky to get out of Dodge and leave a certain young Amish woman in peace? Surely not. Rocky ducked his head. His jeans, so worn they were a pale blue with skin peeking through thick threads at the knees, were dirty. His jacket had bloodstains on it from where he'd cut his hand chopping firewood, and he probably smelled a lot like Chocolate.

Leroy parked near the gate and descended from the buggy. Once both boots were on the ground, one hand went to his back. He was slow to straighten. "Evening."

"Evening."

Rocky waited. He'd learned in his dealings with the bishop to let the man do the talking. He got in a lot less trouble that way.

"Tomorrow is the annual auction." Leroy wiped his face with a bandanna that might have once been white but now looked a dingy gray. "It's our annual fundraiser for the school and our emergency medical fund."

Rocky shoved through the gate and latched it behind him. "I might have heard something about that."

Leroy propped both arms on the top plank of the wooden fence and leaned against it. "Have you finished your readings?"

The older man's shift in topics from the auction to a barely legible translation of the Dordrecht Articles of Faith and its eighteen articles had meaning, but Rocky couldn't say what it was. "I'm working on it."

"Those articles are very important to a Plain man of faith."

"Yes, sir."

"Don't 'sir' me."

"Yes, sir—Leroy." Why had the man made this trip out here to repeat a conversation they'd already had? More than once. "I know that."

"You talk to your mother lately?"

Now that was indeed a new topic. "I gave up my phone."

"You don't know how to come to the store and use the community phone?"

Surely that was a privilege meant only for the members of the district. "Well, yes, I mean, I didn't know, I didn't think—"

"Never underestimate how much a parent misses a child who's left the nest." Leroy cleared his throat. His gaze drifted over Rocky's shoulder. Surely he thought of his own son, whom he refused to see and with whom he would never break bread again. "Mother or father. It's as God intends when a grown child strikes out on his own—for the most part—but that doesn't mean it doesn't hurt a parent's heart."

"Understood."

He'd talked to his mother every night from his hotel room on the trip down, regaling her with stories of the people he'd visited within the diners along the way, describing parks where he'd stopped to eat a sack lunch and take a quick snooze. She thought he would pick up Frannie and bring her home. If things didn't work out, he wouldn't have to tell her how close he'd come to assuming a Texan citizenship. Texas had been its own country more than once, and some still thought it was or should be.

Writing letters was a lost art in the English world, but one he had given due diligence since coming to Bee County. His mother deserved to know what was going on with her only son.

"Tell me something about your mother."

Leroy's abrupt command blew away Rocky's reverie. "Beg your pardon."

"Your mother raised you to be a decent human being, best I can tell." Leroy stared at Rocky over streaked wire-rimmed glasses that rested halfway down his long nose. "Tell me something about her."

Food always came to Rocky's mind first when he thought of his mother. That and the way she used to put vapor rub on a cloth diaper, warm it on the gas register in the living room, and then pin it around his neck when he had a bad cold. Her hands were always cool on his hot forehead. She always hummed a George Strait song under her breath when she made chicken noodle soup from scratch. "She makes the best fried chicken in the state of Missouri."

"And your father? What do you remember about him?"

"What does this have to do with me joining the church?"

"You are who you are because of your parents. They taught you what's right and what's wrong. They taught you what to value."

"My dad mostly taught me what not to do." Rocky let the rough wood of the fence absorb an anger that never really went away. It bubbled under the surface and reared its ugly head at inopportune times. "He wasn't a real dad. My Uncle Richard, he was my dad."

"The boxer who became a farmer."

"Yes."

"He raised a good man."

Rocky ducked his head, his throat tight at the unexpected, matter-of-fact assessment from a man he'd come to respect. "He used to take me to auctions up in Jamesport. I loved the auctioneers. I used to practice all the way home, in the backyard, at the kitchen table, until my mama finally told me to hush."

"Any good at it?"

"Uncle Richard said I could always become an auctioneer if the NFL thing didn't work out."

Leroy sniffed and straightened. He turned and ambled toward the buggy, his limp more pronounced than it had been earlier. At the buggy he turned. "I reckon I could use some help tomorrow."

"Help?"

"Are you deaf? *Jah*, help. At the auction. It's a long day and my legs aren't what they used to be. Throat gets mighty parched too."

A chance to be at one of the most important events in the life of this district and he was invited, by the bishop, no less. Rocky squashed the urge to pump his fist and whoop. As an added and particularly sweet bonus, Frannie would be there. "I'll be there with bells on."

"No bells needed. Show up before dawn."

"I'll be there."

"Don't be late."

"I won't."

Leroy touched the brim of his hat, hauled himself into the buggy, and drove away.

When his visitor was well down the road, Rocky succumbed. He pumped his fist, did his best Snoopy dance, and whooped until Mrs. Cotter came to the window and looked out, a perturbed expression on her face. Chocolate simply nickered.

CHAPTER 8

Englisch folks sure worked up an appetite at auctions. Still pleased that *Aenti* Abigail had trusted her with taking money and making change, Frannie recounted the bills in the shoe box. More than two hundred dollars just from the food shack since the beginning of the auction. More money than she'd ever seen in one place. From the number of cars and trucks parked in front of the Combination Store, the crowd would equal or surpass those she remembered from previous years. From her vantage point seated by the tables laden with pans of hamburgers, meat loaf, green beans, potato salad, and coleslaw, along with bread and pie, she couldn't see much. All the same, the stream of *Englischers* and the steady singsong sound of the two auctioneers said all went well.

Her mouth watered as she batted away flies buzzing the table. The women wouldn't eat until the flow of customers became a trickle and then disappeared. This event, held the first Friday every November, was about raising money for the school, their medical fund, repairs, stocking up for winter, and preparing for emergencies that might occur during the year. Everyone understood that.

"I'll have the meat-loaf plate."

She'd been so sure Rocky would know better than to seek her out here, in front of Aunt Abigail and the other women. She'd been so careful to avoid him since the impromptu basketball game. She'd taken her *aenti's* words to heart and accepted a handful of invitations to go riding with Joseph. He asked almost nothing of her, and he'd never brought up the topic of Rocky again. He was a nice man. Smart. Funny. A hard worker. Easy on the eyes, if that counted for anything, which it didn't. Not much, anyway.

She counted off his attributes on her fingers at night in bed. She told them to Rebekah in the dark as they both tried to sleep. Rebekah cheered her on every time, and every time Frannie found sleep eluded her for hours.

She patted damp sweat from her cheeks with a paper napkin. Even in November, she felt warm. Or maybe it was his presence. "Good choice. Five dollars." She glanced up at Rocky for a split second. Blue shirt, black pants, boots. All he needed was a straw hat and suspenders to look the part. That's all it was—a part. "It includes your choice of wheat or white bread, apple, cherry, or lemon pie."

"White and apple, of course. You should raise your prices. You could get a lot more for good grub like this." He tugged a worn leather wallet from his back pocket and handed her a crumpled twenty. "Can I take something to Leroy? He must be getting hungry. He's been up there auctioneering for hours."

She fumbled with the box lid. It took her two tries with trembling fingers to count out the three fives for his change. "He'll eat when it's over."

"You could at least look at me. I'm just trying to help."

"If you want to help, take your plate and have a seat at one of the tables." *Aenti* Abigail slipped into the space next to Frannie. Her tone was polite, but her expression stern. "What kind of pie would you like?"

"Apple, but I can't sit. I have to get back. I'm helping spot the bidders. Leroy invited me to help out when I met with him last night." Rocky's tone had a *so-there* quality to it. He'd met with the bishop. He'd been invited. Would wonders never cease? "I may spell him after a bit as auctioneer. He looks pretty tuckered out."

Frannie held out his change, trying to ignore her aunt's surprised stare. Leroy had invited Rocky. That was a good thing. Besides, a man had to eat. She hadn't done anything to encourage him. Not one thing. "You know how to call an auction?"

"Uncle Richard used to take me to the livestock auctions up in Jamesport all the time." Rocky waved away his change and picked up his plate instead. "I loved going and I used to imitate the auctioneers in our backyard. Uncle Richard said I got to be pretty good."

"You forgot your change."

"*Nee*, this is a fund-raiser, isn't it? Consider it my donation."

There he went using a *Deutsch* word again. Frannie eyed her aunt, whose eyebrows knotted in a fierce line across her forehead. "We appreciate it."

Humming a soft tune that sounded like a Christmas hymn, he sauntered away, already picking at the meat loaf with his plastic fork.

"He is quite the talker, isn't he?"

"*Jah.*" Frannie counted the bills again. And again. Sitting here in the food shack far from the auction had become unbearable for no apparent reason. The first time she met Rocky outside the restaurant had been at a Jamesport school fund-raiser auction. The memory of his smile and the way he asked her if he could call on her sometime—that's the way he put it—was so sweet it hurt to think of it. "Maybe I should take food to the boys at the water table."

"I don't think so." Aunt Abigail pursed her lips, her eyes narrowed. "But you could take a plate to Joseph. He's partial to hamburgers. And lemon meringue pie, it's his favorite."

"There's nothing between Joseph and me." And there never would be. Both of them knew it.

Smiling, her aunt whipped from one end of the table, wrapping a burger with all the trimmings in a paper napkin and placing it on a Styrofoam plate, along with a baked potato steaming in its tinfoil and a thick wedge of pie. "Sometimes you have to work at it a little. Give things time to grow. Get it to him while it's hot."

Frannie sighed. She needed a breath of fresh air. She needed to be someplace else. Anyplace. Skirting folks who stopped in the middle of the road to chat and sip sodas or bottled water covered in condensation, she trudged past the Combination Store intent on her errand. At least Joseph would get a decent meal out of it. He would appreciate that.

"Where're you headed?"

Frannie stumbled. Rocky grabbed her arm. She tugged away. "Are you following me? You're supposed to be eating your meat loaf."

"I lost my appetite after you gave me the cold shoulder. We have to talk."

"I know." Frannie glanced around. A crowd of *Englischers* pressed them, no one she knew, but that could change any second. "Not here."

"I was thinking of buying some chickens. The Cotters don't have any." He pointed toward the livestock area. "Maybe you can help me pick them out."

Joseph's plate clutched in her hands, Frannie veered to her right. Her mind said, Nee, nee, nee, but her heart seemed to be in control of her body. She slipped between the sheds to the pens that held chickens, pigs, goats, and sheep. The stench nearly knocked her back a step.

"Remember the auction in Jamesport?" The smell of manure didn't seem to bother Rocky. He leaned on a fence post with one elbow and surveyed a mama hen and her chicks.

"I do."

"You looked so cute with your sunburned nose. Your freckles tripled in one day."

His teeth had been white against his tan, and his eyes, always so vivid blue, were made even more vibrant by his blue shirt.

"It was so hot that day, at least a hundred and two."

"You drank three cups of lemonade and ate two helpings of homemade ice cream."

"You kept track?"

"I didn't want to get you in trouble. So I gazed upon you from afar until I realized I wouldn't get another chance like that to ask you out."

She giggled. "From afar?"

"Yeah, haven't you ever read a romance? Mr. Shakespeare or something." His hand came up and his fingers brushed at her cheek. They were so warm. "I keep telling myself to follow the rules, to wait, to be patient, but when I see you, all I can think about is . . ."

He leaned so close she caught a whiff of peppermint on his breath. She found herself stretching on her tiptoes to meet him. "Think about what?"

He pulled back. She felt as if she'd been dropped into a deep well of cold water. "Rocky!"

His face flushed, he straightened. "Sorry, I'm sorry."

"I feel the same way." The words came out in a stammer. "I'm trying so hard to do the right thing."

"But sometimes it's hard to know what the right thing is."

"Exactly."

Rocky returned to the fence post, his hands gripping the wood as if determined to stay put. "Remember the sewing machine?"

"The Singer treadle?" It was a nice machine. They had one just like it in their front room. Most Plain folks did. "Of course I do."

"My mom embroidered a tablecloth and draped it

on top." He shook his head, his expression sheepish. "She set her begonias on it. Looks very pretty."

Frannie chuckled. "Not much of a sewer, I guess."

"Nope. She likes the way it looks in her living room, but if she wants to fix a hem or something, she drags out her Sears electric and lets it rip."

The chuckle they shared had a homey feeling, as if they'd known each other years and years.

"My parents bought a used wringer wash machine." Frannie rubbed her hands across the slats of the fence, the wood rough under her fingers. "Can you ever imagine them filling it with dirt and planting begonias in it?"

"Or using the canning jars you bought for them as planters?" Rocky shook his head. "They're practical people who live in a practical world."

"Our worlds *are* different." For one thing, her parents couldn't afford to buy something for looks. "Besides, when you work the land, you have a lot of dirty clothes."

His sigh had a strange, sad echo in it. "That doesn't mean never the two shall meet."

"You are in a funny mood today."

"Very literary."

His college education sometimes bled through, making Frannie feel worlds apart. As if she didn't already. "I don't know what that means."

"I know. Do you understand why I'm meeting with Leroy?"

"To talk to him about . . . being Amish."

"Exactly."

"What does he say?"

"He says it's a very big change, not one most *Englischers* can make. They try, but they fail."

"What do you say?"

"I'm not big on failing or losing. I'm not doing this because I want a simpler way of living. I don't have any illusions about how hard your life is."

"Then why are you doing it?"

He shook his head without meeting her gaze. "There's something in me that needs filling up, I guess."

Not for her. That was good. Very good. "Because of your dad and your uncle?"

"Because of my life." His gaze leveled with hers. "Who's the burger for?"

Frannie glanced down at the plate in her hands. She'd forgotten about it. Grease had begun to congeal on the bun. "Oh, that."

Rocky took only one step back, but the gap between them widened to a chasm. "Joseph?"

As much as she wanted to deny it, she wouldn't. She could never lie to Rocky. "Yes."

"These chickens look a little small." He took another step back. "I should spell the boys in the auction barn. It might not be a hundred and two, but it's warm and muggy. They might need a swig of water."

"Taking a plate to someone doesn't mean anything." Only to her aunt. Even Joseph knew where he stood, and he didn't seem all that upset about it. "He's a friend of the family."

Rocky's face twisted with pain. "I love you."

He whirled and strode away.

The words floated in the air around her. She wanted to collect them and hold them close to her heart where she could hear them over and over again in the middle of the night or in broad daylight, morning and afternoon. "*Ach*, Rocky!"

He kept walking. Soon he disappeared into the steady stream of folks moving between the auction barn and the food shed and the buggies for sale in front of the Combination Store.

She closed her eyes. *Love you too.*

In her world, love might not be enough. Faith and community also counted. Rocky knew that.

They both did.

A chicken squawked and the goats bleated in response. The smell choked her. She glanced at the plate in her hand. The offending hamburger needed to be delivered. She plodded toward the honey table, glad only the animals could see the misery and pain riding piggyback on her shoulders.

Joseph leaned over the table, sacking an array of jars ranging from honey to wild mustang grape jelly to strawberry jam for an elderly lady leaning on a walker that tilted unsteadily on the uneven ground. He smiled at Frannie and went back to his chore. She set the plate on the table and touched the woman's arm. "Can I help you carry that?"

"Thank you, young lady, but my grandson is around here somewhere. He'll be back any second to help me to the car. Sweet of you, though."

Indeed, the young man in overly tight blue jeans and a fluorescent orange T-shirt that matched his orange-and-green sneakers returned just as Joseph handed the lady her change. "Enjoy, ma'am."

"I plan to. Deacon here loves strawberry jam on English muffins. Don't you, Deacon?"

The teenager's big ears turned a deep shade of purplish red. She leaned on her walker and tottered away, Deacon's arm around her bowed shoulders in a surprising—to Frannie, anyway—show of affection.

"That was sweet of you to offer to help her." Still smiling, Joseph snapped the plastic lid onto the battered coffee can that served as his cash box. "You do have a sweet disposition under all that sassiness."

"Sassiness?"

"*Jah.* You give a lot of lip, but I see more to you."

None of this was his fault. It was her Aunt Abigail's fault. "I'm so sorry."

"Sorry for what? For being lippy and not the best housekeeper? Don't be." He rearranged the jars on the table, from four in a row to five, still smiling. "You may not be the most ordinary Plain woman, but I like you just the way you are. Life with you would be interesting."

More likely irritating and annoying in the long run. The shiny would wear off. Most Plain men would wish for a *fraa* who could make gumbo without burning it and bread that wasn't hard as a rock. Men like Joseph would want a *fraa* who knew her place and also knew how to sew a tear in his pants so that it held. "You will find your special friend one of these days."

"And you don't think she'll be lippy?"

"I think you know what you like, and you're too nice

to tell my aunt to leave well enough alone." She slid the plate toward him. "I brought you your favorite pie. *Aenti* Abigail said you'd rather have a hamburger than meat loaf, but I can always take it back and trade it."

"It's too bad Abigail is already taken. She does make a fine pie."

He grinned at her despite the *Englisch* girl in a pink T-shirt—why did young *Englischers* wear their clothes a size too small—who flashed a five-dollar bill at him and said her mother wanted to know if she could get two jars of honey with that. The answer was no, but Joseph ignored her for the moment. "Your *aenti* is only trying to save you from a world of hurt."

"You have a customer."

He tended to the girl, who seemed happy with her one jar. Whether the mother would be was another question. She traipsed away and he turned back. "Abigail is a wise woman."

"Sometimes the heart doesn't listen to wise words."

"For your sake and the sake of your parents, you should try harder." He plopped onto an overturned bushel basket, unwrapping the hamburger. "Don't worry. I won't tell anyone your secret. I can even keep coming around to take you on rides if you want."

"That's okay. You shouldn't waste your time on the likes of me."

"It wasn't a waste. Abigail is a good cook." He grinned. "And Rebekah is a firecracker."

"She is indeed." Frannie grinned back. "See you around."

"Not if I see you first."

As she walked away, the sound of the auctioneer floated from the big shed. "I've got two, who'll give me three, there's three, how about four, anybody give me four . . ."

Rocky's voice, deep and sure and full of delight. Leroy had let him take over.

Wonders would never cease.

Frannie could use unceasing wonders about now.

CHAPTER 9

Rocky snapped the reins again. Chocolate picked up his pace. Such a good piece of horseflesh. Rocky felt guilty monopolizing Seth's horse all the time, but the elderly farmer assured him it was no imposition. Seth paid Rocky well, and he squirreled away every penny he could in savings. Even with his nest egg, it would be awhile before he could afford to buy his own horse and some property for settling down. If he was here that long. *Gott* willing. The soupy gray sky hung so low it felt as if it weighed on his shoulders. He wouldn't miss the south Texas weather, that was for sure. November in Missouri meant crisp fall weather with leaves turning brilliant oranges, reds, and golds. Frost sparkled on the grass in the mornings. "Downright dreary" described Bee County this time of year. Dreary matched his disposition this morning.

On the bright side, warmer weather meant winter strawberries could be planted, along with cabbage, broccoli, onions, and English peas. Which gave him an excuse to head to the district to help out. Maybe Mordecai would extend an invitation for Thanksgiving.

Stop it.

He hadn't seen Frannie since the auction. Frannie with her plate for another man. Leroy said Rocky must leave her out of the equation. Regardless. Make a decision based on a desire to live out his faith according to the Bee County district's *Ordnung*. Could he do it? Did he want to do it? Did God call him to do it?

Leroy asked all the hard questions. Rocky turned the buggy onto the farm-to-market road, contemplating his answers. The sun broke through clouds that began to scud across the sky in a chilly breeze that hadn't been there a few minutes earlier. The sudden brightness blinded him for a second. Chocolate snorted, whinnied, and began to pick up speed. "Whoa, whoa, what's gotten into you?" He tightened the reins with one hand and pushed down the bill of his cap with the other. If he planned to stay, he really should get a straw hat. More of a visor. Chocolate whinnied again, the sound high and nervous.

Rocky saw what had the horse worried. A buggy capsized in the ditch just beyond the turnoff that led to the highway and Beeville. A horse, still tethered to it, bucked and tried to free itself. Mordecai's Morgan. A vise tightened around Rocky's chest. Fear choked the flow of blood to his heart. "Come on, Chocolate, let's go."

He gave the horse free rein for several hundred yards and then pulled him in as they approached the overturned buggy. "Easy, easy does it."

Don't let it be Frannie.

He hopped into the ditch and shot across the muddy terrain, slipping and sliding despite the tread on his work boots. "Hello? Are you okay?"

A moan greeted the response. The orange SLOW triangle dangled to one side on the rear of the buggy. He squatted and shoved it back. Abigail lay on her back, her right side under the buggy. Mud covered her face. Blood streaked her forehead.

"There you are. Can you move?"

"Help me out of here." Abigail's voice was soft, but determined. "I'm stuck."

"Are you sure you can move? Is anything broken?"

"I'm fine."

He took the hand she held out and gently pulled. She groaned and jerked away. "My wrist. Something's wrong with my wrist."

"Okay, we'll do this a different way." Rocky slid his hands under her arms. She stiffened but didn't protest. "I'm going to lift you out now. If anything hurts, tell me and I'll stop."

Seconds later he had her out from under the buggy. Mud, bits of dead grass, straw, and weeds covered her apron and dress. One of her shoes was missing. Her *kapp*, normally so perfectly situated, had slipped down her back. Her hair, now tousled and falling from its bun, was a deep blond highlighted with a few strands of silver. He wanted to push the *kapp* back into its rightful place, but he didn't dare. "Where does it hurt?"

"I'm fine. A little headache and some pain in this arm." She clutched her wrist against her muddied apron. "It's nothing. I need to get home, that's all."

"*Nee*, you need a doctor."

"No doctor."

Finances were tight. If anyone understood that, he

did. "Then let me take you up to the Cotters. It's closer than home. Mrs. Cotter will have first-aid supplies. You can get cleaned up, and we can decide if that will do it, or if you need more medical attention."

She touched a finger to her forehead, winced, and drew it away. The sight of the blood seemed to give her the answer she needed. "Home. We have first-aid supplies too."

"The Cotters are right down there at the end of the road. It's much faster. You're bleeding."

She shook her head. "I'm fine."

"You're not fine."

Their gazes locked. She looked away. "Fine. The Cotters."

A lifetime of letting men take the lead couldn't be overcome in a day. Rocky would never take advantage of her upbringing, but in this instance, he felt relief. She needed his help. "Let me help you up."

"I can do it."

Stubbornness definitely ran in the family.

Abigail scrambled to her feet, slipping in the mud, then managing to hoist herself upright. Her knees buckled. Rocky caught her before she went down again. "There's no shame in letting a person help you."

"I know. It's good of you to stop."

Something about the emphasis on *you* puzzled Rocky. Was it because he was an Englisher or because he was Rocky Sanders, the man trying to steal her niece away from her family?

"Of course I stopped. Who wouldn't?" He lifted her into his buggy—surprised to find she weighed not much more than a child—and settled her on the seat. "Tuck this blanket around you. You're shivering. I'll take a quick look at your horse."

Even though her expression could only be described as dubious, she pulled the scratchy, stinky wool blanket up to her chin without a word.

He took two minutes to unhitch the Morgan and tie him to a nearby tree. It wouldn't do to have him take off and get hit by a semi on the highway. Adding another expense to the repair of the buggy. If it could be repaired.

"All set." He climbed into the buggy and picked up the reins. "What happened?"

She clutched the blanket tighter. Her teeth chattered. Shock. "A deer ran across the road and spooked Brownie. I couldn't get him under control."

"That would do it."

"I should've been able to handle it. I don't know if the buggy can be repaired."

And they couldn't afford to replace it. "It would've happened to anyone. Especially when it takes you by surprise like that. Leroy and his boys are excellent at buggy repair. I have no doubt they'll give it their best shot."

"*Jah.*"

"What were you up to?" Maybe conversation would take her mind off her predicament. "Going into town?"

Women didn't usually go alone.

"Mordecai had to fix the shed. The wind blew off some of the roof overnight." She swiped at her face. Her sleeve came back with a trail of blood. The distinct sound of her teeth chattering filled the pause. "He'd promised a box of jams and jellies to Belle Lawson—the one who has the This and That antique store. I told him I was quite capable of taking a box of jellies into town."

A hint of tears tinged her attempt at a laugh.

"It could've happened to anyone," Rocky repeated.

After that his dogged attempts at small talk were met with monosyllabic responses. She allowed him to help her from the buggy when they arrived at the Cotters' farmhouse, but she moved away when he attempted to put an arm around her to hold her up on the walk to the front door.

A book in one hand, Mrs. Cotter answered the doorbell on the second ring. She took one look at the two of them through thick dark-rimmed glasses that made her look like a horned owl and shooed them in.

"Goodness gracious, whatever happened to you?" She drew Abigail into the living room made cheery by a fire in the fireplace and pretty Tiffany lamps on either side of two recliners that faced the pine bookshelves that filled one entire wall. The room smelled of coffee and mesquite. "Sit, sit. It's Abigail King, isn't it? I'm Lorraine. Lorraine Cotter. You probably don't remember me. I stop by the store for honey and jam all the time now that I'm too lazy to make my own homemade jams."

At seventy-five the woman didn't have a lazy bone in her body, as evidenced by the pristine cleanliness of her house.

"*Jah*—yes, I remember you." Abigail still clutched the blanket, which stank a bit of wet horse, with one hand as she edged toward the fire. The other hand stayed limp at her side. "I'm sorry to barge in like this. Rocky said—"

"She's had a buggy accident. I thought we might use your first-aid kit."

"Absolutely. Of course." Mrs. Cotter dragged an oak rocking chair across the thick, evergreen carpet toward the fireplace. "You sit here and we'll be right back. You need a good cup of coffee to warm you up or would you rather have hot chocolate? I'm a bit partial to hot chocolate, as Richard will tell you."

Mrs. Cotter always called him Richard. She said Rocky reminded her too much of an aging action-film star.

"Don't trouble yourself. I'm fine."

Again with the fine. Rocky shook his head. One stubborn woman. "Have some hot chocolate. You know you want to."

"Fine, hot chocolate would be fine."

He followed Mrs. Cotter down the long hallway to the kitchen and watched as she bustled about, filling a basket with medical supplies and a warm washcloth. "Are you sure she doesn't need a doctor?"

"No, but she wouldn't let me take her."

"No money?"

"I reckon."

"You know what to do?"

"Yes, ma'am. Part of my recreation training. Sports injuries and such."

"Good, skedaddle in there and figure out if it's something we can deal with. I'll bring the hot chocolate. After we get her warmed up, we'll let her fix herself up in the bathroom. She'll feel better once she gets cleaned up."

He felt better already. "Thanks, Mrs. Cotter, you're a peach."

"I keep telling you, call me Lorraine."

He'd like to call her Grandma. He'd never had one of those. His mama's mother had been gone by the time he was old enough to remember. His father's mother had never been in the picture, as far as he could tell. "She's not going to want me to touch her."

"I'll be right behind you with her hot chocolate. I understand their need for propriety, but it's no different than having a doctor tend to her wounds with a nurse present. Go on."

He scooped up the basket of medical supplies and headed to the door.

"Rocky."

"Yes, ma'am."

"She's the aunt of your Frannie?"

He'd spilled the beans about his reason for coming to south Texas over the very first supper of ham, mashed potatoes, gravy, green beans, and coconut cream pie what seemed like years earlier. "Yes."

"Things have a way of happening for a reason, don't they?"

"God caused that deer to run across the road in front of Abigail's buggy?"

Mrs. Cotter chuckled and shook a long, bony finger at him. "I wouldn't go that far, but it's possible He placed the right person there to help her out when she needed it."

Fortified by that thought, Rocky settled the basket on an end table and tugged it closer to Abigail. She'd smoothed her hair. The *kapp* was exactly where it should be now. She looked almost asleep with her blanket tucked around her and the wood crackling and popping in the fireplace. Shock did that to a person. He hated to bother her. "Abigail?"

Her eyes opened and she peered up at him. She sat up straighter. "*Jah.*"

He pulled up Mr. Cotter's fancy cushioned footstool and plopped down in front of her. "Can I see your arm, please?"

She drew back. "It's fine."

"Don't start with the 'fine' again." His tone was sharper than he intended. "I mean—"

"It's okay. I'm being silly." She extended her right arm and took a sharp breath. "Is it broken?"

With as tender a touch as he could muster, Rocky pushed up her long gray sleeve and began to probe and bend. She pressed her lips together but didn't cry out. He smiled at her in what he hoped was his best reassuring manner. "I think it's just a sprain. No broken bones. What I'm going to do is wrap it in an Ace bandage. If you were anybody else I'd suggest ice, but in this case, you'll rest it for a couple of days, swallow some ibuprofen, and let the girls take care of business around the house until it heals."

"I don't think so."

That was Abigail. "You'll be there to oversee their work."

"True." She sounded less snappy.

He slipped the stretchy beige bandage around her wrist and began to wrap toward her elbow. "It could've been so much worse. When I rode up on that buggy tumbled by the side of the road, I . . . I don't know. I didn't know what to think."

"You were afraid it was Frannie and relieved it was only me. That's human."

"That's harsh. And not true." He picked up the washcloth and dabbed at her forehead. She jerked back. "Try to relax, I need to clean it. Yes, I was relieved it wasn't Frannie, but I wasn't relieved to see it was you."

"Sorry. Clean it." A pulse throbbed in her jaw. "Don't fib. It would only be human, especially considering I haven't been very nice to you."

"I'm not fibbing." He picked through the bandages in the basket until he found one that would cover the gash on her forehead. Better dab on some antiseptic ointment first. "I understand your concerns, but you have to believe me when I say I never want to do anything to hurt Frannie or take her away from her family. If I'm not accepted into your community, I will leave here without her. That's a promise."

Tears welled in the woman's eyes, whether from pain or emotion, he couldn't say. "I only want to do what's right for her. I promised her parents that. After what happened with my Leila, I know what pain the wrong choice will cause them. Not seeing my daughter is a hard cross to bear, but it's worse knowing she might not have eternal salvation, which is even more important."

"I understand." Rocky smoothed the bandage over

her cut and leaned back to survey his work. Leila still worshipped, she still had her deep faith, from what Frannie had told him, but he wouldn't argue with a mother's fear. "I don't want Frannie to spend her life apart from her family or from God. But being with me doesn't have to mean either of those things . . . if everything goes as planned. Nothing is more important to me than Frannie's eternal salvation, as you put it."

She ran her fingers across the bandage. From her high cheekbones to her neck, her skin was stained red. Rocky figured his was the same color, what with having such a personal conversation with a woman so important to his future. "Staying with her family, being baptized, living her faith, marrying a Plain man, and being a mother, that's what is best for her."

"Agreed, but love's also important. You married for love, didn't you?" He held up his hand. "Sorry, I don't mean to be so personal. It's none of my business."

The red deepened to scarlet. "She told you . . . about me?"

"It's obvious whenever you and Mordecai are in the same room." They had a look about them, like newlyweds, that he tried hard not to covet. "You still get that glow I imagine you had on your face the day you married the man."

"In this case, there's more to be considered. Even if you stay, if you are accepted into the faith, how do we know it will work out?" Her voice quivered, but her gaze stayed on his. "It almost never does. It's too hard for your kind to give up all the things that make your life easier."

"Easier or more cluttered and difficult to navigate?"

"If anyone can do it, Richard can." Mrs. Cotter carried a tray filled with three huge mugs of hot chocolate topped with dollops of whipped cream. "I've never seen anyone more determined. He never turns on the TV or the DVD player or even the radio in the bunkhouse. He's showered us with gifts of his cell phone, his laptop, an iPad. He's turned the place into a workout room instead, with barbells and such. Of course, we don't know what to do with most of that electronic stuff. We just turn it over to the grandkids, being fairly simple folks ourselves."

She couldn't have done better if she were writing him a job recommendation. Rocky shot her a quick look of thanks. "Besides keeping in shape, I've been reading books in the evenings instead of watching TV." He pointed at the Cotters' extensive library on the nearby shelves. "Being a jock through high school and college, I missed out on a lot of good books while I was on the road playing whatever sport was in season."

Abigail looked at him as if he spoke Greek. To her, he probably did. She nodded slowly. "Mordecai reads."

Which was how he knew so much about so many things. "We have that in common then."

Among other things. Like concern for Frannie's well-being.

The silence held for a full thirty seconds.

Mrs. Cotter placed the tray on the other end table with a soft thud. "Now, let's get some hot chocolate in you and get you warmed up. There's nothing that chocolate doesn't help, is there?"

"Will it fix the buggy?" Abigail's tone was tart, but she smiled at the older lady as she accepted the mug. "Your kindness is appreciated."

Her gaze moved to Rocky. "Yours too."

CHAPTER 10

Nothing like a good game of softball to get the blood circulating. Frannie hoped it would give her brain a jump start. Susan managed a blooper into center field over second baseman Hazel's head. The six-year-old was so short it wouldn't take much. Frannie hitched up her dress and raced for third. The *kinner* screamed for her to head for home. *Why not?* Her legs were strong and her lungs stronger. Sally Glick hurled the ball with a much better arm than most boys. It smacked into catcher Jacob King's mitt seconds after Frannie crossed the plate, letting her momentum carry her toward the school porch.

"Woo-hoo! We win, we win!" she shouted in glee, even though she knew no one was keeping score. A fact that would've made Rocky crazy. She shooed the thought away. She hadn't seen him since the auction. Aunt Abigail's story of his rescue after the buggy accident had warmed Frannie's heart, but she saw nothing in her aunt's face to indicate she'd changed her mind about the man. Her aunt continued to try to invite Joseph to supper, even though he'd found a variety of excuses to turn her down. "Good hit, Teacher, good hit."

Susan laughed and two-stepped away from the old rug that served as first base. "Too bad it's time for recess to be over."

"*Nee, nee.*"

The chorus of scholars' voices couldn't have been more in unison.

"One more batter, Teacher, one more," Caleb called from his shortstop position. "Let Frannie hit again. She hits good."

"She hits well or she's a good hitter." Ever the teacher, Susan corrected with firmness. She made the *kinner* practice their English at recess when she played games with them. They seemed to find it a good trade-off. Everyone wanted her on their team. "One more hitter, then it's time for *Englisch*. We need to practice our grammar."

"Let Sally hit. I'm old and tired." Not old, but tired. Frannie hadn't been sleeping much, and when she did, her dreams were filled with an aching sadness over unborn babies and people who were invariably lost to her. Her parents roamed the fields looking for her. Her little sister Hannah cried at the supper table, her hand patting the empty chair next to her. "Go on, it's not fair. You know I'll get a hit."

Sally picked up the scarred wooden bat, leaving Frannie to slip down the makeshift first-base line to where Susan hopped on and off the base as spry as a kindergartner. Uncle Mordecai's sister was a shorter, rounder version of her brother with the same dark-brown eyes and unruly black hair trying its best to escape from her *kapp*. Give her a beard and they'd be twins. The thought made Frannie giggle. She hadn't giggled much lately.

"So what are you doing here?"

"Huh?" Frannie kept her gaze on pitcher Luke Hostetler, who kept peeking over his shoulder as if he expected thirty-something Susan to steal second base. "*Aenti* Abigail made an extra big batch of fry pies. She thought it would be a nice treat for the *kinner* so I offered to bring them over. I thought it would be fun to visit, and it gets me out of *Aenti* Abigail's hair for a while."

Her aunt had been unusually quiet since the buggy accident. She didn't wear the bandage on her wrist anymore, but the wound on her head seemed to be taking its time healing. She had bruises up and down her right side from shoulder to ankle. Most were now an ugly yellow and green color. Frannie had been on her way for a cup of *kaffi* this morning when the sight of *Onkel* Mordecai kissing his *fraa's* forehead in the kitchen had caused her to slip back to the front room. Her uncle's love for her aunt was written on his face every day. Theirs was a second chance at love, yet it seemed as strong and as sweet as any Frannie had ever seen. She longed for a tenth of what they had.

Which brought her back to the school yard and her reason for wanting to escape such a lovely scene.

"I know better. You couldn't wait to get out of the schoolhouse a few years ago." Susan edged from the base, her skirt hitched up around her shins. "The only time you come around is for the Christmas pageant. And then it's for the cookies."

"Not true. I love the hymns and the scholars' performances." She studied her sneakers. "I was thinking maybe you'd need a helper now that Esther is married."

"Get a hit, get a hit, Sally! I have essays to read!" Susan clapped her hands. Her high voice carried over the *batter-batter-swing* chant of the infield. "I can always use help, but I'm having a hard time imagining you here, inside, every day. At recess, *jah*, but doing reading with the little ones, *nee*."

"I have to do something." Frannie fought the urge to stamp her feet. "I can't stay at *Aenti* Abigail's all day long, doing laundry and washing dishes."

"That's what she does. That's what *fraas* do."

"I didn't mean it that way. She does it for her *mann* and her *kinner*."

"You don't think you'll have your own *mann* and *hoplin* one day?"

"It's not looking that way."

"Oh, ye of little faith."

"Susan!"

Susan stomped on the base with both sneakers. "You don't know what *Gott's* plan for you is. You don't. So right now, the best thing to do is wait upon the Lord. Wait and be patient."

"Is that what you did?"

"What do you mean?"

"You never married. You never had your own *boplin*."

"*Nee*." Susan clapped and shouted encouragement to Sally, who took a big swing and missed. Strike two. "Things might not have turned out exactly as I planned, but they turned out as *Gott* planned. In that I am certain and I'm content. When Mordecai's first *fraa* was killed in the van wreck and Phineas nearly died, Mordecai needed me. They needed me. I was there and ready and able to step in when I was needed. I thank *Gott* for that. I know Mordecai does too."

Feeling thoroughly small and chastised, Frannie crossed her arms over her chest. "You're right."

"*Jah*, I'm right. And *Gott's* plan for me is not at an end yet. Who knows what the future will bring? Only *Gott*. The same is true for you. Be patient. Wait to see what He has in store for you. It'll be greater than anything you can imagine for yourself." Susan grinned at her, unaware that Frannie had heard all this before from Aunt Abigail. It bore repeating, no doubt. "Besides, as a teacher, I get to play games every day at recess. Who could ask for more?"

The crack of bat against ball filled the air. Susan took off, arms and legs pumping. "See you at home plate."

Stop being so self-centered. That's what Susan meant to say, only she was too kind to use those words. Stop thinking of only herself.

· · ·

Frannie climbed into the wagon and picked up the reins, still picturing Susan's cheerful face. *Sorry*, Gott. *Thy will be done. If that means Leroy sends Rocky home and I end up an unmarried aunt to a boatload of nieces and nephews like Susan, so be it.*

"Hey, Frannie."

She looked back. Susan scampered across the yard,

her hand on her side as if running had given her a stitch. "Come back tomorrow. I'll talk with Leroy."

"You mean it?"

"If nothing else, you can be my recess monitor."

"I'll do more than that."

"No eating their lunches."

"Just their cookies."

"It's not forever, Frannie."

Maybe not. "*Danki.*"

Susan laughed. "You'll be sorry when I make you practice their times tables with them."

"Two times four is nine, right?"

Susan's laugh followed her as she drove the buggy from the yard and out onto the dirt road that led to Mordecai's. It wasn't forever. *Nee*, maybe not. But this was her show of faith. She had a job. She would move on with her life if that was what *Gott* required.

Thy will be done.

She repeated the words over and over on the ride home until they sounded like a hymn sung to the *clickety-clack* of the wagon wheels on the dirt road and the *clippity clop-clop* of the horse's hooves.

Finally, she began to say them aloud, sure she could learn to mean them.

CHAPTER 11

Some folks might think hunting was about camaraderie among men more than the sport itself. It might be, but Rocky could see that Mordecai and Caleb were serious about bagging a wild turkey or two. Otherwise, most likely they'd be eating chicken for Thanksgiving. Not that anything was wrong with chicken when a person had an empty belly, but Thanksgiving by all rights should include turkey. Being asked to come along on this hunting trip was an honor. He had to remind himself of that. In the dusk before dawn, the air was soupy with rain that misted on their faces and dampened their coats. His boots made a squelching sound in thick mud that made it difficult to pick up his feet. If only he could help them put a big bird on the table. Today was their last chance. So far they'd seen not a feather nor heard the *kerr-kerr* of a hen.

"This land has been picked clean." Caleb shoved his hat down on his head with one hand and nestled his shotgun against his chest with the other. He sounded like a grown man, not an eleven-year-old. He'd likely been hunting for years. "We might as well head home."

Mordecai put a finger to his lips and smiled. "It's early. They're still roosting. You know turkeys don't like getting wet in the rain any more than we do. When it's raining they can't hear predators approaching. They'll head out to the fields to look for insects for breakfast any minute now."

As always, Mordecai was a fountain of information delivered in a soft, gruff voice. "Until then, I could use a spot of hot *kaffi*." He tugged a thermos from a knapsack on his shoulder. "How about you, *Englisch* man?"

Something about the way he said "*Englisch* man" made it a term of endearment, which surprised Rocky to no end. He accepted the offering, popped the cup from the top of the thermos, and unscrewed the lid. "I was surprised when you asked me to come along."

Mordecai eased onto a fallen tree trunk, seemingly unaware or uncaring that it was damp from end to end. "Would you be surprised if I invited you to Thanksgiving tomorrow?"

"Yes." Might as well be honest. If a man couldn't be honest on a hunting trip, then there wasn't much left to do on this earth. "Why would you put me in close proximity to—"

"To my family." Mordecai shook his finger at him, his gaze on Caleb, who squatted nearby drinking hot chocolate from his own small thermos. "First, it's a way of thanking you again for the kindness you showed my *fraa*. When I think of her alone there on the side of the road, hurt, well, I . . ."

His voice had grown hoarse, as it had the first time he thanked Rocky for stopping to help Abigail when the buggy overturned. Who wouldn't have stopped? Anyone with a heart surely would help a woman on the side of the road. "No need to thank me for being a decent human being—"

"I also have been following your progress with Leroy and in general," Mordecai interrupted, also surprising as it wasn't something Plain folks generally did. The man had something to say, it seemed. "You've worked hard and walked quietly among us, following the lead of the other men. You seem earnest in your endeavor."

"I am earnest."

"It's a hard row."

"It is."

"Are you prepared to learn German?"

"I am."

"Not just *Deutsch*, but High German as you've heard in the services?"

"I am."

"Is your heart prepared?"

Rocky contemplated the question, trying to follow Mordecai's thinking. "If you mean do I understand the calling to faith and how it's practiced in this community, yes, my heart is prepared. More than prepared. I feel as if I've waited my whole life for this."

"No more competitive sports. No more boxing matches."

"I wouldn't be here now if those were more important to me than my walk in faith."

Rocky paused, the images from his past life painting a montage in his mind. Parent-pitch and T-ball with his dad, Pony league with his uncle, flag football, tackle football, YMCA basketball, competitive basketball, tryouts, making the teams in multiple sports in junior high, high school, college. Championships and trophies. Cheerleaders, bonfires, and pep rallies. His life had revolved around something Mordecai would never understand. But if Rocky knew anything, it was that sports were simply games. Games that taught children leadership, teamwork, loyalty, and social skills, but still games. They didn't make a life, but they helped hone character. Sports crafted leaders, but they did nothing to fill the void in his chest where his faith should reside.

"Don't get me wrong. I don't apologize for my previous life choices," he said finally. "I believe in sports. As a teaching tool for good values, but also for health and physical fitness. For helping kids blow off steam at recess so they can sit still and learn in class. I'm sure you've seen this at your school and with your *kinner*, so you know what I'm saying is true."

"I don't question your past choices. I'm only trying to understand your current choices." Mordecai took a swallow of coffee that steamed in the chill of the early morning. "And to make sure you won't regret them."

"*Nee*, I won't." Rocky elbowed Caleb, who grunted and nearly spilled his hot chocolate. "I fully expect to play a lot more basketball and softball in these parts, given the chance. I'll even play volleyball if nothing else presents itself."

Caleb stood. "Yeah, after we eat tomorrow we can play ball."

"Sure. We'll work off all those carbs."

"Carbs?"

"Wait." Mordecai held up a hand. "Hear that?"

His voice had dropped to a whisper. A sound like yelps and then the *kerr-kerr* sound of hens talking to one another. "Kerr-kerr. Yamp, yamp, kerr, yamp," Mordecai called back, mimicking the sounds perfectly. "Kerr, kerr, yamp, kerr, yamp."

Rocky reached for the thermos. Caleb tucked his in the knapsack and stood, his Winchester at the ready. With luck the calls would bring the birds their direction. Time to hunt.

A *crack* broke the silence. Like a firecracker or . . . a gunshot.

Something whizzed over Rocky's head, so close he felt the cool breeze. A pinging sound echoed from behind him.

A shot.

A second bullet *thunked* as it dug into the trunk of a mesquite tree behind them.

His cup hit the mud near his boot.

Feeling as if he moved in slow motion, Rocky hurled himself at Caleb. The boy let out a *humpft* as they hit the ground face-first in the mud.

Another shot pinged over their heads.

"Cease fire!" he hollered, aware of Mordecai flat on his stomach next to them. "Cease fire."

Mordecai yelled something in *Deutsch*.

Adrenaline pumping through him like an out-of-control geyser, Rocky inched up his head and waved his cap. "Stop shooting now!"

Voices clamored. A few seconds later two *Englisch* men in drab brown-and-gray camo tramped toward them, their shotguns pointed at the ground. Both looked stricken. "Hey, are you guys okay?" The shorter man with a full Duck Dynasty beard and thick glasses had a cigarette-roughened voice. "So sorry, man, I thought I saw a tom fly out of the trees in this direction."

Rocky scrambled to his feet. Mordecai and Caleb did the same. For a few seconds, the only sound was their heavy breathing.

"This is private property." Rocky spoke first. Mordecai was busy inspecting every inch of Caleb as if he couldn't believe his stepson hadn't been hit. "You must've wandered through a gate without realizing."

The taller man shoved back a hat with GUARD YOUR SECOND AMENDMENT RIGHTS embroidered on it. "Sorry, man, we might have gotten a little off track, what with following the droppings and the molting." Curiosity etched across his face, his gaze fluttered to Mordecai and Caleb. "You're Amish folks? I didn't know you hunted. I thought you were pacifists."

The shaking in his legs made it hard for Rocky to stand. He eased onto the tree trunk Mordecai had vacated. "We only hunt what we eat." The *we* came out like the most natural thing in the world. "You'll find the road off this property up there to your left. Follow the path."

"Sorry about that. We'd didn't see y'all."

"Like I said, no harm done."

He watched them trudge away until they were out of sight, somehow not convinced they would actually leave if he didn't.

"We're fine." Mordecai squatted next to him. Caleb

flopped down on his knees, seemingly oblivious to the mud, bits of weeds, and grass that covered his clothes. "Like you said, no harm done."

"Way too close for comfort."

"It's one of the risks of hunting season. Too many folks, too little territory. Some of them are weekend warriors who don't give a hoot about safety or don't know any better." The pallor on his usually brown face reflected more concern than Mordecai seemed to want to admit. "You handled it right."

"How so?"

"You thought quickly and moved quickly under fire, however shaken. Then you were firm but calm with those fellows." Mordecai brushed leaves and dirt from his black jacket and pants. "Just as you should have been. Oftentimes a scare like that will cause a person to react with anger."

Rocky examined the last few minutes in his mind's eye. Anger had been there, but also the understanding that it was an accident. They didn't seek out fellow hunters at whom they could shoot. It could have been tragic. Thanks be to God, it wasn't. "I think the time I spent over the years coaching kids has a lot to do with the way I react to things. Usually calm works best."

"Agreed. It's good to know you're not one to fly off the handle under duress. Plain folks don't abide by that much." Mordecai gave Caleb's shoulder another squeeze. The boy's face still looked pasty. "You good?"

Caleb nodded. "We're still hunting, aren't we?"

"*Jah*." Mordecai clapped Rocky on the back. "My

fraa will be very disappointed if we come home without a bird for the table tomorrow."

Rocky blew out air. One thing was for certain. He couldn't afford to disappoint Abigail.

CHAPTER 12

The once heady aroma of Thanksgiving turkey now made Frannie want to open a window. The food had been wonderful. She'd eaten too much of it, in fact. Like the others, she wasn't used to such a bounty of rich foods. That second piece of pecan pie had been the breaking point. Or maybe it was the second yeast roll slathered with fresh butter. Wishing she could loosen her dress somehow, she placed the last of the clean plates on the shelf above her head. Since she'd chosen to dry, she was the last one in the kitchen. Rebekah had dragged Hazel off for a much-needed nap. Frannie could use one herself. Hours to prepare, minutes to eat, hours to clean up afterward. That's what her *mudder* always said with a certain air of satisfaction. Men might bring home the turkey, but womenfolk did the lion's share of the work when it came to this holiday and most others.

A wave of sadness swept over her. This was her first Thanksgiving away from her parents and silly little Hannah and baby Rachel, who wasn't a baby anymore. Her brother Obadiah would be there with his *fraa* and *kinner*, as would Rufus. Joshua was courting, according to Hannah, but they weren't sure with whom. If Frannie were there, she'd figure it out. She had a way of doing that.

Someone else was spending the holiday away from his family. Rocky. It hadn't hurt his appetite. He'd put away two helpings of turkey, exclaiming over how much better the darker meat was than a store-bought bird, cornbread stuffing, mashed potatoes, sweet potatoes, gravy, cranberries, and two pieces of pie—one pumpkin, one pecan. Not that she was watching or counting.

They hadn't spoken since the auction. Since his declaration. He hadn't shone his flashlight in her window. Or sent her a note. Nothing. Right now he was out in the front room by the fireplace playing card games with Caleb and her other cousins.

Which was why she would head out the kitchen door for a nice, long walk far from temptation. She needed to work off the food anyway. Grabbing her shawl from the hook by the back door, she bundled up and put her hand on the doorknob.

"Where are you going?"

She bowed her head. Almost made it. Her heart began to thump like Butch's tail against the porch railing when she petted him. "You have to stop doing that."

"What?"

"Popping up everywhere."

"I didn't pop up. I came for another glass of lemonade. Is that a crime?"

Crime? So often he talked nonsense. Still, Frannie wanted to smile. "What kind of question is that?"

"Are you going for a walk?"

What was his first hint? "*Jah.*"

"Can I go with you?"

"*Nee.*"

"Don't be that way."

"My *aenti* is out there."

"She went to her room for a nap. *Onkel* Mordecai is passed out in the rocking chair. The boys are going to play kick the can or some such game I've never heard of."

"I thought you promised Caleb a game of basketball."

"I did as soon as the food settles. I ate so much I might vomit . . ." Rocky's grin spread. "Not the most romantic thing I've ever said to a girl."

The potential existed that she might do the same, but it wouldn't be from playing games. Frannie tightened her shawl around her shoulders and opened the door. "And there's been a lot of them, I'm sure."

With his long legs he caught up with her all too quickly, zipping up his black leather bomber jacket as he went. "A few, I won't deny it. But none like you."

Frannie had no doubt of that. She pounded down the back porch steps and lengthened her own stride, picking her way around rain puddles and dodging droopy nopals that didn't care for the winter weather's penchant for hiding the sun. They walked in silence, Rocky's last statement ping-ponging between them. She truly didn't know what to say so she said nothing.

At the stand of mesquite and live oak that separated Mordecai's property from the Hostetlers', Rocky caught her hand. His fingers slipped between hers and tightened. He stopped walking, forcing her to do the same. "About what I said the other day at the auction."

"The other day? That was three weeks ago." She tugged at her hand, but he wouldn't give it up. "A person doesn't say that and then let three weeks go by."

"I had no choice."

She swiped at her face with her other hand. "I know." She did know. That was the trouble.

"I meant it."

"I know."

"I'm trying to do the right thing."

"Me too." She gazed at his face, memorizing the way his curls sprang up around his ball cap, damp and wiry. "I took a job as Susan's helper at the school."

"You did?" Uncertainty washed over his face. "I thought—"

"Single girls take that job, that's what you thought?"

"Sort of. I mean, it was kind of understood."

"It is."

"So you're thinking you'll remain single."

"That's what I'm thinking." Her knees shook, but she forced one foot to move, then the other, until she stood in his space. "I love you too."

"And what does that have to do with you working at the school?" He took a step toward her, enveloping her in that tantalizing Rocky scent. "Exactly?"

"It means that if Leroy decides you should go back to Missouri and never see me again, I'll abide by his decision." His fingers tightened, the white knuckles matching her own smaller ones. "I'll ask you to do the same."

"I will." The words sounded raw, his voice husky. "I promised myself I wouldn't keep you from your faith or your family."

"Joseph isn't coming around anymore. He was more interested in *Aenti* Abigail's cooking than in me anyway. Says I'm too lippy."

"You are lippy." The muscles in Rocky's jaw contracted. His breathing quickened. "You'll not court another? That's what you're saying?"

"I love you. That's that."

His free hand touched her face. He shook his head. "I never thought loving someone would make me so crazy."

"You know how to pick them, I guess."

He laughed, more pain than mirth in the sound. "Don't I, though?"

"Look at it this way. You'll be home for the holidays with your family, instead of missing them on days like today."

"Missing you instead."

She acknowledged the truth of that statement with a quick, hard hug, stepping back before he could respond. "We shouldn't make it harder."

His arms came out, then dropped to his sides. "What do you mean?"

"Don't come around anymore."

"I may only have a few weeks left and you want me to waste the chance to spend time with you?"

"We can't court unless Leroy decides you'll stay. It's best that we not see each other until he makes a decision."

"I'll get to say good-bye?"

Mourning already soaked his words. *Don't make it worse.* "We'll see."

"I have two more sessions with Leroy and then the interview."

"I know. Mordecai mentioned it." To Aunt Abigail. But in front of Frannie, giving her the gift of knowing what was going on. "That means you'll be here through Christmas."

"Yes."

"A sweet time of year to be with family."

"My family's here." He wrapped his long arms around her in a bear hug against his chest. His heart beat in her ear. His breath touched her forehead, warming her. "You're my family."

"Rocky."

His arms dropped, leaving her cold and bereft in a gray, sunless day. "We better get back to the house."

They walked side by side, not touching, but Frannie savored the lovely sensation that he still held her hand. All the way home.

CHAPTER 13

Rocky paused on the school porch to remove his ball cap. Balancing the pan of pumpkin bars Mrs. Cotter had made against his chest, he used one trembling hand to slick back his unruly hair. Leroy would make a decision in the next few days. The interview had taken only an hour after all those long, frustrating days of study and discussion. Depending on Leroy's decision, the Christmas pageant might be Rocky's last gathering with folks he'd come to like, admire, even love.

Including Frannie. If he were anyone else, he would rue the day he'd trotted into Callie's Bakery and Restaurant in Jamesport, Missouri, to see this skinny girl with hair the color of carrots and more freckles than a guy could count hefting a rubber bin of dirty dishes almost as big as she was. He would never regret meeting Frannie Mast. Everything that followed had made him a better man—a better person—with greater faith, new friends, a passing knowledge of south Texas and all that region encompassed. It had brought him love, bittersweet though it might be in the end.

If Leroy decided against allowing him to join the

church, Rocky would have to go back to Missouri, whether he liked it or not. He'd agreed to that provision. He must've been out of his mind. The pan of pumpkin bars weighed heavy in his hands. Laughter and chatter wafted from the building. Another buggy pulled in next to his. Time to get in there and get it over with.

Enjoy it while he could, better yet.

The door opened and Caleb grinned up at him. "Whatcha doing standing out there? It's cold. We're getting ready to start."

"Cold for south Texas. This would be balmy weather up north." Rocky took a breath and summoned a smile. "Merry Christmas."

Inside, a wood-burning stove created a warm glow that matched the happy faces that filled the room. It might not seem cold to him, but these folks wore coats. A chorus of Merry Christmas's greeted him. Mordecai, Deborah, Phineas, Abigail, even Naomi Glick seemed to have put aside differences for the moment. After setting the pumpkin bars on a table already loaded with sweets, Rocky took his time, made the rounds, greeted each one, memorizing faces and making memories to carry home.

Frannie offered a tiny half wave from across the room. She wore her Sunday gray dress and had managed to arrive without a single stain on her apron. Her hair behaved itself behind a clean, neat *kapp*. He nodded. No sense in getting her in any more trouble than he already had. They'd agreed not to see each other, and they'd kept their word over the past few weeks. A simple hello wouldn't be too much, would it? He sidestepped little Timothy King and angled his way past the second row of benches.

"You should have a brownie. They're really good." Joseph stepped in front of him. "I heard Hazel say Frannie made them, but I'll believe that when I see her mixing the batter."

Rocky looked over the shorter man's shoulder. Frannie sank onto a bench between Rebekah and Abigail. "I was just going to—"

"Say hello?" Joseph inched closer. His voice dropped. "Don't spoil the night for her. Half of courting is knowing when and where."

"I'm not courting."

"I know." Joseph chucked him on the back. "That's what she says."

"Really, I—"

Susan clapped her hands twice. Silence fell as her scholars trotted to the front of the room and disappeared behind sheets that had been tacked up across one corner for a makeshift backstage. Much giggling and whispering ensued. Rocky swallowed his retort. Truth be told, the man was right. This was the crux of the matter. He couldn't choose the Plain life for Frannie's sake. It had to be for the sake of his own faith. He inhaled and lowered his head. Gott, *Thy will be done.*

The children sauntered from behind the sheet in their costumes. Caleb made a fine Joseph. Leroy and Naomi's Sally struggled to straighten her head covering while nestling a baby doll against her skinny chest. Mary and the infant Jesus. Sweet.

Their enactment of the "no room at the inn" scene

brought smiles to the faces in the audience. Singing of Christmas songs followed. What they lacked in musical talent, these youngsters made up for with their enthusiasm. Rocky found himself watching the faces in the audience. The Amish didn't have a speck of pride in them, but he could pick out the parents, the way they watched their children, the way they smiled with pleasure to see them celebrate the birth of Christ. God incarnate sent to earth to die for each one of them.

Such goodness. Such sweetness. He bowed his head and swiped at his face. *Good Lord, Father, Abba, give me strength. Whatever Leroy decides, I know it will be the right thing. If I need to go home, so be it. I'll go because I know You'll be with me wherever I am.*

Abigail and Mordecai's little Hazel rounded out the show with a cute poem she'd written with the help of her classmates. One hand on her cheek as if to hide her face, she managed to make it all the way through with only one prompting from Susan. Then she ran from the impromptu stage right into her mother's arms. Cheering and clapping rocked the room with choruses of Merry Christmas and blessings for the New Year.

Rocky swallowed hard, stood, and slapped his hat on his head. No matter what happened, this would be the best Christmas of his life.

. . .

Frannie's hands hurt from clapping. Her throat hurt from holding back tears. Christmas would always be her favorite time of year. Nothing could be allowed to change that. This was not about her. Exactly as Rocky had said on Thanksgiving Day. So eloquently and then he left. She hadn't seen him since that day a month ago. She'd heard of how he helped bale the last of the hay and chopped wood for the school and helped load the horse trailer with the Kropfs' furniture when they decided to move back to Carrollton in Missouri after only a year in Bee County. He had to do what God called him to do, as did Leroy. If only Leroy would make a decision, ending her suffering and Rocky's.

Aunt Abigail turned and leaned close. "Patience is a virtue."

Indeed. That didn't make it any easier. Frannie gave Hazel a big hug and a quick shove. "Go get a brownie before they're all gone. Bring me a cutout cookie with lots of frosting."

Hazel frowned. "But I want that one too."

"If there's enough, you can have one of each."

Grinning from ear to ear, the little girl took off. To be so young and innocent that a cookie could make her day. Frannie allowed herself to do what she hadn't done all evening. She sneaked a glance across the room. Rocky stood near the dessert table, a gingersnap the size of his palm in one hand and a cup of hot chocolate in the other. He looked content.

As he should.

"Don't even think about it." Deborah offset the sternness of her words with a pat on the shoulder. "You've been doing so well, don't give in now."

Frannie studied her sneakers. "He looks like a doofus chewing on that big cookie."

Deborah giggled, sounding like Hazel. "Don't be mean."

"I'm trying to put myself in the right frame of mind."

"You don't have to say good-bye just yet."

"You think Leroy will say no?"

"I think Leroy is praying and heeding *Gott's* word. He'll do what is right and wise."

The ache in Frannie's throat threatened to choke her. "That's what I'm hoping."

Rocky tucked the last bite of cookie in his mouth. He picked up a napkin and handed it to Hazel. They seemed to be having a conversation. He rubbed his bare chin, looking serious. After a minute or two, he placed a cookie, and then another, on the napkin. He patted Hazel's head and gave her a little shove before turning back to the table without looking in Frannie's direction.

The girl trotted back to Frannie. She held the napkin with both hands as if conveying a precious gift. "Rocky says to give you the star. He says it reminds him of you because you shine so bright."

Frannie closed her eyes. *Don't cry. Don't cry. Don't cry.*

"Are you going to eat it? If you're not, I will."

Frannie opened her eyes and took the cookie from her cousin. "Of course I'll eat it."

She lifted the cookie to her mouth and glanced across the room, hoping Rocky would be watching.

He wasn't.

Leroy stood between her and Rocky. They were talking; rather, Leroy talked, and Rocky simply nodded. The older man's hand came out. They shook.

Then Rocky shrugged on his coat without looking at a single soul.

And he left.

Leroy trudged across the room. For the first time, Frannie realized he was limping a bit. He looked old and tired. He tipped his hat to her and smiled. "Merry Christmas."

Joy dawned in those words. No matter what happened, God still reigned in heaven and on earth. "Merry Christmas."

Leroy limped on, this time stopping to talk to Uncle Mordecai, who nodded. Her uncle began to circle the room, speaking to the older folks, the married ones. After a moment Frannie realized he was speaking to all those who'd been baptized. The members of the church. She sidled up next to Abigail. "What's going on?"

Abigail settled onto the bench, a paper plate filled with Christmas goodies in her hands. "Leroy has called a meeting."

"For when?"

"Now. Everyone's here. He's putting it to a vote."

"Everyone will decide?"

"He says that's the proper way. Take Rebekah and Hazel on home. We'll get a ride from Phineas."

Pinpricks of purple and light flickered in Frannie's eyes. She tried to breathe and found she couldn't.

"Go on, child." *Aenti* Abigail smiled up at her. "Go home. Say your prayers and remember, *Gott's* will be done."

She wanted to ask how her *aenti* would vote, but

Frannie didn't. That, too, was between Aunt Abigail and *Gott*.

She tried to form her own prayer as she helped Hazel bundle up and slipped into her own shawl. The only word that came was *Please*.

CHAPTER 14

Chores first, of course. Rocky didn't mind. He dumped feed into the horses' trough and inhaled the crisp morning air. He'd awakened with such a sense of peace. Even though Leroy hadn't said he could stay, he hadn't sent him away. His handshake had been firm, his words of farewell kind. Either way, Mordecai's last-minute invitation to join his family for Christmas Day had been the frosting on the cake. Christmas with Frannie. Truly a gift all its own. His gifts for them were small, a new faceless doll for Hazel, a baseball mitt for Caleb, basketballs for the rest of the boys, orange spice tea for Abigail, a book of crossword puzzles for Mordecai. He had nothing for Frannie because he simply couldn't decide yet what that gift should be. He would give her something special before he left for Missouri.

If this was to be their only Christmas together, it had to be a special gift. Memorable. Lasting. He would figure it out. Just not today. She would understand.

"Come on, it's time for breakfast," Caleb hollered from the barn door. "Hurry up. We get presents now. Maybe we can play some basketball later."

Rocky had to laugh at the boy's exuberance. Kids were all alike when it came to gifts. Even Plain *kinner*.

He went to the kitchen first to wash his hands. The water was icy. He ducked his face and splashed it, trying to wash off the sensation that this would be the last time he did each one of these tasks with these people. A tiny piece of tissue floated in the water. He'd forgotten the wound along his jawline. Learning to shave with a razor had taken a daily toll on his face. Maybe that particular struggle had ended. He straightened and grabbed a threadbare dish towel from the counter, taking his time memorizing the warm kitchen. A stack of pancakes as tall as a toddler sat warming on the stove next to a huge pan of scrambled eggs. The house smelled of maple syrup and fresh baked biscuits and bacon. His mouth watered.

"Come on, come into the front room." Hazel tugged on his hand. "Your seat is next to Caleb's."

Rocky followed. He sank into his chair, glad to sit. He'd never felt so blessed or so welcome or so sad.

"Presents first?" Hazel danced around Mordecai, keeping him from making much progress from the kitchen to the table. "Presents are first, aren't they?"

"Not if I stumble over you and break my neck." Mordecai scooped her up and carried her on his hip like a sack of potatoes. She shrieked, her giggles contagious. His low rumble of laughter mingled with the girl's. "Patience is virtue, my child."

Even though he'd heard that phrase a hundred times, it had never meant more to Rocky.

Frannie set a basket loaded with biscuits on the table.

At the sight of him, she smiled, a broad, happy smile the likes of which he hadn't seen in a month of Sundays.

"Morning."

"Morning."

"Presents?" Hazel touched a small stack next to her plate, but she didn't pick anything up. "Now?"

"Prayers first." Mordecai bowed his head. Everyone followed suit.

Silence swept over the room, bringing with it a sense of peace and a kind of prosperity that had nothing to do with material goods. Rocky prayed for each person in the room and for his own salvation.

"Since we have a guest this bright and beautiful morning, I think we should start with his gifts." Mordecai broke the silence. "What do y'all think?"

"There's no need to give me gifts." Rocky squirmed in his seat. These folks had no extra of anything. They worked hard to feed and clothe themselves. There was nothing left after that. "Honestly, I wouldn't feel right."

"A person should never reject a gift given from the heart." Mordecai shook one long and calloused finger at Rocky. "Accept and be blessed by these offerings."

Nothing could be said to that, especially with the tightness in his throat and the heat behind his eyes, so Rocky opted for a simple nod.

"Me first, me first!" Hazel scooted from her chair and ran around the table, a small brown bag in her chubby hands. "Open it, open it."

Rocky obliged. The bag held two apples and three long carrots. Uncertain, he smiled at her. "Thank you. I love apples and carrots."

"For your horse. For Chocolate." Hazel held up her hands as if amazed she had to explain this. "Horses like Christmas too."

Silly Rocky. "Of course they do."

Caleb went next. A hunting knife wrapped in newspaper funnies. A nice one. "Are you sure, Caleb? This was expensive."

"*Jah.*" The boy shrugged, his grin philosophical. "I had two."

"Perfect."

"We have to go deer hunting soon."

"Absolutely." If he was still here. "It will come in very handy."

Deborah handed him a box across the table. Phineas sat next to her, his arm thrown across the chair behind his *fraa*. The word came naturally. *Mann* and *fraa*. Something Rocky might never have. He focused on the box, afraid they would all see the emotion that threatened to overwhelm him. No fancy paper or bows. A simple box with the flaps entwined to keep the lid shut.

"Y'all shouldn't have done this."

The *y'all* made everyone laugh. He would take a bit of Texas home with him, no doubt about it. He tugged open the flaps. A beautiful, pristine straw hat. He lifted it with gentle hands. "You shouldn't have." It was the nicest hat he'd ever owned. "I mean, I—"

"I hope it's not too big." Deborah slapped a hand on her husband's broad chest. "Phineas insisted you have a big head."

"To match my big feet." Rocky managed a laugh. It sounded strangled in his ears. He set the hat on his head. It fit just as it should, a little snug so the first south Texas wind wouldn't send it sailing. If he were to look in a mirror right now—if there was a mirror in this house, which there likely wouldn't be—he'd see a man the spitting image of an Amish person. He had no doubt of that. "He's right. It's perfect."

Abigail went next. "From Mordecai and me."

A small package wrapped in white tissue paper. Suspenders. This time he had to take a long breath. What were they saying? Did they know something he didn't? A straw hat, suspenders, a hunting knife, food for his horse. It seemed to add up to an enormous gift he hadn't expected to receive.

"*Galluses*, right? That's the word for suspenders?"

Abigail nodded and smiled. "*Galluses*."

"Thank you." He cleared his throat. "I know you don't stand on ceremony, and you're not much for flowery sentiment, but I have to say it. Thank you for making me feel so welcome and so a part of this family today. It's the best Christmas ever."

"That's not all."

Frannie slipped from her chair and picked up a box nestled on the floor next to the fireplace. When she turned, tears shone in her eyes. He'd never seen her cry. Not that she would admit to crying now. The box was heavy. He unfolded the flaps. An enormous English–German translation of the Holy Bible sat on his lap. He lifted it from tissue paper that protected it. Leather bound. Substantial in his shaking hands.

He lifted his gaze from the book and let it travel to Frannie. Her smile trembled. "Nothing is more important than your path with God. Our journey through this world is short. You'll need that to navigate."

She plopped into her chair, her hand over her mouth as if to keep from saying more.

He cleared his throat again. "I'm not sure I understand what this means."

"You already have the most important tool." Mordecai leaned back in his chair, his expression expansive. "You have faith, despite or because of the travails you've experienced. You've shown Leroy and me and the rest of our community your commitment, your willingness to set aside the trappings of the world, to keep yourself apart."

Rocky heard the words, but they still didn't compute. "Leroy made a decision?"

"We all did. The district voted after the pageant."

"All y'all said yes."

Mordecai's laugh rumbled deep in his chest. "We all did."

"*Jah, jah!*" Hazel crowed. "Merry Christmas."

"I'm in?"

"You have to take the baptism classes in the spring and be baptized."

"Hence, the Bible." He touched the black leather cover. His jaw ached with the effort to corral his emotions. He wouldn't start out by bawling like a baby in front of members of his new community. "I'm speechless."

Caleb smacked his fork against his plate in a beat reminiscent of a Christmas song. "Enough talk. Let's open our presents so we can eat pancakes."

Indeed. All the important words had been spoken. Almost.

• • •

Frannie scraped the last of her scrambled eggs and bacon into Butch's dish on the back porch. The dog's snout turned up in an obvious smile under one eye with the "pirate patch." If the *schtinkich* of his doggy breath was any indication, he'd already bagged a rabbit or some such critter for breakfast. Regardless, his behind wagged a stubby tail. Tightening her shawl around her in the chilly December breeze, she glanced back, feeling only slightly guilty. *Aenti* Abigail didn't like for her to feed table scraps to Butch, but even the dog deserved a Christmas treat. After the gift exchange, she'd found herself with little appetite. She wanted to run after Rocky when he left the table with *Onkel* Mordecai. Ask him, What now? What does this mean for us? A woman didn't do that. Especially in these circumstances. It wasn't about her or her feelings for Rocky. This was about Rocky's path on this earth. Nothing was bigger than that, no matter how she felt.

All the same, it wasn't fair, making women wait until men grew enough smarts to know what they wanted out of life. Women always got down that road first, it seemed. Always.

"There you are."

A shiver swept through her that had nothing to do with the damp winter weather. She turned. Rocky loomed over her. The Rocky scent engulfed her. He wore his new straw hat. He looked so Plain. Appearances meant nothing, Frannie knew that, but the sight of him made her want to sit down right where she stood. Her feet were lumps of wood. If she tried to walk, she'd keel over. "Here I am."

Rocky scratched Butch behind floppy ears. The dog panted in sheer delight and went back to eating. "Does Abigail know you're feeding Butch bacon? That has to be some form of sacrilege."

"Hush. He's a good dog. He deserves a treat."

He shrugged those massive shoulders. "I reckon you're right."

His hand came up and his thumb brushed against Frannie's cheek. Suddenly she didn't need her shawl after all. "What are you doing?"

"At least you're not still asking me what I'm doing *here*." The humor in the words didn't match his serious expression. "You had a smudge of syrup on your face."

The plate clattered against the wood beneath her feet. She bent to pick it up. Her head collided with his. "Ouch. Ouch!"

"Yikes, ouch, sorry!" They both straightened. Rocky held the plate, by some miracle, unbroken in his hand. "Sorry. That's what happens when I try to be helpful."

Would it always be this hard for them? Frannie wanted to find out. She couldn't wait to find out. She snatched the dirty plate, tempted to press it against her apron for fear it would fall again. "Was there . . . something else?"

"Yep. I mean, *jah*."

"What is it?"

"I'm so happy about being allowed to stay. I was wondering . . . are you happy too?"

"Of course I am. It's what I wanted. For you. And for me. If it's what you want."

"It is. It truly is. I'm looking forward to spring and the baptism classes."

A question not asked echoed through his words.

"Me too."

"You'll be baptized with me, then?"

With or without him, of course, but Frannie knew what he meant. "I'll be baptized."

Rocky shuffled his big feet, his smile almost shy. "I feel bad. I don't have a Christmas gift yet for you. I couldn't decide."

She'd already received the gift of his continued presence in her life. A chance that they could be together. "You don't have to get me anything. It doesn't work that way—leastways not around here."

He would learn that now. It would be a pleasure to watch him embrace this new season in his life. If he planned to share it with her. Surely, he did. Still, a girl didn't like to take these things for granted.

"There are so many things I thought of getting you." He stared over her shoulder. "I just thought . . . well, now that we know I'm staying, well . . ."

Come on, Rocky. "Well, what?"

"I wondered what that means for us."

"What do you think it means?"

"I know what I hope it means."

The man was seriously addled. Frannie set the plate on the porch banister. She grabbed his hand and entwined her fingers in his. "Do I have to do all the work here?"

"No. You don't." His Adam's apple bobbed as his gaze fastened on their hands. "I hope it means you'll take a buggy ride with me—a lot of buggy rides. That I'll need lots of batteries for my flashlight, and neither of us will get enough sleep anytime soon because we'll be driving around the countryside talking all hours of the night."

"That's all you've got?" Frannie tugged her hand from his and crossed her arms. "You can do better, Rocky Sanders, I know you can."

He snorted and shook his head. "You make me crazy, Amish woman."

"You make me crazy, *Englisch* man."

His belly laugh mingled with her higher, softer giggle. Frannie loved that sound almost as much as she loved Rocky.

He sighed and wiped at his eyes with the back of his sleeve. "I keep thinking about how patient God is with us. It takes us so long to figure everything out. We moan and carry on about His will and His plan, trying to figure it out."

She certainly had done her share of moaning and carrying on in the last year. "We do."

"We need to be patient."

"We do?"

"I love you. I want to marry you. But I have things I need to do first. A lot of learning. A lot of changing to do. Can you understand that?"

Love you. Marry you. Frannie's brain was stuck on the first two sentences. *Fraa. Mann. Boplin.* The life for which she'd prayed and hoped. "*Jah.*"

"Do you understand?" He looked so worried, so uncertain. "Will you wait?"

"Of course I'll wait." Frannie inhaled. Finally. A breath. "I love you too."

He sighed as if he'd been holding his breath. "What will your parents think of all this?"

"Leroy called and left a message at the phone shack last night. They left their own message this morning at the store."

"No argument?"

"They trust folks here. They trust Leroy."

"What would you think about going home then?"

"Back to Jamesport?" Sweet relief ran through her. No more holidays without cheeky Hannah and baby Rachel, who surely wasn't a baby anymore. Obadiah and his brood. Rufus. Joshua and his mystery special person. "Back to my family and yours? I'd like that, but truth be told, I only want to live wherever you live."

"We'll go home, then, when the time is right."

His gaze, full of emotion, full of love, wandered across her face. His expression held her there, unable to look away. *Aenti* Abigail could storm onto the porch at this very moment, *Onkel* Mordecai bringing up the rear, and Frannie wouldn't be able to move.

His hands came up, both of them this time. They cupped her face. His expression gave her a hint of what was to come, but she didn't have time to brace herself. He leaned down. His lips touched hers. She closed her eyes, wondering at the softness of his skin on hers. She reached for something to hold on to before she fell into the whirling vortex of emotion. Her hands found and gripped his solid biceps. He would always be the rock to which she could cling.

Her heart quivered and opened like a sunflower seeking the warmth and brilliance of the sun. Rocky filled up every nook and cranny that had been waiting for him to simply come home to her. He tasted of *kaffi*, maple syrup, dreams, and hopes. The kiss deepened and lingered with a sweet promise of many more such kisses.

After a time, he raised his head a scant few inches. His arms dropped. For an instant, Frannie felt cold. Then he wrapped them around her waist, lifted her off her feet, and pressed her against his chest. "How about that?" he murmured. "What do you think of that?"

Frannie felt as if she were flying, wings spread for the first time in her life. She rested her forehead on Rocky's shoulder. "You found the perfect gift."

"I reckon it's the first of many such gifts."

He proceeded to make good on that promise.

DISCUSSION QUESTIONS

1. Rocky follows Frannie from Missouri to south Texas, knowing her family disapproves. Do you think he is right to pursue her, knowing she'll have to give up her faith and family to be with him if he doesn't join her faith? Do you think love is more important than approval?

2. Frannie and Rocky both say they will abide by Leroy's decision. Rocky will go home and Frannie will become a teacher's aide, knowing she'll never marry. Do you believe in a love so strong, you'd be willing to forego all other chances for marriage and family because of it?

3. Rocky has never felt close to God because he identifies him as "abba" or "father." His father abandoned him and left his mother for another woman. Do you have trouble relating to God the Father because of problems in your own life? How do you overcome those feelings?

4. Rocky is willing to give up electricity, computers, his phone, even his beloved Dodge Ram pickup in order to put distance between himself and the world so he can be closer to God. What are you

willing to give up in order to have a closer relationship with God?

5. Abigail tells Frannie that English people are rarely
   successful when they join the Amish faith. They're
   unable to adapt to such a plain, austere lifestyle.
   What can you do to lead a simpler, more Godly life
   without going so far as to give up electricity, cars,
   computers, and phones?

ABOUT THE AUTHOR

Kelly Irvin is the bestselling author of the Every Amish Season and Amish of Bee County series. The Beekeeper's Son received a starred review from Publisher's Weekly, who called it a "beautifully woven masterpiece." A former newspaper reporter and retired public relations professional, Kelly lives in Texas with her husband, photographer Tim Irvin. They have two children, two grandchildren, and two cats. In her spare time, she likes to read books by her favorite authors. Visit her online at KellyIrvin.com; Facebook: Kelly.Irvin.Author; Twitter: @Kelly_S_Irvin.